DUALITY OF CHANGE

AN IDENTITY ODYSSEY

A Tina Marin Adventure

D L COOPER

This is a work of fiction. Names, characters, places, business establishments, and incidents are either the product of the author's imagination or are used fictitiously, and any resemblance to actual persons, living or dead, is entirely coincidental.

Cover design and Illustration, Maps by Lucy Dirksen, lfdstudios.com

ISBN: 978-1-966632-01-6

DEDICATION

To my lovely and loving life partner and spouse

Renée

CONTENTS

ACKNOWLEDGMENT

John Donne was right, no man is an island. First and foremost my loving gratitude to my wife, Renée, for her everlasting support and patience in all my endeavors. My thanks to select friends for their valuable input on my journey creating this work. Last but not least, my thanks to our friend, Lucy Dirksen, for her sage advice, excellent cover art, and illustrated maps.

PROLOGUE

SHE

A Few Years Ago – No Man's Land

She was too much of a predator to accept fatigue, so she stalked on. It was more an animal trace than a footpath they were following, rock with crunchy snow, just under the upper edge of a jagged timberline. She was cold, especially in her hands and feet, despite her heavy clothing. The figure She had been trudging behind for the past hours, the past days, halted, then squatted in the snow. She took another step then stopped, panting hard. Appreciating the break. She considered her situation. They must be well south of the Siachen glacier by now, deep within the Indian area of influence. Pakistani troops, Chinese troops, and now the front line of Indian troops, were all behind her.

She looked up and around. A pleasant change from matching the footsteps of her guide. It was the first clear day in a while and the sights, white on rugged rock, took her breath away almost as much as the altitude. There were certainly easier ways to infiltrate this country, but She was seeing such raw beauty that few ever did. And it was essential to be untraceable. Those were her terms for taking the job. As far as the Indian government would know, She had been born and raised in Kashmir and had never left it. Her employers shared her desire for secrecy. No links back to them, not physical, not electronic, nothing.

All this took time. She appreciated their patience. It took plenty to even find her. After all, it wasn't like She advertised. But they were playing the long game, willing to wait, and pay, for their results. The Sherpa stood and resumed his relentless pace. She took another moment, just an instant really, making a memory of the landscape. Then stalked on.

PART ONE

NOW AND THEN

CHAPTER 1

TINA

Today – New York City

Tina leaned close to the mirror supporting herself on the sink. A critical study. *I look like shit.* She felt like shit too. And tired. Very tired. Had those rings under her eyes always been there? Perhaps, but not so pronounced. Nothing a few days of serious R&R wouldn't cure. But when? She straightened up, squaring her back. Were her breasts a little lower than they once were? She knew they were. But only a bit. For now. The ballerina build of her youth was still there. A hint of soft about the belly button and hip, but again only a little. In fact, she had a figure that any man her own age would appreciate. And even some that were younger.

Tina heard movement in the bedroom and cringed. But the sense of satisfaction was stronger than any embarrassment. Far stronger. Good old-fashioned physical satisfaction. Can't beat that. To hell with convention. Coupled with discretion, anyway. She bent over the sink splashing cold water on her face. Clearing the cobwebs from her head and the oil of a slightly drunken sleep from her face.

In the mirror, Tina noticed the lean twenty-something was out of bed and on the move. Her eyes widened as she realized the young man's eyes were riveted on her bare butt. Fully awake now, Tina watched his approach through the reflection. She gasped audibly as he sprang to attention, instantly erect. He grinned a response. A quiver shot through her already aching thighs. *Lord, give me strength.* Firm forearms wrapped around her midriff. But she wore a grin too. And it was genuine.

"Well, good morning," Tina said. "You're up early."

***

Too much later, Tina was walking briskly down the Perry Street sidewalk. A bit weak in the knees, but still on the go. Almost breaking into a run, she was late and she knew it wouldn't do. Not that she'd catch too much trouble. Her boss, the editor of the political desk, needed her. Hell, he loved her. Tina knew that. But she shouldn't take advantage. Didn't want to go to the well too often. Not even if she could.

Tina swept into the crowded conference room, refreshed instantly by the coffee steaming from every hand. Loving the lively embrace of investigative journalism. An aggressive exchange was already underway. Tom flashed her a tight smile from the far end of the table that said it all: could have used you here sooner. He'd already loosened his tie. Not good. Two of the boys were debating, standing nose to nose across the center of the long table. Borderline to a fight. Competing, as usual. A half dozen interns sat on the sidelines as did some other reporters who didn't have a dog in this particular race. If it got too out of hand, Tom would settle it. Like a thumb on a bug. Tom was a good boss, but had little subtlety. In Tina's experience, not many men did. Rick and Bobby went at it like two rams trying to prove whose horns were harder. Nothing new in the newsroom. What started as creative and constructive confrontation often turned into competition. Tina could settle them down and reach a conclusion blending and bettering both points of view. Assuming Tom didn't knock their heads together first.

"Take a breath, gentlemen, and wish me good morning." Tina flashed a smile. Bobby, immediately distracted, dropped back into his chair.

He laughed, "Might as well since we'll end up doing it your way."

"Not this time," Tom growled. "Grab a toothbrush, Tina. You're heading to Kashmir."

"What?!" Bobby was back on his feet, but Tom stared him down.

"Come on, Tom," Tina said. "I'm neck deep in this border mess. In another couple of days, I'll blow the lid off this story. Send Bobby."

"Thank you!" said Bobby, vindicated.

Rick rounded on Tom, jabbing a hand in his direction, "You can't send a woman on this one, Tom. No offense Tina, but this is Muslim country in the back end of nowhere. And you can't send a rookie either," he added, looking pointedly at Bobby. "None of you can handle the risks like me."

"So she'll put a scarf on her head," said Tom. "Better get going, girl."

"But I know the languages for Chrissake!" said Bobby, back on his feet, he came at Tom. "Hindi, Urdu."

"That's two out of 24," Rick said, closing on Tom from the other side of the table. "Big whoop."

"I'm Indian after all, if you failed to notice!" bristled Bobby, "You won't be in Kansas anymore."

"I'm from Weehawken actually, but it doesn't matter," Rick said, "I'm the better reporter."

"Than Tina?" Bobby shot back.

"Than you!" shouted Rick.

Tom's fist came down on the table, coffee cups bounced. The room went silent. "Nobody calls the play in this huddle but me! Beat feet, Tina!"

***

"Knock, knock," Tina said as she opened the door, letting herself into Tom's office. Tom waved her in from behind his disheveled desk.

"I've been expecting you, girl," Tom said, "have a chair."

"No time for that, boss," Tina said, remaining in the door frame. "Just letting you know that the perfect solution to this India assignment is to send both Rick and Bobby together. They fight now, but they could end up like Woodward and Bernstein. In any case, as I said before, I don't have time for it."

"And the paper's made of money, right?" Tom said. "You managing the budget now, too?"

Tina shrugged, "I'm sure you could swing it, in an emergency."

"Have a chair, Tina."

"No thanks, Tom. In a rush, I've solved your India problem," Tina said, turning to leave.

"Sit down!" Tom was glaring at her now. "And close the door."

Tina sat down with mock subservience. "We're going to have another talk, are we?"

Tom's face softened to sadness. "Goddammit, girl, what am I gonna do with you?"

"What? Does my writing suck? Am I missing my deadlines?"

"No and no."

"Well?"

"Damit Tina, you know damned well that border story doesn't compare to Kashmir. Not as a deep investigative dive. What's wrong with you? You used to fight tooth and nail for the biggest and toughest assignments. And another thing, these late arrivals have got to stop. Unless you're on the job, nobody can be late for meetings."

"Who says I wasn't on the job?"

"Look Tina, I know that on occasion," Tom started.

"When the chips were really down," Tina interjected.

"When the chips were down," Tom went on, "you've shtupped information out of men before, and I've looked the other way, but somehow I don't think last night,"

"And this morning," Tina added.

"And this morning, I stand corrected, was all for the good of journalism."

"It's not your business, Tom. My private life. Even you can't cross that line."

"Tina, I'm worried about you. Talk to me. What's going on?"

"Oh I don't know," Tina said, relenting. "What was enough before somehow isn't anymore."

"Enough of what? Sex?"

"No, not sex."

"The job?"

"No, I still love it, but…"

"But what?"

"I don't know. It's somehow not enough anymore. I don't feel…whole."

"It's not easy," Tom agreed. "Being married to the job."

"It's worked for you."

"But I've got Nancy guarding the homefront. And the girls, although we won't have them for long. Growing up fast."

"She's a good egg, Nancy," Tina agreed.

"She's so much more than that," Tom said, "you have no idea."

"I believe you, Tom." Tina shrugged. "There certainly aren't any male Nancys out there. At least not in the circles I run in."

"You don't know that. Don't give up hope."

"Who are you trying to fool? They are all as career driven as I am. Or used to be," said Tina. "And it's just that I'm on the move all the time. All over the world. I mean, it's great and all,"

"But you're never home long enough for a relationship."

"Oh, I've had plenty of them," Tina said airily.

"I know. For what, three months, maybe four?"

"They still matter, Tom," Tina said. "Deep down each of them has a place in my heart forever. And not a man of them ever parted from me in bitterness."

"I know. How could they, girl," Tom said softly. A pause, "I think what you're feeling, Tina, might just be middle age."

"Oh wonderful. You think I need to be put out to pasture already?"

"You know I don't. My job is waiting for you if you can just hold on for another few years. The boys upstairs know my plans for you and they are all in. Just hang on a bit longer in the field." They lapsed into silence.

"Alright," Tina sighed. "Enough of this wallowing in self pity. I'll go to Kashmir."

"Now you're talking," Tom said, leaning in. "Pass Rick your notes on the border business. Now you're familiar with the broader Kashmir issue. India has most of it, but Pakistan and China have pieces of the pie as well. All three of them want the whole shebang, and the current borders are in such dispute that in some areas there aren't really borders at all."

"And they all want control of the water from the Siachen glacier region. But Tom, this has been going on for years. What's your angle?"

"I got a tip from a guy in State that they think the Chinese are really upping their ante in covert operations within India and it's somehow about Kashmir."

"But there's more?"

"Damn right there is," Tom said, "I felt he was playing me."

"Those government types are always playing us. Or trying to."

"Exactly. And here's what I think. Well not think really, more like feel. That it's actually the good old US of A that is upping their ante in covert operations in India."

"Misdirection. I'm on it, boss," Tina said, rising to her feet.

"Thanks Tina. Want to bring Bobby along with you?"

"Think I need a caregiver to help me with my cane?"

Tom laughed. "Truly no. Forget I mentioned it. Just take care of yourself. And bring home the bacon."

CHAPTER 2

NIKIAS

Over Two Thousand Years Ago - Greece

Nikias studied the dirt road leading up to his position. A bit of dust stirred, but it was just the breeze. Sweat trickled down from ear to jaw. Only mid-morning, it was going to be a hot one. And today was the day. He could feel it. Turning back into their encampment, Nikias surveyed the scene. They were hidden behind their recently completed earthworks from anyone coming up the road from the north, but they were unsheltered from the sun. Everyone was moving slowly. Lethargic from a week of waiting since finishing the earthworks.

"Why do you keep watching, Nikias?" one of the soldiers said, "We'll have plenty of time."

"Too much time. I'm sick of squatting here in this stinking oven," said young Aristol, the platoon's only officer.

"And I'm sick of you wailing like a babe without a tit," growled Agi. He stood up, stretching to his full height. "I want blood. Corinthian blood, but if they don't show, yours will do, my baby boy."

The young patrician's sword was out in a flash and he moved toward the big man. Nikias lunged off the embankment, intervening chest to chest with Aristol, grasping the wrist of the young officer's sword arm.

"Let him come, Nikias," laughed Agi. He'd unslung his big shield off his back, but drawn no blade.

Nikias ignored the fool behind him, focusing on the potential in front. "There's a time and place for everything, sir. We'll need every man before the day is done." He said that last line loud enough for everyone to hear.

"Hah!" grunted Agi, walking away.

Nikias released his officer as he felt the tension flow out of the young man. He resumed his perch on the embankment considering their situation. His eyes strayed to Agi. Clearly the strongest man in the platoon, he wasn't new to combat. But Nikias doubted Agi had the sand that would be needed this day, which had the makings of a last stand. Not every man can keep up the fight knowing that an honorable death would be his only reward. By some other sense than the behavior of the newcomer to the platoon, Nikias knew that Agi had no honor. And so, at some critical point, he would cave.

Aristol had returned to the bit of shade where their wall met the rocky crowns of the mountain summit, honing his blade, absorbed in the activity. Nikias had seen him spar and appreciated the young man's expertise. He was quick. Very quick. Though tall, Aristol still had the baby face of youth. He wasn't a leader of men. How could he possibly lead men half of whom would like nothing better than to bend the lad over a rock?

Nikias felt a stir in his loins at the thought then forced his mind back to the coming fight and the men here that he would die with today. Most of them were solid. Tough men in a melee, able to fight with both weapons and skin. Not elegant swordsmen like Aristol and others of the upper classes, but able to get the job done up close and personal. Skilled with the knife, the fist, the throw, and the kick. Aye, they'd do Sparta proud this day.

He looked back down the broad expanse that only narrowed at the summit where the Spartan platoon stood guard. The scattered green gray brush on the right side of the path sloping up unevenly would offer little cover for more than a few men. The grove to the left, a mixture of trees, was more dense, but abruptly ended about a javelin throw below their position. There the path widened to a plateau at the summit before narrowing just before the path led down again to the south. And Sparta. They had a good command of the approach to the pass that allowed travel through the mountains into the southern Peloponnese.

Somewhere to the south, not more than ten miles away maybe, an army of Sparta was bivouacked. Might as well be on the moon. They'd done well to force march so far and so fast, but now they were resting for the battle to come lest they be too tired to fight. Unless the Corinthians were softer than their reputation, they would reach the pass before the Spartans. Except for the thirty-seven Spartans already here. Dust stirred on the path again. Only this time, it wasn't the breeze.

CHAPTER 3

AJITA

Today - Delhi, India

Ajita was worried about her brother. He had gotten himself way too deep into this brotherhood, or whatever it was. It had gone from politics to activism to protests to…she dared not give it a name, but some of Rohit's new "friends" looked and acted like thugs. They scared her. One of them barely concealed his lust for her. That one, the one they called Haji, scared Rohit too. Big and brutish, common decency wouldn't protect Ajita if Haji ever got his chance. He wouldn't respect anything.

And then there was the woman. Ajita had only seen her once. So quiet, but somehow in command. Unsettling, she scared Ajita even more than Haji did. Last night, Ajita had begged Rohit to quit them all before something horrible happened.

"These Hindu fanatics you are consorting with," Ajita told him. "They are no good for a Sikh boy. They still believe in burning widows alive when their husbands die."

"That's just street talk, Ajita. We aren't about religion, Hindu or otherwise. We're about an independent Kashmir. Remember that Kashmir used to be Sikh country before it was partitioned. And we're against this globalization too. It consolidates wealth and power in the hands of only a few. Mostly foreigners. It's imperialism all over again."

"Quit them, Rohit," she had begged.

"It's too late for that," was all he had said, but Ajita had detected a hint of remorse in his voice.

Now Rohit had left their flat very early for the city center and Ajita knew there would be trouble of some kind before the day was done. She had stayed indoors all day, waiting. Pacing and fretting. Sweating it out in the stifling heat. She threw her lean length on the settee for the umpteenth time today and flipped quickly through channels, not even noticing what passed by.

Just come home, you fool. They were all each other had, Ajita and Rohit. She was six years his senior and had practically raised him since their parents had died.

Ajita left the station on the local news channel and rolled off the settee to the floor for some more yoga. *Breathe, girl, breathe.* She arched slowly, from the upward facing dog pose to the downward dog, a slender yet curvy upside down V, ignoring the background noise of the news as body, mind, and spirit met in her mantra.

***

Ajita was aware of the carpet against her cheek. She opened her eyes, dizzy. Blood pulsed through her temples, echoing in her ears. She closed her eyes again, as her memory returned and Rohit's image rushed back to her. She saw him through her eyelids. He had been on the television with that horrible Haji doing those horrendous things to that poor woman. Then there was Rohit in the picture. A part of it. *Rohit! What have you done? The police will kill you. Haji will kill you. Run little brother, run!* No, Rohit would help the woman. But he couldn't fight Haji. Then it had all been a blur. The camera and the action had combined to create chaos on the screen. She saw Rohit fall. And so had Ajita.

She pieced it back together in her mind. Tried to. Rohit had rescued the woman. And then the news reported that she had killed him. Why? Ajita staggered back to the settee. Her hands went to her head as she wailed in mourning for her baby brother. Had there been a funeral pyre, she would have thrown herself upon it.

CHAPTER 4

TINA

Tina lay flat on the hard floor of a bank in New Delhi, India trying to fight off the panic, willing her body to meld into the cool tile to escape. Her head jerked back brutally as she was hauled up by her hair. Stifling a scream, a hoarse grunt still snuck through her clenched teeth. Haji strode to the security camera, wrenching Tina off her feet. She staggered and scrambled to keep up and relieve the pain on her scalp. The big man pulled her upright so that she went to her toes to keep some of the strain off her hair.

"Here's what we do, until you do what we say." Haji said, looking up into the camera. "This western slut is the perfect start."

Tina hacked at Haji's thick wrist with all her strength. Once, twice, three times. No good. A pathetic attempt. The big man's grip on her hair was unerring. He looked at her, catching her eye and holding it. A small smile broke his lips through a disheveled beard. It was almost gentle. Then his left fist struck Tina in the solar plexus and as her body collapsed around the force of the blow, the brute released her hair. She crashed to the hard surface floor on knees and elbows. In shock, and with the wind knocked out of her, she couldn't breathe. *I'm going to die!* Finally, after what seemed an eternity, her lungs refilled. Tina pushed herself up to hands and knees just as rough hands tore her slacks from her hips half way down her thighs. She tried to rise but a heavy forearm forced her back down. Her cheek pressed painfully against the hard floor. Haji grabbed her right wrist and twisted her arm behind her back. Agony seared through Tina's mind and soul. She sobbed. Her arm was close to the breaking point, her shoulder and elbow near to popping. Holding her down via the arm lock Haji put his left index finger in his mouth with slow relish. Then he thrust it into her exposed anus.

"Aagh!"

On his knees behind her, Haji jerked his finger out.

"That was just to loosen you up," he gloated.

***

Rohit watched the scene in horror from the far end of the bank lobby. This wasn't what it was supposed to be about. His glock was slippery in his hand. "No," whispered Rohit, moving to intervene. It was only a walk. "No!" he shouted, breaking into a run.

***

Never again! The rage burst out of Tina just as Haji released her arm to unbuckle his belt. She instantly whipped back from the hips sending the back of her head with lashing velocity into the nose of the big man. Cartilage cracked, then a second strike landed with no less force. Still on his knees, Haji rocked back to sit on his heels, both hands over his face, groaning in muffled pain as blood flowed through his fingers. Her legs still bound by her pulled down pants, Tina went from knees to a half handstand, and with a two-legged scissor kick, struck her enemy in the throat. Her toes pointed to allow them to slip between the forearms of her enemy. She coiled again, still on her hands, and extending her arms in a single pushup, vaulted to her feet.

Her pants were back up freeing her legs. Another attacker, smaller and younger, was running at her, shouting. A kick down on his forward leg just at the knee and there was a crack of bone. As he fell toward her with a cry of agony, his head landed conveniently in her grip, seemingly planned. His scream was cut off by a quick snap of the neck. Another wicked sound of wreckage, as she let the inert body fall, seeking new foes.

People were running, shouting and screaming in a strange tongue in this strange place. They were all dark and oddly clad. And they were scared. Terrified. There was nobody familiar. *What is this place?* It was indoors with a vaulted ceiling as high as a temple. But not of stone. Had to get out. See the sky and breathe fresh air. The very air was alien. *What is this place?* Circling warily, these strange folk kept their distance. They were many, but they had fear and that was a weapon. Then Tina saw the sky through the wall. Distracted for a mere moment, what a marvel. To see through a wall. *It's a window. Of course, it's a window.* She rushed through the revolving door. *The sky! The blue sky! Sweet Zeus be praised, the sky!* Then darkness descended.

CHAPTER 5

PALLY

Sub-inspector Pallavi "Pally" Agarwal studied the slender, almost petite, woman sleeping softly before her. She appeared at peace, belying the leather restraints around her wrists and ankles. She had a pretty Anglo face, Pally decided, framed by flaxen blonde curls and rather full eyebrows only slightly darker. A soft snore escaped the woman's parted lips, which were a bit thin by Pally's standards, but they suited the rest of her face.

Alone in the hospital room with the sleeping woman, Pally enjoyed looking at her without discretion. Uninterrupted with nobody watching. Savoring the moment, yet feeling guilty. What was the matter with her? Last night at the dinner for the family to meet her cousin Raj's fiance, Pally had been smitten by the new girl on sight. With just a glance across the proverbial crowded room. But fortunately, Pally's glance hadn't been returned. What with all the bustle of meeting so many people, Pally was mere background noise to the girl, who was some ten years her junior. But Pally had snatched many discreet glimpses of the pretty girl from a distance. Quickies. Eyes can't linger lest you be caught out by someone. Or worse yet, make eye contact with the girl herself, revealing all of Pally's shameful passion in an instant. But now she could look to her heart's content upon this strange sleeping Anglo woman. She had her all to herself. Pally's hand came to rest inside her own thigh, then catching herself, moved it out to rest on her knee. Be careful you fool! The woman stirred in her sleep causing Pally's mind to return to her work.

It was hard for Pally to believe that this woman had killed two men, terrorized many more, and was only taken down by a knock on the head from behind by a police baton. She was lucky this one, only a concussion, but didn't appear to appreciate it. The Sub-inspector studied the press credentials and passport yet again in disbelief. Tina Marin, 51 years old, United States citizen, NY, NY. Old enough to be my mother, she thought. At a glance, Pally would have guessed her as ten years younger, maybe more. But on closer study, she could sense the woman's maturity more than see it. Pally had seen the bank films of the incident. Incident. It would have been a terrorist attack, but for this Marin woman. Now they didn't know what to call it. But the American woman had broken it up, that was for sure. As she awoke to a hero's welcome in her hospital bed, with her doctor taking her pulse, she had broken the poor man's wrist and flipped him across her bed. The staff had scattered as she sprinted seemingly directionless through the hospital corridors until a security team had finally cornered her and taken her down with a taser, followed by sedatives. Now the drugs were wearing off and Pally was here to place the pieces of the puzzle together. She studied the credentials again.

"Hello," said Tina. Startled, Pally looked up from the credentials to the woman. Her brown eyes locked onto big baby blues.

Pally flashed a smile. "Hello. How do you feel?"

"Ugh," Tina moaned, but managed a grin. "I feel awful." She suddenly was aware of her restraints as she tried to put a hand to her wounded head. She shifted uncomfortably, arms, legs and torso. "Hey, what gives? Where am I? Who are you?"

"Settle down," Pally said as Tina struggled to move, seeming surprised at her predicament.

"Where am I?" Tina asked again. Then, "Why am I tied down like this?" she demanded. The attending doctor entered the room, his arm in a sling and heavily bandaged.

"Do you know this man?" Pally asked Tina.

"No."

"He is your doctor. You broke his wrist a couple hours ago," Pally said. Tina's eyes grew wide. "Recognize him now?"

"I said I didn't," Tina shot back. "I don't think so," she added, with less certainty. "Oh, I don't know." This was practically a wail. She thrashed against her bonds, but there wasn't much heart in the effort.

"Settle down," Pally said. "Just relax. We will sort this out together."

"That would be wise, not to move so," the doctor said. "You have a concussion. Only a mild one surprisingly, but any concussion is serious. Try to stay calm and, please, no sudden head movements."

"What, what happened to me?" Tina asked.

"You were clubbed on your head," Pally answered.

"I've seen worse results from a policeman's baton," added the doctor, which produced a grimace from Pally. "You were lucky."

"What?" Tina exclaimed. "Why would a policeman hit me?"

"Because you were running amok, incoherent, and scaring everyone to death," said Pally.

Tina slumped, all resistance gone. Tears welled up. She took a deep breath. "Tell me. Everything. From the beginning."

Pally flashed another smile, "That's my line. You tell me."

"But I don't know!" Tina shouted. "Settle down," she immediately corrected herself.

"Again," Pally said with a chuckle, "That's my line." She looked kindly into the eyes of the American. "Ms. Marin, I am Sub-inspector Pallavi Agarwal. Call me Pally," she said, starting over.

"I'm Tina."

"Tina," repeated Pally. They smiled at each other. "Kind of a ridiculous circumstance to meet in."

"It makes no sense to me," said Tina. "Did I really hurt you, doctor? I'm sorry."

The young man appeared smitten by her soft sincerity. "Apology accepted, ma'am"

"But you don't remember it?" asked Pally.

"I, I don't know. It's all a fog."

"Let's back up a bit. To get on solid ground," started Pally. "You're American. You're a journalist. You know that, right?"

"I do. Yes, I do."

"And you're here in India for work?"

"Work. Yes, I'm on my way to Kashmir."

"Kashmir. Do you remember why?"

"Sure. The India - Pakistan conflict. Yes, that's it."

"But you stopped in the bank while still here in New Delhi," Pally prompted.

"Yes," said Tina, thinking back.

> *Running. Charging shoulder to shoulder. A jolting clash. Blood flows. Jaw to jaw, sweat, skin and bone grind together. Grunts. Cries. Thrust and parry. From me. In me? Sweaty skin again. Meshing. Intense, ecstatic. Strange. Familiar.*

Pally saw the confusion in Tina's face. Her eyes widened. She seemed to convulse, writhing within her constraints.

"Doctor?" asked the police sub-inspector as Tina's eyes looked right through them.

"Wait," he replied quietly. Tina clenched her eyes shut now. She thrashed against her bindings, panting hard. Blood trickled from her bit lip. Her thighs and knees locked together with rapid pelvic thrusts. She arched. Shocked, Pally suddenly recognized orgasm. And felt some moisture in herself.

Tina murmured something unintelligible to the two Indians. They both leaned in over the woman, listening, studying the clenched jaw and flared nostrils. Suddenly, her eyes flew wide open showing shock and fear. More words, clear now, but still unintelligible. She thrashed against her bonds.

"Ms. Marin!" barked the doctor. "Come back!"

Recognition returned to Tina's eyes. She looked quickly all about her, as much as her predicament permitted. Her total body tension suddenly drained, Tina collapsed into a soft sob. She looked at Pally, who saw fear and shame in the American's face.

"Don't think, Ms. Marin," the doctor said softly, "just breathe, focus on your breathing." He motioned the police officer into the hallway. Pally minded the doctor's advice for herself, feeling flushed as she followed the doctor.

"I can't let you question her further, Inspector," the doctor stated once out of earshot.

"What was that?"

"I am not certain, but I believe it was triggered by her attempt to recall past events."

"I understand your concern, doctor, but I have a terrorist attack to investigate that is becoming an international incident. I don't doubt that someone from the American Consulate will be here shortly. I need answers."

"I'm sorry, but you can't question her. My chief will back me up on this. I'll arrange a psych consult immediately."

"Then I'll just sit with her. Observe."

"Alright. For the present. But no questions. I will return shortly."

CHAPTER 6

AGI

The Corinthian column slowly poured into the view of the thirty-seven hidden Spartans waiting for them. Three officers came forward closer than the rest, just out of projectile range, studying the Spartan position while the long column behind them wheeled and maneuvered from a marching line into attack posture. After a few moments, Aristol, the young Spartan officer, stood upon the earth rampart in open view silently surveying the three opposing officers and the multitude of motion behind them. From his crouching position peering over the wall, Agi saw the same sight. But his tongue clove to the roof of his bone dry mouth. With an effort, he finally forced a swallow and licked his lips, chalk on rock. Agi looked up at Aristol standing tall above him, appearing so cool and calm, with something like hatred. *He'll be the death of me!*

The Spartan rampart was man high from rocky wall to wall where the pass narrowed. Before it, facing the Corinthians, was a ditch half again as deep as the rampart was high so that a man would need to climb a steep incline from the bottom of the ditch to reach where the young Spartan officer now stood. With two companies defending, it was a position that ten times that number would find difficult to breach. The Corinthians couldn't know that they were facing a single platoon, that arrayed from wall to wall the Spartans could only man the rampart as a single column with no reserve. A two platoon reserve would have been ideal. At least there would be plenty of room for each Spartan to fight, Nikias had told the platoon earlier. Agi knew, they all knew, that the spacing between each man was too much. Way too much.

The three Corinthians returned to the main army just as the maneuvers completed. A mass of men in close formation as wide as the pass moved forward as one. Aristol appeared to watch them with professional interest for a moment then jumped down from the rampart. His men were on their bellies peering over the top of the rampart as the enemy approached. Distributed evenly from wall to wall, it was a very thin line indeed. An exhausted Spartan runner entered the camp from the direction of the southern plains they were defending. He fell to his hands and knees before Aristol.

"Stand your posts everyone!" Aristol ordered. "Nikias, get this man some water." The runner waved away the water as he gulped precious air. Aristol and Nikias waited for his news. Agi strained to overhear from his place on the wall. The thunderous footfall of the approaching enemy was overwhelming.

"Speak, man," Nikias urged the runner.

"Two companies," he gasped between breaths, "an hour behind me." The officer and his sergeant looked at each other, but said nothing. Agi wanted to scream. *It will be too late!*

"Send a runner back down the pass, Nikias," Aristol said, "Tell them to make all speed. If they don't arrive in half that time they should fall back to the main army."

"Agi" Nikias called, "there are two companies coming up the pass to support us. We need to hold until they arrive. You run down to them. Tell them to get here in 30 minutes or not at all. Leave all your weapons here. This man will stand your post." Agi peeled off his gear.

"Agi?" Aristol asked quietly of Nikias, "he's our strongest."

"And our weakest," Nikias replied just as quietly. But Agi heard. He sprinted back down the path without a word.

Inside, Agi was bursting with relief as he ran. He would live another day. The only man in the platoon who would.

***

Back at the wall, having finally recovered his breath, the runner drank deep then took up Agi's place in the line with Agi's shield, sword, and javelins.

The Corinthian host stopped as one. Silence slowed down time. At a single command, two companies trotted another thirty steps forward to optimum javelin range. Any defender standing on the rampart would be marked and taken down immediately. Another command barked and three more companies surged forward in tight shieldwall formation, shield to shield, and covered by the javelin throwers.

The Spartan line remained under cover. When the forward three companies were halfway to the ditch a final command ordered the main body of the host forward. The first three companies leapt into the ditch unopposed, but they didn't try to scale the rampart. Instead, they slung their shields over their backs and shoulders to form a ramp for the following companies to march over and up to the rampart. It was awkward for the soldiers to walk on the shield floor. Some few fell through into the ditch, but other soldiers gained solid ground at the base of the rampart. In a few steps, the first soldiers would be at the top. Still the Spartans waited.

Just as the first Corinthians staggered to their feet on the apex of the rampart, Aristol shouted, “Forward soldiers of Sparta!”

Thirty-seven Spartans were on their feet in unison pushing with shield and striking with sword at the Corinthians, before they could regroup. The rampart was only two strides wide at its apex. On that narrow strip of earth, with hundreds of Corinthians swarming up the rampart, the thirty-seven Spartans stood staunchly at bay.

CHAPTER 7

AJITA

Ajita turned away from the hospital receptionist, not sure if she could go on, but needing to. She knew this place. Had never been inside, but passed by it regularly for most of her twenty-seven years. Following the directions given to her, Ajita found the morgue in the basement. An attendant led her inside, then motioned her to wait. He approached one of the many tables in the room where three men stood around talking softly while studying a corpse on the table. Ajita choked out a gasping cry as she realized it was Rohit on the table. She sank sobbing to the floor, which caught the attention of the men. One of them came to her, a policeman, while the other two continued their discussion.

"You're here to identify this man?" the policeman asked.

Ajita nodded, staring past the cop to what had once been her beloved brother. A firm hand supported her elbow, lifting her, guiding her forward. One of the others pulled a sheet over the body just as she arrived, leaving the head and torso exposed.

"Is this your brother, Rohit Singh?" the burly cop asked gently.

"Yes," she whispered. She began to shiver and her knees weakened. Strong hands were there to catch her before she fell. They guided her to a nearby chair.

"Rest here until you feel strong enough to walk. Would you like some water?"

Ajita shook her head.

"Then rest here for now. I am sorry for your loss. We will talk later, when you feel up to it."

The policeman returned to the other two men studying her brother. They seemed to forget about her as one man, the doctor, silently performed a slow methodical physical examination.

"Most impressive," the doctor told the police officers when he had completed the examination. "Most impressive." After a moment, he continued without prompting from the two cops. "The break of the leg and knee couldn't have been done better if it had been choreographed in advance. Not only did the strike hit a moving leg at just the perfect angle to render the limb completely inoperable in an instant, but it caused the victim to fall forward in the direction of the strike. Whether it was all by design or chance, I can't say. The second injury, the fatal one, is a clean break of the neck and spinal cord at the cervical area. It needed minimal effort by the attacker because the momentum of the victim's fall provided most of the force. Putting the two injuries together, it appears the work of an expert in martial arts. I heard of such training within the special forces when I was in the army medical corps."

"Well doctor, that fits with the bank video except for the expert part. She's no expert as far as we know," the burly policeman said.

"An American woman, of all things. And not a big person at all. Maybe 5'6", 115 lbs.," added the other cop. "In fact, the earlier portion of the tape showed just how helpless she was. That big guy on your other table there was manhandling her like a play thing. And not in a nice way, I might add."

"You mean until she decided to break his nose then crush his larynx?" asked the doctor. "Another precise move that required minimal force."

"Yeah well, all I can say Doc is that she was completely helpless until she went all ninja on these two fellows. Not that I'm feeling bad for them. They had it coming, especially the big one. That video would have played a lot worse if she hadn't...changed."

"I would like to see this video. And the woman," the doctor said.

"She's up on the fourth floor right now. Our people are with her. Didn't you hear about all the commotion earlier today?"

The doctor shook his head. "This was supposed to be my day off. I just got here a few minutes before you arrived."

"Well, this woman was put out cold when our people nabbed her at the scene. She came to in the hospital, broke a doctor's arm and knocked hell out of a few more trying to escape. Hospital security took her down with a taser. Good thing too. We'd have had to shoot her otherwise."

"Well that fits with how she dispatched these two. I'm sure you will find out where, when, and how she got all her training in due course. Probably American special forces. They and the British wrote the book on this kind of thing. Meanwhile, I'll write up my report."

"Thanks Doc. I guess that wraps things up for now."

Ajita was out the door and heading up the stairs as she heard the policeman say, "Oh, Ms. Kaur? Are you well enough to talk now? Now where did she get off to?" She fled light footed up the stairs before they could look for her.

CHAPTER 8

NIGHT VISITS

Tina woke from another restless sleep. The dream was vividly violent. She tried to grasp the images even as they faded. Her breathing slowed. Movement in the shadows caught her attention.

"What do you want?" Tina asked, still waking up. A white lab coat was visible in the dim light. Tina relented and relaxed. "I suppose you need even more blood." she said with a chuckle to make up for her previous harshness.

"No blood," came the soft reply, "not yet." Tina was on her guard, sensing something. She was acutely aware of her bonds. Her helplessness.

"I can scream."

"I know."

"What do you want? Who are you?" Tina asked.

"My name is Ajita. And I want to, need to, understand," a pause, "who killed my brother. And why."

"You're not supposed to be here," Tina barked. "I'll scream." But she didn't.

"Now tell me." Another pause. "Your name."

Tina didn't reply. Her own name, the name she knew, didn't seem to be true. But there was nothing else, was there? The figure stepped closer. An Indian woman, Tina's own height. But much younger. She had a knife in her hand. Tina recognized it as one of the ceremonial knives Sikh men wear. The knife came closer. Toward her throat. It stopped still, barely touching Tina's neck under her left ear. Tina went rigid. She felt a hand unfastening her left hand binding, then her right as the knife stayed stock still on her carotid artery.

As soon as her right hand was free as well, the American's left hand quickly gripped the knife hand at the wrist and forced, knife and hand together, up toward the chest of the Indian woman. Her right hand took the Indian by the throat with a thumb digging deep under her jaw. During this quick reversal, the knife had nicked the American half an inch vertically on the jawline not far from her ear, but she ignored the blood dripping down her neck. The Indian girl tried to shrink away from the blade just under her ribcage, but she was held fast. The American woman, who was still bound at the ankles, increased pressure on Ajita's throat, knowing the technique inflicted a mix of pain and partial paralysis. Ajita went down to her knees before Tina, who remained sitting upright in the bed, still bound at the ankles. A quick twist of the wrist, a gasp from Ajita, and Tina had the knife in her hand. She studied her would-be attacker.

> *Dark of skin, an attractive girl. A Nubian. Not often seen in Hellas, they were usually slaves. This one must be a slave. But sent by whom? On what orders?*

The knife slashed sharply to Ajita's throat, but it was the only knife hilts that struck the Indian on the jawline. She collapsed to the floor.

***

Her throbbing head was Ajita's first experience coming back to awareness. Then slender pale ankles atop bare feet, right at eye level, came into focus in the dim lighting. The American woman.

"Please," Ajita whispered as she brought herself up to her hands and knees. Still shaky.

The American replied, but Ajita didn't understand the language. It certainly wasn't English or Hindi. Then the knife was under Ajita's chin bringing her to her feet, face to face with her captor.

"Please," Ajita repeated.

Even in the dim light, Ajita was captured by the intense blue eyes considering her. There was no anger or hate in the eyes. Only intensity. The eyes released Ajita. While the knife remained on her throat, the eyes scanned the dark surroundings of the hospital room. Ajita focused on her breathing, to combat the panic rushing through her veins. The American woman mumbled words Ajita couldn't understand. Then she asked Ajita a question. Ajita could tell it was a question, but nothing more. It was in no language she had ever heard. She asked again in a sharper tone, clearly frustrated by Ajita's silence.

"Please," was all Ajita could repeat, not understanding what was wanted of her.

"Please," the American repeated, looking around the room. "Please." Then she slowly, deliberately looked Ajita up and down, adding a discomfort to Ajita's fear. A smile came to the woman's face. Ajita had seen such smiles before. On men.

The American woman pulled the T shirt by the collar and cut Ajita's shirt down her front. She studied Ajita's bra with seeming surprise, then Ajita gasped as that too was cut and her full breasts fell free under the open lab coat. Ajita fought the sudden impulse to cover herself with her arms, but she dared not move for the knife. Focused on her breathing, Ajita slowly recovered her composure somewhat. At least it didn't appear that the crazy American would kill her. The eyes upon her nudity, a first time for Ajita, was strangely stimulating.

The American murmured admiration and gently fondled Ajita with a single hand. The knife was ever present before the Indian girl's eyes. Ajita stood stock still. Despite her fear, she felt herself physically responding. With the knife, the American, again, slowly cut Ajita's skirt and panties down the front. The point of the blade tickled, but didn't cut, Ajita from belly button down to her pubic line. Ajita felt dizzy. She widened her stance a bit to steady herself. A soft purring sound came from the blonde woman in response.

The American stepped in closer. Ajita could feel her warm breath on her face. Enter her space as she too breathed. The American's free hand followed the path of the knife lightly from her breasts down her tight belly to below. Ajita closed her eyes, trying to fight the physical instincts of her body. Yet part of her was euphoric. The American murmured softly again in the mystery language. Her free hand went from Ajita's sex to her own. A muffled cry came from the American. She dropped the knife, urgently pulling up her hospital garb with both hands over her head. Both of her hands were between her thighs now groping and probing. The American was shaking as her hands headed north to discover just a handful of breast for each. With a tragic cry that resonated beyond the room and through the hospital corridor, the American collapsed unconscious.

Ajita was almost in a state of shock. She heard footsteps pounding. Taking all her strength, she heaved the American woman up under her armpits, tossing her on the bed. Then she grabbed the knife and bunched up her cut up clothes in her arms and slid bare assed under the hospital bed just as the door swung open.

CHAPTER 9

TO A MAN

Agi was still breathing steady as he toiled in step with the rest of the forward company, double time, up the trail toward the pass. Some of the others around him were gasping for breath. But they were stoically still keeping time. How any of them were expected to be in fit condition to fight once they got there was beyond Agi's understanding.

He tried to keep the panic at bay that was pumping through his chest and coiling up his throat. Focus on your breathing. Stay strong. And Agi was strong. He had always been one of the strongest since childhood. Now at twenty-nine years of age, he was at the height of his physical prowess, martial expertise, and combat experience. Yes, Agi knew combat. Bigger and stronger than most, and faster than some, he was an apex predator. Agi had been in any number of small patrol skirmishes as well as several major army actions. Any natural fear he had felt, and Agi knew that all men felt fear as he did, had always been tempered by his confidence in his own abilities and his trust in the superiority of the Spartan army. Of course he could die in any combat, but more likely he would kill instead.

The soldier next to him staggered. Agi steadied him for a moment with a strong hand under the man's armpit. The man steadied himself and managed a grin of thanks through his heavy panting. Agi let him go. A stumble like that was a sign of fatigue. A foot isn't quite lifted high enough to clear a rock or a root, and a man stumbles. Agi returned to his own breathing. His body was still strong. The man in front of him went down and with no time to help, Agi hurdled him and resumed his steady pace. Two men behind Agi dragged the fallen man back up and as he got his feet back under himself, he too soldiered on. The company's quick march scarcely missed a beat.

Agi had fairly flown down the trail to meet the approaching companies after Nikias had ordered him off. Running downhill from certain death had been easy. His speed had made his own wind on his face in that sprint. On one turn in the trail, the mountain opened onto a broad shallow high altitude valley on his right and Agi could see the distant plains of his homeland below.

It was an elating sight, filling him with hope. Somewhere down there was the main host of Sparta and soon he would be amongst them. Safe and strong.

The past month had been a slow agony for Agi. It had been so for everyone in the platoon, stationed up there all alone. At first, they had been too busy to worry about attack, building the earthworks for the rampart. Before it had been built, of course they would have withdrawn if a larger enemy force had arrived. But as the defenses took shape, Agi knew it would become harder to fall back in the face of a superior force.

Then came the word a week ago that the Corinthians were on the move and the Spartans were hastening north to meet them at the summit. Their orders: hold the pass until relieved. The dread had been slowly growing in Agi ever since.

The two Spartan companies rounded the last bend to reach the summit pass. Running four abreast, Agi was in the third row. On command, the companies came to an abrupt halt. Less than a hundred yards away, the pass was swarming with Corinthians. Thousands of them. A mass of Corinthians more than double the number of the arriving Spartans were already on their side of the rampart.

"Sweet Zeus," gasped Agi under his breath, "we're too late. Retreat."

"Charge!" shouted the Spartan captain.

He led his 200 men toward the mountain wall where a handful of Spartans, the ragged remnant of Aristol's platoon, still fought on, back to back. Agi's legs went to jelly as he lunged forward on command toward the melee. The Corinthians were aware of the newcomers now and with a shout javelins rained down amongst them. Agi was already weak in the knees with fear when the spear struck him full on his shield. The force of the blow halted his momentum, backed by his own hesitancy. Other warriors pushed past him.

Agi's head was spinning. He stopped fighting it and let himself collapse, only knowing that he couldn't continue charging into certain death. His comrades surged on. The pounding of sword on shield, grunting and swearing, cries of agony, permeated his mind. He lay still, face down on his shield, eyes squeezed shut.

***

The fight to hold the rampart was brief and bitter. Even as Nikias struggled to hold his place in the line, expending every ounce of his energy at an incredibly rapid rate and the bloodlust of battle raced through his veins, there was a place of fatalistic peace deep within him. Today was a good day to die. It had been shield work at first for the Spartans, using the man high devices like battering rams forcing the enemy back into the pit before they could catch their footing at the top. But it couldn't last. Nikias had turned his shield sideways to push two men back at once, but a third slipped by. A deep thrust with a short blade pierced Nikias just above his left hip. Nikias pivoted and knocked the man over with his shield even as he dropped to one knee. The heat of battle kept him active even as his life's blood flowed. He drew his sword just as another Corinthian swung his blade to behead him. Nikias ducked it, but the enemy's sword still struck his helmet hard. Nikias staggered, dizzy and weak. Then he was down. Unconscious and bleeding out. Warriors stepped and tripped over his body, swearing savagely as they came to grips with their enemies.

***

His slashing blade seeming everywhere, the Corinthians facing Aristol were only forced forward by the overwhelming surge behind them. Several had already fallen to his sword. Bellowing his commands over the tumult even as he slashed and sliced, Aristol rallied his remaining soldiers toward the right end of the rampart, still temporarily holding the high ground of the rampart, building a shield wall. But they were soon forced off the rampart, sliding down to the southern side. And still their shield wall held with only ten Spartans left, their backs to the mountain face. Over the cacophony of screams, swearing, and grunts, Aristol heard the shout of the Spartan relief force's charge. Their shield wall finally broke just as the Spartan companies, already greatly reduced, reached them.

It was a man-to-man melee from then on. The Spartans fought savagely, but the fight was over in less than ten minutes after the Corinthian attack had begun. Aristol was struck by the flat of a blade to the back of his neck. Not a drop of his blood was spilled, but he was out of the fight. An elegant inert lump of flesh amongst the wreckage and slaughter.

***

"He's worth keeping." Harsh laughing of many voices followed the comment. Aristol opened his eyes, but no sight came to him. Strong hands gripped him. He felt movement, but didn't understand. He tried to move, but couldn't.

"He's waking up."

"Always better when they're awake." More laughing.

A horn blared and the laughter settled into grousing. Commands barked. Aristol was dropped heavily. Pain erupted through his head to his right shoulder. He was briefly confused, fell back into oblivion as the Corinthian officers bullied their men to cease their looting. Forcing them back into formation. The main host of the Spartan army had been sighted marching up the trail toward the summit.

CHAPTER 10

VISITS REVISITED

Two nurses and a policeman poured into the hospital room only to find the American woman face down naked, groaning as she pushed herself up on the bed, as if coming out of a deep slumber. The policeman drove his forearm with all his weight behind it onto Tina's back. As he forced the woman face down back on the bed, he twisted one arm tightly near to breaking point, handcuffing her other wrist. Tina was cuffed before she was fully conscious.

"Stand back you oaf," the senior nurse shouted, pushing the cop aside.

"That lady is dangerous," replied the cop, "how did she get out of her bindings?" He stepped back a few paces and pulled his sidearm.

"Here, let's get her turned and get her ankles bound again," the nurse said to her younger colleague.

"There's blood," the younger nurse said, "where is she bleeding?"

The two nurses worked quickly. Tina groaned in complaint, but realizing that they were helping her, didn't resist. The nurses found, gauzed, and taped the small cut on Tina's jaw. Then they covered her nakedness with a sheet.

The night duty doctor arrived rubbing his eyes with his one good hand. It was the same young doctor whose wrist Tina had broken less than 24 hours earlier. "What do we have here?" he directed his question to the older nurse. Then he saw the cop with gun in hand. The doctor stepped back a bit. "Nurse, stand back. Everyone stay six feet away from the bed. Is the patient secured?"

"I cuffed her hands behind her back," the policeman told him.

"And her ankles are strapped down again," the younger nurse added.

"But we found her totally free, face down on the bed, bleeding, and completely naked," explained the senior nurse. "And you must have heard the same cries that we did."

Tina was fully alert now. The doctor approached her.

"Do you know who you are?" he asked. Tears flowed from Tina's baby blues down soft pale cheeks. She didn't answer. "Do you understand me?" the doctor continued, "The words I am speaking to you?"

"Yes. My wrists hurt, doctor."

The doctor chuckled. "Believe me, I understand how you feel," he said, holding up his own injured wrist, "but let's see about getting you more comfortable."

"I can't uncuff her, doctor, and rely on the bed straps until we learn how she got free in the first place," the cop said.

"A fair point, officer," said the doctor. Then to Tina, "can you tell us what happened?"

"I was dreaming. There was a beautiful young woman. She had a knife. He...I...I can't remember. Nothing makes sense."

"Ms. Marin," the doctor said earnestly, "you passed all your psych evaluations with flying colors. Your head wound won't keep you in this hospital long. Tomorrow morning, or today I should say, it will be police investigators asking you questions, not doctors. Now is there anything you can tell me to help me understand, from a health perspective, your behavior over the past 15 hours?"

"No. I'm sorry. Nothing makes sense."

"All right, it doesn't make sense," the doctor said. "Tell me anyway. Whether you understand it or not."

Tina took a deep breath. "I woke up. The room was dark. A beautiful young woman was standing before me, just where you are now. She had a lab coat on, unbuttoned, just as you wear yours. Then she showed me a knife, I thought she would kill me. I was so scared. Then I seemed to go away. It seemed I was dreaming, watching someone else. No...I," Tina gave up in frustration.

"When you first woke up, Ms. Marin, and saw the woman, do you think you were still dreaming?" asked the doctor.

"It doesn't seem like I was, but I must have been. It must have all been a dream."

"Except that you were found out of your restraints. With a cut on your jaw. Did any of you see a woman come into this room? Officer?"

"Well, I was down at the nurse station," the cop replied uncomfortably, "still in sight of the hallway and this door though."

The doctor looked at the two nurses, "Can you two say with certainty that nobody entered this room from your position at the station?"

"No doctor," the older nurse replied, "but nobody passed our station in that direction that I saw."

"Oh, there was somebody," said the younger nurse, "from the hospital staff."

"Who was it?" the older nurse and the doctor asked in tandem.

"I don't know," she replied, flustered, "I didn't really notice and I don't know everyone on the staff. I've only been here for two months."

"When was this?" asked the older nurse.

"When you were on your rounds."

"So while I was checking on patients, you two were talking too much together to pay attention to anything else," the nurse said severely to the cop and the younger nurse.

"We'll deal with that later," interjected the doctor. "It appears Ms. Marin, that you weren't dreaming. Did the woman unstrap you?"

"As I said, she pulled out a knife. I got scared. I was helpless, strapped in as I was. I panicked. Then everything gets hazy." There was a long pause. Tina closed her eyes. "Someone else was here. In bed with me. A man. Yes, she unstrapped us. He took the knife from the woman. Held it to the young woman's throat. She was lovely. We cut her clothes off. Her skin was soft and smooth. Her breasts responded to our touch." Tina paused. "That's all. Very strange. I must have been dreaming."

"Can you describe the woman to us?" the doctor asked. The policeman pulled out his notepad.

"Oh yes. I saw her quite clearly, even though it was dark. She was medium height, maybe 5' 6" or 5' 7", mid-twenties, Indian of course, a bit darker than you, doctor, but only a bit. Her teeth, yes her teeth were very white and even, she didn't ever smile, but I bet if she did she would be dazzling. Hmm, black hair parted down the middle and braided down her back."

"The woman I saw in the hallway had a long braid. That must have been her," said the younger nurse. The doctor silenced her with a look.

"Tell me about the man, Ms. Marin," said the doctor, "what did he look like?"

"The man? I didn't really see him. I mean, he was here, but I was looking at the woman. I was so scared of her knife, but he wasn't."

"Why wasn't he afraid?" asked the doctor. "Even if you didn't see him, what can you remember about him?"

Tina closed her eyes and didn't speak for a moment. Then softly, "He's a soldier of Sparta."

"Sparta?" said the doctor.

"The Corinthians," whispered Tina, "They are coming." The doctor didn't ask any more questions because Tina had drifted into sleep.

CHAPTER 11

BOBBY

Bobby fidgeted in his airline seat. They seemed to be getting more uncomfortable every time he flew, which was often. He didn't mind the narrow seating, being a lean man, except when the neighboring body spilled over into his precious space. But being also a tall, gangly, young man, the lack of legroom was downright cramped, particularly on these longer hops. Right now, he was halfway through the London to Bombay leg of his journey to Tina. Nine hours in the air.

He had never been on an overseas assignment with Tina before, just the two of them. Bobby was partially worried for her - that video footage was horrific - part reveling in the chance to spend one on one time with her, and part nervous.

Tom had wanted to come himself, but eventually his protectiveness for Tina was overcome by his commitment to the job, the paper, the profession. He was an old school newspaperman and always would be. Bobby on the other hand, was a techno geek as well as a writer. He'd found the video on the web showing that horrible bank scene. Tom was working through State to get a copy of the bank surveillance videos. But they didn't have audio. The cell phone version provided a different angle and audio. Bobby shivered just thinking about it.

He tried to pull his mind out of emotional mode toward the analytical. He had a job to do. Two jobs in fact because Tina's assignment hadn't disappeared just because she was attacked. He had to move on to Kashmir, with or without Tina, depending on her condition. But Tom was enough of a newspaperman to recognize that Tina was a story herself. Finding out how big a story was Bobby's first task. He was ordered to spend a precious day with Tina then report back to Tom, who would decide whether to drop Kashmir or Tina as a story. The Kashmir situation was volatile. It could literally blow up in their faces on both sides of the border. That in itself was not unique, but the possibility of the current crisis having been precipitated by the United States government was.

His mind went back to the two videos. One shot from an elevated angle looking down at the action. That monster holding a helpless Tina up by her hair in front of the bank camera. Then the other shot from the floor taken by a hostage, from behind and a bit to the left. That had gotten lots of views in India, perhaps because it displayed a beautiful blonde's bare bottom, but it hadn't really gone viral internationally. The audio was weak, but Bobby had been able to identify Tina's voice amidst all the chaos that erupted when she had killed those men. It wasn't clear what she was saying, what with all the screaming and shouting going on, but he was pretty sure he made out the word 'Zeus'. He had run it many times and at least that one word he clearly heard. Tom had technical staff working on the audio to see if they could clean it up. Remove all sounds other than Tina's voice to understand what she was saying. Zeus. That made no sense. The Greek god? Why would she say that? In what possible context?

Bobby flagged a passing stewardess, "another Manhattan, please." The British woman nodded a crooked, cute smile in acknowledgement without breaking stride. Bobby took another sip off the drink still in hand. It would be empty before the next one came. He needed something to help him relax. It was impossible to meditate in such crowded, confined quarters. Intermittent turbulence sealed the deal against meditation. Flying didn't frighten Bobby, but one couldn't help feeling helpless. Better to focus on other matters or nothing at all. With meditation denied him, Bobby used alcohol instead. And still he couldn't stop thinking.

Bobby wasn't sure what attracted him most, Tina's slender figure which seemed to glide as she moved, or that petite featured face that could flash a smile from ear to ear. She wrinkled around her eyes when she smiled, which was often. It seemed to Bobby that Tina was a joyful person. Her flaxen blonde hair blended subtly with gray, particularly where it curled a bit at her temples. Bobby let out a sigh. He will see her tomorrow. Eager yet tentative.

He couldn't stop thinking of that video. The one he had found on the web. From floor level, the iPhone couldn't have been more than 15 feet from the action. Bobby felt guilty knowing what had almost happened to Tina, but he kept returning to that freeze frame he stored on his phone. The video quality was terrific and he was able to zoom in. For one brief moment, that bastard torturing her had moved back, and the instant before Tina went on the attack, Bobby now had the most vivid snapshot of Tina's beautiful bottom. In detail. Pure loveliness. To be treasured. Revered even.

Bobby didn't have carnal thoughts for Tina. Well, not many anyway. To his mind, she was so over his head, so out of his league, that just to work with her, be around her, was all the reward he ever hoped for. He knocked back the rest of his drink when the stewardess arrived. Armed with the fresh cocktail, Bobby nestled his length as deep as he could into his tight seat and pulled out his iPhone.

CHAPTER 12

AJITA

Ajita slammed the door shut to her flat and leaned against it for support. She was practically panting. Then she started to shake and sob. Three unsteady steps and she collapsed onto the settee. Curled up into the fetal position, her emotions took full control and her nerves, stretched to the limit over the past two days, sent signals helter-skelter throughout her body, twitching and shivering. Her eyelids. Her thighs. She felt cold despite the heat. She clutched a cushion close. Wrapped the hospital bed sheet tight around herself. The only covering she had worn when she escaped the hospital. Minutes passed, then an hour. Her heart rate began to slow to normal.

Hunger and thirst drove her upright. On her way to the kitchen, she stopped at the hallway mirror. Shocked at what she saw. Sweat beaded her upper lip, flowed free from the bit of black satin hair of her armpits trickling all the way down to her hips, slid across her breastplate twixt her cleavage and the crease under her breasts, down the inside of her thighs.

But her eyes haunted her the most. The shame of what had happened to her, pushing even her grief for Rohit aside, cascading more shame. She moved on to the kitchen in nothing but her shoes. The only thing she had worn into the hospital and wore out again. Ajita devoured some hummus on naan, chasing it with water.

That woman. Why had she humiliated her so? Aroused her so? She couldn't even admit that to herself, but it was lurking just under her consciousness. Ajita had wanted to meet the woman who had killed her little brother. To tell her about him. How he was growing into a fine young man. That she had practically raised him. Ajita had wanted to set the woman free so they could sneak out together, find a quiet space, maybe back to her home, her and Rohit's, to tell the story of Rohit's life. So she would understand what she had done. That woman had been attacked. Ajita knew she wasn't a cold blooded killer. But she had killed her Rohit. She needed to know what she had done. Perhaps even mourn together with Ajita.

But that woman was not who she appeared to be. She was crazy. No, not crazy, she was a killer after all. A professional. Ajita was still trying to digest all she had heard from under the bed. She had lain there for hours, had wanted to scream when the woman talked about a man. What man? There was no man! And yet the doctor had believed her. Or humored her, Ajita couldn't tell which. But it was she who had humiliated Ajita so. Not some mythical man. A Spartan warrior? Ajita didn't even know what a Spartan was.

Finally, the police had taken the woman away the next morning. Ajita had remained under the bed trying to summon the courage to make a move. Someone had come in to strip the bed sheets and left them in a bin by the bed. That is when Ajita had grabbed the sheet, wrapped herself in it like a Sari and strolled boldly out into the hallway. It had been agony. She got some strange looks from people and staff, but nobody challenged her. And so she had made it all the way home. It was over. It was still daylight, but Ajita went to bed. She was physically and emotionally spent.

***

There was knocking. And more knocking, louder than before. Why wouldn't it stop? Ajita came reluctantly out of a deep sleep. Without raising her head she checked her cell on the nightstand. 9AM. She must have slept for 16 hours straight. The image of Rohit in the morgue flashed. The feel of the foreign woman touching her where she had never been touched, except by herself. Her phone buzzed. She must have slept through many buzzes because she had messages waiting. The knocking returned with a vengeance.

"Alright already!", Ajita shouted. She got up, threw some clothes on, splashed water on her face, and reached the front door just as another round of pounding began.

"Who's there?"

"Police, Ms. Kaur," replied a female voice, "We'd like to talk to you." Ajita opened the door to find five people on her doorstep.

"Hello Ms. Kaur. I am Sub-inspector Agarwal. May we come in?" Pally asked.

Ajita stepped aside and motioned them in without a word, regarding them warily. The big policeman Ajita recognized from the morgue followed Pally in with a nod and a shy smile.

"Inspector Khera, Intelligence Bureau, Ms. Kaur," said a stocky, middle-aged man in a dark suit. Ajita's eyes widened. So the IB was involved.

"Terrence Grey, United States consulate," said the thirty-something man.

"Special Agent Miller, ma'am, United States Federal Bureau of Investigation," said a woman.

There wasn't enough seating in Ajita's small flat and she was in no mood to entertain, so she just stood there, silent and sullen. The five of them half-surrounded her in a semi-circle.

"Tell us about your visit to the hospital, Ms. Kaur," opened Inspector Khera.

CHAPTER 13

AGI

Agi lay stock still. He had been that way for hours. The fear was ever present, but the great god Pan no longer controlled him. Agi lay there focusing on a slow shallow breathing technique. Not only did that keep the panic at bay, but it also wouldn't likely be noticed by the Corinthian garrison on the rampart. The rampart that Spartans had built. That he, Agi, had sweated over. Agi wanted revenge for this insult to Sparta. And that was a good thing. He was thinking more about killing than dying. But before he could kill he had to survive. He was lying in an exposed area under Corinthian control. Playing dead amongst the dead. He dared not move or even twitch.

The main force of the Corinthians had headed south down the trail to meet the Spartans. Fortunately, he hadn't been trampled too much. After all, no soldier wanted to turn an ankle. The Corinthians hadn't returned. Agi figured the two armies had fought to a standstill. Had the Spartans won they would be here by now. Then Agi could feint recovery and rejoin them. But that hadn't happened. Nor had the Corinthians returned victorious. While Agi wasn't able to look around to see anything, his ears were working fine. Runners had been going back and forth between the battle and the pass all afternoon.

It had been a long day for Agi. When he had awakened in the morning, Agi had been the newest member of a platoon that had been together for quite some time. He had been assigned to the unit only a month ago. He and that pup officer Aristol. That boy was attractive. And Agi resented him for it. Much as he wanted him, young Aristol was off limits to Agi. Unlike in other city-states, like Athens and Corinth, love and lust between men was frowned upon in the disciplined Spartan culture. Of course, a citizen could use his slaves as he saw fit, but while Agi was a citizen he was not rich enough to own slaves. He was a simple soldier of Sparta. As such, he was honored in Sparta as were all soldiers, but it brought no pleasures. The female slave prostitutes were of course available and Agi enjoyed them as often as time and money allowed, but boys were off limits.

Agi had gotten his taste for boys during his youth training. All Spartan boys trained rigorously from childhood to adulthood, when they became soldiers. And while not openly permitted, growing boys spending long hours together in training, and cut off from girls to boot, they will indulge themselves. Agi had always been bigger and stronger so it had been easy to cut out the smaller and younger youths that had appealed to him. But upon adulthood and entry in the army, that avenue was cut off. And Agi's frustration had grown with his lust. It had been that way for years now. Then came this new platoon assignment and there was young Aristol looking like Cupid himself. Those curly locks drove Agi crazy. Attraction had quickly grown to yearning, to frustration, and ultimately to resentment. He hated Aristol because he couldn't have him.

Now Aristol was probably dead. Agi couldn't know. And it didn't matter. Agi had to survive. He very much wanted to survive. But it was his duty as well. Agi knew he had disgraced himself when he fell. Knew it and accepted it. But he was not lost to all honor. He couldn't lay here forever. His muscles were starting to feel the forced stillness. The arch of his right foot was really bothering him. Agi breathed through the spot to alleviate the cramp, but it was getting bad.

He heard another sickening thud as a spear was plunged into a prostrate body. A death sigh followed. So that's done, Agi thought. Another one dead. As soon as he had heard the movement, Agi had known it was just a matter of time. A grunt of pain, a fallen man just coming to will groan or move. If a Corinthian, a few men would come down from the rampart to lend assistance. If a Spartan, they would finish the job. There weren't enough of the Corinthians stationed at the rampart to deal with the fallen in any organized fashion so they were dealing with them ad hoc.

The sun was setting and still no army had returned, neither Corinthian nor Spartan. And the battle hadn't worked its way up the trail either. So the Corinthians were at least holding their own. Maybe even winning, although Agi had a hard time believing that. As soon as the sun went down Agi would make his move. There were woods to his right where the trail widened. That's where Agi would go. He would ease his way as silently as he could. With luck he could get clean away before dawn. If detected, he would make a run for it. The entire garrison couldn't chase him and in the darkness of the woods with only a few pursuers, anything could happen. Agi was weaponless, but there must be plenty still lying on the field of battle. Just as with the fallen, the Corinthians had no time yet to collect weapons. He could snag one on the way.

***

Daybreak wasn't far away. It had been a slow agonizing night. Agi had been on the move the entire time. At the speed of a slug. But he hadn't been detected. Nor had he made his escape. And he had moved too slow. He was going to have to run for it now. Maybe at this hour, just at daybreak, the guards would be dozing. Agi prayed to Apollo, then was on his feet and sprinting toward the woods. He was half way there and still no alarm. He was going to make it. Then a shout went up and the hunt was on. Agi had failed to find a weapon in his direct path and wasn't going to start looking for one now. He pelted for the scattering of trees ahead of him. He could hear the pursuit but didn't look back. A misplaced foot would be fatal.

He was in the woods now. The trees weren't dense, but there was some cover. A faint morning sunlight scattered among the foliage. It was a gradual downhill and Agi kept a good pace. He was hungry and thirsty, but still strong. He limped a bit. That damned right foot. The enemy was behind him. He hated to run from them. How many were there? He couldn't know, but he would guess at least four. Four to one and he was unarmed. Agi kept running.

He broke into a clearing and sheep were scampering in alarm out of his path. Bleating and pushing. Agi almost tripped over one. His pursuers would have a clearer path due to his efforts. He was almost on top of the small figure with a mass of dark hair before he saw her, without breaking stride he sidestepped as best he could, but sent her sprawling with a glancing blow of his shoulder. Agi kept running. A cry went up from the Corinthians. They had entered the glade before he had reached the woods on the other side. They saw him and sped up, the blood lust upon them.

The decline steepened considerably once Agi was back in the woods and he was scrambling, half sliding down the hill. He lost his balance, fell, and rolled abruptly to a stop with his chin hard against a fallen tree. With a burst of adrenaline, he was on his feet in an instant.

A cry rang through the woods. A woman's cry. She kept screaming, over and over. Then stopped. So did Agi. The shepherdess. Those Corinthian scum must have found her. Agi took a few steps down the hill and stopped again. He listened. There was no pursuit. He was free and clear. The woman? She was no concern of his. Many was the time he had vented his fear into lust after a battle on the women and boys of the fallen enemy. That was life. And death.

He took another step, but there was another cry. Faintly, he could hear hoarse laughter. The fun would start soon. Agi stood rooted, undecided. He owed that woman nothing. Still, this was Spartan territory. Maybe he could yet wipe his honor clean. And if there were only a few and he caught them by surprise...

Honor had never mattered to Agi before. He'd never given it any thought. Sure, it had been talked about all his life, but it had never registered with him before. He had taken it for granted. Until he lost it. Still he made no move. Then finally, almost reluctantly, he began to trudge back up the hill. Time to kill.

CHAPTER 14

TINA

Tina wondered if she should call her mom. Because Tina was under arrest. Not for the killings at the bank, that event was still under investigation, but for assaulting the doctor and other staff as well as damaging hospital property. The American consulate had intervened on Tina's behalf and managed to keep her out of the Indian prison system, however there was no dispute that Tina was a public danger and a flight risk. The FBI was working with the Indian Intelligence Bureau on the overall terrorist attack, but there was some dispute between the two organizations regarding Tina's role. Inspector Khera suspected Tina was an American covert operative while the FBI insisted that she wasn't. Numerous interrogations had failed to resolve the issue to the frustration of all, including Tina.

No, Tina wouldn't call her mom. Not because she couldn't use her support and not because her mom wouldn't be in India to the rescue in a fast minute if she could, but mostly because Tina just didn't know where her mom was exactly. As far as Tina knew, she was somewhere at sea in the Pacific Ocean. After years of bridge and golf since Tina's father had died, her mom had recently taken to exotic travel to the far corners of the world.

An only child, Tina was always daddy's little girl and had grown up seeing her mom as the ruling belle of the ball in local social circles. There had always been a subtle unspoken rivalry between daughter and mother for the affections of the man of the house. They competed in many things actually, with her mom teaching Tina tennis and golf, and never giving an inch of ground in any match. Tina's mom becoming a mother at a young age, she and Tina were often mistaken for sisters once Tina reached high school. Still, theirs was a healthy relationship much as would be expected in a father - son scenario. Tina's dad, a rags to riches engineer, had died prematurely while Tina was in college at Swarthmore. The grieving had been hard for both Marin ladies, bringing them even closer together during the lost semester of Tina's academic career. It was then that Tina gave up her childhood journaling, her father's death a breakpoint in her life, and began writing letters to her mother when she returned to college. She still wrote to her mom, sharing her heart and hopes, longhand the old fashioned way, once every couple of weeks or so. Her mom, showing great restraint, replied with acceptance rather than advice or judgment.

Tina was struggling to keep her spirits up under the intense interrogation, but it was getting more and more difficult with each passing hour. She thought of her father. He wouldn't have provided just support, he would be her champion. And woe betide anyone who would harm his little girl. The consular officer had been generally supportive, sitting in on every interrogation and representing Tina's rights as a United States citizen. Pally, police sub-inspector Agarwal, had remained friendly in her demeanor, while Miller, the FBI special agent, had been poker-faced and professional. But the Indian Intelligence Bureau officer, Khera, was openly suspicious, bordering on hostile. Tina had been shown the videos of the event in the bank multiple times. At first, they let her view each video twice without interruption, then asked her to comment. Tina reacted in horror. Viewing the attack on video and watching herself fight back, killing two men, none of which she remembered at all, evoked confusion and left Tina emotionally spent. Then came the slow motion replays with agonizing and sometimes humiliating pauses for questioning. She answered honestly and thoroughly through the first part of the videos, although it was difficult to talk about. But she was unable to provide any insight about the part where she is shown breaking free and killing her attackers.

Khera, the IB officer, thought she was stonewalling. He kept returning to the iPhone video and freezing it just at the point before Tina fought back, repeatedly demanding to know what Tina was thinking at that very moment. Finally, FBI special agent Miller put an end to the interrogation by commenting dryly that the gentleman had studied Ms. Marin's ass more than investigative procedure required.

So after a long frustrating morning, they had agreed to break for lunch. Now, after a much needed toilet break with Pally serving as escort, Tina was back at the same chair and table in the interrogation room they had been in all morning. She was still manacled at her ankles and chained around the waist to a floor to ceiling iron column. At least her hands were free so she could eat lunch without assistance. The Sub-inspector was the only person in the room eating with her.

"How are you holding up, Tina?" Pally asked.

Tina gave a brief bitter laugh, "How would you be holding up?"

"I'm not sure, actually," admitted Pally, "I've been trying to put myself in your shoes, but I can't quite pull it off."

"I don't know which is worse," said Tina, "having to repeatedly watch myself get raped which was already seared into my memory forever, or to watch myself do things which as far as my memory is concerned never happened. I'm actually glad you are bringing in a couple shrinks this afternoon. I must be going insane."

"I don't think you're insane, Tina. For what it is worth."

"You don't? Why not? I'm beginning to doubt myself, I can tell you that."

"Look at it this way," Pally explained, "You demonstrated skills and training that you don't have. That you have never been taught. So something different is going on here."

"You mean you really believe me? You don't think I'm a secret agent?"

"Totally I believe you, Tina. I didn't know what to think of you in the beginning, but I never doubted your sincerity," Pally said. "Meanwhile," she went on, "the FBI is doing a deep dive into your background, looking for the type of training and service that would produce the skills we have on tape. I don't think they'll find anything."

"That's okay, I doubt that IB agent, Inspector Khera, will believe even the FBI. But if I'm not some kind of secret agent, where do you think I got my fighting skills? Even I can tell from the videos this wasn't just luck."

"Well, I haven't raised it with the others yet, but I think you are in touch with a past life. And in that past life you were a real badass," said Pally.

"You believe in reincarnation? Really?"

"This is India, Tina. And while I am not Hindu, yes I believe in reincarnation."

"But you don't remember past lives, do you? I mean, nobody does, right?"

"There are rare instances where it does happen. That past lives resurface. Rest assured the psychiatrists will consider that possibility. Remember this is India, and can you think of another alternative?"

"I'm thinking of the man who was in my bed at the hospital," Tina said.

"Exactly!" said Pally, "Maybe you were that man."

CHAPTER 15

AGI

"You hit her too hard, you fool."

"Relax. She'll come around in a minute."

"I can't wait."

"You'll wait. Because I go first and I like 'em awake."

Agi was watching the Corinthians hovering around the woman. They had her in a sitting position, but she wasn't conscious, or only just. She wouldn't know where she was or what was happening. They had stripped her down, but so far they were doing nothing more than handling her small breasts. One of them was stroking himself.

"Do that too much and you'll have nothing to give her."

"I reload quick enough."

"Quick at both ends," somebody said to general laughter.

Agi had come up the hill about fifty feet to the left of where the Corinthians had seen him go down, just in case they decided to look. But they had clearly let him go with this more interesting prey before them. There were five of them. They had stripped themselves in anticipation of the fun. Their weapons were scattered on the ground, but on the far side from where Agi watched. He couldn't get to a weapon first. They were clustered around the woman about a hundred feet from the tree line. The woman's head lolled around. She groaned as her eyes opened.

"Here we go!"

"Wait for it," the Alpha said sternly.

"She's a pretty little wench. A bit skinny."

"The closer to the bone, the sweeter the meat." General laughter. The woman was suddenly aware of her situation. She gasped harshly.

"Shss," said the Alpha softly, a knuckle under her chin to hold her eyes. "Don't fight it and we'll let you live. And we'll be gentle." He paused for a moment. "But no screaming," he added sternly, "I won't tolerate screaming."

The woman whimpered where she sat in the tall grass, but made no move or further sound. With her head bowed, her thick dark hair draping her in all directions, she presented an erotic contrast to her bare body. Agi felt himself swelling. What was he doing here? These men were only going to do what he had done many times himself. It is what you do after a battle. Small enough reward for surviving all the horror and slaughter. Still, Agi stayed. Watching and waiting. Only the occasional bleating of sheep was heard over the hoarse breathing of the men. Heavy with anticipation.

"Here, each of you take an arm or leg," the Alpha ordered as he kneeled down and pushed the poor girl onto her back. "I don't want my eyes gouged out at just the wrong moment if you know what I mean." They all took their positions and the woman cried, writhing in pain.

"Don't tear her apart you fools or you'll have nothing left for yourselves."

"Here we go!" one said as the Alpha hovered over the small woman on his hands and knees, taking a moment to feast upon her delicate physique with his eyes.

"Just relax, little lady," the Alpha said with gentle mockery, "and we won't hurt you." Leaning down, softly, slowly he suckled each small pale breast. Shivers erupted across her lean frame, but still she didn't struggle. He dipped a finger into her sex, probing in and out.. More shivering. Then he entered her wetness, gently as he had promised. Agi watched aroused, bringing back memories. Still, another thought came to him, the oppressive weight of the man upon the small woman must be suffocating the little thing.

"Ahh," moaned the Alpha, "a virgin." The others grunted and guffawed, each eager for their own turn.

"Shss," he whispered as he pressed gently against her "This will sting a bit, just for a moment, then you'll like it well enough."

Then he was in. A stifled cry escaped from the woman, then a mixed moan.

"Release her legs," the Alpha ordered his men, "let her move, but keep hold of her wrists." Then, "That's it, little lady," he said.

Only muted rhythmic grunts slipped past her clenched teeth. Her thin nostrils flared, struggling to draw much needed air. Closed eyed tears rolled down her pale cheeks, the evidence immediately eradicated by the steady scrapes of coarse beard against her soft skin.

Agi had watched and waited until the men were fully distracted. The Alpha arched, increasing his speed. Now. Decision made. Agi was approaching soundlessly. About halfway to the group, one of them noticed Agi's attack out of the corner of his eye and shouted. Agi went into a full sprint, charging right into the gang rape. He snapped the Alpha's neck even as the man emptied his seed into his victim. The assault avenged in his instant of ecstasy. A wicked left cross to the jaw put a second man down. Another tackled Agi and they both fell hard on the woman as she lay defenseless on her back. Agi heard thin ribs crack under his muscled shoulder. He rolled off and to his feet, but took a kick to his jaw before he could get upright. Agi went down hard. Seeing stars he scrambled on all fours, got hold of a leg and forced a man down. Agi pounced on him like a lion, swinging through a blur of blood with both fists. Some of his shots landed. Shouts and grunts, mixed with more bleating from the frightened sheep, resounded across pasture. Another kick caught Agi in the head. He went blind. Then two more to the ribs. His wind left him as he collapsed face down into the grass then curled into the fetal position. The kicks kept coming as he faded from consciousness.

***

"I say we cut his nads off and make him eat 'em," a voice said savagely.

Agi's head hurt. He wanted to put his hand on the hurt, but he couldn't move it. He tried the other hand, but that didn't work either. He ached all over but his groin and ankles hurt acutely. Getting his attention. Opening his eyes, for a moment everything was blurry. As his vision cleared, a face was leaning over him, badly mauled and bloody, still oozing and dripping out of his left nostril and eye from the mauling of Agi's fists.

"Take a good look at me," FistFace said, then spat in Agi's eyes. There was blood in it. "When we are through, you'll look a lot worse than I do. And you'll feel a lot worse too."

He started to strangle Agi with both hands. Slowly. Deliberately. Up close and personal. His hot breath was foul. The hideous face was framed surreally by blue sky beyond with a scattering of green-gray leaves from low hanging branches. Agi struggled to resist, then realized with horror that he was strapped spreadeagle on his back across the flat of a large stone near the edge of the clearing. Agi's wrists were bound tightly to stakes in the ground left and right leaving his body stretched and exposed. His ankles, also bound, were tied painfully wide and upward to nearby tree branches.

He flexed and pulled with all the strength born of terror, but he could not break free. Fistface grunted with pleasure, enjoying his victim's fear. Agi's butt was suspended in air beyond the edge of the stone. He thrashed as much as he could. His hips and torso could pivot only a few inches in any direction. The pressure increased on his throat. It was collapsing. His neck in agony, Agi gasped for air. Then just as he started to black out, the throttling stopped. His violated throat didn't reopen fully, but he could breathe somewhat. He could still hear the sheep. And then he noted a sad rasping sound nearby. Someone else was struggling for air. And failing to get it. The sound and feel of frail ribs caving in under his weight came to his memory. The little woman. And even in Agi's dire circumstance, a newfound feeling welled within him. Pity.

"How's that feel?" FistFace asked viciously, and spat on Agi again.

"Lighten up, man. First things first," said another Corinthian.

"Look what this bastard did to me, Dicus," FistFace said bitterly, not for the first time.

"I know," Dicus replied, "and you'll get to finish him however you want. But he's the only sport we have now that the skinny slut is as good as dead."

"I'm gonna cut his balls off," said FistFace.

"By Zeus, you won't," said another voice. With authority. The new Alpha of the now smaller gang. Agi strained his neck around to try to see the source of the voice from behind him. The voice, Agi recognized, that held his fate. A tall man loomed over him. He sipped on a water sack. Agi hadn't eaten or drank in two days.

"What's your name, Spartan?"

Agi paused before answering. He knew he was a dead man, but still prayed for escape. "It doesn't matter," Agi finally replied hoarsely. "I am a soldier. Like you. A warrior. Kill me, if you must, but as a soldier." He paused for breath through his bruised throat before croaking out a final, "With honor."

"Honor? Bold words," replied the Alpha, "But fear is in your eyes, and in your voice. Your very breath reeks of Pan. And you ran away from the battle. Playing dead, were you? Where are your wounds, warrior?" he mocked.

"I was knocked out," Agi replied feebly.

They all laughed at that. "Hercules himself!" "Hail the conquering hero!" "We'll crown him with laurels!" "Let's just kill him."

"No," said the Alpha. "He lives." Agi gasped audibly in relief as the others protested.

"Listen up," continued the Alpha as the others groused then settled down. "We'll use him as we wish, in payment for ruining the wench. We'll take our time. And when we have fully slaked our lust, which may take a few days" the Alpha continued with relish, "You," this to FistFace, "get to geld him. But we don't kill him. We'll hamstring his right leg, take his right hand, his right ear, and his right eye." There were murmurs of approval now.

"Then we'll leave him a knife. By whether he has the courage to kill himself will the gods measure his honor."

CHAPTER 16

INVESTIGATORS

"You didn't want to have lunch with me for my company," Khera opened, "What do you want?"

"What's going on with you, Khera?" Miller snapped, in no good humor.

Khera considered the big black woman sitting across from him. He sensed a danger within the FBI agent, under control, for now. "You don't like my interrogation methods?" he asked mildly.

"You're overly concerned about this incident and the Marin woman."

"Don't you find her peculiar?" Khera asked.

"Of course, but she's no Mata Hari. You seem to be looking for one."

Khera took a sip of tea, but didn't answer right away. Miller's stare was relentless. "I'm hearing rumors," Khera began quietly, "Not even that, whispers. Hints really," Miller's stare softened, but she remained silent. "Something is coming, or is already happening. And there is talk of a woman."

"Doing what?" asked Miller.

"I don't know. I don't have anything really."

"Marin is a known quantity. Known to the public. She's not who you're looking for," Miller insisted.

"Maybe not," replied Khera, "Or maybe she has been operating across the globe under the cover of a reporter. Maybe India is her next job. But something went amiss. She was in the wrong place at the wrong time. At the bank, it went too far and she had to blow her cover. The amnesia story is her cleanup."

"Maybe," Miller conceded. "Just maybe. But she's not one of ours."

"And this other woman," Khera went on, "Ajita Kaur, the sister of one of the dead terrorists, she spoke of a woman in the group, but the other two terrorists we captured didn't say a word of a woman."

"You'll break them."

"Sooner or later," Khera agreed, "but I'll bet they won't know anything more about her than Kaur does."

"Well, if that is the woman you are worried about, it can't be Marin."

"I know. Two separate theories," agreed Khera, "But also consider the strangeness of the bank attack. Well planned, well executed, but completely pointless."

"They're all pointless," said Miller.

"Agreed," said Khera, "but this attack was more than pointless. It was stupid. Attacking a bank to strike a blow for an independent Kashmir? They didn't even try to rob the place. And they had no exit strategy. How were the four of them supposed to get out of there?"

"Maybe there was a second phase," offered Miller, "that never happened because Marin broke everything up."

"If there was, our two captives didn't know about it. According to them, they were going to escape from the bank guns blazing. It's all too stupid. Whoever set this up, it wasn't any of those four fools who did the job. And it wasn't supposed to succeed, I am certain of that."

"So what was its purpose, who set it up, and what comes next?" Miller asked.

"Exactly my point," said Khera.

"And you're thinking of your mystery woman."

CHAPTER 17

NIKIAS

Crows were circling low over the bodies scattered across the ravine off the side of the road. The work of clearing the road of corpses had interrupted the Corinthians with the approach of the Spartan host. Local human scavengers competed with the crows for the bodies, but the crows were persistent. Some even landed with a loud "CAW" on the dead despite the close proximity of the living. Nikias opened his parched eyes as one of them landed on his arm, which twitched instinctively. The bird and several others nearby took wing in complaint. But not going far.

"Here, this one is alive," a woman said.

Her husband came over. "Probably won't be for long. He's awfully pale."

By chance, by fate, the woman locked eyes with Nikias as his eyes opened. "Let's take him home, Neston," she said.

"What for?" Neston asked.

"We haven't found anything else worthwhile in this lot. Don't want to leave empty."

"He'll be mighty heavy, of no use, and will probably die anyway."

"If he heals, he'll be a strong hand," the woman explained. "We could use the help. You aren't getting any younger."

"If he heals he won't listen to us. And will likely kill us."

"No. Not this one," the woman said, looking Nikias over.

"By the lord Apollo, Delia, he's a Spartan soldier. You can't keep one of them like a farm animal."

But Delia was already probing Nikias for injury and staunching his wounds with grass and damp earth. She gently cradled his head in her lap and kissed his forehead softly. The cool touch of her lips tingled Nikias. She dabbed water lightly to his parched lips. Then gave him some sips, stroking his hair.

"He won't be any trouble," Delia told Neston. "Trust me."

Nikias looked up to see a white haired goddess with loving green eyes smiling upon him and he felt the first hint of life returning. The spot where she had kissed his forehead continued to tingle. Soft dry fingertips caressed his cheek. He managed a small smile then closed his eyes. At peace. Neston stood over the two of them dubiously, but made no complaint. He searched around the pile of bodies that they and a half dozen other scavengers had been going over, looking for anything the Corinthian looters might have missed. He sighed. At least they'd be dragging the Spartan downhill for starters, but it would be a struggle after that to get him home.

***

Nikias drank deeply from the mountain stream, enjoying the spring sun on his bare back. He glanced at the three brown trout he had to show for his morning efforts to bring back home. Home. It was a simple life he had been living these past years, but not an altogether unpleasant one. Nikias had bound himself to the couple who had saved him with the fealty owed to a lord and his lady. They lived a quiet remote life alongside a mountain stream deep in Arcadia. A life of fishing, a bit of hunting and gathering, Demeter's bounty was plentiful with olives and wild grains, fruits, and herbs. It was a humble life, but not a hard one.

Other folk of the area, and they were few anyway, kept their distance from the couple's small homestead. While never discussed, Nikias was aware that the pale white haired woman was special. A lady. He suspected she had the sight as well as other gifts and was perhaps a wood nymph or even a goddess. How she had ended up as the wife of the dour Neston was beyond Nikias' understanding. It didn't appear to be a particularly loving relationship the two of them had, but there was some unseen understanding or connection that bound them as one, and not in a possessive way, but as if part of the natural order of things. Nikias accepted them as they were and served them as those who gave him life.

Footsteps approached and Nikias turned to see the gaunt gray Neston approaching as expected. He eased himself into the cold stream. Neston disrobed as well and joined him in the water, letting the quick current cleanse them. Eventually Neston lay on the grass to dry in the sun, Nikias followed suit, lying on his back, silently waiting. Neston stood and retrieved some olive oil from his things. Nikias looked at the older man's member, which was already swelling before he applied the oil. Nikias remained on the grass, spreading his legs so that Neston could apply oil to his hole. Neston kneeled upright above him stroking himself fully firm. Then he hooked a forearm behind each of Nikias' knees. They both knew the drill.

Later that day as he was tending the farm animals, Nikias reflected on his lot in life. His thirty years of life in Spartan society until the battle at the mountain pass had drilled many skills into him, but little learning of an intellectual nature. Combat, discipline, and certainly obedience were lessons well learned. Nikias' own character, innate to himself from wherever such traits arrive, tended to see and accept people as they were, the good and the bad, protect those weaker than himself, and above all be unwaveringly loyal to those who are worthy. The lovely white haired lady, Delia, held his love and loyalty since that moment of eye contact when his new life began. Nikias knew that somehow the lady had recalled him back from death. He had been born again that day. What purpose she had for him was not yet clear, but Nikias was a patient man. Until that moment came when all was revealed, he would help as he could and do what he was told by the master of the house. If that included a weekly buggering, then so be it. Neston was after all the head of the household and as such was entitled, even expected, to insert his phallus into whatever orifice suited him. Yet the Lady Delia was never so handled, as far as Nikias could tell. Neston would kiss her cheek, sometimes she would take his hand, but there appeared to be no other contact. She would bestow a smile upon the older man occasionally, which would immediately soften his mood every time.

They lived only a few miles to the west of the Arcadian mountain pass that led southwest into the Spartan dominated part of the Peloponnese. The forests and small mountain pastures of the region were only lightly populated, more with sheep and goats than people. It was a land living on an incline, of streams and the occasional misty morning lake on small high plateaus sprinkled amidst the evergreen woodlands.

While officially in their domain, the Spartans of the Laconia plain paid little attention to the area, it having no economic value, little strategic importance aside from the pass itself, and not enough people to be a source for soldiers. The Corinthians controlling the northeastern side of the mountain pass paid no more attention to the region than the Spartans. But there were animal traces and trails through the mountains connecting north and south unknown to the soldiers of the city-states. The Arcadian rustics of the mountains held no fealty in their hearts for the city-states that presumed to rule them. The soldiers or any commercial traffic in time of peace seldom strayed off the road over the mountain pass. An ancient people, the Arcadian herders and their flocks had graced the mountains long before Sparta and Corinth were built. And they would be found in the high meadows and aside the upland streams long after the lowland city-states had fallen into decay and ruin.

CHAPTER 18

ARISTOL

"I am an officer of Sparta!" Aristol roared, not for the first time. He was ignored by the men who handled the pulleys from outside at the four corners of his cage. Controlling his arms and legs like a puppet.

"Why do you treat me so? Have you no honor?" The servants remained mute, exchanging glances between them, but otherwise showing no expression that Aristol could detect. The cage had been his traveling home for a week now. He was shackled at the wrists and ankles. For his comfort, leather bindings mitigated the chafe. But what was chafing on his mind was the lack of information or communication of any kind. Those that guarded him, fed him, and otherwise tended his needs told him nothing.

The cage was exactly that. Wooden bars on four sides and the roof with soft skins and cushions on the flooring. Nonetheless, it was a bumpy ride. The cords attached to his shackles were slack most of the time allowing him to move around his cage, which was just tall enough for Aristol to stand up.

He had awakened groggy after the battle already bound in this caged cart and underway. How he had gotten in this predicament, Aristol knew not. His last clear recollections were of the battle. Fast thrust and parry work it had been. Several men had fallen to his sword, but he and his platoon had been driven off the rampart. Still, his remaining men had answered his shouted commands, holding formation. He remembered his elation hearing the charge of the Spartan relief force. Then nothing until the cage. Where he was being taken and why, Aristol had no idea. He assumed north toward Corinth, but couldn't know that. Once out of the mountains, he had seen other traffic going to and fro, mostly civilian. For several days of travel, the evidence of increasing population density had led Aristol to believe they were approaching a city, but then they had turned onto a smaller road. The terrain was unlike the plains of his family's estate in Laconia, and untended, with no order. They had passed through a few villages, but never stopped. The locals had gawked at Aristol, stripped naked as he was, as they rolled by. Aristol had been tempted to talk to them, try to find out where they were, but had decided it was beneath his dignity. Sooner or later, there would be a showdown with his captors. He would just have to wait. Their caravan consisted of two wagons in addition to Aristol's cart, some half dozen soldiers and more than twice as many domestic servants on foot.

The caravan came to a stop. Aristol noted it was early in the day to make camp, but it was level ground. There was nothing in sight to indicate they were near any kind of settlement or other people. The servants slowly pulled on the lines so that Aristol could adjust himself comfortably into the supine position without being forced. Incapacitated, but not in discomfort. He wondered at that because he had already been fed and cleaned. They always spread-eagled him before the servants entered the cage so they could tend to his needs in safety. But whatever was happening now was out of the routine.

The tarps were lowered down on all sides of the cage, but the roof remained open as it had every evening. Aristol appreciated seeing the stars at night. The weather was comfortable even in his nudity. He could hear the servants walk away, leaving Aristol alone. Movement of men and animals was evident to his ears, but some distance away from his cage. Aristol tensed up in anticipation for he knew not what. He tried to focus on his breathing as he had been taught, but couldn't.

Time crawled on. Footsteps. Aristol looked down past his feet to the rear end of the cage where the door was. A tall man ducked under the tarp, unlocked the cage and entered, closing it behind him. Aristol had never seen this man before.

"You are obviously in charge here," Aristol began, recognizing a fellow nobleman, "explain yourself, sir." The man stood over Aristol. He had to stoop a bit to keep his head clear of the cage roof.

"Beautiful," the man said in admiration, more to himself than to Aristol, as his eyes scanned the young Spartan slowly from head to foot. "Truly beautiful." He met Aristol's eyes, "It is a blessing you were spared. Such as you should not be wasted on war."

"Explain yourself, sir," Aristol repeated, trying to keep his voice level. He was suddenly very aware of his own nudity. He had been admired by men before, even propositioned. But he had always been, if not in complete control of the situation, at least on equal footing. And he had always said no, a disciple of Spartan dogma. Now he was completely helpless.

"Patience. The young never learn patience. I have been very patient these past days. But now that I can see you. Really see you, well, I have no patience left, don't you know?"

The older man, maybe forty or forty-five, lay down and placed his hand gently in the center of Aristol's chest. Aristol stared at the hand upon him, inert but warm. He began to address the man, but his captor was looking away in the direction of Aristol's feet. He began gently caressing Aristol. "So smooth and yet so hard," he said as he probed Aristol's musculature. The hand strayed over a nipple, then back again. Aristol had never been so touched. An offense to his dignity. But he quivered under the soft strokes.

"Here, what are you doing? Stop that!" Aristol demanded.

"Or what? You'll scream?" the man asked with a smile. "I think I'd like that." But Aristol didn't scream. "Oh god," Aristol whispered as the hand slid agonizingly slowly down his torso. He felt the blood rushing into his member, watched himself swell. Fingers stopped at the pubic line. Dignity forgotten, Aristol ached with anticipation. First a firm hand, then a moist mouth engulfed him. "Oh god!"

***

The wagons pulled to a stop again the next day early just as they had the day before. Again, the servants silently restrained him then left him alone in the covered cage. Aristol waited, not knowing how to feel. Yesterday, he had to admit, had felt glorious. Unlike taking a prostitute, the man had drawn his juices out of him. He reminded himself that this man was his enemy. He was a bound prisoner. Yet as he awaited the man's arrival, Aristol throbbed in anticipation. He heard the man's approach.

"You're glad to see me," the Corinthian said with a smile, noting Aristol's arousal. "Torture is not so bad after all, is it? I suppose it is time I introduce myself," he continued, as he quickly disrobed. "My name is Homedes, your host. And you are?"

He should have said 'an officer of Sparta' but replied simply, "Aristol."

"Aristol. It is a pleasure to know you, Aristol," Homedes said.

He kneeled before Aristol's outstretched thighs, purring softly as Aristol felt lingering kisses tingle him all over. A sigh escaped Aristol as he closed his eyes, his thoughts far from Sparta and war. A jolt ran through him as Homedes oiled Aristol with a few strokes.

"How does that feel, hmm?" Homedes murmured. Then he squatted on his knees over the young man, easing Aristol slowly up into him.

"Oh god," they moaned in unison.

CHAPTER 19

TINA

Tina watched Pally's figure sway down the aisle to the WC. Wide hips, slender waist. Built for bearing babies. She looked so much younger out of uniform and wearing an outfit quickly bought in the New Delhi airport, a sleeveless blouse and shorts fitting snugly round her bottom. Perfect for the start of the season in Greece.

The plane shivered and the fasten-seatbelt sign lit up immediately. Another shiver, a bit rougher this time. Tina leaned back and closed her eyes. Nothing to do but enjoy the ride until it ends one way or the other. She stretched her legs, trying to relax. Breathe. Her hand went to her jaw, to scratch. The bandage stopped her, doing its job protecting the scab from mindless interference.

What was she doing? Did this even remotely make sense? Did anything? At least she was free. Pally was returning now. Their eyes met and they exchanged instant smiles. The younger woman's wide toothy grin and the elder's soft upturned lips. Pally fell into her seat as turbulence struck the plane again, practically spilling into Tina's lap. A brown hand landed on the pale flesh of Tina's bare inside thigh. Their heads knocked lightly together.

"Your head, Tina. So sorry," Pally gushed, "and you, with a concussion."

"No worries, youngling," Tina said, "only a love tap. You okay?"

"I'm fine," Pally replied, righting herself. After a long moment she withdrew her hand from Tina's thigh. "I better buckle up or my head will be up through the overhead compartment next," then, "Tina, what's youngling?"

"It's something you call a younger person. Someone you care about." They lapsed into a comfortable silence as the plane bounced along. Tina's mind wandered back over recent events. They were an hour's flying time away from Athens.

Tina could still feel the warmth of Pally's hand on her thigh, tingling, long after her touch had ended. What was happening to her? When had she ever had such a reaction to a woman before? Like most teenage girls she had hung out with in high school, Tina had always been boy crazy. Sure, she had stolen covert glances at the other girls in the locker room and showers, but that was more curiosity than anything else. It was always the male form that had attracted Tina. Fascinated her. Coming in all shades, shapes, and sizes, Tina had been an active explorer of the male body in high school. She was always in love with one boy or another, sometimes more than one at a time. Tina had never minded that she had developed a reputation back then. She was selective with who she dated and had sex with, but there were so many choices she was never in want. Plus she could always select from the top of the barrel. In retrospect, Tina knew she had left a few broken hearts in her wake, but she had always been upfront with every boy, whether she was in love with them or not. Now it was almost as if she was looking at everyone with new eyes. Men and women. And she was still very much attracted to men, but even that was somehow different.

The last two days had been a flurry of many meetings and quick decisions. The US consular service had pressured the Indian government to keep things moving, in turn responding to influence at home from their Washington news bureau, according to Bobby. The investigation concluded that Tina had acted in self-defense at the bank. No charges leveled. The hospital dropped all charges against her too with the encouragement of both the doctor she had injured and the Intelligence Bureau.

From what Pally said, Inspector Khera, the IB officer, was still convinced Tina was a US government covert agent despite the psychiatric and religious opinions supporting the reincarnation theory. The FBI, meanwhile, was adamant that Tina was not an operative of any kind and certain that she had no close quarters combat or martial arts training in her background. They had found childhood ballet, sailing, high school tennis, and a smattering of social athletic teams and events, such as co-ed softball and volleyball. Inspector Khera couldn't say the FBI was lying, not directly to Special Agent Miller's face, but his skepticism was obvious. The compromise was that Tina was free to go, provided that she left the country at once.

The press had made a circus of Tina's every move in India. The bank incident had caused a sensation, as the too frequent terrorist attacks always do. But this one was different. Only terrorists were killed and there was live footage for the world to see. Tina, while not a known figure in India, and only known via her By Line to her readers in the States, was enough of a public figure to be easily, if only superficially, researched online by any inquiring mind. Her background, education, and career, were all active subject matter for many people in and out of India. The bank video was released of course, or leaked, and several others made by people in the bank at the time were also circulating. Indian and American officials were interviewed both in New Delhi and in Washington. Freelance martial arts experts were rendering their judgements about Tina's skills both on the air and online. And of course, the theory that the source of her fighting skills was from a past life had got out too. That was an added sensation. When it came time to release Tina from police custody, it was impossible to do so without her being swarmed by both the press and the public. The US ambassador had invited her to stay as a guest, but Tina had opted for Pally's offer of the police barrack. Once in the hand of the velvet yet powerful grip of the US government, Tina thought it could become at least awkward to make her next moves independently. And the reach of the ambassador didn't extend beyond the embassy without the support of the local police anyway.

So when it was time to leave India, of course there were reporters, paparazzi, and the public on hand at the airport. Despite the fact that she was officially free to go where she wished, Tina had agreed to being handcuffed in exchange for police escort all the way to the plane. IB Inspector Khera had insisted and even Tina saw the sense in the precaution. She still didn't trust herself, particularly with this unfamiliar stress of public attention. The last thing she wanted to do was hurt anybody else before getting out of India.

There had been some last minute confusion and consternation at the airport gate when the airline had refused to let her board. The optics of having the cuffs removed just before boarding had put both the passengers and crew in an uproar. Only IB intervention, Khera had been part of the escort to the airport, had settled the matter. He seconded Sub-inspector Pally Agarwal to the IB on the spot to escort Tina until such time as she chose to return to the USA. That, and Tina's own disarming demeanor, mollified all concerned once her background and what had happened to her was explained to the airline officials.

Tina suspected that Khera wanted an eye on her for as long as he could keep one, and Tina wasn't objecting to Pally's company, but had been crystal clear that she would refuse any other escort. Khera had agreed because he had no legal ground upon which to insist otherwise. He clearly didn't approve of women in police work, and knew the young sub-inspector believed the reincarnation theory, but he also admitted that Pally had an excellent record. Meanwhile, Pally said she was open to changing her opinion as events unfolded.

And so Tina found herself with a companion she innately trusted and liked on a journey to discover who she was in a past life. The whole idea appealed to her investigative reporting instincts, but she still wasn't convinced herself, being a skeptic by professional necessity. She still tended to agree with Miller's and the FBI's opinion that Tina's self-defense was a panic response and the successful outcome of a one in a thousand fluke. Her temporary amnesia was due to the trauma she had experienced and not because she had been controlled by a ghost. They expected the amnesia to fade away with time. That had been the USA psychiatric conclusion upon seeing all the videos and reviewing all the interrogation transcripts, albeit remotely.

Tina unfolded her small map of Greece for the umpteenth time. Her iPhone was so bombarded with input she didn't even want to turn it on. Surprisingly, Tina was enjoying this temporary reversion to paper maps.

"So where are we going?" Pally asked. "One of the islands? Mount Olympus?" The Indian girl's knowledge of Greece had been next to nothing at the time of the last minute assignment to fly there.

"South I think. Maybe start with Corinth. Yes, Corinth."

"Corinth. Have you ever been there?"

"We'll see, youngling," Tina laughed. "Actually I have only been to Santorini as part of a Med cruise. Funny. With all the travel my work has taken me throughout the world, I have never been assigned to Greece. And now I am heading there. For this, whatever it is."

"Well, all I can say is that it feels right to me," said Pally. "But what do I know?"

"No more or less than I do, that's for sure."

"So Corinth it is. When reason fails, trust your instincts."

"Who said that?" Tina asked.

"My mother always says that. Whether she made it up or not, I can't say. It's how she convinced my dad to let me apply for the police academy."

"I'm glad she did. It fits you well. Being a cop, I mean. I don't know why, but it does."

"Thanks Tina. I have wanted to be a policeman, and a detective, as far back as I can remember."

"Well good for you is all I can say. I can't imagine it has been easy for you in India from what I have read about the culture, if you don't mind my saying so."

"Is it any better in America? A woman being a cop, I mean. Or a reporter?"

"We've still got a long way to go, but it's getting better. Not because men are giving ground, mind you. But because we're taking it, inch by inch. The best you can expect from any man in the USA is passive support. Not because they are against women. Nothing like that. They just can't comprehend that an obstacle exists."

"I know what you mean," agreed Pally.

"Oh, they think they support us," continued Tina. "And they say they do. But they don't. They can't really empathize. Maybe there are some black men, or other minority males, who have experienced oppression, so they get it. Really understand. But even they self-identify by gender before race as far as I can tell. I swear, female inequality is the root cause of everything that is wrong in this world."

Pally didn't respond and they lapsed into silence. As the plane continued to bounce along, Tina's mind wandered to thinking of young Bobby heading off to Kashmir. She didn't resent losing the assignment. Her new assignment: an in depth autobiographical essay on one Tina Marin. After speaking with Bobby, she had called Tom. She told him that she needed some downtime after her ordeal. Tom was reluctant to agree, taking his best player out of the lineup, so he came up with this autobiographical angle. Tina didn't mind because the paper was covering most of the costs and giving her a free hand.

Only Bobby had been so obviously disappointed. Tina enjoyed the adoration of such a young good-looking man and only the fact that they were work colleagues had prevented her from taking advantage of him before. In fact, for some reason that she couldn't explain right now, the work relationship didn't bother her as much anymore. Even at the barrack, when they had first been alone together, Tina had trouble staying focused on work. She had done absolutely nothing inappropriate in that meeting, or even outwardly behaved any differently to Bobby than she ever had, but as soon as they were alone, Tina had become monstrously horny. And not just generally horny, she had wanted Bobby. Right then and there on the spot. It had taken all of her focus to control herself. This was a situation beyond her experience. And Bobby had sensed it, she was sure. That had made it worse. Thinking back on it now, while the plane rattled its way to Athens, Tina felt moist. She took Pally's hand in hers. Her clasp was returned. Their eyes met with smiles.

"So how does it feel, Pally? Flying to Greece?"

"Honestly? It feels liberating. I mean I'm still on the job, but there are no bosses looking over my shoulder. And I am leaving India. Indian attitudes. Family, whom I love, but it's nice to be released from the pressure of…expectations."

"Good for you, youngling. I hope you enjoy it. And I promise not to be too difficult."

***

Further back in the plane, Ajita Kaur was seated wearing the hijab of a moslem woman. She had been part of the public crowd that had followed Tina's every move. That had been easy. Getting a last minute plane ticket to Greece had been tricky, and lucky. The delay of Tina's own boarding and IB intervention in holding the plane had bought Ajita the time she needed. She had only been out of India once, and that had been to Bangladesh, but now she was on a mission. She needed closure for her brother one way or another.

CHAPTER 20

AGI

Helen reached down between her legs to tousle Agi's tawny head. He could feel her breathing subsiding in the afterglow of her orgasm.

"Crawl up here and kiss me you big beautiful brute," she said with a sigh. Agi gave her one final vaginal kiss that made Helen squirm then joined her at the head of the bed. He gave another slow wet messy kiss on her mouth then rested on his back, content. Helen snuggled into his broad hairy chest. Daphne knocked on the door as she and Lorae entered the one room home without waiting for a response.

"Are you two finally done in here?" Daphne asked with a laugh.

"More than done my girl, almost dead," Helen replied to her sisters.

Daphne sighed, "Be sure to get some rest, Agi. There are three of us."

"Not to worry, little one. I'll be ready," Agi replied.

"Hey, I thought I was your little one," Helen said.

"No, I'm your little one, Agi," said Lorae, "after all, I am the youngest."

"But you're also the tallest," protested Helen.

"And I am the lightest," declared Daphne.

"Not by much," Helen and Lorae protested in unison.

"You are all my little ones," said Agi in response to the sibling bantering, "and never was a man so blessed with such a family."

Daphne and Lorae jumped on the bed, "Dog pile on Agi!" Helen shrieked with laughter while Agi moaned in mock despair.

It was a continual wonder to Agi that his life had turned out the way it had. Left for dead, to kill himself if he so dared, Agi had come close to doing just that. But Helen's sisters had found the two of them lying helpless among the sheep after the Corinthian renegades had gone. Helen had truly been near death and her recovery had been slow. Agi had been in shock. Multiple rapes had been a numbing and humbling experience for Agi. He had always been the predator. Now he realized what he had been to others. And true to their word, his captors had castrated him, blinded one eye, lopped off an ear, a hand, and then hamstrung one leg. They had used fire to stop the bleeding, their final torture, to staunch his wounds. To make him suffer a long life if he lacked the courage to die, as they suspected. And in truth, he lived every day of his life in some pain. It was never far from his consciousness.

But the joy, the love, far outweighed the pain for Agi. These three little sisters, orphans at a young age and alike to strangers as three peas in a pod, had taken him in. Nurtured him back to health, if not wholeness. After Helen had been a victim of the rape, the very idea of men repelled all three of them, but the big eunuch was never a threat from the start. They took him to their hearts as a fellow victim. To them, Agi's wounds were symbols of his sacrifice in defense of Helen's life and virtue, vain though his attempt had been.

But even women who have suffered can still have longings, and sisters don't naturally attend to such needs for each other. Daphne, the oldest but still a virgin, feared men for what had happened to her sister, but Agi suspected that deep within her there lay a latent longing. Agi had no such stirrings left within him, but he worshiped the beauty of the three sisters with his eye, touch, taste, and all his heart. It gave him the ultimate joy to give them pleasure. They'd had a hard life, the three of them. Even with Agi to help it was still a life of work to survive. But it was a loving life now for all of them and a happy household. The shame of Agi's past, his character, he kept hidden.

Now some years later, life was more secure for the sisters than it ever had been before Agi joined them. Crippled though he was, in his hobbled state, Agi was still a formidable man. He could throw a spear as well with his left as he had with his right, and he had been a fine javelin thrower even by Spartan standards. Under Agi's instruction, the girls had crafted a good supply of ash spears and Agi taught them how to use them, both throwing and at close quarters. He had also taught the sisters how to injure a man with little force with their bare hands, a knee or a kick. Word had gotten around the neighboring area to treat the small homestead with respect.

CHAPTER 21

AJITA

Before leaving India, following Tina with no clear intention, Ajita went to the bank where her brother was killed. She emptied her account. It wasn't much, but it would get her started on her journey. It had been strange to stand on the spot where her brother fell. Very strange. She had let him go in her heart. She had seen him die on the TV news. Had seen his body on a cold hard slab in the morgue. She had let him go. His body at least. Now she was completely alone in the world. Better me than him, she thought grimly. Rohit would have been lost without her. Some things are worse than death in that the suffering doesn't end. Rohit's suffering was over. And she could handle hers.

Yet there was much to be undone. She couldn't leave her beloved brother with the reputation of a terrorist. Such a tender boy. He deserved better and she would see his honor restored to the world. And that woman was the key. Ajita didn't quit her job. She just never went back. She didn't know what she would do. Where she would be going. How she would live.

Ajita had been fourteen when her parents had died in the accident. Rohit only seven. With no immediate relatives, the local Sikh community had helped support the children, with a rotation of boarding from family to family every month or so. For two years, Ajita and Rohit had lived like that. On the charity of others. Ajita had felt the compassion from the families bleeding away with the continuous stress of caring for additional children. Looking back, Ajita knew that she and Rohit hadn't helped. Her poor little brother, who had been doted upon by their mother, had simply shut down. He seldom spoke, or even responded to adult authority, and failed in school. Ajita on the other hand had been angry, and she took it out on everyone, except Rohit. The two of them had left numerous emotionally exhausted families in their wake.

Finally, as soon as Ajita had turned sixteen, she had secured an entry level sales job in a clothing store. That had been with the help of a Sikh friend of her father's. To the surprise of all, Ajita did well, managing to control her temper and stay focused on her work. What they didn't understand is that

Ajita saw this one precious opportunity as a path to independence. After two months on the job, she and Rohit moved to their own flat. It wasn't much and not in a good neighborhood, but it was theirs. Their needs were simple as long as they had each other. Over time, Rohit had come out of his shell and turned things around at school. He had even gotten a small scholarship awarded via the Sikh community to attend university.

Meanwhile, Ajita had worked. Her education was only minimal, but she was a quick study and committed to sustaining freedom for herself and her brother. Advancement was minimal, but her job was safe at the store. She was an able and hardworking employee. Ajita had no social life outside her work colleagues with whom she was on friendly relations, but that didn't extend beyond the workplace. There was too much to do to maintain a life for herself and Rohit. She kept their home, their attire, and their bodies clean and neat. She consistently discouraged social interest from men, which had been considerable as soon as Ajita had been out from under the protection of the Sikh community. A social life of any kind was a distraction she couldn't afford. It was a risk that she dare not take. Abject poverty was only one mistake away.

And so the past thirteen years since her parents had died had created a disciplined person, routinized in the daily task of survival. Her social skills were as limited as her interests. Her serious demeanor tended to discourage would-be suitors of what could only be called a lovely young woman. Those who didn't know her background assumed her a snob, thinking such a beauty thought too much of herself to lower herself to the standards of others. Ajita let them think as they wished, as long as they left her alone.

Now her routine life was shattered. She was ill equipped for the difficulties before her. Except for her discipline. She had a new mission. Unclear as it was in her own mind, Ajita would somehow see it through.

CHAPTER 22

ARISTOL

The dark eyes glared back at Aristol, full of anger and fear. "Sshhh," Aristol whispered. He spoke only basic words to them in Greek. They didn't understand a word of it, nor did Aristol, Homedes, or anyone on the estate speak their strange tongue from Africa. Aristol's idea was not to push education, but to let them understand that he was trying to communicate with them. They would have months and years to learn from each other.

Aristol had been sitting quietly between the two of them for about a half hour when Homedes entered the gymnasium. The two prisoners recoiled in horror at his entrance, to the extent that their bindings permitted. They were both restrained in the same manner as Aristol's cage when he was transported to the estate some years earlier. Aristol looked up at Homedes, annoyance on his face, but said nothing.

"Sorry," Homedes whispered, backing out of the room, "we'll talk later."

Aristol nodded and flashed a brief relenting smile in response. He turned back to his charges and began singing softly. Aristol had a fine tenor voice. He sang a slow lullaby common in Greece, but new to the Nubians. The two of them were bound ankle and wrist in the supine position comfortably on inclined bedding facing each other. Aristol sat across from them, but back several feet so that the three of them could easily view each other at the same time. He looked each of them over carefully yet again. They were naked as he was and stunning to Aristol's eye. Both had very dark skin and brown eyes with an unruly head of curly hair. The young woman was tall with an aquiline nose set between strong deep set dark eyes that missed nothing. The man, perhaps a year or two younger and an inch or two shorter than Aristol, was broad and well-muscled in the chest, back, and shoulders yet very narrow at the hips. Strong limbs completed the physique of a natural athlete. They were securely bound, but comfortably so. Both were also gagged, but could breathe easily enough.

The two of them had been transported to the estate together in a cage, but not bound during transport as Aristol had been. Such an apparatus was not commonly used in the slave trade. Homedes preferred the devices and had them custom built as a means of avoiding discipline via corporal punishment. The report Aristol got upon receipt of the beautiful dark pair was that they couldn't be handled and indeed upon first inspection Aristol could see that was true. He had decided to drug their drink so that they could be cleaned and bound before starting the breaking process. Aristol, like Homedes, believed in breaking in new slaves gently, with love, if at all possible.

Homedes' first attempt with each of them, alone and out of sight of the other, had been a failure. He had begun with nothing more than a soft touch of his hands on arms, legs, and torso, but in both cases they shrank away and shivered in fear. This new experiment would be slower and run only by Aristol. Patience. That is what Homedes had taught Aristol years ago. Patience.

These two newcomers were a few years older than Aristol had been when he first arrived so the three of them were about the same age. Their prime years were still before them. Aristol wanted their life here on the estate to be as happy as his was.

Every few minutes, Aristol would stand and stroll around the large room that was the gym and bathhouse then return to his seat. He would fondle himself absently while he walked, as if habitually, but always stopped before full arousal. At first, his self-pleasuring caused his captives alarm, but when nothing untoward happened the two prisoners settled down again. After a while, they were no longer alarmed that he did this.

And so a patient week went by. Aristol stayed in the room almost all the time. He slept on the floor near them. He ate with them and slackened the ropes to their bindings enough for them to clean themselves and stretch. Several times daily, Aristol performed some basic gymnastic exercises. Eventually, the new slaves copied him, feeling the benefit of the motions and poses. By the end of the week, the three of them had developed a synchronized routine.

Aristol let them talk to each other periodically. It took a while, but eventually they learned not to shout or yell. If they did, the gags returned. Often they were gagged anyway just so they were as used to being gagged as not, for no apparent reason. He touched them occasionally, just casually as he attended to their needs, until they got used to that as well.

***

One day, Homedes met Aristol during a short break.

"Tomorrow I think," Aristol told him..

"Well, it is about time," Homedes said, "What is your plan for these two? Beautiful as they are, I am skeptical that anything can be done with such savages."

"Buyer's remorse? Maybe you shouldn't visit Corinth so often," Aristol chided his master. "You seldom return empty handed."

"It was on impulse. I hadn't really been shopping when I visited the slave market. These two, no surprise, were causing quite the sensation. Once I saw the pair, I just had to have both. They cost me a pretty penny, I can tell you that."

"I can well imagine."

"So what's your plan?" Homedes asked again.

"Dani first, for sure," replied Aristol, "If he enjoys it, he won't be so upset when it is Ife's turn. And hopefully neither will she."

"Dani and Ife?"

"Their names. He is Dani and she is Ife."

Homedes smiled, "My, you have made progress."

"They're people, Homedes. Just like you and me. This will work," Aristol said. Homedes looked at him quizzically, but let the issue slide.

"And the boy first, hmm? Dani. I'm wondering, Aristol, if that is strategy or simply preference," Homedes said with a smile.

"Normally I'd say both, but even you have to admit that Ife is stunning. I look forward to the day when she comes to us free and joyfully. Meanwhile, I just hope Dani will enjoy my attentions."

"Oh, he'll enjoy you alright. At least his lower parts will. Once you have their bodies, my boy, their hearts will follow. Look how it worked for you."

"But I was such a novice. That helped. And I had nobody that I left behind. We don't know anything about these two. Even you have never dealt with a language barrier like this. And remember, they don't even know each other, having been captured from different areas."

"There is risk for sure, but we won't know until you try. I have confidence in you," Homedes said, gripping the younger man's hand.

Aristol smiled in response, but continued. "And then there is Ife," he went on. "I don't know enough about women in general, let alone her culture, to even guess her reaction."

"Come on, Aristol, you've lain with Dulce lots of times."

"Of course, but Dulce is so accommodating, so contented a person. She's really quite wonderful in that regard, but Ife appears to be very much the opposite."

“Yes, there is a nurturing quality in Dulce that is quite unique in a slave,” said Homedes

“A person,” corrected Aristol. “But back to Ife. Hopefully, she also will see that we mean no harm. So even before I lay a hand even on Dani, they will both watch me alone.”

Homedes was surprised. “A brilliant idea, my boy. I envy them the education you will give them,” Homedes said.

“Will you observe?” Aristol asked.

“Wouldn’t miss it for the world.”

“Just stay hidden. And remember to watch them watch me. Then watch her while I am with him. I won’t be able to.”

“You shall have a full report on their reactions. Good luck, my boy,” Homedes said. He gave the younger man a kiss. Aristotle felt that special tingle on his lips. He responded hungrily, the kiss lingering, the hug tightening.

***

The next morning, Aristol gently gagged both Ife and Dani after breakfast. Then Aristol strolled around fondling himself as usual. However this time he did not stop, as if unplanned, he couldn’t restrain himself. He stood where they could both see him, closing his eyes, into a fantasy with the two lovely people just a few steps away. Fully aroused now, Aristol slowly ran his hands up and down his body while his member quivered stiffly. He was dreaming they were brown hands touching him. His hands returned to his phallus, his entire body shivered, deep in the moment of his ecstasy, until he spouted through several spasmodic gyrations. Then Aristol collapsed back on his chair, almost missing it.

“By Zeus,” he said, knowing they couldn’t understand him, his eyes still closed. “I hope you enjoyed the show. I know I did. I should do that more often.” Then, he looked at both of them sheepishly, as if embarrassed, but noted that the man had swelled somewhat while the woman had fully blossomed. They were both looking at him wide eyed.

CHAPTER 23

SHE

The American reporter woman had thwarted her terror attack. It wasn't a major setback by any means, but She didn't like a loss. The attack wasn't supposed to actually accomplish anything other than bring the Kashmir independence issue into the heart of the nation's capital. Shake people up. Now She was walking briskly on a crowded street in the New Delhi business district. People, dodging traffic and chattering on cell phones as usual, didn't look shaken up at all. The American woman had become the story so the whole event was a wasted effort. On top of that, the authorities had two captives. None of those terrorists were supposed to survive. She had even been outside the bank herself to make sure of it if the police hadn't killed them all. A few extra shots in all the chaos would escape immediate notice. But the fools never got out of the bank thanks to the American, so the police caught two of them. Not that they knew much, but they would be able to say a woman was the planner. It added risk. She could handle it.

Now the American woman was off to Greece and good riddance to her, for now. She wouldn't forget Tina Marin and there would be a reckoning. But no rush. Meanwhile, Marin had left an assistant behind to continue snooping. Bobby Singh would need watching. Good looking kid so that wouldn't be too much of a hardship. Maybe she would even make contact. Get on the inside. She could use some entertainment. In the meantime, she had other plans to unsettle the everyday Indian on the street. More importantly, to turn them against each other even more than they already were.

CHAPTER 24

NIKIAS

Neston was dead. He died at the supper table after a long workday. Just collapsed face down into his bowl, still on his stool. Nikias looked to the Lady Delia. Her eyes were on Neston with an expression of peaceful understanding. Serene. Nikias did nothing, waiting for his lady. She closed her eyes, and raising her slender arms skyward, began a soft slow song in a tongue Nikias had never heard. Without understanding a word, he seemed to know that it was a song of Neston's life, from womb to tomb and everything in between. It was neither happy nor sad, just accepting. Serene.

Nikias woke the next morning just before dawn, as always. Neston had been buried the evening before in a manner as was his due. Nikias went to the fountain to fetch water for his lady as he did every morning. It bubbled from a stone more than twice his height into a pool on the side of the stream. The mist and endless splashing always soothed his senses. A child-high waterfall in the stream blended with the fountain water from the pool at the bottom of the fall. Nikias was surprised to find Delia already there and bathing in the frothy current. Her head was back so her silver hair flowed behind her. The fall cascaded upon her pale bare bosom. Soft moonlight gleamed in her locks. Delia opened her eyes and looked upon Nikias. The moonlight in her glance smote his heart.

Delia spoke, "I am priestess of the fountain of Aphrodite. I abide by the goddess. Will you abide by us, Nikias?" Nikias fell to his knees by the bank of the current. Delia held out a long white arm to him. "Come to us, Nikias. Companion of the fountain. Now is your time. Our time. For all time."

It was much later when the sun rose high enough to peek through the leaves, making Nikias squint. He enjoyed the warmth on his face. Chest deep in the pool, the warm fountain water flowed across his body and limbs as he leaned contentedly against a large stone, smoothed over time by the fountain flow. Delia was suddenly with him, under his outstretched arm. He closed his arms about her as she snuggled in. Completely at peace, but curious.

"Neston wasn't one with you," Nikias said.

"No."

"What was he?"

"A helper," Delia replied. "I was waiting for you."

"Waiting for me?"

"Not only you. We didn't know of you, but we were looking for someone like you."

"What am I like?"

"Humble, accepting, selfless. In other words, loving."

"Well, Neston certainly wasn't all that."

"No, there was never any thought of Neston in any other role than that which he played."

"Which was?"

"A man to be at my side, in a man's world. It simplified things."

"And he accepted that?"

"Of course. Why would he not?" said Delia. Why not indeed, thought Nikias and said nothing more.

CHAPTER 25

PALLY

The plane bumped and lurched in its approach to Athens. Pally leaned forward to look past Tina out the window. Their hands were still clasped, tightly now. Pally's hand was wet from sweat. She was not an experienced flier and was trying to hide her panic from the petite goddess she found herself traveling with.. Tina turned back from the window to her, smiling reassuringly. Gasps and a few cries rang through the cabin as the plane dropped suddenly and Pally felt momentary weightlessness in her belly. She swallowed hard against the burn of bile in her throat.

"Well, that was a wild one," Tina said loudly. Pally said nothing. Her eyes were riveted on the window where the Earth was almost upon them as the pilots attempted to land in a blustery crosswind. Tina turned as fully to her friend as her seatbelt allowed.

"Look at me, Pally," she said firmly, "Look at me."

Pally met Tina's eyes hoping she didn't look as frightened as she was. Almost beyond caring.

"I've been through some rough rides over the years," Tina told her, "but the last few minutes of this jaunt has been hellish. Almost as bad as that drop from the sky into Gibraltar about ten years ago. Which I survived." Pally heard her, but wasn't really registering what was said. "When the time comes in just a few minutes," Tina went on, "I doubt the captain will try to put her down. At least I hope not." Pally started to sob.

"No, focus on me, youngling," Tina told her. "This is not how we die." Tina reached around with her far hand behind Pally's neck for emphasis, rubbing her gently.

"Will we die?" Pally managed to whisper through her whimpers.

"Today? Maybe. But if we do, it will be as soldiers. Warriors. With honor." A pause. "Trust in your gods. Trust in your friends."

Another wicked weightless drop, and hearts were racing. Tina's hand came from behind Pally's neck to her soft dark cheek. The touch reached through Pally's fear. What a beautiful woman. Suddenly, Tina kissed Pally full on the mouth. Pally's mouth opened to hers, tongues entangling as the plane lurched sharply to the side. Screams erupted through the cabin. Pally felt Tina's hand on her breast, slipping the cup of the brassiere up over it. Pally leaned into her, moaning into Tina's mouth, feeling the pressure on her nipple race down to her sex. The plane leveled off then lurched hard onto the tarmac, the force of deceleration pervading the cabin. The women held their embrace. They broke away as the plane slowed to a controlled taxi. A collective sigh amidst scattered clapping echoed across the cabin. Tina squeezed Pally's breast hard, then released her. Pally slipped her left breast back into place, still holding Tina's hand. They both looked down at their locked hands, then smiled into each other's eyes. Pally wiped her wet eyes with her free hand. Breathing deeply through her nose as she regained her composure. Still alive!

***

Tina waited outside the women's bathroom, looking at the airport signage in both Greek and English. She studied the Greek lettering. The Euclidean alphabet as she recalled from her college days. Fortunately, visitors could get by with English in this country for the most part. Tina had never studied Greek, but the lettering was familiar from her sorority days. Could she still recite the alphabet backwards? She doubted it and wasn't going to try now.

And try as she might, Tina couldn't shake off the feeling of coming home to a place she'd never been before. She was still trying to sort out what had happened on the plane. The episode was not nearly so foggy as the bank was, which she could hardly credit as having actually happened if not for the videos. Then in the hospital when that girl had entered her room. It was like someone else had been there with her, but she remembered some of it. Sort of. But on the plane? That was all clear. It was her who had kissed Pally, who has never been so attracted to another woman in her life. And she was still attracted to her. Just as she was now so sexually drawn to young Bobby. She wasn't bi. Who was she?

"I'm ready," Pally said, startling Tina who hadn't seen her approach from the ladies room.

"And so you are. You look quite recovered." Pally smiled in response. Tina reached out for a brief awkward handhold. "Let's find us a rental car. Hellas is waiting." *After so long…*

CHAPTER 26

ARISTOL

Aristol noticed Ife entering the gym out of the corner of his eye. She had a sulky look on her face. Her full lips pouted. He and Dani were wrestling, and distracted by Ife's arrival, Aristotle felt Dani's arm slip behind Aristol's knee, putting him on his back. Laughing, Aristol tapped his defeat on Dani's shoulder who rolled off him with a grin.

"Did you see that move, Ife?" Dani asked her.

Without reply, Ife turned and shut the door then disrobed to be nude as the boys already were. Two years had passed since Ife and Dani arrived at the estate yet Aristol never got tired of seeing Ife naked. Her long lithe figure was darkly magnificent, highlighted by the deeper blackness of her areolas and thick tangle of pubic hair.

"What's the matter, Ife?" Dani asked.

"Homedes," she answered, "I am sick of him taking me whenever he wants to."

"He didn't hurt you, did he?" Aristol asked.

"No. He never hurts me. He is always as gentle as a lamb. I just don't like it."

"Well, it's a small price to pay for paradise," Dani said.

"Do you like it?" she asked Dani.

"Well," Dani paused, "yes. He always gets a rise out of me, but I know what you mean. With the rest of us, we get to choose, I love it. Never gets old."

"It was Homedes who opened my eyes to the wonder of love," Aristol said. "I will always be grateful."

"We are slaves here," Ife said.

"We are safe here," replied Dani. "We are fed here. We are free here to do as we wish."

"We aren't free to say no to Homedes," Ife said bitterly.

"No we aren't, but there is no place in all of Hellas where the master of the house doesn't take the same liberties. With everyone in the household, free or slave," explained Aristol.

"Homedes is gentle and good looking for a man his age. And he is just plain nice. We are lucky," said Dani.

"Well, he makes me sick. Come, the both of you. Help me get him out of my system," Ife said as she waded into the bath. The two boys followed her in. Ife dove under.

"Better?" Aristol asked when Ife surfaced.

"I can cleanse the man's sweat off my skin. But I can't cleanse him out of my soul. Or his seed out of my body."

***

Later, the three of them lay together on the soft matting of the gym floor. Ife on her back staring holes through the roof, Dani and Aristol on either side of her snuggling to her bosom, drowsily contented.

"Let's run away," Ife said suddenly. Both boys sat up at that. "To the mountains you told us about, Aristol."

"Arcadia?"

"There we can be free."

"It's wild country," Aristol warned. "Few people live there, so high up."

"Sooner or later I will have babies," Ife said. Both Dani and Aristol showed concern. She had their full attention now.

"But Homedes follows the calendars for all of you girls," Aristol said. "He never takes you when you're ripe. None of us do."

"Believe me, the both of you, sooner or later I will have babies. I want them to be only yours," Ife continued. "For the three of us to be a family. To make our own household."

"That would be nice," Dani confessed.

Aristol said nothing, troubled. He cared for Homedes, but his feelings for his two friends ran much deeper. The three of them had truly become one in body, mind, and spirit. Homedes just didn't fit in. He treated everyone in the large household the same way, as Aristol had done until Dani and Ife had arrived. Aristol was second in authority on the estate, with the exception of the platoon of soldiers who answered only to Homedes. Now he only occasionally played with any of the others, women or men, of the large household.

"What about Aria?" Aristol asked Ife, referring to a petite olive skinned Persian slave girl a few years older than them. "You two are so beautiful together."

"I was coming to Aria. I won't leave her behind, if she'll risk it. I would miss her," Ife acknowledged.

"So would I," said Dani.

"Then let's ask her to join us. After all, it wouldn't be fair to you Ife to have only us men to love," Aristol suggested.

Ife laughed, relieved that Aristol was agreeing to leave. "And you boys wouldn't mind the variety either."

They all chuckled then sobered up as they realized the dangerous decision they had just made. Two slaves had tried to run since Aristol had been here, before the two Africans had arrived. Both had been tracked down, hauled back, and their toes cut off on one foot so they could never run again. Running away came at a price if you couldn't pull it off. Not many slaves had tried, because life here was easy and free within the confines of the estate. But none who had run had ever succeeded.

Aristol had been born to a wealthy family, a citizen of Sparta, and no man's slave. But what freedom he had experienced in life had been here as a slave on Homedes' estate. What pleasure he had experienced had been here. And the love he had learned, starting with the sensual from Homedes, but growing to the spiritual with Ife and Dani was outside the strictures of Spartan society. He missed his mother, true, but he'd rarely had the opportunity to see her before, when he had been in the army. No, there was nothing for him back in Sparta.

The fact was that Aristol never thought of himself as a slave since the day Homedes had first taught him the sexual pleasures, even though he knew he was one. But now his friends, his lovers, were discontented. Theirs was a different experience and perspective. Hellas was not their home. The entire Hellenic culture was alien to them. So they hungered for a new place, where they could build their own micro-culture. And they wanted Aristol with them. Could he ever be content again here on the estate without them? Did they have any chance of escape without him? He knew they did not. And yet he knew they would try.

CHAPTER 27

IFE

Ife lay wide awake in bed reflecting on her life here at the Homedes estate. Aria snored gently, her small frame nestled on Ife's hip. The daughter of a local chief from a village on the banks of the upper Nile, Ife had been a virgin when she had been abducted. She missed her family and friends from the village terribly. She had never known Dani before they met in captivity, but his home village had also been on the Nile. Dani had treated her with respect from the start and had viciously tried to defend her as best he could whenever their captors approached. Ife's own fiery spirit and behavior was equally as savage, if not more so, whenever the slave traders had tried to handle them. They had never known that the reason both of them had been unspoiled sexually, well fed and treated, was because virgins brought a higher price on the slave market. Eventually, the slavers had crossed the Mediterranean Sea to Hellas where Homedes had been infatuated with the pair at the Corinth slave market and purchased them.

The blonde Aristol had been a vision of exotic beauty to Ife. Even among the Hellenics, blonde hair was uncommon. Raised in a rigid conservative culture, nudity was unheard of in Ife's experience. That first week on the estate, Ife had been fascinated with the frequent changes in size and shape of the genitalia of the virile young Aristol and Dani. She had been mesmerized watching Aristol as he stroked himself until he was stiff and his empurpled bulb came out of its cape. Dani's bulb, darker than Aristol's, had come out without even being touched. Aristol had stroked himself until he erupted. Ife had felt funny all over when that happened. It was scary, but she ached in a strangely good way. She had wanted to touch and feel the boys all over and herself too but, of course, she had been bound. That made the aching agonizingly sweet. Then after a few minutes, Aristol's shaft had shrunk down again. He seemed somehow happy. Contented.

Next he went over to Dani who was still standing stiff. It seemed to be pulsing. He too couldn't touch himself. But Aristol could, and did. He stroked him slowly. Dani moaned through his gag. Ife moaned too. Then Aristol licked Dani's bulb. Ife could see it all. It shivered and shook. Then he put Dani's shaft in his mouth. Ife was shocked. Was he going to bite? But he didn't. Ife could see that Dani loved it. Ife was beside herself. Then Aristol began stroking Dani again, slowly, but with a firm grip. Dani's eyes bulged. So did Ife's. She strained against her bindings, longing to touch the boys, herself. Dani's hips thrust into the air and the white oil flew out, but as soon as it started Aristol put his mouth over Dani until there was nothing more to drink and Dani was softer and smaller.

Ife noted that Aristol was aroused again, but he didn't touch himself. He strolled over to Ife with a soft smile on his face. He said something to Ife with his sweet voice, but of course she didn't understand. Their eyes met and she saw understanding. And love. He put a hand lightly on each of her shoulders. Ife shuddered sweetly in response. His touch moved lightly down to her breasts and the touch ran right from her nipples to between her thighs. Ife felt delightfully dizzy, watching Aristol's face as he focused on where his hands were. She had touched her own breasts before and felt a tingle down there, but this was so much more than a tingle. He lightly brushed the back of his fingers against her erectness. It was wonderful, but not enough. She didn't know what she needed, but she needed it bad. Aristol knew. He bent between her legs. His lips, then his tongue touched her wetness. Entered gently and slowly. Ife felt she was floating. Later a finger went in, but not deep, while his tongue and lips still caressed her. She moaned through her gag. Don't stop. Don't ever stop. And he didn't. He added his thumb to her bottom now wet from her own juices. He glided, and pressed, but didn't penetrate. Finger and thumb danced in tune with his tongue, soft and slow, but relentless as strange sensations welled within her. Then it struck clear through her, her sex, her heart, and her head. With her first orgasm, Ife fell in love with Aristol.

That next day, Homedes had entered the gym. The two Africans, still strung up, listened to the two Hellenics speak together without understanding. Eventually, with a departing smile of reassurance to each of them, Aristol was gone. Homedes remained looking them over carefully, humming to himself. He approached Ife. She looked at the man who had bought her at public auction with suspicion. He ran his hand lightly across her taut belly down to the pubic line just grazing her black bush as he lifted his hand. Goose bumps followed his fingers.

He said something, more to himself than to Ife, that she didn't understand. Then he sauntered over to Dani and disrobed. Homedes was already swelling with anticipation. Dani noticed and his own member reacted despite himself.

***

Homedes had waited until the next day to take Ife. He was gentle with her as he always was with all his slaves, but they both knew that there was no sympathy between them. He spoke softly to her as he entered. It didn't help. She felt him meet the resistance of her chastity. He probed twice not forcing a breakthrough. Ife's eyes were closed, her full lips compressed under the gag. Suddenly she felt both her breasts squeezed. Her eyes opened at that, and in that moment he held her eyes and pierced her. Ife gasped. It hurt. Homedes held his position stock still for an eternity. Then a slow rhythm commenced and continued to completion. It was Ife now that held his eyes the entire time. A slave in body only.

Ife was remembering that moment over two years ago as the three of them discussed escape. She remembered it every time Homedes took her. Ife knew that while Homedes was proud and pleased to own her beauty, his preference was for the boys. Yet he had taken her most every day since that first time two years ago. Because he could. He needed her to know that. She knew it had to stop. Ife did not want his baby. Once several months ago she thought she was pregnant. While a false alarm, it had been on her mind ever since. Since then, escape had been on her mind too.

CHAPTER 28

DANI

Dani had been sold into slavery by his own village. He was orphaned at a young age. The elders of the village saw to his welfare until he was old enough to be of value. Unlike Ife, who was abducted, Dani witnessed his own transaction and understood that he was intended for and would likely go into the sex industry. While not thrilled with his fate, he realized he had just been a work slave to his village anyway. At least he wasn't fated to be worked to death in a mine somewhere. Not yet anyway. Prior to being sold, Dani had enjoyed pleasuring himself when he had the chance for privacy. The slave traders had inspected and tested him before closing the deal. They were impressed with Dani's size and stamina. While he felt humiliated to be manipulated so, he was acutely aware that sex could keep him alive and hopefully safe. He had conveyed all this to Ife on their journey to Hellas. Slavery was a reality of life in the world. They had both been aware of it since childhood. Now they were a part of it. Dani had in fact been expecting it.

To the Africans, the appearance of Aristol was a surprise and a blessing. Here was this beautiful young man, a fellow slave wearing the same collar, but an influential one helping them. He appeared to be actually concerned for their happiness. Like Aristol, Dani had never really thought about his own sexual orientation. Everyone appeared off limits anyway. That day, the day after Homedes first raped Ife, they were waiting in the gym still strung up as they had been for a bit over a week. Aristol entered. Ife caught his eye. She started to weep. Aristol was at her side immediately. He untied her, set her free. Then Dani too. Ife just sat on the floor sobbing. The two boys attended her, comforting her as best they could. Dani told her that the worst was over. Aristol took both their hands and walked them around the gym. Showing them the pool and warm laconica bath. Then he left for they knew not why or for how long. The Africans hugged each other. Dani in joy of release, Ife mourning her loss. With the lovely Ife in his arms, Dani couldn't help but become aroused. Embarrassed, not wanting to offend her, he let her go and turned away. But she hugged him from behind, told him it was ok. That it was natural. She put a hand around him to his penis. He stiffened to full. She turned him around smiling into his uncertain eyes. Then Ife bent over his member to study it closely. How it looked from all angles. Dani was fascinated watching Ife fascinate over his penis. She seemed to purr. Then she did what she had seen Aristol do. She covered as much of it as she could with her mouth. Dani felt a shiver run through his thighs and chest. They went to the floor together. Dani rolled fully on his back spreading his legs. Suddenly Aristol was there with an armful of fresh clothing. He dropped the clothes and joined them on the floor. Focusing on Dani, he made eye contact with Ife then moistened his fingers and fondled Dani's bottom. This was a new sensual experience for Dani, he struggled briefly not wanting it to end, then erupted into Ife's mouth as he convulsed and contorted, ecstatically out of control.

CHAPTER 29

BOBBY

Bobby marveled at the luscious landscape as the train chugged him deeper into Indian Kashmir. No wonder three countries were fighting over the place. It was paradise, or could be if not for politics. Bobby stretched his legs onto the empty seat across from him, slouching his long frame, trying to ease the tension out that this assignment put upon him. A saried matron seated nearby immediately looked down at Bobby's feet in disapproval. Bobby put his feet down again and sat up straight, returning his focus to the countryside and the assignment that brought him here.

That interview with special agent Miller had really been something. What an intimidating person. She kept her hair in a close-cropped afro. Clearly practical, but contrary to the styles of the day among many black women back in the States. All business and no nonsense, that was Miller. Being tall, Bobby was used to looking down at most people physically and while a bit taller than most women, with Miller it was no different. Except it was. Miller exuded a physical presence. A power. She reminded Bobby of Serena Williams of whom Bobby was a big fan and admirer. Tennis being his game, Serena was the closest person Bobby had to a sports hero. Thinking back on that interview, Bobby realized that Miller never looked into his eyes. So she never looked up at him. Her eyes were always elsewhere in the room, staring as if lost in thought, as she rapped out her questions and orders. Yes, orders. She had no legal authority over Bobby, but he felt like he was working for Miller now. Tom wouldn't like it, that was for sure and Bobby still didn't know how he would handle things, but Miller expected regular updates on what Bobby learned, if anything. And that was another tension. The big one. What if he failed? What if he got nowhere at all? Fell flat on his face?

The truth was Bobby felt overwhelmed taking on his first solo assignment. He sure wished Tina was here with him, but then if Tina was on the job he wouldn't be here at all. How could he even reach Tina? Miller could find her. That was it, Miller could do anything. Bobby knew that deep down he was going to need Tina's help before this assignment was done.

What was really wrong with her anyway? She hadn't been raped, after all. Abused for sure, but she got her own back in spades. She sure seemed on the ball when Bobby had met her about his assignment. Giving guidance and discussing the points of contact Bobby needed to track down, how to do it and then how to handle them when he found them. God, how could he possibly cope with all this by himself? He was just two years out of journalism school. Naturally confident, if you had asked him a month ago if he could get the story on his own of course he would have said yes, but watching the world go by through the train window Bobby's confidence was ebbing away as quickly as the scenery.

He would need Tina. And he would need Miller to find Tina. Tina and Miller. Two totally different women in appearance, but alike in that they were both masters of their crafts. Miller, Bobby reckoned, was some five or ten years younger than Tina. Bobby's mind drifted back to his interview with Tina in the police barrack. God, it was good to see her. Except for the bandages on her forehead and jaw, Tina had looked as radiant as ever. And she certainly seemed to be on her game professionally, as always. So why wasn't she working on this assignment? And yet, Tina had been somehow different. Always glamorous in Bobby's eyes, he had sensed something new in the older woman that day. As if she was some sort of predator, under control for sure, but there. Come to think of it, Miller had been the same way. As if they both knew that they could take him whenever they wanted, if they wanted, at their leisure. And they were right. Bobby noticed the saried matron was frowning at him again. Why? Then he realized he must be wearing a shit-eating grin.

***

The babble of Kashmiri all around him on the train platform was bewildering as Bobby disembarked at Srinagar. Surely, they were all talking about the stranger. At 6 foot 3, Bobby stood out like a sore thumb. A man brushed by him. Was that intentional? But the man moved on. I'm getting paranoid, Bobby reflected. He forced a smile hoping he could feel some bravado inside to go with it.

"What are you grinning about?" the woman asked. It was Hindi! Bobby understood.

"I, I, nothing really," Bobby replied in the same language.

"Well don't stop. You have excellent teeth. Very straight. Very white. Very American."

Bobby blushed, opened his mouth to speak and then closed it, not knowing what to say.

The woman smiled, "I didn't expect an American to be so shy. You own the world and usually act like it, don't you?"

"If we ever did, that was before my time. Maybe the Boomers or the GenXers act that way."

"I don't know those terms," the woman said, switching to English, "but since you aren't one of them, what are you?" The change of language shifted Bobby's perception of the woman before him. Looking into hazel eyes, he suddenly realized that this nondescript woman was nondescript on purpose. The heavy gray jacket she wore against the early mountain spring was overlarge. Cut for a man.

"I like to think I am the first of the Z's. The latest generation." Bobby said after a pause.

The woman turned and with a mild gesture invited Bobby to walk with her, which he did.

"Nice to meet you Z. Call me Lucky."

"Lucky? Who are you?"

"I'm your cousin, here to pick you up."

"Oh," Bobby said, brightening up. "I was expecting someone older. My mom's cousin."

"My parents, but I am here for you instead," Lucky said. "Let's go. What are you thinking of, Z?" Right now, this instant?"

"You know my name is Bobby, right?"

"Of course, but indulge me, Z. What are you thinking of?"

"You."

"Good. Because I am thinking of you. Stay in the moment."

"But where are we going?"

"That didn't last long," Lucky said with a sigh. She stopped Bobby by spinning in front of him. She took a fist full of beard to pull him down to her, nose to nose. "Don't ask questions. Just be. Be with me. Focus on the person with you. Don't ask, don't judge, don't analyze, just accept. You were feeling alone, but you never are. And now you know that, because you are with me."

They continued walking. "The questions are streaming through your mind," Lucky continued, "Let them come, but let them go on just as quickly. Unanswered. All that you see is registering in your mind. Let it register, but don't dwell on it. Focus on us."

She took him by the hand. It was small in his, but strong. She worked with her hands in some way. They continued strolling. It was a slower pace than natural to Bobby's long stride, but he adjusted to his companion.

"I'm sorry," Bobby said, "but I need to go to the bathroom. And I'm hungry."

"Of course. Your needs will be attended to."

"No, I really need to pee. It is distracting me from focusing on us."

Lucky laughed. "Fair enough. Get in the car."

They were on a side street just off the train station that, while not bustling, was busy enough and lined with cars, mostly compacts. Lucky unlocked the door and hopped into the smallest car Bobby had ever seen. He sighed as Lucky reached across to unlock the passenger side. After wedging his rucksack into what couldn't possibly pass for a back seat, contorting his frame into this clown car didn't do Bobby's bladder any favors. With a couple of quick back and forths, Lucky had the small car bouncing along in fine fashion.

"What is this thing?" Bobby asked, with his knees practically under his beard.

"This is a 1967 MK I Austin Mini Cooper," Lucky said with obvious pride. "Relax, we don't have far to go."

"I feel like we are off road," Bobby said after a particularly vicious bounce.

"Spoiled American," came the response.

"Well some of our roads aren't much better, but we don't revel in them." Lucky accelerated in response as they turned onto a main road along a large lake. There was a row of picturesque square floating structures lined up along the banks of the lake.

"What are those colorful barges with buildings on them?" Bobby asked

"Houseboats, you fool. One of them's mine." She sped into an impossibly small parking space, even for this matchbox car, and after a short walk were aboard and inside her abode.

"This is incredible," Bobby whispered as they entered. He was overwhelmed by the color red, rich and deep, on the walls and floor, covering the windows. The very air glowed a soft reddish hue. Being a houseboat, it wasn't a big space and the furniture had clean simple lines, almost nondescript, but the rugs and walls dominated his senses.

"Through there," Lucky gestured to a narrow door. "You can bathe and get the travel off of you while I prepare a meal." Bobby opened his mouth to respond as Lucky pulled the faded gray beanie off her head and piles of rich black hair poured down her face and shoulders to her elbows. He just stood there gawking.

"What are you, a fish waiting for a hook?" Lucky asked. "You have to pee, remember?" Bobby closed his jaw like a trap and turned to the door without a word.

"And make the shower a quick one," she called after him, "my fresh water tank isn't huge."

There was a clean towel hanging next to hers so he used it. Stepping back into the small bedroom he noted a Buddha on the nightstand. There had been a smaller famously familiar figure in the standup coffin that passed for a bathroom as well. Soft music began as Bobby pulled a fresh T-shirt out of his rucksack. He decided to bypass briefs all together, not wanting to put on the ones he wore on the train and not wanting to burn a second clean pair on a single day either. Pulling his skinny jeans back on, he zipped up with care. It was a cool mountain April morning in Kashmir, but it felt comfortable enough inside so Bobby left his hoodie behind as he stepped out of the bedroom. Through the music, Bobby sensed something sizzling. He couldn't tell what it was, but the aroma was pleasing.

"There you are, all shipshape and Bristol fashion as those English used to say." Lucky said, sticking her head out of the tiny kitchen alcove. "Making magic in the galley here. Be with you in a moment."

"You almost sound English yourself," Bobby replied.

"Only almost? I studied the Queen's English at university. It's a shame to hear from a native speaker that I didn't quite get it right."

"You studied. That's good to know."

"Why is that?"

"Because I haven't been able to tell whether you are 15 or 35."

"Somewhere in between," Lucky laughed as she stepped out of the galley. Bobby's jaw dropped again. Lucky laughed even more at his gaping face. Her big hazel eyes with a hint of Asian sparkled.

"You're a sweet young man," she said as Bobby continued to stare dumbfounded. The black mane still flowed all around her heart shaped face that finished from the round cheekbones under those large eyes down to her soft rounded chin. Her nose was pert over a mouth that was not wide, but well lipped. But Bobby was transfixed by her classic hourglass figure. He'd never seen anything like it. Lucky was wearing a burgundy T-shirt with cut off sleeves and waist that was so short that Bobby caught glimpses of the underside of her breasts as she moved. And she was bare down to the widest point of her hips where burgundy sweatpants were held up only by the roundness of her rear. A few long black pubic strands had teased their way over the top of her sweatpants. If that was by design, it was effective on the young man. But Bobby was mostly riveted on her long midriff. A strikingly pale contrast to Lucky's dark face. Amid the most slender point of her waist, which while narrow was also soft, was an inny belly button you couldn't see into. Bobby imagined a deep crevice to be revealed if he could only penetrate it. With his tongue. He could feel himself swell against the denim coarseness of his jeans.

"I admit I am showing off, and happy that you are so pleased with me. And that said, I think we had better take care of something before we eat," Lucky said, pushing against him.

"Hey! What gives, Lucky?" But Bobby didn't resist as Lucky pressed him, forcing him to take a step back. She opened his beltless jeans in one motion as a small sofa was magically against the back of his legs. Bobby sank back into the deep cushions.

"Relax, cousin Bobby, American reporter. I'm on your side." Big beautiful eyes smiled up at him before they turned their attention lower.

"Circumcised, how adorable," Lucky murmured as Bobby sprang to attention once released from his jeans. A few admiring strokes, then Lucky immersed him in her mouth. Bobby groaned, as she pushed her breasts against his thighs as additional stimuli. Her hands slid under his buttocks, gripping him tight. It didn't take long, after a brief struggle to hold back, building to a crescendo, Bobby exploded in Lucky's mouth. She drank until he was dry, but he still stood firm.

"My God, what is happening?" Bobby gasped.

Lucky looked up at him from where she was between his thighs. "I've just had my first course of the meal. More than a mouthful, I must say. Now help me up. I'm feeling rather dizzy. Time for nourishment for both of us."

They were soon seated across from each other at the small two-chair dinette. The food was familiar, similar to what he had grown up with out of his mother's kitchen in Brooklyn. It was good and Bobby ate with gusto and drank lots of a fruit juice blend with mineral water. She kept filling his glass.

"Drink up," Lucky ordered, "you need to replenish your fluids."

Bobby pushed back from his plate, sated in body, but not in mind. "Thank you for the meal and," a pause, "everything."

"You are most welcome," Lucky replied with a grin.

"And we're related how, exactly?"

"I think we're cousins. Or maybe I'm more of an aunt. Technically, my dad is your grandparent's generation. At least I think that's how it is. The whole family tree thing is a bit of a blur." Aghast, Bobby was speechless. "Relax, nephew. What do we share, the same great grandfather? Or great great grandfather for you. So its not like we're inbreeding or anything."

"This is surreal. How did we get here?" Bobby asked as much to himself as to Lucky.

"Your mother called my mother saying that you were coming on a news assignment, although what the assignment is wasn't clear. We'll get to that later. My mother told me yesterday and showed me the photo of my handsome American kinsman that your mother had sent to my mother. My parents were going to pick you up," Lucky went on, "but my mother is always so late for everything, she just can't get herself out of the house, much to Dad's chagrin, so I got to you first and whisked you away before they arrived. They are probably still at the station or searching the neighborhood wondering where you wandered off to. So I headed you off at the pass, as you say in your Western films, and here we are."

"I understand the technical details, Lucky but what is going on? This has been like out of a school boy's dream, a wet dream I should say, but now is time for some answers."

"Now we see Bobby Singh, American journalist. Ask away."

"Okay then. To start with, are you as crazy as you seem?"

Lucky stared into her drink for a moment before answering. "Not crazy…just different."

"Different how, if I may ask. And I think I am entitled to, all things considered."

"Can I trust you?" Lucky asked seriously.

"Well, sure. How so?"

"I mean really trust you. You're a stranger here so it's not like you know many people to blab to, but you will meet my parents. And you are a newspaperman."

"Are you about to tell me something newsworthy? Look, if you don't want me to write or tell anyone about something then I won't. We reporters must always protect our sources. Which is the long way of saying you can trust me. But if you really don't want to tell me something, then just don't. I don't want to pry. It's just that today, meeting you, has been kinda crazy."

"But I do want to tell you. And I know I've acted crazy. I don't go around giving blowjobs to strangers. But living in the closet just slowly saps one's will. I've needed to talk to somebody for ever so long," Lucky said. Bobby said nothing, waiting her out. Meanwhile he fantasized how she would look naked.

"I'm poly," Lucky blurted out. "More philosophically than in practice. Well, for the most part. We're too traditional here in Kashmir. And in all of India for that matter."

"Poly?" Bobby asked.

"Polyamorous, at your age and being an American I thought you would have heard of it."

"Of course, I've heard of it. I've just never run into it. And I've certainly never heard of closeted poly people."

"Of course you wouldn't have, they're in the closet. But now you have, so keep it quiet. My parents would freak and I would be in real danger if the millions of other religious psychos throughout India were to hear. So I'm serious, my life is in your hands."

"That must be an exaggeration. Come on."

"Please don't take this lightly," Lucky pleaded.

"No worries, Lucky, relax, I won't tell a soul. But how did you become polyamorous?"

"How?" Lucky practically snarled. "Let me tell you something you can investigate and write about, you can be born gay, you can be born straight, you can be born bi, but nobody, nobody, is born monogamous! I was born poly and so were you."

"But," Bobby started.

"You're single, right?" Lucky pressed on, "Are you monogamous?"

"Well, no."

"Of course not, why would you be?"

"But I am not married."

"And when you do marry, your poly nature, the way you were born, will magically change? Nonsense! Complete and utter nonsense! What's your American word? Bullshit!" Bobby sat silent, absorbing all this. Thinking of Tina, of Miller, and the luscious lady before him.

"You don't talk much, do you Bobby?" Lucky said, less aggressive now.

Bobby smiled, "I was just thinking you can talk a blue streak."

"I have a multi-talented mouth," Lucky said, smiling too.

"I can't argue with that," Bobby said, "Now let me say more. Again, your secret is safe with me. Really. And thank you again for this…uniquely warm welcome." Lucky laughed and clapped her hands in delight, which sent her ample breasts quivering much to Bobby's distraction. But she waited quietly.

"I suppose poly can mean a lot of things to a lot of different people," Bobby said.

"It can."

"So what I am wondering is, and I mean no disrespect, do I need to be worried about STDs?"

"No," Lucky said emphatically. Then she opened her mouth wide and stuck out her tongue for him to see from all angles before continuing, "and no shankers so your penis is safe with me."

"I didn't mean anything by it," Bobby said.

"No, it was a fair question." Her smile returned.

"Do you get tested?"

"No. As I said earlier, I am more philosophically poly than practicing. So I am safe assuming you are safe. You certainly haven't contracted anything from our blowjob."

"Well in that case I am kinda hoping," Bobby said, blushing, "there might be more than just the blowjob."

"Oh, you are, are you?" she asked with a raised eyebrow.

"I mean, I replenished my fluids and everything, just as you said."

"So you did. Well then."

She stood up from the table and swayed to the center of the small living room. The soft background music had been playing all along and Lucky began to undulate to the rhythm. Her arms snaked in all directions to the music. They were fleshy but by no means fat. They just fit the rest of her body. Without warning, the bit of T-shirt was gone, exposing round orbs as pale as her belly that moved in time with the music. Bobby gawked and Lucky responded as her nipples hardened her pink areolas protruded. Bobby started to stand, which was awkward considering his crowded crotch, but with a wave of her hand he sat back down. Meanwhile, the burgundy sweatpants had been inching down as Lucky danced, although whether by design, simple gravity, or both was unknown. Quite a bit of rich black thatch was visible. Finally, Lucky pulled her drawstring and the pants slid to her ankles. She danced out of them and swayed to the music, fully free.

Bobby struggled to be shorn of his jeans. He stood and with some difficulty managed to get them off as his dancing partner giggled. Finally upright, in more ways than one, Bobby peeled off his T-shirt to be as nude as she. He had the long limbed sinewy musculature of the tennis player he was. Curly black hair ran up from his ankles to his crotch and on his forearms as well. His chest hair was less dense. Lucky took in the sight of him with relish as Bobby goggled back at her muscled thighs, her legs a bit short in contrast to her long torso yet wildly erotic to Bobby. She danced toward him.

There was a loud rap on the outside door.

"Khatri? Are you in there?" a muffled male voice penetrated in Punjabi.

"Coming Daddy!" Lucky shouted back.

CHAPTER 30

HOMEDES

Homedes toured the length and breadth of his estate on horseback most every day. It took the better part of the morning being a good 500 hectares. In addition to the cluster of buildings, including the villa, on the highest hill in the center of the place, there were meadows and woodland, pastures and two mountain streams that ran into a deep lake, part of which lay within the confines of the estate. The estate was not a farm as such, producing only some food and items as interested Homedes to grow. He owned a much larger commercial farming enterprise a long day's travel from his home estate, but the bulk of his wealth was in mining further north. A dozen slaves worked the estate as landscapers. Then there were the domestic servants, also slaves, another dozen or so who saw to the needs of those who lived in the main buildings. Then there were ten slaves who had no working role at all. They were the sex slaves and Aristol was first among them.

They were free to wander where they wished and do as they wished on the buildings and grounds of the estate. Sports and outdoor games were their primary pastimes. While at the beck and call of the master, the sex slaves, or companions as Homedes liked to call them, were free to form relationships among themselves, which they did. Homedes didn't have a jealous bone in his body. He liked to see all his slaves happy and healthy. Even the field hands and domestics had good housing, clothing, and food. And they were encouraged to couple among themselves. Homedes fully embraced the teachings of the decadent philosopher Aristippus of Cyrene, whom he had heard lecture once in Corinth. The soldiers were free to take any of the domestic and field hands for their pleasure. Those slaves had no say in the matter, but the soldiers had to follow the rule of gentleness. There were no whips on the estate. Not to be used on slaves, that is. Once a soldier was caught being rough with a field slave. It was the soldier who was stripped and lashed severely by Homedes himself, then expelled from the estate.

Homedes returned from his tour one day in a wistful state of spirit. It was often the way. Such a paradise he had created, but for whom? His son had been lost in the war some seven years ago. That ache never went away. This estate had once been his family home, and technically still was, but with his wife and son both dead, Homedes had no family. After his son died, Homedes eventually found that he could escape his sorrow, at least temporarily, in sensual pleasures. It had started with an attractive domestic slave boy that he grew perhaps overly fond of. Soon the boy was released from all domestic duties to focus on pleasing his master's sensual desires. Then he bought another slave for the same purpose. And so began the start of a collection. Homedes thought himself a decent man. He treated all of his slaves with tenderness, even affection, as one does with pets. But they were not equals in his eyes, not even people.

Except Aristol. Here was a rare thing, a slave of noble birth and bearing. Most of the other sex slaves weren't even Hellenic, let alone civilized. Homedes enjoyed variety. But he recognized Aristol as his equal, which indeed he was, except in the knowledge that comes with experience. Aristol was a slave by the fortunes of war only. Nonetheless, he still wore the same collar as the field hands and domestics. These were symbolic rather than functional. Light thin filets, they were practically jewelry. But they were known for what they were, should any slave leave the estate.

As much as he loved sex with Aristol, Homedes shared other pleasures with the younger man as well. They broke bread together often over rich conversation. Philosophy, music, art, and literature were common discussions. A question often on his mind, though he never shared the thought with the boy or anyone, should he make Aristol his adopted son and heir?

CHAPTER 31

PALLY

The sun was low in the sky, soon to drop behind the hills at their backs, as Tina and Pally waded up over their ankles into the cool clear sea. There were only a few people scattered along the narrow beach. Their tiny bungalow was a mere few hundred feet behind them off the beach, one of a cluster in a complex that was half motel, half campground. A local family with two small children frolicked on the water's edge not far away. Making memories. This place was the recommendation of an ebullient rental car agent at the airport when they asked for something quiet, away from the city, not too long a drive, and on the road to Corinth. The agent had called his cousin then and there, booking them a bungalow. In Greece, ask for help and you'll get help.

Pally breathed the last of the tension from the airport landing out through her feet to dissipate into the endless saltwater. The breeze was soft and pleasantly cool. It had been a mere few hours since they had bounced to a landing in Athens, and Pally was still swimming in mixed up emotions. She glanced at the older woman next to her who was looking out to sea seemingly lost in her own thoughts. Was this troubled American in her charge Pally's chance to finally find love?

***

Tina was thinking of the young woman next to her. Of their fast friendship. Of the episode on the plane. The madness that was her life over the past week or so. Tina was wildly attracted to Pally. It had struck her on the plane and she had acted on impulse. Now her impulses were under control, but her desires hadn't subsided. Her mind went back to the image of the strange young woman in her hospital room, frightened and naked before her, and so hot. God, she was gorgeous. She remembered the touch of her skin against her fingertips, that full breast in her hand. The girl had been ripe despite her fear. And now here was Pally next to her.

Tina glanced at her friend, they exchanged small tentative smiles. Then Tina noticed the mother playing with her two kids not far away. Nice thighs, well muscled. Tina shook her head as if to shake the thoughts away and returned to the sea horizon. She'd never been attracted to women before. Appreciate the look of a woman, sure. The occasional wonder of what it would be like, yes. But not like this.

"Pally, are you hungry?" Tina asked.

"I think my insides have settled enough now to hold down food," Pally replied with a nervous laugh.

Tina chuckled too. "Relax, youngling. I don't bite." Yet.

***

Tina opened the second bottle of red and refilled Pally's glass who was dipping the last of her bread in olive oil with black pepper. She popped it in her mouth and chased it with a gulp of wine. A red line trickled down the side of her chin, making her laugh. Pally covered her mouth with a giggle. The remnants of dinner; bread, feta, olives and oil were strewn across the end table between their two single beds. It was a cozy one-room bungalow with an adjacent bath. The two open windows were beginning to make the room too cool. Tina got up to close them.

"So you've heard most of my life story over dinner," Pally said once she had swallowed down the bread and wine, wiping her chin with her paper napkin. "And me, the detective. What's Tina's backstory?"

"Of course you talked," Tina replied. "After all, I'm the investigative reporter."

"I suppose our professions aren't so different. Still, I think you're better at it."

"Well, I've been at it longer."

"So tell me," Pally said as Tina returned to her bed, "Who is Tina Marin?" The American didn't reply immediately, but responded with a pointed look as she refilled her wine and took a deep swallow.

"As you know, I've been asking myself the same question recently."

"Oh I know what you're dealing with now, at least somewhat, but tell me about your childhood. What are your parents like? You already know my dad didn't want me to be a cop. What about your dad?"

"Well, where to begin? You've seen the FBI bio so you know I was born and raised in Maryland."

"That's a state near Washington, D.C., isn't it?"

"Yes, just a short drive away, but culturally I'm not a Washingtonian. I'm an Annapolis girl."

"Annapolis?"

"The Maryland state capital. And the sailing capital of the world, I might add."

"Sailing. There was a bit about that in the bio brief. But you weren't in the navy."

Tina laughed. "Good lord no, nothing like that, although my dad was a navy man in his youth." She sighed. "I still miss him."

"He passed away?"

"Yes. Mom is still alive, but Dad died a longtime back. When I was still in college. Now HE was a sailor. We had a boat growing up so we were always out on the bay for weekends, vacations, sometimes racing."

"The bay?"

"The Chesapeake Bay. A sailing paradise. I miss it."

"Racing sailboats. The FBI noted that too, but it was all Greek to me, pardon the pun. What's a 420?"

"That's a small two person one design, Pally. And was my summer passion once school was out. In my teen years. We raced all kinds of boats, but at the end of the day, I'm a 420 girl."

"Sounds like I'm on to something. Spill, Tina."

"Time for the bright lights and rubber hoses?"

The detective laughed. "I'm curious. You light up when you talk about sailing."

"God, I love it. I miss it." Tina paused for memories. "Well, a 420 is, well, perfect for teenagers. A small race boat. Lots of fun. A bit tender, or would be now if I tried it again at my age."

"Were you good at it?"

Tina laughed again, thinking back. "Let's just say we had fun. The kids I ran with back then. And raced with. We could compete, for sure, but didn't take many guns." Tina was silent for a moment. "But it was a wonderful childhood, growing up on the Chesapeake. Good times." She sighed.

"So different from mine," Pally said. "I know nothing about the sea, or sailing."

"Well, you'd better learn, youngling. Here in Greece you can't go far without getting your feet wet. The Aegean Sea is right outside our door with a thousand islands to visit," Tina said, then paused in thought. "That's it! That's what we'll do, Pally. I'll take you sailing."

"Is that why you're here, Tina?" Pally asked, immediately nervous at the prospect. "For a vacation?"

"Why the hell not? You know, maybe I should recall some of Tina Marin before trying to recall someone else. What do you say?"

"Sounds exciting." Pally smiled, "Just don't drown me."

"You can swim, can't you?"

"About as well as I fly."

"Oh dear, we have some work ahead of us. We hit the water first thing in the morning."

"You helped me on the plane," Pally said, suddenly serious, looking her in the eye. "I place myself in your hands."

"Chill out, Pally," Tina said, " Sailing won't be anything like the plane."

Tina rose and taking Pally by both hands brought her to her feet. She smiled sadly into the younger woman's eyes, then hugged her. Fully, head to toe. Pally melded into her, Tina knew she was waiting for the next move.
Tina pulled back a bit to look into big brown eyes. So pretty, so innocent. She touched her soft cheek. Noted a wisp of peach fuzz under the ear. Cute.

"We'd better get some shuteye," Tina decided. "It's been a long day."

"You regret what happened on the plane." It wasn't a question.

"Not a bit of it. Well, it's just that I don't want to take unfair advantage."

"I'm 32 years old, Tina. Hardly a child anymore."

"And you've always liked girls?"

"Yes. And boys. But girls more I think."

"And you've never been with either, have you? Good Indian daughter that you are."

"It's not so easy. It can be bad in my country. My family would freak."

"I understand. You know Pally, I've been with men younger than you. Recently. I'm fifty-one years old and truly in my prime. Men of all ages come to me, I don't have to play cougar."

"I'm coming to you," Pally said softly, giving Tina a gentle kiss.

"I know," Tina replied after the kiss. "But I've never been interested in women before. Before the event. Men too still, but my urges for women, for you, well, they don't feel…feminine."

"Tina, listen to me," Pally said urgently. "Right now, it doesn't matter how you feel about me."

"I feel a lot about you Pally," Tina interrupted. "I care very much about you."

"And I for you. But either way it doesn't matter. Not right now. I'm aching Tina. Please."

CHAPTER 32

ARISTOL AND HOMEDES

Some of the soldiers of the estate were paired off in Pankration practice as Aristol and his friends strolled by. They were heading for the lake today. While pretending not to show interest in their martial technique, Aristol watched them spar with a professional eye. The troops on the estate kept fit, Homedes wouldn't permit otherwise as much for aesthetics as effectiveness, but their fighting skills were weak by Spartan standards. Soldiering on this estate was light duty. Even with a regular training regimen, these men had lost their edge, if they ever had it. The living was just too easy.

Aristol was an obsessive athlete. He and all of the sex slaves were active every day. When not practicing their trade, they were attending to their bodies in all other ways. With the master's permission and approval, Aristol held a wrestling school and competition with his colleagues, including the females. It was a rigorous sport, keeping the young bodies lean. Aristol himself was fully trained and competent in all aspects of Pankration, but the strikes and kicks he practiced alone on dummies. Homedes believed that the weaponless martial art was only fit for citizens, and Aristol had always agreed. Now he was wishing he could train his friends fully for their flight. They would all be fit enough for the rigors of travel, but he was the only professional warrior. That burden weighed heavily on him. He knew he could match any Corinthian on the estate, with the possible exception of Homedes. But he was still only one man.

Approaching his fifties, the tall Homedes still had the sinewy build of a much younger man. When he worked out with his soldiers, he was teaching as well as training. Aristol knew he was faster, and probably as strong as Homedes, but skills? He wasn't sure. Except maybe with the sword. Aristol was hell on wheels with a sword, but he hadn't handled one in over five years. Aristol found himself thinking of how such a confrontation would play out. Now that they were plotting escape, he had the dreadful feeling of inevitability. Only through that line of thought did he suddenly realize how much he truly loved Homedes. How could he leave him? How could he fight him? Perhaps even kill him.

***

"Am I intruding?" Aristol asked as he entered the library.

"Never, my boy," Homedes replied, pleased to see the young man seeking him out. That hadn't been so common lately.

"I was wondering, well, I'd just like to be with you."

"Here I am. Always. Is there anything troubling you? That you wish to talk about?"

"Not really. I just want to be here," Aristol replied, taking Homedes by the hand. Homedes led him to the sofa and sat down. Aristol remained standing.

"I know you have developed deep affection for our Africans. Is that perhaps confusing you?"

"You, you don't mind?" asked Aristol.

"Of course not, my boy. The human capacity to love is infinite. You know that. We've discussed this at length over the years. Additionally, I am, as you know, a Cyrenaic of sorts and having suffered enough pain in my life, my focus is now and forever on the sensual pleasures of the moment. For me and mine."

"I know, but it has never hit me in the face before. Love. This isn't philosophy. It's real. And they're real Homedes. Real people, I mean."

"Are you saying that you have developed intellectual love for them? Even for the woman?"

Aristol laughed grimly. "Maybe even especially with the woman. Ife is so discerning. It's like she can read my mind, and my heart. I know they are not Hellenic and of another race, but Ife is from a noble family."

Homedes noted how the young man's eyes lit up as he talked about the Nubian female. "She certainly has spirit," Homedes admitted. "I admire that. She doesn't like me very much, that is for sure. Is that why you came here, to plead for her?"

"Truly no. That is just how the discussion has turned," Aristol said.

Homedes accepted this answer and allowed the matter of Ife to rest. "Then allay any fears you have on my account. Love them to your heart's content," said Homedes. "I confess that I miss your attentions these days. But I understand. It is the way of things. The heart has infinite room for many loves, but there isn't infinite time to explore and enjoy them all. That commodity is limited. We all just need to learn to share."

Aristol beamed at him. "Thank you Homedes. Bless you for your wisdom. Your generosity of spirit."

Homedes laughed. "Don't praise me too much, my boy. You'll have me believing you. Then where will we all be?" Aristol didn't reply, he just stood looking at his mentor shifting his weight nervously from one foot to another.

"Great Zeus, Aristol, what is it?"

"I want you. Now," Aristol whispered hoarsely. "So bad I can taste it."

Homedes was deeply moved. "Then taste it," he whispered back. He clasped his hands behind his head, leaning back in submission, and spread his long legs slightly. Aristol leaned over him, kissed him long and slow on the lips, their tongues tangling together. Aristol pulled away with a shivering sigh. Homedes waited, tingling with anticipation. He didn't have to wait long. The young man ran his fingers across the sheer material of Homedes' tunic whose nipples ripened, shooting signals south through his senses.

"Oh, ah. The magic touch."

Aristol removed the older man's top, kissed his neck and chest. Tugged some chest hair gently with his teeth. Homedes closed his eyes, straining to remain passive. He felt tears welling up behind the shutters to his soul, tried to suppress them, then accepted the truth as some seeped out and rolled down his cheeks.

Homedes never summoned Aristol for sex as he did the others and it had been a long time since they had been one on one. As part of a group, yes, as chance allowed, but not alone together. It had been such a long time. Hands ran from his shoulders down his arms. They were holding hands again. Soft lips kissed his wet face, ever so gently, taking his tears.

"I'll never stop loving you, Homedes," Aristol whispered. "Father."

Completely overcome, a small single sound, high pitched, somehow feminine, escaped the older man's lips. Then Homedes felt a tongue on his belly button. Conscious thought succumbed to senses. His waist robe came away as if it had a mind of its own. Still with eyes closed and hands idle, Homedes felt a flood of contentment take his body. Oils were on his chest, his muscles jumping in reply, then settling. A wave ran through Homedes, permeating, penetrating beyond his body. He felt he was floating. Then more oil tickled him where the sun never shines. Aristol guided him to the soft woven floor matt. Their breathing was audible. In sync.

Aristol lay on his back. He pulled a Homedes leg across his midriff so that the older man straddled him, sitting upright. Looking down, Homedes saw the young man tearing up too.

"Look at us," Homedes said. "A couple of crybabies."

Homedes felt the familiar bulb slick with oil caressing the crease of his crack. It had been so long since he and Aristol had been alone together. Too long. Homedes held himself high. Only lightly touching the tip. His firm thighs carried his weight with ease. Not in a hurry. In the moment. Aristol guided the older man to massage his own nipples. Then Homedes felt a firm palm on his penis, Strong fingers wrapped around, gave a squeeze that brought a groan, and a slow stroke began.

Homedes saw wonder, loving wonder, on the young man's face as he gazed at the phallus in his hand. Homedes' phallus. Overwhelmed by the love of the young man, his tears flowed freely now. He closed his eyes again, sobbing for joy, losing himself to the sensory.

Homedes continued to caress his own nipples to the pace of Aristol's strokes. He began to dip tentatively onto Aristol. Backing off to the resistance, not letting him fully enter, but with every dip just a tiny bit deeper, keeping to Aristol's rhythm. Letting Aristol set the pace. They continued this gentle gyration as anticipation built. Aristol began to stroke faster on Homedes in his hand and thrust his hips upward to the rhythm. Homedes responded, dipping deeper and faster, plunging unto Aristol recklessly now with a grunt, then almost withdrawing with every lift. His powerful thighs were quivering, his knees spread wider. He was panting heavily now, straining to keep himself from releasing into the hand engulfing him. Just as Homedes knew he could hold no longer, finally thrusting and shooting, Aristol gave a final thrust skyward.

"Oh god!" they chorused as Homedes sprawled collapsing with Aristol deep inside. Homedes fell forward on Aristol, sobbing, "Thank you, my love."

***

"I can't do it. I can't leave him. I love him," Aristol stated.

"Had a good time last night, did we?" Aria asked dryly.

"It's not funny," Aristol protested. "It's real. If I leave, it will break his heart." Nobody spoke for a moment.

"You break my heart," Ife said.

"Ife! Listen to me," Aristotle pleaded. "Life here is good. It is practically paradise."

"Good for you, maybe," Ife said. "You pretty much run the place. The rest of us are slaves."

"Hey, I wear the collar too! But slave or not, I am freer here than ever I was before. Homedes loves us."

"He loves you, for sure," Aria agreed.

"He loves all of us," said Aristol. "Look at the freedoms we have here. Look at you two girls. Do you really think you two could explore your affections for each other openly without fear anywhere else in the civilized world? In Persia, Aria? In Africa, Ife? You know you couldn't. Not anywhere. And if caught you would be stoned to death. You two think about that."

"Every time he touches me it is against my will," Ife said.

"But he is never violent," Aristol replied.

"You keep fooling yourself," Ife practically shouted, "The act itself, no matter how gentle, IS a violence. Your lover rapes me, Aristol. Every day. Every damn day. I know it. He definitely knows it. And it's high time you knew it too." Ife wiped tears from her eyes, turning her back in rage and shame.

Aristol shook his head in denial, weeping too. "Dani, in the name of the gods, say something. Tell them." They all looked at Dani.

Dani shook his head slowly. "Aristol is right," he said. "Homedes loves us all." Then he looked pointedly at Aristol, "He loves you as a man. An equal. He loves the rest of us like he loves his dogs." Aristol shook his head in disagreement, but Dani pressed on. "You ever seen him kick one of his dogs? Never. He feeds them himself, pets them, plays with them. We're like his dogs. Not you, of course," Dani continued, "you are an officer of Sparta. And good for you. You are worthy of all the love you receive. Not just from Homedes, but from all of us. We love you as a person. And you love us the same way. But to Homedes? The rest of us are just dogs."

Aristol shook his head. "I can't leave him. It wouldn't be right."

"You have two choices," Ife said, "You can lead us, or hunt us. But we're going."

CHAPTER 33

BOBBY

Bobby was following Lucky in his rental car to his hotel. It had been difficult to extricate himself from a relentless invitation to stay at the home of his older relatives, which truth be told, was practically a mansion. But Bobby insisted that he was not on vacation and had much to do. His paper had already booked his room and he had to get there to check in with his editor. Yes, even at this late hour in America. His was a time critical assignment that he was not permitted to discuss. Still he had gratefully accepted the afternoon and dinner invitation that had been proffered when they met at Lucky's houseboat.

When the surprise arrival of her parents had interrupted them, Lucky had quickly enough been back in the androgynous outfit she had worn when she had picked up Bobby, but Bobby had hopped around trying to force into his skinny jeans an angry erection that had other ideas. Wasting no time, with another bang on the door reverberating in their ears, Lucky had herded her naked young cousin into the shower and blasted on the cold water, then left him while she answered the door.

Now he was off to check in at his hotel with Lucky graciously leading the way through the strange city. He really did have much to do now that he was getting settled, but the unfinished business at Lucky's houseboat was all that was on his mind. Assignment be damned. In his Audi sedan, a luxury to the youngster, Bobby had no problems keeping up with Lucky's Mini Cooper. Lucky's father had arranged the rental car to be delivered to the house before dinner, which seemed a strange convenience to Bobby. But when in Rome…

***

"You know what's been on my mind on the way over here?" Bobby asked. Lucky replied with a quizzical look. "We haven't even kissed yet," he finished.

They were finally together in Bobby's hotel room after Lucky had insisted on taking a separate circuitous route through the hotel to meet him there. She took both his hands in hers. He looked down on her adorable face still framed by her gray beanie and overly large jacket. No one could guess at the curves underneath. She was of medium height, but he still towered over her. Lucky sat him on the bed and planted herself across his lap so they were nose to nose. They kissed, gently, slowly, deeply, tongues intertwined. She felt him hardening under her right butt cheek.

"So here we are," she said when they came up for air. She pulled off her beanie and let her hair flow down. Bobby ran his fingers through her locks.

"So thick, and yet so silky," he admired.

"I have a variety of potions I use to make it so."

"Potions? Am I ensnared by a witch?"

"What do you think?" Lucky said.

"I don't think you need to use potions on me." He kissed her again and drew her down on the bed so he was above her. His hand went inside her jacket. She let him explore for a bit, but he made a mess of it, trying to get through her garments.

"Here get off me big boy and let me drive."

He let her up. "If you want to do a strip tease again," he said, "you'll get no complaints from me."

"A strip tease? Do you take me for some kind of slut?" Lucky seemed suddenly annoyed.

"Slut? Of course not. I just meant that your dance at your place was wildly erotic," Bobby told her.

"It was, was it?"

"Well, wasn't it supposed to be?"

"Yes, but not in a cheap or coarse way."

"And it wasn't. Believe me. I didn't mean to compare you to a pole girl."

"What's wrong with pole girls? They have to make a living too, you know."

"Nothing wrong with them, I just mean that you aren't one of them."

"You don't think I could be?"

"Of course you could. But you're not, are you?"

"Would it matter?"

"Not to me, but hey wait a minute, time out, we took a wrong turn somewhere. What gives?"

"Nothing really. Except you seem to be taking me for granted. Like our impending coupling is a done deal."

"Well, isn't it? I mean, you didn't plan for your parents to interrupt us when they did."

Lucky smiled at that. "No I didn't."

"So don't you still want to?" Bobby asked.

"Yes I do, but timing and setting the mood is all a part of loving. And here we are in a hotel room and I'm still in my travel clothes."

"All right," Bobby said standing up, "what do you suggest?"

"Let's talk. Get to know each other. That's what I had hoped we would have done after loving at my place, before my parents showed up."

"Didn't we talk enough at your parent's house? I feel like I was put through the third degree."

"That's just it. All that talk has whetted my appetite. I want to learn more about you, cousin. And I want you to know more about me too."

"That sounds wonderful to me too. But, well, I'm kinda excited right now. Distracted if you know what I mean."

Lucky smiled. "Fellatio before I fed you and now fellatio before I can even talk to you."

"If we can't do more, then yes please," Bobby said sheepishly. "I'm ready to explode."

"God love you, Bobby. You're like a little boy who can twist his mum around his little finger." Lucky sighed. "Alright then."

CHAPTER 34

LUCKY

Lucky looked at herself in the bathroom mirror. What a wild day this had been. She could feel she was on the edge of a grand adventure, something much needed in her dull life. But two blowjobs in a single day, really? Euphorically dizzy, Lucky took a deep breath, put on a smile and left the bathroom.

"There you are. I've never figured out what girls can do in a bathroom for so long," Bobby said.

"And you'll never learn the secret from me," Lucky replied.

"Fair enough, but now let me put my reporter hat on and start with the basics," Bobby said, "name, age, and occupation."

"Now who's getting the third degree, but okay. As you quickly caught onto, and bless you for it, my name is Khatri and my parents don't even know of my Lucky nickname. I use that as another persona. The real me that I am sharing with you. And I'm actually 37 years old, I hope you don't mind. And I don't really have an occupation in the sense of a job, but I write. Under an assumed name of course."

"Really, what do you write?"

"Underground articles about the many oppressions in our culture. And educating people about polyamory."

"Cool, I'd like to read your work, but are you really in danger?"

"I think so. I mean, if I was just quietly practicing polyamory with a few others, I don't think I would be. Ostracized from family and friends for certain, but not in physical danger. Of course, it would break my parents' hearts and I can't do that to them. So I live in the closet."

"In the closet. That can't be a good place to be either."

"I cope. But it wears on me. It's like a long slow relentless burden. But today is a happy one, because I am out of the closet with you. Now three people know about me. You've upped the global knowledge of my orientation by 33%. That's a big leap."

"What orientation? Are you gay?"

"No, my love orientation. I am poly, not mono."

"So you only like men, but not just one."

"I have the ability to love many people. We all do. That's what it is to be poly. And not just men."

"Oh, so you are bisexual as well as polyamorous."

"I think we all have a little bit of bi in us. Or at least some curiosity."

"I don't know about that."

Lucky laughed."Maybe you don't know it yet. But you're still young."

"Tell me about the other two people that I share your secret with," Bobby said.

"It is their secret too so I can't tell you much. Definitely no names. Simply put, they are my lovers and best friends."

"Also in the closet?" Bobby asked.

"Most definitely," replied Lucky.

"So if India is such tough terrain to live poly, how does one find anyone?"

"It's not easy. In my case, we were childhood friends so the trust has been there forever. The three of us were thick as thieves all through school. The two of them eventually married."

"So how does that work?"

"We are a secret triad. As old friends we get together for dinner a couple times a month. When I host them here, we have the privacy for more than just dinner."

Bobby laughed. "You go, cousin Khatri."

"Please don't call me that."

"What, Khatri?"

"Yes, I am Khatri in another world. Please let me be Lucky in your eyes."

"Of course, now and forever," Bobby promised. They hugged in a long silence, her cheek on his chest. Lucky could feel his hard, lean strength through his clothes, and was tempted not to let go.

"But I sometimes feel like the third wheel in the triad," Lucky said, returning to the topic of her lovers. "I mean, the two of them are openly married in the eyes of the world."

"They love you, don't they?"

"Of course. I don't doubt that, but as a couple they get to be out in the open with each other every day." Lucky looked away out the hotel window into the evening. Lost in thought.

"So how did you come by the name, Lucky?" Bobby asked, bringing her back. "Your lovers should have named themselves Lucky."

"It's just a nickname I made up for myself after Lakshmibai, the Rani of Jhansi. She's a hero of mine."

"Who?" Bobby asked.

"Don't you know your Indian history? Have you heard of what our British overlords called the Sepoy Mutiny back in the nineteenth century?"

"Oh sure, I believe we Sikhs stayed loyal to the British. But I never heard of this Rani."

"She was a leader against the British. A strong woman in a time dominated by men."

"Admirable. What happened to her?"

"She died in battle."

"Hmm, take heed of her fate, Lucky."

"Speaking of fates, let's talk about yours? What is this assignment all about?"

"I don't want to get into all that. Tell me about your lovers."

"Later. Maybe I can help with your work. You're going to reach out to contacts, won't you? And you should develop your own, right? Well, I can be your first."

"This isn't about polyamory. It's geopolitics."

"Look, you're here in Kashmir so of course it is about geopolitics. We live it every day. The Pakistanis make the news, but it is China you need to watch. They play a long game, the Chinese. They think in terms of generations to reach their goals. Look at Hong Kong. The British left in 1999 and they have been relentlessly bending the treaty terms ever since, but oh so slowly. Only twenty years later did they come out in the open."

"Hey, I didn't know you were a student of politics. Maybe you can help."

"Of course I can. Now spill. What's the assignment?"

CHAPTER 35

ARISTOL

"Well, I am off for a bite to eat and then early to bed," Dulce said. The buxom Sicilian girl rose in the warm water and waded to the steps.

"But not to sleep, right?" Dani offered, still lounging with Aristol in the bath.

"I do recall Xerxus saying he would turn in early as well," she said with a sly grin over her shoulder.

The boys watched in admiration as she dressed then departed. Aria and Ife entered the gym hand in hand. They smiled hellos to the passing Sicilian girl. The two had a healthy satisfied glow about them. Dani and Aristol were still lounging in the hot laconica bath, relaxing their muscles, after an afternoon of sport. The setting sun glancing through uncurtained windows provided a soft setting in the gym.

"How'd it go?" Dani asked.

"Fine," said Aria dreamily.

"More than fine, I'd say," Aristol said with a smile. "A scent of love is upon you."

"You have the same idea as me, Aristol?" Dani asked.

"You know it."

"Well count me out," Ife said with a tired grin. "This little bit of lightning was all I needed for the day. I'm exhausted." Aria turned her head up as the two girls embraced and kissed.

"Aria?" Dani asked

The dusky girl grinned mischievously, "I suppose I have a bit more lightning in me for you two."

"I'll just watch," Ife said, "I am plum worn out," her tone changed, "but first some business. The cache is ready. It's time."

The three of them looked at Aristol. After a pause, he said, "It is still too early in the year. I'd like the weather to warm up for a few more weeks.."

It was quiet when the soldier stuck his head through the door. "Ife, the master wants you." The tall girl stiffened.

"I'll go," Aria said.

"You know it doesn't work that way," Ife said. Then she followed the soldier without a word. The boys were downcast. Silent.

"You guys still want to?," Aria asked softly, wading into the bath, "I know I'm not Ife, but I'm always here for you." Aristol stood and hugged her tightly, lifting the small woman off her feet.

"You don't ever need to compare yourself to anyone. You are Aria."

"The beloved," Dani added.

"Poor Ife," Aria sighed.

"Last time," said Aristol, "last time."

CHAPTER 36

IFE

Ife entered the master's suite. The guard closed the door shut from the outside. The girl stood silently just inside the door. Homedes was standing over a table on the far side of the room. He absently petted the big head of one of his dogs as he studied a map. Minutes passed. Ife stood stock still. Both man and dog ignored her. The man sighed, and looked up from the map.

"Ah, there you are. Go say hello to Ife, Hercules."

The big hound bounded over to the tall girl and resting his paws on her shoulders licked her face enthusiastically. Ife tousled the dog's thick neck rigorously with both hands, giggling at the tickles of tongue on her cheek and neck.

"I wish I could get that reaction from you," the man said. Ife dropped her furry friend to all fours and met the man's eye. She was stiff and stoic again. Hercules whined, pushing his head into her hand. She scratched the dog behind his ear, but otherwise didn't move a muscle.

"Everyone and everything loves you, including me, yet you love everyone and everything, except me," said Homedes. Ife began to disrobe.

"Where do you want me?" she asked.

"Stop." It was as close as Homedes ever came to a bark. Surprised, both girl and dog froze. Ife let her hands fall to her sides, one breast already open to the air.

"Look at you," Homedes said with a sigh. "With the possible exception of Aristol, you are far and away the most beautiful creature I have ever seen." He walked to a long sofa. "Come, sit by me. We need to finally talk."

Ife obeyed, keeping some space between them on the sofa. The man's eyes fixated on her lone exposed breast.

He sighed again. "I have gazed upon you, caressed you, suckled you so many times these past few years," he said, seeming to address her right breast directly. "And it never gets old. Magnificent. Perfect in shape, size, and complexion." He raised his glance to her wide almond shaped eyes. "And those bottomless black pools of yours. I long to dive through their depths to your soul. And every time I try, I drown in the attempt. Why is that?"

Ife said nothing, thinking maybe it was better that they didn't converse..

"Please speak." She remained mute. He smiled sadly, shaking his head. "I am not giving you a polite command, Ife," Homedes said, "I am truly asking. Begging even. For understanding. You don't have to answer. Of course, I won't do anything to you if you don't. Have I ever? But please, I do beg you, why won't you love me?"

"Like Hercules, here?" Ife asked. The massive animal had followed them to the sofa and lay sprawled across their feet, managing to touch both of them as dogs do.

"Yes, of course. And why not? Dogs love a pile. So do people. Most do anyway. I have never made you join our orgies. And you never have. But of course it isn't that you don't enjoy them. You do with all the others. You have great passion. But not if I am in them. Never with me. Why? I know I am older, but I am fit enough. Am I so disgusting to look upon in your eyes? What is it about me that you hate me so?"

"You are a handsome man," Ife said evenly. "And the kindest master as could be wished for. All the others say so."

"Well then, what?"

"You are the master. You can't help that, but that is what you are."

"And, and you resent that?" Homedes asked. The very idea seemed to stun him. "Great Zeus, Ife," Homedes went on, "some are slaves and some are citizens. It is the way of the world. There is no disgrace in the former, and truth be told, no great honor in the latter. It is just an accident of birth."

"I was not born so!" Ife shouted.

"An accident of circumstance then. And I didn't enslave you, Ife. You know that. I simply acquired you. Simply, did I say? No. I paid a fortune." He sighed. "And you're well worth every drachma. Truly, the most beautiful woman in the world. My ebony Aphrodite. An opposite equal to the goddess herself."

He brushed his knuckles lightly against her exposed breast, which puckered in response. Ife was mortified. She closed her tearing eyes. Leaning in, he cupped her breast underneath then suckled her with slow strength. Eventually he released her. When she opened her eyes, his were waiting.

"You see? You can't help yourself. Can't control your body to do other than what it was made for," Homedes said gently. A sob escaped from the girl. "Accept it. Be true to your nature. Be true to your role in nature," he said soothingly.

Ife recoiled. "You own me," she accused.

"Of course I do. You make it sound like a bad thing. By my nature and philosophy, I am a gentle man. What more would you have me do?" he replied. A pause. "And if I took you to wife, Ife?" He touched her hand, but now she pulled away. The first time she had ever refused his touch. He took her hand firmly in both of his. She didn't resist it this time. "And if I took you to wife?" he repeated. He held her eye. "No difference," he finished softly. "No difference. You are a woman. Destined for servitude, whether here in Hellas or in your home country. Practically speaking, slave or free changes nothing for you or any woman."

"I resent that too," Ife said.

Homedes nodded thoughtfully. "Aristol says you have a strong mind. Equal to a man, he says. I can't believe that. Clever you may be, but he overestimates you. You do have the ambition of a man. That I grant you." He paused. "If I free you, would you stay? Not as a wife, to be owned still. But as a free person. Will you stay and be my lover as a free woman?"

Ife eyed him fiercely. "That would be a false freedom and you know it. And I would not anyway. How could I? No, never can I forgive what you did to me."

Homedes was incredulous. "Forgive? Forgive? It is not your place to forgive, or withhold forgiveness. You are a woman AND a slave." He stood up, towering over her. "No. I have been too lenient. Too soft. And now you forget yourself. But I have not forgotten. Why I called for you. Disrobe slave girl."

Ife stood and reluctantly obeyed. Homedes gazed at her in wonder, as if for the first time. Immediately mollified.

"Oh the perfect symmetry of your form. Hips and shoulders perfectly aligned as are bosom and bottom. Leg to arm. Limbs to torso. So beautifully balanced." He ran his hands slowly up and down her smooth arms from wrist to shoulder and back. "Such musculature. Strength and softness. And the form of your face. Perfect. Lips and mouth to balance with those deep, wide-set eyes and brow. With your magnificent nose amidst it all. In command, but not dominating. There aren't words to do you justice."

He sighed and gently kissed her lips. She didn't respond, but Homedes moved on. His hands went from her shoulders down her torso inside her arms, coming to rest on the curvature of her hips. He sat her back down and spreading her legs he nuzzled her pubic bush, breathing deeply. Taking in her scent. He kissed the lips of her sex. As his tongue probed, she began to respond. The silent tears flowed, then Ife couldn't stifle her sobs as she blossomed. Homedes came up to her, caressing her breasts.

"Don't you understand?" he asked, gentle again. "Accept what you are. Embrace it. And most importantly, enjoy it. You were made for this, Ife. As was I." He slid into her warm wetness. Her hips replied.

***

"There you are! Finally." Aria said, running to Ife as she entered the gym. They embraced. Ife burst into tears, completely wretched. The boys hung back. "Oh, my dear," Aria whispered to Ife, "I'm here. I'm here." Weak in the knees, Ife slowly collapsed. Aria guided her down to the matts. "Oh my dear. Sshhh. It's over. It's over."

"It's never over." Ife gasped out as she continued crying uncontrollably.

"What, what happened?" Aria said. " Tell me."

"Yes, talking is better," Dani said. The boys had edged closer.

Ife took a deep breath. "No it's not. Not always. He talked to me. Homedes. For the first time ever, he talked to me. We had a conversation." The crying took over again.

Aria kissed and caressed her hair, gently rocking the taller girl in her arms. "You don't need to talk, if you don't want to," she whispered to Ife.

"You have to know. You have to. I failed. He won. For the first time. I didn't just lay there. I…" Ife broke down.

"It's okay," Aria cooed soothingly. "It's okay. You didn't fail. It's natural."

"Don't you dare say that!" Ife barked. "That's what he said."

"But it is, Ife," Dani said. "I've embraced my sexual nature since that first incredible day with Aristol here. And I am the happier for it. Master he may be, but Homedes is also an incredible lover."

"So have I," Ife replied through sobs, "With the rest of you. But never with him." A pause, "until now," she finished breaking down again.

"We have to go," Aristol said, "now." They all looked at him, but didn't respond. "Dani," he said pulling his friend upright, "let's go. Ife. Aria, get her up. We move now."

"Give them a minute," Dani said.

"There's no time. Don't you see? He's onto us. Or at least suspects. We need to move now. He knows Ife is in no condition now. He won't expect us to make a move tonight after what she has been through. We have a brief window to escape. Come, on your feet, Ife. Pull yourself together. You have a chance to best him still."

CHAPTER 37

TINA

"Just relax, Pally. Focus on your breathing. Meditate." The calm sea was a bit over waist deep. Pally was floating on her back, or trying to. Tina stood beside her lightly supporting Pally with her hands under her lower back and bottom."

"I can't relax with your hands on me like that," Pally said.

Tina looked down at her bikinied friend. The water lapped gently around her breasts and across her midriff. The wet thin fabric of her bikini bottom hinted at the outline of pubic hair. Tina couldn't keep her eyes off it, or her mind. She was acutely aware of her left hand supporting Pally's butt cheeks. Deliciously aware.

"Okay, let's break for lunch," Tina said.

"Let's break for something for god's sake," Pally replied.

Tina laughed. "You win, youngling. You've worn me down at last."

They were shortly back in the bungalow, toweling off. Pally was openly goggling at the pale slender symmetry that was Tina. And Tina found herself enjoying the admiration without any awkwardness. In fact, it was arousing her as much as the form and hues of her friend. A bit wider at the hip, narrower at the shoulder, slim at the waist topped by a full, but not overly so, bosom. Her shoulders and torso complexion was much lighter than her face and hands. Pally threw her towel on her bed, facing Tina. She took a step forward. Tina stopped her with an upraised hand.

"Slowly. We need to get to know each other. Our bodies, I mean. First with our eyes. Completely, head to toe and everything, every orifice, in between. I'll start." Tina slowly removed her top, allowing Pally to see her breasts for the very first time. The girl gaped, spellbound.

"We're allowed to talk, you know," Tina said. "Tell me what you're thinking as you look at me. Ask me questions if you want."

"I've never seen such beauty."

"Describe me."

"Oh Tina. Your breasts. Incredible. Pale nipples against even whiter flesh. So small and yet round and perfect." Pally took a deep breath.

"Hanging a bit lower than they used to," Tina replied. "Oh well. It is what it is." Pally took a step closer.

"No touching," Tina ordered. "Not yet."

"But I can look as closely as I want, can't I?"

After a pause, "You may." Tina stood erect in response to close inspection. Goosebumps all over. Never had she exposed herself so to another woman before. Tina felt vibrantly alive, separate from her mind, seeming a distant observer of the scene. Pally's face was inches from Tina's skin. Feeling rhythmic hot breath on her nipple, an uncontrollable shiver ran through Tina, shaking her pale flesh. Pally cooed, longing to put lips to nipple.

"You have light tiny freckles across your décolleté," Pally said. "I didn't see that before."

"Too much time under the sun in my youth," Tina replied nervously. "Didn't pay much attention to sun damage back then. It was all about getting dark."

"For us in India it's all about being as pale as possible. Funny."

Pally explored Tina's waist and hips in silence. Resisting the urgency within her. To kiss the precious flesh. To touch. Tina raised her arms to expose her sides and under her arms.

"Lovely," Pally whispered as she rounded behind to explore Tina's back.

"Now I'm really nervous," Tina said. "What do you see? One never gets the chance to study one's own back."

Pally's cheek grazed Tina's shoulder. A jolt ran through both of them.

"Pally!"

"Sorry! I got dizzy for a moment. This is maddening."

"I know. I know. Just tell me what you see."

"Okay," said Pally, taking a deep breath. "Some more freckles on your shoulders. And very fine white hairs, hardly to be seen at all, but begging, begging to be stroked."

"Not yet, Pally. Not yet," urged Tina, but her own heart was racing.

Pally laughed. "Your idea, Tina. A sweet torture. The intimacy of it all." A pause. "Oh, you have a little tan mole on your back, just off your spine."

"I know, at least I've felt others touch it."

"It's cute. Very cute. It gives character."

"Gee, thanks."

"And here, more pale hairs, a bit longer, in the small of your back leading down under your bikini bottom. I can't wait to see where they lead."

"Well, you've got to," Tina took a deep breath, "Because now it's my turn to see you before we lose our bottoms. And all control of ourselves."

Pally stood back and unclasped her halter behind her back but held her top in place with her arms.

"Are you waiting for a drumroll?" Tina asked. "Please don't tease me."

"I'm not, Tina. Really," Pally said. "I'm shy. I've never done this."

"Well, neither have I, but I did it. It was delightfully difficult, I can tell you that."

"What if you don't like them?" Pally asked.

"Oh, for goodness sake." In two steps, Tina was kissing Pally feverishly on the face and mouth. Pally moaned as her dark arms wrapped around the paler woman. Tina's lips were on her neck now. She slipped the halter top up and over Pally's head, throwing it over her shoulder. She filled her hands with the Indian's eager breasts.

"*It's been so long*," Tina whispered in Greek.

Pally didn't notice. Her eyes were closed as she reveled in the hands, lips and tongue that seemed to be everywhere. She was on her back now, on one of the beds, her legs high as Tina quickly pulled off Pally's bikini bottom. Then Tina froze, gazing in awe down at open, welcoming, glistening pink amidst black curling strands, the closest hairs to her sex already damp. Tina ran a hand slowly from each brown knee down the inside of Pally's thighs. Her fingers stopped as they touched the black curls. Pally was dizzy, audibly gulping air. Then Tina's hands slipped under Pally's bottom as she dove face first between tingling thighs.

CHAPTER 38

ARISTOL

The ultimate goal was to head south into the Arcadian no man's land between Spartan and Corinthian territory. But first they were moving north. The Peloponnese peninsula was mostly mountain country between the Gulf of Corinth and the Laconian plain to the south where Sparta ruled. The Homedes estate lay northwest of the main north-south pass connecting Sparta and Corinth. Off a well-traveled east-west road that was dotted with villages, inns, and estates, Homedes lived in a settled region, albeit several days away from the city. The road was easier terrain for travel, but no place for runaway slaves. The north side of the estate ended in rugged hill country, foothills to a range of an east-west mountain range that blocked access to the leveler ground of the Gulf of Corinth basin.

Partially splitting those hills was a long lake running north-south, the southernmost end of which abutted the Homedes estate. The four fugitives were making for the lake in the early evening. Bathing in the lake, and loving on the shore, were favorite pastimes for Homedes and his companions during the dog days of summer. The four knew the route well even in the dark. On the shore, a small cache of food and supplies had been secretly gathered over the last several weeks to provision them for their journey. They would make their way north up the lake. For a time. The hope was that Homedes would pursue them the full length of the lake toward the Gulf of Corinth. While actually they intended to turn west into the mountains then south along the Corinthian – Achaean border.

They had just reached the lakeshore when a baying of hounds erupted in the distance. The hunt was up. Adrenaline gushing, the girls gathered their provisions from their hideaway in the shrubs while the boys launched a small raft they had built and hidden afloat a short distance away. They poled the raft to the girls. Once the stores were aboard the four of them disrobed, rubbed each other all over with grease stolen from the carriage house, then wrapped themselves tightly in their robes. Dani gasped audibly as they eased themselves into the chilly water. They swam north pushing the raft before them. Aristol grimaced as they left the shore. The water somehow seemed colder knowing they would be in it for a long time. The raft was too small for any but Aria aboard with the supplies. She lent her strength to propelling the raft by pole until the water was too deep. Then she too slipped into the water and helped with pushing. It was slow going, but Hercules and the other hounds wouldn't be able to track them over water.

Aristol looked back to the shore. He could see small twinkles of light in the distance. Torches. None of them had ever been so far out on the lake before, but it appeared that the western shoreline was impassable by land, due to rocks, a league from their launch point. Aristol hoped there would be a spot north of there where they could return to land.

CHAPTER 39

BOBBY

"Well that was a complete waste of time!" Bobby exploded as soon as they were alone in the car. They had just completed an hour long interview with one Colonel Gupta of the Indian Army mountain brigade.

"Oh, I don't think so," Lucky said cheerfully.

"He told us nothing that we didn't already know."

"Really? You know what I heard?"

"What?" demanded Bobby.

"That it's really cold up there."

"They are operating at over 10,000 feet above sea level!" Bobby exploded again, "of course it's friggin cold. Hardly newsworthy."

"Language, Bobby," Lucky admonished him. "And take a breath. Relax."

"Sorry," Bobby said, still on edge. "It's just that I am really feeling the pressure, you know?"

"I do know, but you're not alone. Now back to the interview. Colonel Gupta said they spend 24 hours a day up there, not fighting the Chinese or the Pakistanis, but Mother Nature, just to survive."

"Again, that isn't news."

"Don't you think the Chinese and Pakistanis can freeze to death too?" Lucky pondered aloud. "I mean we're all the same species, right?"

"Of course, but they're hardly able to invade India without your troops noticing despite the horrific weather. So it's a stalemate. Again, that isn't news."

"True, but you know what that also means, don't you?"

"What?" Bobby asked, as calmly as he could.

"Individuals or small groups could probably walk across these borders passing not far from the military units stationed up there without being noticed. In any direction. This might be the most porous border in all of India."

"Huh." That got Bobby thinking. "Maybe that's our angle. The three countries are infiltrating each other to destabilize their areas of control. I mean the local populations are all the same ethnic mix, look the same, speak the same languages."

"Exactly," Lucky said. "There are still old people alive on all sides of the borders that lived under a single British rule before the current borders existed. And the British held Kashmir for less than a hundred years. And us Sikhs ruled it for less than a hundred years before the Raj. For us locals, the current map feels, well, temporary. It is just a matter of time."

"Until what?" Bobby asked.

"Until trouble. Bad times that hopefully will result in a greater good on the other end."

"I could be a foreign agent and you wouldn't even know it," Bobby said, "on any side of the borders."

"So could I," said Lucky. Bobby felt a shiver go down his spine.

"But the trail we are following," he said, "that I was sent here to follow, is foreign interference beyond the three actors on the border, specifically the United States."

Lucky laughed. "I suppose that makes you the secret agent, not me."

They were now driving back to Srenagar from base camp headquarters 5,000 feet lower than where the troops were actually deployed. It was still a cold April afternoon, but nothing unusual. Similar to Bobby's weekends out of the city in upstate New York or in New England.

"One thing I did learn," Bobby said, "is that we got a lot more interview time with the colonel because you came along."

"Well, as he said, he was just back after a month on the front line," Lucky said. "If they have women up there, with all the gear they have to wear, you wouldn't notice."

"The colonel noticed you, that's for sure," laughed Bobby. "You are wicked in a sari, Lucky. Absolutely wicked. Glad you didn't wear that outfit to meet me at the station. You would have been swarmed by men and we never would have met."

"You'll have the same impact on any females we interview. They will pour their hearts out to those innocent eyes of yours."

"Which leads us to my next interview."

"Who?" asked Lucky.

"You," Bobby said. "Tell me about all the local activist groups in Kashmir, regardless of their causes. It could be that they are being influenced or even led by foreign agents."

"I see, destabilize behind the lines to weaken the front lines before an assault."

"Less structured than that, I think, but more nefarious. Attack the cultural glue that holds society together as one. Get the whole house of cards to collapse on itself. That will even creep into the military. After all, they are citizens too."

"You can take a country without firing a shot," exclaimed Lucky.

"Exactly," said Bobby. "Civil war. Regime change."

"I think I know of the person you should talk to next."

CHAPTER 40

HOMEDES

Homedes sipped on his wine, feeling completely satisfied. Not only physically, but spiritually. That magnificent Ife had finally succumbed. For two patient years, Homedes had gently copulated while the girl just lay under him limp as a warm corpse. Oh, her erogenous parts reacted, she couldn't help that, but she had always managed to keep conscious control of her musculature. Had refused participation regardless of what her urges had demanded. Truly a disciplined mind for a woman. But not today.

It was Aristol that had unwittingly given him the idea. Aristol had praised her intellect. While doubtful, Homedes engaged her intellectually. He talked to her. He listened. She responded. And what a ride it had been. That girl had stamina. She was strong. Homedes could still feel it in his lower back.

What a week, Homedes reflected. Aristol earlier in the week, which had truly moved him, and then Ife. Sure there were still issues with the girl, but there was no doubt that a breakthrough had occurred. She'd come round now. The last bit of resistance in his whole herd. And she'd be the happier for it, Homedes thought contentedly. Good thing he had persevered. He had thought for a while of moving her over to be a field slave. A harder life, but not a bad one. Of course as soon as he saw how Aristol had taken to her, that was out of the question. His companions did not fraternize with domestics or field slaves.

He rubbed a hand across his jaw. Bristly. He should have shaved before laying with Ife. Probably burned her cheek. How could he have known things would get so passionate? From now on, he would shave. She deserved it. He closed his eyes. Dreaming of Ife, dreaming of Aristol. He had watched the two of them become one, blonde on brown. Beautiful. The image of a threesome came to his mind. Never had he participated with those two together. Every other combination of slaves he had, yes, but never with Ife and anyone. She would orgy with everyone else, but never with him. That would change now. Might take a while, but it will happen. Homedes looked forward to it.

A memory came to him, unbidden, 'they're people like you and me,' Aristol had said. Youthful, sentimental nonsense. Aristol, mixed up in his emotions, failed to see the separation of the male mind and female body. And yet, for the first time tonight, with Ife, what had he seen behind those hostile eyes? Intellect? He was getting to be like Aristol. Mesmerized by that luscious physique. And yet?

A ringing bell broke his thought. Homedes leapt to his feet as the bell rang frantically. He grabbed his trusty javelin from behind the door on his way outside. People, soldiers and slaves alike, were coming outdoors in response to the racket.

"Here, what goes on?" he shouted as he stopped a soldier running by.

"I dunno, sir. I think it's coming from the gymnasium."

"Follow me, all" Homedes shouted the command to all in sight as he sprinted around the corner of the big house in the direction of the gymnasium.

Soldiers and slaves raced after him. Dogs were barking, jumping directionless in the excitement, adding to the clamor of the bells. Three soldiers were outside the entrance to the gym as Homedes and his followers approached.

"Stop those bells, Dicus, I'm here now," Homedes shouted over the din. The soldier complied, the dogs continued to howl and bark.

"You there," Homedes commanded another soldier, "corral those animals and settle them down, we may need them." He turned back to the soldier, Dicus, with the bell. There were two others with him. One was prostrate on the ground while the other bent over him, tending his wounds.

"Here, what's all this?" Homedes demanded. Other soldiers were joining the gathering in various states of dress, most with some kind of weapon.

"I'm not sure, sir," the soldier tending his fallen comrade replied, "Dicus and I were making our rounds when we found Artis here, on the ground. Look at his face, sir. Somebody hit him. Somebody who knows how, sir."

"Alright then," Homedes ordered, "All slaves to quarters." Then to the soldiers, "I want a head count of everyone, slaves and soldiers alike. You two, tend to Artis. See if you can rouse him." The slaves scattered to their quarters as the soldiers mustered under the barks of the sergeant.

CHAPTER 41

BOBBY

It was a dingy office on a dingy side street. Litter was part of the landscape, both outside and in. But the business inside was brisk enough. Everyone moved with purpose, whether banging on a keyboard or on one of the half a dozen simultaneous cell calls going on in the small space. Bobby stood waiting patiently for the woman at the desk in the back of the room to notice him, a tall statue withstanding a tornado of activity. He caught her eye and she called something to him over the din in Kashmiri. Bobby approached and introduced himself in Hindi. The woman's eyes narrowed at that, then, after a moment, she waved him to her desk. She gestured to the one chair with a wave of a hand while firing up a cigarette with the other. She tossed the pack and lighter on the desk in front of him. Bobby lit up too and took a deep drag. He rarely smoked except when together with a few specific college buddies.

"You don't smoke often, but when you do you enjoy it. I like that," the woman opened in Hindi, "don't want to waste my smokes on those who don't know how to do it."

"It was more of a college thing. I still believe in no smoking the day before a match."

"Tennis, no doubt. With your length you should have a formidable serve."

"I can put some heat on the ball. You play? With all this traveling it's been a few weeks since I played."

"Doubles is more my game these days. Mixed if I can get it."

"While I'm in town, give me a call if you need a fourth. Or if you want to risk singles."

He wrote his cell on the back of his business card and tossed it on her desk, as she had the cigarette pack. She let it lie. There was a silence. Despite the hustle and bustle all around, this woman was in no hurry. A counter puncher, Bobby surmised, taking his time as well.

"Tell me about Kashmiri independence," Bobby opened finally, "why?"

"Why?" she exploded, "What business do any of them have in Kashmir?"

"Don't you even have a sense of being Indian? And if not, isn't that at least better than the other two options? China would eat an independent Kashmir alive. Bite by slow bite while it still bled."

"So say the Boy Scouts of America!"

"We ARE boy scouts compared to the Chinese!"

"We'll take our chances, thank you very much. What do they say in your New Hampshire? Live Free or Die!" she was glaring at Bobby, truly incensed.

"The Chinese won't let you live free, but they won't let you die either," Bobby replied, softening his tone. "I'm sorry. I am here to report, not to judge. What an amateur mistake. Can we start over?"

"Don't bullshit a bullshitter. It was an opening gambit and it worked. You see my true colors from the outset," she replied, but she was mollified.

She pulled another smoke out of the pack, but instead of lighting up added it to the littered desk with a toss. "Let's get out of here." She was up and on the move before Bobby could even react. He trailed behind faithfully. She stopped to zip up her leather flight jacket just outside and breathed deeply as if to expunge the previous smoke.

She coughed once. "I do too much of that bullshit. It'll be the death of me."

"If something else doesn't get you first."

"Good point, that is more likely." She gave him a wide smile, her first one. It made her look much more oriental than Indian. There was no slouch in her posture, ramrod straight but naturally so, not from military training. It fit her frame, broad square shoulders, a narrow profile front to back, long limbs.

"I'll bet you do have game," Bobby said, she must be only a bit under six feet.

"You know it. And not just in tennis," she said. Bobby grinned in reply. "I mean volleyball, stupid," she added. "Don't get ahead of yourself."

"Sorry," he replied, still grinning. "How old are you?" Bobby asked her.

"Is that germane to your interview?"

"No, well, you seem about the same age as me and that would be a pleasant change. Professionally, I am always Bobby Singh, cub reporter. Everyone worth an interview is old."

"How old are you?" she asked.

"23." A pause. "And a half."

The wide smile again, "We're close enough." She walked and he fell in step with her, not asking where they were going, appreciating her gait. "So what do you want to know?"

"Let's start with your name. Dalha. Do you have a last name to go with it?"

"No," Dalha said abruptly. "I'm not your topic for discussion."

CHAPTER 42

TINA

Tina looked at the daysailer with cautious optimism. It was bobbing gently on a mooring some 100 feet or so off the beach.

"Good boat," said one of the two men with Tina and Pally, studying it from the beach.

They were just a few minutes drive down the coast from their motel. The motel owner had a cousin who, just so happens, had a boat for rent.

"You two wait here for a moment, while I check her out," Tina said to the cousins. She peeled off her T-shirt and shorts down to her suit underneath. "You stay put too, Pally, until I can get a life jacket on you."

"Water not deep. Only one meter," said the owner.

"Well, okay. Come on, Pally."

They waded out together, hand in hand. After a few minutes inspection, Tina was satisfied that it wasn't about to sink. They returned to the beach to close the deal for a day of sailing. The girls waded back out and climbed aboard.

"It looks awfully big, Tina. You sure you can sail this alone? I'm afraid I won't be much help."

"Piece of cake, youngling. She reminds me of a San Juan 21 a boyfriend of mine had back in the day. As a matter of fact, I lost my virginity on that boat in a little cabin just about that size." She sighed. "God, I loved that boy." Pally looked inside the small enclosure dubiously. Catching Pally's expression, Tina said, "Hey, when there's a will there's a way."

The breeze was blowing off the beach so Tina didn't even bother with the small outboard. She lowered the centerboard halfway, then just released the mooring line and hoisted the mainsail. The boat fell away from the beach. Pally looked back nervously. Tina soon rolled the jib out as well and put the boat on a broad reach to clear the beach and keep her from heeling too much, for Pally's sake.

"Not a bad old girl," Tina said about the boat. "Sails are blown, but hell it's a rental. No holes or tears at least. And she's dry enough, which is the main thing." After a bit, Tina altered course to parallel with the beach on a beam reach.

"Here, sit by me, Pally." She patted the spot next to her on the high side. "We should be able to see our place from the water in a little while." Pally joined her without a word, an arm around Tina's waist.

"Hey, are you alright? We can go back, you know."

"No, no. I'll get used to it. And you are so obviously enjoying it."

"What a perfect day. Clear skies, not too much air for a landlubber like you. Water so clear it makes your eyes ache." Tina unstrapped her top, fisted it into a ball and tossed it into the cabin.

"Freedom. That's what sailing is all about." After a moment, Pally followed suit.

"Finally," Tina laughed, "I can get a good clear look at those boobs for yours in the light of day." Then more seriously, "You're beautiful, Pally. Don't ever think differently."

"My boobs are like fat bananas," Pally replied. "And they point in opposite directions, one left one right."

"Oh good lord, Pally. I love them. That's all I can say."

"Look at yours, Tina. Yours point straight ahead, not like mine."

"Silly girl, that's because there's not enough of me to point anywhere else, except down maybe. When I was young, it worried me. Being so small, I mean. Now, well, we are what we are."

They sailed on in silence. Gradually, Pally relaxed and started to enjoy the feel, sights, and sounds all around her. The sea sluiced smoothly along the length of the boat with the occasional slap of a small wave. Pally watched her friend's face as Tina steered the small craft. Her eyes were always on the move, up at the sails, ahead where they were going, and to either side. In her element, Tina exuded confidence, but more than that, she was beaming with joy.

After about a couple hours or so of lovely sailing Tina said, "Looks like it'll be time to turn around soon. We're running out of land, unless we want to hang a right out to sea. But there's a bit of shipping out there, plus if we run downwind we'll have to beat back into it at the end of the day. I wouldn't bet odds on these old rags pulling us upwind."

"We have to turn around?"

"Disappointed?"

"For sure. This is exciting."

"It's been wonderful and I don't want it to end, but exciting? Now if we were neck and neck with another boat, that would be exciting. Or if a storm kicked up. This? This is just dreamy."

"I'll settle for dreamy. After the plane, no storms, please."

"Me too, Pally. Me too." Tina gave her a light kiss.

"What's all that land up ahead?" Pally asked.

"Some islands with Athens not far beyond them."

"Can we go to that first little one before we turn around?"

"Absolutely. Let's be explorers."

The rocky islet was too small to be inhabited, but on the leeward side, the south shore, there was a tiny cove. Tina turned into the wind, dropped the small anchor, and lowered the sails. The place was totally secluded.

"This is lovely," Tina said. "Hard to believe Athens is just a stone's throw away."

Tina fetched her little backpack out of the cabin for lunch and a couple Mythos beers. After the last bite and draining her beer, Tina stood and peeled off her bikini bottom. Pally's eyes went to the small blonde thatch only slightly darker than the flaxen hair on her head. Tina smiled and dove over the side into the cool water. Pally slipped off her own bottom, but stood tentatively on the cockpit bench. Tina looked back up at her.

"Come on in, it's lovely. A bit cold so I can't stay in long. There's a ladder on the stern. You can let yourself down and hold on the boat the whole time."

It took Pally a long time to ease her way into the cold water, but eventually got there. But it really was cold, so soon enough they were both back aboard toweling off and warming in the sun.

"Yesterday, Tina. Were you a man?" Pally asked, out of the blue.

"You mean maybe the Greek guy? Why do you say that?"

"You surprised me. You were…aggressive."

Tina was concerned. "My god, did I hurt you? I'm so sorry."

"No, no, Tina. You were wonderful. I just…thought I sensed something."

"Pally, I, Tina, remember everything about yesterday. Everything. That was all me, I swear. God, I hope it wasn't a bad experience for you."

"No, no, Tina it wasn't really. But it was, well, my first time."

"Mine too, with a woman. What did I do wrong?"

"Nothing, Tina really. You saw how I reacted. It was incredible."

"Well I thought you liked it."

"I did. But…"

"But what?"

"You were so passionate. So urgent, Tina. You seemed in a hurry." Tina sat up at that.

"I was, wasn't I? But I wanted so much to make you happy."

"And you did, Tina. You did. Afterward I fell asleep, remember?" Pally assured her. Tina reached out and took her friend's hand.

"I took that as a good sign, actually."

"You didn't mind?" Pally asked. "That I didn't, you know, do anything for you. I feel like it was my turn. Like I owe you."

Tina laughed. "You do, dear girl, you do. But don't worry, I had a marvelous time watching you sleep while I … pleasured myself. Made love to myself, actually."

"Really? How? Would you tell me about it? Please." Pally pleaded.

Tina smiled. "It's not like you've never done it before, but, well, it's different too. It's slow," Tina said, her face turning red. "The opposite of how I was with you yesterday. Sorry. Anyway, it's, well, mindful, deliberate. And it's spiritual as well as physical."

"Can you teach me?"

"I'd love to. I'll teach you slowly, with a bit of time and practice. You're likely familiar with the Tantric foundations, being Indian I mean."

"Actually, my family is Catholic. So yes, I've heard of Tantra, but don't really know much about it."

"Really? A Catholic girl. Then we have our work cut out for us. But don't worry, it'll be fun."

"What are you?" Pally asked.

"Me? Nothing, really. As my dad always said, 'I'm not going to waste a sailing day in church.' And I never disagreed with Dad on that one. He was a piece of work sometimes, but he got that right."

Pally was looking into Tina's eyes. Tina knew what she was thinking. What she wanted.

"We'd better get back. Time to weigh anchor," Tina said with a squeeze of Pally's hand as she released it and got moving. "Besides, that little cabin is better for teenagers. A welcoming space matters in tantra. We can prepare that in our bungalow."

CHAPTER 43

ESCAPE

Ife's teeth chattered. Despite their exertion of pushing the raft, they were all shivering. It had been an hour of swimming and while the early April days had been quite warm, the lake was fed by mountain runoff. There was a sliver of moon just rising over the hills to the right. Their swimming had been slow, but strenuous, laden as they were, and all were tiring. Only little Aria seemed to be breathing without stress. Aristol guided them to the left, hopefully to find a landing beyond the steep rocks along the shore. There wasn't enough light to make out details of the shore. He took a quick glance over his shoulder. Homedes must be at the shore by now. The dogs would have tracked them to the lake with little problem.

It was another half hour swim before they could get their weary feet into earth. The bottom sand was rocky but welcome nonetheless. The evening air on wet skin made them shiver all the more. They hadn't passed north of the rock wall. They were in the midst of it. They all stood knee deep in water with no obvious way to get to land in the dark. They huddled together for warmth. It wasn't really cold out but their bodies had worked hard to maintain heat and it had told on them.

"Follow the rock line north," Aristol whispered, "the rocks will have to open up sooner or later." Or so he hoped. They slogged through the water as best they could. Ife's feet were feeling numb.

***

Another tear rolled down the tall man's cheek. Homedes was grateful it was too dark for his soldiers to see him cry. Aristol! Why? He caught the scent of lemon trees. It reminded him of little Aria although he couldn't tell why. A veritable acrobat, that girl. Distracted, he stumbled in the dark and regained his footing, keeping as fast a pace as possible behind Hercules and the other dogs pulling on their leashes.

"Looks like they're heading for the lake, sir," the sergeant said. Homedes only grunted in reply. Why? Such a betrayal. Why? But he knew the answer: Ife. The ten men and three dogs trudged on under flickering torchlight. The slim moon cleared the hilltops.

"That won't give us much more to see by," the sergeant noted. Not even a grunt in response this time.

They stopped at the water's edge, not far from where the fugitives had waded in. The sniffing hounds quickly found the very spot. Homedes dipped his hand in the water. They couldn't have. No. They wouldn't survive. Aristol knew that. He regretted he kept no boats on the lake, but the fishing had never been good. His thought was not of capture, but rescue. How long could they last? Even young and strong as they were, not long. You fools. You deluded fools. Why would you run? Was not your every need attended to? Was there a better place in all of Hellas? You all were safe here. Cared for. Loved.

"You four, take Hermes to the left as far as the shore lets you walk," Homedes ordered. "You others take Apollo along the shore to the right. If you find them, detain them, but do them no harm. And send a runner back to me. Maybe the cold forced them back ashore." Then to himself, "At least I hope so."

The two groups departed. Homedes stood alone with Hercules at his heel. A single torch in hand. He scouted the cold sand about him. The markings were clear. They had gone in. He closed his eyes and said a silent prayer. Please live. All of you, just live.

***

Ife was in the worst shape. The dawn found them huddled together on a rough black rock beach. A brief break in the rocks. Once out of the water, they all stripped themselves of their sodden attire. Then they ate some bread. The little raft was beached on an incline. Aristol laid down on his back. The quaking Ife was face down on top of him. The other two lay over their friends on either side with the lone remaining dry blanket stretched over all of them. It wasn't quite big enough to fend off the cool cloudy dawn.

The landscape was barren of any vegetation. Just black rock all around. It was daylight. Gray, but they could see. His feet stung from the cold, but Aristol forced himself to wade back into the water creeping close along the rocks to get a look back south. He didn't have to go far to see around the furthermost rocks. When he did, he drew back quickly. Nearby were four soldiers bivouacked on the beach, separated only by the unnatural jagged black rocks. The hills to the south and the land adjacent to the beach where the soldiers were still had the scrubs and fir trees of home. Or what had been home. A world away and yet so close. A dog's head came up, suddenly alert. Hermes. Aristol withdrew, but dared not move. It wouldn't take the soldiers more than ten minutes to wade around the rocks to their tiny beach. The Spartan snuck another peek, mindful of the hound. But the soldiers weren't looking up the coast at the unfriendly black stone. Now that there was enough light, they were looking across the water. He could hear them talking, but it was too far to make out what they were saying. Aristol's legs were aching with cold. He slowly made his way back to the beach, signaling silence to the others as he came. He sat back on the beach. His three friends rubbed his legs and feet vigorously to support his circulation.

"Soldiers very close," he whispered, "and Hermes."

"How?" Aria whispered back.

"Just strolled up the shore. We didn't get very far. Only just far enough."

"We couldn't have gone any further," Dani whispered.

"No. How are you all feeling?" Aristol asked.

"Ready," Ife said quietly.

Barking erupted. They all stiffened. More than one dog. They could all distinguish the deeper bellow of the mighty Hercules. Aristol relaxed. The dogs hadn't detected the runaways, they were greeting each other.

"What now?" Dani asked.

"We wait. Until they go home. Or wade around the corner."

"And then?"

"We fight," said Ife. "I won't go back."

Aristol stared at Ife intently. There was no hope of winning a fight. Ife didn't even know how.

"If it comes to that, Ife. I will take your life." It was Aria. Wet cheeked, but determined. Ife nodded with a small sad smile. The girls clenched hands.

Aristol looked at the rocks beyond the narrow beach. Could they climb them? He didn't think so. What had he brought them to? "Nobody will go into this water if they don't have to," Aristol told them. "We have to, let's move out. Quietly. Keep the rocks close on our left. Ife, take the lead. I'll take the rear."

Despite the cloud cover, the day warmed quickly. They made good progress with only Dani dropping all the way over his waist once when he stepped in a hole. He gasped as the water shriveled his shocked nethers, but little Aria was there to help him up onto firmer footing. The lakeshore dipped into the rocks a bit further west and soon their beach was out of sight behind them. After a while, they all crawled out of the water onto a big flat rock to let their numb feet and legs come back to life. It was painful. By midmorning the sun had come out to warm their bodies and their spirits. Aristol was pondering this strange landscape of nothing but rock with only occasional moss growing between the cracks when Aria broke the silence.

"Hey look, I think I can see trees on the other side of the lake," Aria said. They all peered into the distance. There did indeed appear to be a tree line across the water.

"Not much good they do us all the way over there. Anybody want to swim across to find a landing?" asked Dani.

"No, don't you see? If there are trees on that side there may soon be trees on this side," said Aria.

"Now how do you figure that?" Aristol asked.

"This lake, the strange rocks. We're sitting on a recent volcano," Aria explained. Aristol started at that. "Not recent like yesterday," she continued, "but recent like back when my mother was born maybe. I've seen this before in Persia. My mom says it takes a long time before things start to grow where volcanoes were."

"What's a volcano?" Ife asked. Dani looked equally mystified.

"I've heard of them," Aristol said. "It is what happens when Hades farts. Smoke, ash, fire. High into the sky. It shakes the very earth itself and kills all it touches." He paused. "Let's get moving."

"Not to worry," Aria said. "This volcano is long dead. If not, the lake water wouldn't be so cold. It would be a lot warmer."

"A warmer lake sure doesn't sound bad," Ife said with a brave grin.

"Be careful what you wish for. I remember at home there were places where steam would rise out of the ground and pools of water would boil," Aria said. She stared off east across the lake, remembering another life.

"Time to move out," Aristol announced, breaking her reverie.

Another hour of slogging through the cold water, with only two short breaks and the black rock began to succumb to growth. Life. First more moss in ever wider cracks, then some shrubs and finally the cracks became gaps. Small at first but ever widening until finally they landed on a broad black, but fine, sandy beach. The beach sloped steeply into a hill of scrub grass and stunted trees with gray-green leafs. There were still plenty of rocks amidst the ground cover, but there was more ground than rocks.

"Time to leave the lake," Aristol declared.

A mid-day sun soon warmed the last of the chill out of their bones as they hiked up the steep craggy incline, sometimes needing their hands at the steeper parts. The trees got taller as they climbed further out of the bowl of the volcanic lake. They finally rested at the summit, exhausted. Hunger compelled them to lunch on some of their meager supplies after having sprawled in the grass for a nap. Aria was the first up, scanning the horizon. To the west and south, the mountains were crusted snowy white. That was the direction they were taking.

CHAPTER 44

SHE

"The American reporter, Bobby Singh, is meeting with that woman called Dalha," he told She. "And another woman named Khatri Singh. She is a writer, strictly freelance stuff but she has a local following. Both of them will be with us for Kashmir independence. I say we reach out to the American. He could be a voice that reaches the world."

"No," She said. "It is too soon. And I distrust Dalha. She is for reclaiming the ancient kingdom of Kashmir."

"And wouldn't that be glorious?"

"Of course, but we must crawl before we walk. Independence for Indian Kashmir first. Pakistan and then China will be much tougher nuts to crack."

"Whatever you say," he agreed. "What next?"

"You keep track of the American. Come to me immediately if he leaves the city. Otherwise I will see you in two days as usual."

"Why can't I just call you with any news?"

"Don't you like to come visit me?" She asked with a smile.

"Of course I do. I'm insane to suggest otherwise. It's just that…"

She interrupted him with a raised hand. "Your kid brother needs some independence, tailing the American on his own. You coming to me in person is a win-win, if you know what I mean."

"Whatever you say," he gave up.

"See you in two days," She said.

"Maybe sooner," he said with a grin, "I'm hoping that young reporter leaves town just so I can tell you about it."

"Be off with you," She laughed.

She watched him walk down the street to his car and take off. What a fool. But a useful fool. In fact, that is what made him useful. Dalha was nobody's fool. She didn't want that American reporter stirring Dalha up and that motley crew she led. Rebuilding the kingdom of Kashmir was a pipedream. It would create violence in three countries across and along the borders. More importantly it ran contrary to her real mission. The

Independent Indian Kashmir movement was her mission, but not for the Kashmiris. For enemies of India. Very specific enemies of India, in fact.

CHAPTER 45

HOMEDES

Homedes turned away from his map, frustrated. Forlorn. Why? Not that it mattered now. Were they dead? Could all four of them just swim out into that icy water and silently succumb? He couldn't believe it. Didn't want to. Do bodies that die from cold water sink as drowning victims often do? They hadn't found any bodies. Not a one. But it was a big lake and they had no idea how far they had swam before dying, if indeed they had died. His wagoner had discovered that a fair portion of his grease supply was missing. That may have been just enough to protect them from the icy waters. For a while. They were young and fit. Maybe they made it. He prayed that they did.

The trudge back home from the lake with his soldiers had felt like a bitter retreat. Upon their return, he had issued orders to outfit a dozen men for an extended campaign. They would march in 48 hours. He hadn't told anyone that he had no idea where to lead them. Returning to his map, he admonished himself for not having gathered more information when he had it made so long ago. It showed the contours of the lake itself, but its only value now as he poured over it yet again was to spur his memory of a surveying expedition by boat some twenty years ago. At the time, he had been more concerned with his property lines than anything else. There had been that lifeless black slab, spawned from the underworld, on both shores. But further north, there had been some beaches and a tree line again. How far one had to go he just couldn't remember. And the map offered no help.

Homedes slumped on the sofa. The grease. This had been a premeditated escape, long planned. Why now? Another month and the lake would have been warmer. Not comfortably so perhaps, but the difference between life and death. Why now? Something must have caused them to move sooner than planned. Homedes jumped up and strode to the bar. Hercules lumbered to his feet in response to his master's sudden move, shook himself vigorously, jowls slapping, and snorted twice. He was ready, watching Homedes for orders. But the man simply poured himself a tall wine and began to pace, deep in thought. The dog fell in step behind him.

Aristol would be the leader, no doubt. But he himself was a happy young man. Why would he want to leave? Didn't he have all he could want? Every comfort? Companionship? Even love? He lacked for nothing. Maybe that was it. Yes, of course. A young man, not just lovely, but strong, intelligent, skilled. In his prime. What were Aristol's ambitions? Where were his challenges? Perhaps life had become too easy, too repetitive for his young friend. Trained as he was, a Spartan officer, could such an one as he be content with mere training and wrestling?

Homedes pondered further. Could it be that Aristol missed war? He was such a gentle lad, like himself. Homedes had seen enough slaughter for more than a lifetime. But Aristol? He'd only had that one taste, and that ending in defeat and capture. They'd talked of combat, the two of them. Shared their experiences, so intimate, but that had been sometime back. Years. Homedes felt a rush of shame realizing that he had neglected Aristol's needs, as he had with his son before him. He should have shared more of his wisdom, hard earned from tragic experience. Instead, he had taught indolence. Homedes stopped. The goblet almost slipped from his hand before he realized it was there and he tightened his grip. *I practically chased him away.* A rush of grief overwhelmed him. Hercules, sensing his distress, nuzzled his massive head against his master's hip. The man rubbed the beast behind his ear, looking down into those trusting black eyes.

"We have to find him, Hercules. To beg his forgiveness. To set him free. And to let him know that wherever he may go, he always has a home."

Later that night, Homedes lay staring at the ceiling of his bed. The comforting warmth of Dulce at his side, a soft soothing snore whispered in his ear. He hadn't even coupled with the curvy creature. Oh, he had intended to, as always. But when the time came, they just hugged for the longest time. First standing, then in bed.

Dulce, a wise woman, had made no advance when summoned. She'd heard all the news through the grapevine and sensed her master would need solace more than sex tonight. She'd felt the tension in him through their embrace. Slowly she'd drawn it out of him through her touch and her heart, murmuring a nurturing mantra from her early childhood.

Dulce herself couldn't understand why the others had been crazy enough to run away. Born into slavery, her own young life in Sicily had not been easy. Here on the estate she had learned to feel truly safe for the first time. And she adored Homedes as much as Hercules did. She envisioned him as the father she'd never known. Wise, gentle, and yet funny too. Dulce always felt better simply being in his presence. Whatever he wanted of her, she gave of herself fully. With joy. Her master would find Aristol and the others then bring them all home. Things would return to normal. Forever. She fell asleep with that reassuring thought.

CHAPTER 46

AJITA

"Before we get started, Pally, this is about love as well as sex." They were back in the bungalow after a pleasant uneventful return sail, then a light dinner, a stroll along the beach, showers. All observed.

"Does that mean…you love me, Tina?" Pally asked.

"Well, let's not get ahead of ourselves," Tina said. "This is sort of the Tantric philosophy."

"You mentioned Tantra on the boat," Pally put in.

"Just so. I learned some of it from a past boyfriend, and the concept that people can choose to love, not just fall in love by accident. Of course I fell totally in love with him the old fashioned way. And then we didn't last long. None of them ever seem to."

"He must be crazy to have let you go," Pally said.

"Not at all," Tina said. "It's just the way of things sometimes. I mean, I still love him, but the relationship just didn't last."

"Why don't you try to reconnect with him since you still love him?"

"No, we were doomed from the start. I travel for work and he's a naval officer of all things so we were never in the same place together long enough to really be a couple. Besides, I have had other loves before and after, some of whom I still love, since he was in my life."

They were quiet for a while. Pally was frowning. "How can you live life like that? With the heartbreak, I mean."

"I won't pretend it's easy, Pally. It isn't, but in retrospect I don't regret the relationships that went really deep, even though they didn't last. Hell, it's the one night stands that sometimes leave me feeling…soiled. But I digress, remember it was Alfred, Lord Tennyson who wrote, 'Tis better to have loved and lost than never to have loved at all' and I can personally vouch for old Tennyson."

"Look, I don't know who that is, but can't say that I agree with him."

"Okay, maybe a more contemporary song lyric will help, 'it's the heart afraid of breaking that never learns to dance'" Tina sang softly. Pally just looked at her, confused. "Nothing?" Tina asked, "Bette Midler? The Rose?"

"Sorry, Tina," Pally said, "I don't know that song."

"I guess we're seeing some cultural divides here, but no matter. The point is that if you don't try, and risk failure, then you may never experience love in the first place and even if it's only for a little while, well, some moments can carry you through a lifetime. But only if you can let the person go, yet still hold the love. Does that make sense?"

"I don't know, Tina. I was brought up that you get married and love one person for the rest of your life. I look at my parents and know that works."

"The monogamous model, I'm sure it works for a lot of people. And good for your folks. And I think that worked for my folks as well. But for me? I know better."

***

Outside their bungalow, with a puff of breeze billowing the curtain, Ajita caught a glimpse of the blonde woman through the window. She was standing across from the Indian woman. Ajita could hear all that was said easily enough from her spot, but hadn't dared yet pull the curtain back even a little bit.

Then the voices grew softer and Ajita couldn't tell what more was said, but the murmurs continued for quite a while. Ajita was intrigued by the conversation and frustrated that she couldn't hear more. Still she remained patient. It was a part of her discipline. These women weren't going anywhere without her knowing it. Finally, after long silence, Ajita pulled the curtain back ever so slightly to sneak a peek. She gasped at what she saw.

The two women were facing each other, just finishing disrobing. Ajita had never seen nudity before, other than herself in the mirror. From her angle, she could see almost a full frontal view of the American, just as the American had seen her back in the hospital. The broad bottom of the Indian woman as well as her back and shoulder is what Ajita saw of the American's partner. But Ajita focused on the pale slender frame of the blonde. The two lovers were focused on each other. They moved closer, they kissed as hands slowly caressed, explored. Ajita held the curtain open with one hand, the other moved to her own midriff.

"Shhhh," the sound purred in Ajita's ear. Ajita stiffened and froze. Then she was led silently away from the window.

"You are an interesting lady," the man said to Ajita once they were both in Ajita's bungalow. "My cousin told me about you." The man was grinning.

Pokerfaced, Ajita studied the man, the owner of the motel. Swarthy or just tanned, he could almost pass for an Indian. Lean and with a full head of black hair, a face framed with a few days of stubble. Like his cousin, this man didn't look evil, or even bad, just sloppy. Ajita didn't like sloppy.

"I heard about the airport. The deal you made with Christos," the motel owner said. He was shaking his head up and down. "We'll make a deal too. You and me."

Ajita cringed inside, but showed nothing. At the airport, she had watched the two women she followed from India rent the car. They had spoken with the man there at great length. Finally, when they left, Ajita approached the same man to rent a car, and maybe get information. Did he know where they were going? The Indian woman was Ajita's cousin. She wanted to surprise her. Of course, he did. He knew exactly where they were going. *Happy to help, but what's in it for me?* Ajita didn't have much money. *No? Other arrangements could be made. It is my break in a few minutes, I walk you to your rental car.*

He took her to a small storage room. Alone. *You a pretty lady. I like dark skin. You show me your skin then I tell you.* Ajita said nothing. Didn't move. *No? No doubt you find your cousin without my help. Maybe call her. I take you to your car now.* He opened the door and walked out. Ajita remained rooted where she stood in the dingy storage room. This was her only hope. The man came back into the room. Closed the door. Waited. *My break is not long.* Ajita disrobed. Reluctantly. Slowly. The man grinned in anticipation, then appreciation at her bare beauty. Tears. Tell me where they went. *Not yet.* A hand reached for her, she recoiled. *No? I don't force you. I don't touch you. You touch me.* He dropped his pants. Ajita put her hands behind her back. *No touch, eh? Okay, you taste instead. You like. Taste good.*

Now she was with the cousin who owned the beach motel. She'd gotten a room and was keeping an eye on the American and her Indian police friend. Ajita didn't have a plan yet. Just a goal. Confront. She needed to get her alone. Away from the policewoman. She needed control of the situation. Wait and watch. And be ready. That was her plan. Patience. But Ajita was truly almost out of money. No credit. How would she live? And now here is this man.

"Maybe I call police. Tell the nice ladies you spy on them. I do that," said the motel owner. Ajita said nothing.

"No? Then what?" he asked.

"Free room," Ajita said softly, not believing what she was saying, "And food."

"Christos say you not like touching," he replied. "Me, Stavros, I like touching. I think I call police."

"No," said Ajita.

"No? Then try touching. Really not so bad. You like, you see. Food first. Hungry? Okay. I get food. Be right back."

***

Ajita could still see the car she was following as she drove over the Corinth Canal. She knew they were heading to the city of Corinth and the ancient ruins outside the modern town, but nothing more really. Stavros, the motel owner, had recommended a place for the women to stay in Corinth, but he didn't know for certain they would go there. Ajita couldn't afford to lose them now. The last three days at the beach motel had been surreal. The women went sailing for hours. And Stavros came to Ajita's bungalow. For hours. Still, Ajita was uninjured and well fed. Had some Euros in her pocket, and today's lunch in the boot.

You no worry. You good girl. That was the last thing Stavros had said to her through the car window as she pulled away onto the road. What did that even mean? Stavros had been surprised when he first entered her. Had withdrawn for a moment, looking at her oddly. She had just waited. Why would he care? Ajita was doing what was necessary to survive. She needed to survive to achieve her goal. Justice for Rohit. She always survived. Discipline. And the discovery of a new asset. Her body. She would survive.

***

"Tina? Can I ask you a question?"

"Sure youngling, shoot."

"When you said it's about love and sex back at the bungalow. Remember?"

"Yes?"

"So we've had sex. And now I'm going to do as you have done," Pally said. She looked over at the blonde woman sitting next to her amidst the ruins of ancient Corinth, sipping on her water bottle. Squinting in the sun, accented the wrinkles around Tina's eyes. And the bit of gray at her temples.

Tina turned to Pally, giving the younger woman her full attention. "Spit it out, Pally."

"I love you, Tina. There I said it. I'm taking the risk like that English lord guy said."

"Tennyson." Tina sighed. "I hear you, Pally. I guess I should say good for you. Well done."

"And?"

"And you want me to tell you that I love you too."

"Only if you really mean it. But god I hope you do." Pally stared at Tina intently, questioning.

"It's not just sex between us, Pally, that's for sure. I know the difference between sex and love." Tina looked away, humming to herself. "Truth is, I think I'm falling in love with you, youngling. The old fashioned way." Then she smiled. "How could I not be? My beautiful girl." Tina patted Pally's round cheek.

Pally took Tina's hand and kissed it. "You make me so happy. I don't understand you, but you make me happy." Pally thought for a moment. "Will you marry me, Tina?" she asked, kissing Tina's hand again. "We can do it in America. I read about it once."

***

Ajita wandered slowly among the ruins, keeping nearer to another group. Wearing a hijab and sunglasses, she observed the two women out of the corner of her eye. How could she get rid of that policewoman?

CHAPTER 47

HELEN

Helen was sprinting at full speed as she topped the ridge and plunged down a steep wooded slope. The battle was before her as she raced downhill to join the fray.

"Daphne!" Helen cried in desperation at the top of her lungs, warning her sister over the chaos of barking, bleating and snarling.

Daphne turned just in time, catching the leaping wolf full in the chest on the point of her javelin. But she hadn't been able to brace her spear properly. It pierced the hide of the beast, which let out a series of high pitched yelps of pain, but didn't impale the wolf deeply. The wolf was still alive yet wounded as its bulk struck Daphne full on the chest, knocking her down. The girl held tightly to her javelin as her enemy thrashed atop her in mindless pain. Helen charged to her rescue. Further down the slope, she could see two other wolves attempting to close on their small flock of terror-stricken sheep. Daphne's dog stood growling at bay in their defense, backing slowly in an attempt to cover a two-sided attack.

At a dead run, Helen speared the wounded wolf deep in the gut, rolling it off her sister and pinioning it to the ground. Her own hound bolted past her, engaging the other two wolves from the rear. A further cacophony of canine noises erupted as battle was joined.

"Oh Daphne, are you wounded?" Helen asked her sister.

"No no, I'm good," Daphne panted as she rolled to her feet, javelin in hand.

The two sisters ran to the action, but with their arrival the two remaining wolves drew off, snarling as they went. Helen called the dogs off any pursuit of the wolves and they returned to protecting their charges. Daphne was bent over panting hard to catch her breath. The dogs, nearby, were tongue out panting too. Also gulping as much air as she could get, Helen kept an eye on the two wolves, which had withdrawn to a safe distance, but were still watching with hunger.

"Are you sure you're not hurt?" she finally asked.

"Mostly scrapes and scratches," Daphne managed to get out between breaths. "This blood isn't mine." The dozen or so sheep were still bleating. They could see the two wolves clear enough a short distance away.

"That was one hell of a running fight. How far have we gone?" Helen asked.

"We topped three ridges, I know that," said Daphne. "It will be a long walk home."

"And with those two at our heels," Helen said, pointing to the wolves. "Look at them. They're emaciated. They aren't giving up. They can't."

Having finally caught her breath, Daphne was upright again. "Where are we? I don't think I've ever been this far from home."

"Me neither, but if we go uphill we should be able to find some familiar landmarks from that last ridge."

"Look at the sheep. They're spent. The dogs aren't much better."

"You're right." Helen looked through the foliage at the sunlight. "I think we have about three hours before dark."

"Not enough time. We need to find water, then fire will be our best defense tonight," Daphne said.

"Let's move further down the hill. If we clear out I think those two will eat their own rather than tackle us again."

At the girls' whistled instructions, the dogs herded the sheep further down the slope onto the edge of a long narrow valley. Daphne led while Helen served as rear guard to watch the wolves. They came across a fast running stream with icy clear water coming down from the mountain peaks. After all drank their fill, they followed its course upstream, hoping for it to be narrow and shallow enough for crossing. The land on the slopes was mostly fir trees and scrub, not much for sheep to graze on. The hope was that where the ground leveled they would find a meadow for grazing.

Then they came upon a scenic spot. A wide pool opened on the far side of the stream just below a small stony waterfall where the current ran. Most of the cold runoff that fed the stream continued down its course after the falls. But on the far side, some of the current swirled in with the pool fed from a frothy fountain gushing out of a crack in a massive stone on the far bank of the stream. Surrounding the stone, blood red poppy flowers were just starting to bloom. There were no bushes in the vicinity of the pool and the trees thinned out considerably amid a pale green lawn. The trees were mostly small manna ash laden with white blossoms. It looked like an untended or natural park, of sorts. Beyond, further away from the stream, they could see tall grassland.

"How lovely," Helen exclaimed, her worries suddenly assuaged, "it's a natural garden."

"Wish we could get over there," sighed Daphne.

"Stay here with the dogs and sheep. I'll scout upstream a little further beyond the waterfall to see if there is a place to cross."

"Will do. I think the wolves gave up," Daphne replied with a look over her shoulder, "Haven't seen them."

"Keep a close eye anyway. Those two aren't the only wolves in these mountains. I won't be long."

And sure enough, Helen wasn't long at all. In a short while, she was back with good news. "There is a spot just upstream where the stream widens considerably, but the good news is that it is very shallow. It is rocky, but the water won't be above our knees. Shouldn't be too much of a problem for the sheep."

They were all soon safely on the other side. The sheep grazed contentedly while the dogs and girls felt their empty bellies growl. They then herded the sheep back near the pool for another drink. They were surprised to find that the water in the pool was pleasantly warm.

"I'm going in," Daphne shouted. "Time to get all this wolf blood, dirt, and grime off me."

"I'm with you."

The girls quickly stripped down and eased themselves into the pool. The closer they got to the fountain water plummeting down, the warmer the pool water became. They found the pool was over their heads not too far from the bank so they didn't go far, but that they could comfortably sit on a bottom of smooth stones by the bank. They felt their fatigue and tired muscles wash away with the sweat.

"Ah, this place is good enough for the gods," said Daphne.

"It is, indeed," replied a lovely lady, who had emerged from under the waterfall. Startled, the girls leapt to their feet still up to their waist in the pool water. Their javelins, left at the water's edge, were in hand immediately.

"This place is sacred to our goddess, Aphrodite. I am called Delia, Priestess of the Fountain." Delia swam a few slow strokes to where she could stand and rose out of the water. She was more than a head taller than the sisters, who had backed defensively against the stone bank.

"Have no fear. You are welcome here. Be at ease. The waters have already soothed your scrapes and scratches. Allow the spirit of the fountain to permeate your soul as well. I will return shortly to attend to your wants and needs."

The girls watched in awe as the pale lady ascended up stone steps to solid ground clad only in her long white wet hair. She smiled upon them, then turning, sprang away in a light-footed sprint. She was soon out of sight.

"Do you think we should stay?"

"I don't know. I'm afraid of the gods."

"You've never seen one."

"And don't want to."

"That lady seems nice. I trust her."

"So do I. It's settled then."

The sisters eased themselves back neck deep in the pool. The sun had lowered beyond the next ridge when the dogs barked, then the girls heard a wagon approaching. Finding Delia's stone stairs, they stepped up out of the pool. A man was driving a wooden two wheeled cart pulled by a white ox. Delia sat by his side now wearing a white gown.

"Well, here are two pretty peas from a pod of three," the man said, openly admiring the naked sisters. Delia laughed. "Don't mind Nikias. He too is a servant of the fountain."

Surprising themselves, the girls didn't mind at all. On the contrary, their hazel eyes sparkled with appreciation. Nikias and Delia came down off the cart. They both went to the back of the cart to unload. The dogs bounded up when Nikias waved two hocks of dried meat on the bone and tossed them to the hungry hounds. Delia provided Helen and Daphne with simple white gowns open on one shoulder as Delia and Nikias wore them. The gowns came down to the ankle on the short sisters while the other two were cut to fit just above the knee. A large blanket was soon laid on the lawn with an array of simple rustic fare. At a nod from Delia, the girls dove in with gusto. Delia and Nikias nibbled with them in silence with only the murmurings of the sheep to be heard. Eventually, the girls were sated. There was only a bit more bread and olive oil left anyway. They thanked their hostess effusively for her generosity.

"You're far from home." Delia said, "You are welcome to stay the night here."

"Our sister and Agi will be worried, but it can't be helped. We thank you for your hospitality."

"Agi? I didn't know there was a man in your household," Nikias said.

"Yes, a dear friend, but how do you know of us at all?"

"We sometimes wander across Arcadia in the service of Aphrodite," replied Delia, "While we've never seen your homestead, we know where you run your sheep and have seen, at a distance, you three sisters tending your flock."

"I'm surprised our dogs never alerted us," Helen commented. "They're very protective."

"And wise too, they could sense that we are friends. Just as they do now."

"If I may ask," ventured Daphne, "how does one enter the service of the gods? And Aphrodite in particular? We know nothing of such matters, but hear rumors that Pan runs the length and breadth of Arcadia."

"And so he does," Delia replied, "that is one of the reasons for our travels. While not in conflict with the great god Pan, our Aphrodite tempers and calms some of the influences Pan's presence has on her flock in Arcadia."

"Flock?"

"Yes, the people of Arcadia. You are Aphrodite's flock, although we do not herd you. You are free to live and love as you wish. Or as Pan would have it, to lust as you wish. But we will talk more of that tomorrow. Nikias, ladies, let's prepare your lodgings for the night."

Nikias retrieved a tent from the cart and the four of them set it up near the pool with the sheep and the dogs between the pool and the tent. A campfire was soon cackling outside the tent. Bedding and blankets were laid out in the tent as well. Delia gave a long shrill whistle that startled and impressed the two shepherdesses, expert dog whistlers as they were. A few minutes later, two large dogs bounded out of the gathering darkness to join the company. They seemed to already know Helen's and Daphne's dogs, much to the girls' surprise.

"They are called Cupid and Psyche." Delia said, "They will help your dogs guard your camp tonight. We'll be back in the morning to break fast with you." And with that, amid waves and goodbyes, Delia and Nikias mounted their cart and the white ox lumbered away. Soon, the tired sisters fell into a deep sleep to the soothing sounds of the fountain and fall.

***

Early the next morning, both girls woke at the same time, startled. Still fuzzy with sleep, they didn't know what had awakened them. The vague memories of an erotic dream slipped away from Daphne's consciousness. She felt wet between her thighs. She saw Helen had a strange look on her face, but didn't inquire. Without a word, Daphne bolted out of the tent at a dead run, and peeling her gown free as she ran, dove bare assed into the pool. She arched her back under water feeling the warm wetness tingle her tight bare breasts. Drifting to the edge of the current, and feeling the sudden chill, she swam quickly under water back to the bank of the pool. Breaking the surface as she reached the edge of the pool, Daphne was startled to find Nikias right before her sitting at the pool, his legs in the water to his knees.

"Good morning, Daphne," he said with a chuckle and a knowing glint in his eye. But Daphne didn't notice his look, she was staring astounded at his erect phallus less than two feet from her face. She was mesmerized by something she had never seen before.

"Daphne!" Helen shouted, coming out of the tent tightly wrapped in a blanket.

Just then, Delia pulled up in the ox cart. She leapt down and taking Helen by the hand strode to the pool. Nikias stood and approached Delia and Helen as Daphne came up the stairs out of the pool to join them.

"Pan has passed by. I can smell him in the wind and sense him on you girls," Delia said, "Nikias, you're rather obvious," she added with a grin. "Come, Helen, shake off your fearful memories," and Delia shook the girl gently at the shoulders as she spoke, "be at ease. There is nothing to fear at the fountain. Pan can influence the body, but Aphrodite rules the heart and soul. Fear not, Nikias is no satyr."

Nikias bowed before Helen, still erect. "I mean no harm or disrespect to you or anyone," but an idiotic lusty grin was on his face. Daphne sauntered up behind him from the pool, still wet and naked, giving the strapping Spartan a hug. He took her hands in his across his chest.

"Now, now," said Delia lightly, "back in the pool, both of you. Be cleansed of Pan and embrace the love of Aphrodite. Learn love before passion." The two of them dove back in. Delia turned to Helen and embraced her.

"You have suffered a past horror that haunts you still. That much is clear. Pan affects different people in different ways. He draws out either lust or panic. Lust without love is beneath Aphrodite's dignity, but can be harmless enough, even fun. Lust in one and panic in another is a different matter. Be comforted, child. For I am a priestess of love, fear does not abide in my presence." Helen buried her head in the taller woman's bosom in relief, the terror and tension easing out of her.

CHAPTER 48

DAPHNE AND NIKIAS

Nikias escorted Daphne home to bring Agi and Lorae to the fountain. Delia kept Helen and her dog with her as well as the sheep. She would conduct a love healing ritual to exorcize Helen's horrors forever. Preparation for the ritual required one-on-one time between the priestess and the sufferer.

The ritual itself worked best when Helen's trusted loved ones participated with her. Daphne and Nikias had no difficulties finding the way back to Daphne's homestead since Nikias knew the terrain. After reaching the summit of the nearest ridge, Daphne was able to see the path the running fight with the wolves had taken. The weather was clear and warm for early April in the mountains. They walked in silence until taking a midday rest and a light meal of bread and olives.

"Are you and Delia lovers?" Daphne asked suddenly. There was an intensity in her voice.

"Yes, of course," Nikias replied with a grin. He popped an olive in his mouth and chased it with a sip of water. Daphne pulled a bite off her bread, chewing thoughtfully with a frown.

"You're a virgin, aren't you," Nikias said after a while. It wasn't a question.

"I have no husband."

"How old are you, Daphne?"

"26. I'm the oldest. Helen is a year younger and Lorae six years younger."

"And no husbands for three such pretty girls?"

"You said that yesterday. That we were pretty. I've never thought of myself that way. I doubt my sisters have either." She pondered for a moment. "When you think about it, we're a litter of runts. Throwaways."

"You are little, yes. But that doesn't mean you aren't lovely."

"Just skin and bones. Nothing more. It's a good thing really. Nobody is attracted to us, I mean. The real risk is to be mistaken for boys."

Nikias smiled sadly, "That too would be a risk. Boys of a certain age, just a few years before full manhood, are at the height of their beauty."

"I wouldn't know about that. We live alone. Nobody lives near us. After our father died, we hid when anyone came by."

"How old were you?"

"Thirteen."

"And your mother?

"She died earlier, when Lorae was born. Mother lives with us still in our little Lorae." A smile returned to her solemn face, "although she always likes to remind Helen and me that she's the tallest."

"Your mother lives on in all three of you. Her soul, and her beauty."

"Did you know our mother? Or see her from a distance?"

"No, I didn't mean to imply that. I haven't lived around here that long."

"You are a servant of the fountain," Daphne said. "Of the priestess. Of Aphrodite. Of love. Yet your body tells another story, the old wounds of a warrior."

Nikias chuckled, "And here I thought you only had eyes for my phallus." Daphne blushed and lowered her eyes. Nikias lifted her chin gently, looking into her big hazel eyes. "Don't feel shame. There is no cause. Hell, it's probably the best part of this beat up old body of mine."

"You don't know how badly a body can be beaten," said Daphne sadly, thinking of Helen and Agi.

"I do," he replied with soft earnestness. "I was only joking. Making light to make you less self-conscious."

Daphne held his eye. "May I see it again?" she whispered, blushing even deeper through her olive complexion.

"Of course. Never have I received such a courteous request from such a lovely lady. Stand up, Daphne, before me."

Nikias stood a body length away and removed his cape, robe and tunic, watching her watch him. Her eyes explored the man slowly from head to toe. The dark brown hair shorn above the shoulders, the diagonal scar over his left brown eye, the bit of gray on the chin of his cropped black beard. Down the strength of a hairy torso to his nethers between muscled thighs. She noted the various scars and healed over spear wounds, wondering how he had ever survived. Her thoughts returned to the matter at hand.

"Where is it?" she asked.

"It only comes out when aroused. Just as with your rams and dogs. You must have seen that."

"Surely, but they are rams and dogs."

"Surely," he said with a chuckle. "Allow me to see you, and you shall surely see me."

Daphne nodded, blushing again. His face was calm yet solemn. She let her cape fall off her shoulders behind her. Then after a moment of hesitation, removing the gown from her left shoulder, the overlarge clothing slid freely down to her ankles. She stepped forward, clearing her feet of the white garment. Nikias took a single step back.

Daphne enjoyed the cool spring air on her bare body. It was her turn to watch him watch her. He began at the top. Her thick black hair braided tight away from her face running long down her back. Her head and face matched the girl's body, slender. The big hazel eyes with long lashes crested by a black brow were the dominant features. Centered by a thin straight nose flanked by high cheekbones. The lips were also slender over a small firm chin in keeping with the rest of the girl. His eyes drifted south. Daphne's breast and belly were taut, a hint of her ribcage on her sides. The skin lighter than her sun kissed face and arms. Her breasts had only a bit of softness around and under her pale areolas, which stood tall to his gaze. His eyes moved down to the bushy black thatch. Thick like her head on an otherwise hairless body. Daphne spread her stance a bit instinctively in response to his gaze, putting her hands to her hips. Her thighs were equally as pale as her belly and as smooth as her arms, gradually darkening below the knees. There was a hint of black hair just above her ankles and under her arms.

Nikias then took in her beauty holistically. She was fit and slender. Shoulder and hip aligned. Not overly skinny, a narrow waist accented her hips, yet hers was a body that had never experienced idleness or overfeeding. Throughout this process, Daphne had beheld the gradual waxing of his phallus, entranced, until he was fully stiff and exposed.

"I feel funny," Daphne said suddenly. "Like I did yesterday when Pan woke me up."

"Of course you do. I feel funny too. But we can't blame this on Pan."

"What should we do?"

"Now?" Nikias sighed. "Nothing. I am a servant of love, not lust."

"And you love Delia," said Daphne, crestfallen, as she turned and picked up her gown. Nikias appreciated the firm roundness of her bottom.

"Yes, I do indeed love Delia. But rest assured there is room in my heart for you as well. My sweet nymph Daphne. At least you don't run from me as your namesake did from Apollo."

"I am no nymph of the fountain," she said. "But a poor shepherd girl."

Nikias sighed again, as he put on his clothes. "Only time will tell." Daphne's dog suddenly awoke from his nap. Shook himself vigorously to standing and let out a snort. "Right on time, Hector," Nikias said to the animal. "Right on time."

***

They walked in silence for a while. At length they were near Daphne's home, walking through fields and woodlands she knew well.

"Can you talk about your time before? When you were a fighter, I mean."

"I was not a fighter, Daphne. I was a Spartan soldier. A sergeant. A citizen."

"Then you must know our Agi. He too was a Spartan warrior."

"Perhaps, although Sparta has a large army and Agi is a common name. Tell me about him."

"Oh, he's wonderful. Kind and gentle. Funny too."

"Doesn't sound like many Spartans I served with. Certainly none named Agi."

"But he's noble too. He suffered grievous wounds and torture at the hands of the Corinthians. That is how we found him. Our Helen, poor Helen was being…," she couldn't say it.

"I understand," Nikias interjected quietly.

"Agi came along and tried to save her. But he was alone against five. And still he engaged them, killing their leader. He was eventually worsted, of course. Helen almost died. And the torture and abuse they heaped on Agi was sorrowful to see."

"You saw it?"

"Lorae and I. We found them after the fight. The Corinthians were still there so we hid on the edge of the woods waiting for them to leave. They did horrible things to Agi for two days. They paid Helen no mind at all. We thought she was dead."

"That must have been horrible for you two," Nikias said. Daphne didn't reply, lost in the past. "But Helen didn't die," prompted Nikias, rousing her back to the present, "and Agi joined your household. You are glad to have a man around. It's safer."

"Yes, Helen recovered fully after a long time. In her body, that is. She still has waking sadness and nightmares from time to time. Agi, he couldn't recover. They did wicked things to him. Humiliating things. Then they took an eye, an ear, a hand, and they cut him deep right here," Daphne motioned with her hand across her own hamstring, "so he couldn't run again." Nikias remained quiet. "Still," Daphne continued, "such is his joyful nature that we all feel it, even Helen. And he has taught us much to defend ourselves. Like this." The girl suddenly hurled her spear with great force, embedding it into a tree fifty feet away.

"I thought you girls carried your spears like you knew how to use them. Like they were a part of you. No wonder those wolves never got any of your sheep," he looked over at Hector trailing alongside his mistress, "I had given you and your brother too much credit."

"Hector was very brave too," Daphne said, rubbing the dog's big head fondly as he approached upon hearing his name, "as was Helen's Ajax."

They crossed a final field, stepped through a trickle of a stream and entered a wood on a mild incline. Far enough into it that it couldn't be viewed from the field stood a humble yet well-built log cabin. A dog barked and Hector replied, bolting forward to the house. The door opened and a large dog, as like to its brethren as their mistresses were to each other, bounded out in greeting. Lorae was right behind, running to Daphne who met her half way in a deep embrace.

"Daphne! We've been so worried," Lorae was practically shouting in excitement. "Where's Helen?" suddenly fearful and now aware of Nikias.

"Helen is fine," Daphne assured her. "Be at ease. We have much to tell." A large tawny haired and bearded man loomed in the doorway. He had a spear in his one hand.

"Zeus be praised, you're both alive," he said leaning against the doorjamb. Then looking past the girls, "It's been a long time, Nikias," Agi said warily.

CHAPTER 49

BOBBY

Bobby felt his ears pop as he made another turn on the mountain road. He and Lucky were working their way up a road that, as best they could tell, went as high into the mountains as could be driven.

"Did your ears pop too?" Lucky asked

"For about the third time. But I'm a New York City boy, a flatlander. You live in a city as high as Denver. And Kargil that we just passed through was 3,000 feet higher than that. And we're still climbing." Bobby swallowed a few times trying to clear his ears. "I should have joined the navy."

"Whatever for?" Lucky asked.

"Ships stay at sea level."

"The navy has planes too. And submarines."

"Okay. Bad idea."

They'd been driving from Srinagar for over five hours in the direction of the Siachen glacier. It was in that region where Indian, Pakistani, and Chinese influence and lines of control blur the most. A left turn onto an unmarked road between Kargil and Leh had them climbing even higher. It soon changed from pavement to bouncy gravel. They drove on in silence through wooded uplands with the snow covered peaks of the Karakoram range of the Himalayas looming over the trees.

"Good thing we brought your rental and not my mini," Lucky said.

"It shouldn't be too much further," said Bobby. "Dalha said there is some kind of abandoned logging camp at the end of this road."

The road took another turn to the right and abruptly stopped another hundred yards further. Bobby drove to the dead end slowly, then stopped the car. There were two barnlike buildings at the end of the road with a few more sheds scattered around. Everything was coated white in crusty snow. They were both looking around for any sign of life, but no luck.

"You like her, don't you?" Lucky asked. "Dalha."

"Sure, don't you? You sent me to her," Bobby replied.

"I guess so. I don't really know her very well, but I figured she'd be a good person for you to start with. After all, if anything is going to wreak havoc on this region it is a coordinated independence movement in all three occupying countries."

"Are you jealous?" asked Bobby.

"Of course not," Lucky replied. "No. I'm poly, remember? I can only feel happy for you if you find love in another. That said, I can feel concerned if you get into a destructive or dangerous relationship."

"And you think Dalha is destructive and dangerous?"

"Oh, I don't know, Bobby." Lucky sighed. "I think you are investigating dynamite. Dalha is involved. That doesn't mean she's bad, but, well I just feel that the closer you get to this story the more dangerous it will get." They both got out of the car, closing up their coats against the cold.

"Dalha was a wealth of information, that's all I can say," Bobby said. "This border is like swiss cheese. In all directions."

"Feels a bit lonely up here, Bobby. We won't want to stay here long."

"Dalha said this was the pickup point for guides across the border. But now I'm wondering if I have the directions right. I had to swear not to write them now, but as long as this trip was, it only had a few turns."

"You're a good guy, Bobby."

"Why?"

"Because you keep your word. You didn't have to after you left her. She'd never know."

"Before you think too highly of me, remember that a reporter can never burn his sources or soon the word gets around and nobody will talk to him."

"Still, I trust you with my secrets," Lucky said, hugging him, then kissing his cheek. Bobby smiled at her, but then was distracted by movement to his left.

"Here we go," Bobby said. A man had stepped out of the woods and was walking toward them. "This may be Dalha's father. She said he might be the guide today." Bobby and Lucky met him halfway.

"Hello, we appear to be lost," Bobby said, opening the coded dialogue for wannabe border crossers. The man just stared at him, then looked at Lucky.

"Hindi. You spoke in Hindi." Lucky repeated the line in Kashmiri.

"Where do you wish to go?" the man asked in the same language.

"To oblivion and beyond for some milk," Bobby said softly to Lucky. She repeated in Kashmiri. The man smiled and patted their shoulders in greeting.

"Hello," another voice said from over their shoulder, "now where do you really want to go?" They wheeled around startled, then did a double take back to the first man. They were identical. Face, build, hair, even their dark clothing.

"Dalha sent us," Bobby said. Both men picked up Dahla's name and repeated it. Lucky took the lead in Kashmiri.

"Yes, Dahla sent us but we were hoping to meet her father," Lucky explained.

"And so you have," the first man said. "two of us, anyway."

"Wait, what?" Lucky asked and then it dawned on her and she laughed at her own stupidity.

"What's going on?" Bobby asked her.

"These men are Dalha's dads." She told Bobby, enjoying his confusion. "It's called fraternal polyandry, not very common these days, but still practiced by some here in Ladakh. Come to think of it, maybe I should move here."

***

"This is a bad idea, Bobby," Lucky said earnestly on the drive back to Srinagar.

"I can't tell this story from only one perspective," Bobby explained. "I've got to have all three."

"Think Bobby. If the mountains don't kill you, the Pakistanis surely will. The Chinese? We'll never know. You'll just disappear to rot in some cell after they have sucked every ounce of essence out of your soul."

"This is my job, Lucky. Why I was sent."

"You think you'll blend in? You'll stand out like a sore thumb, just as you did at the train station. You won't fool anybody. And nobody will speak Hindi for heaven's sake."

"I have a bit of Urdu as well."

"Urdu. God, you are so not ready for this."

"I'll hire one of these guides."

"You can't even talk to them without me."

"Well, you're not going, Lucky. It's too risky."

"You're damned right I'm not going!" she shouted. "And neither are you."

Bobby didn't say anything. But focused on the road back to Srinagar.

"Call your editor," Lucky insisted. "What's his name? Tom. Call Tom. See if he wants you to go."

"Of course he wouldn't let me go. But he doesn't want the call either. After the fact, he'll congratulate me."

"No he won't," Lucky said with force. "He'll never get the chance."

They drove on in silence for a while.

"I love you, Bobby," Lucky said.

"Love?"

"Yes, love. I didn't know I would until I saw you at the station, although I admit I was predisposed to for a number of reasons of my own, but I have opened my heart to you. Truly I have. Fully and forever. We are one you and I, now and forever."

"This is wild talk, Lucky. After this assignment I go back to the States for my next assignment. You know that."

"If you get a chance to go back to the States. Just go back now. Tell your editor that it's too dangerous. Or that you were overwhelmed. Not ready for such an assignment. Just go home. And you never need to see me again either."

"Good lord, Lucky. Listen to yourself. You just said we were one forever. Whatever that means. Now you never want to see me again."

"To keep you safe, yes."

"You're not making any sense, Lucky. I mean I know you're scared but this is crazy talk."

"Listen, Bobby. You have my unconditional love forever. We don't need to live together. Come and go as you please, when you want me or need me I will be here for you. Call, and I will come to you as soon as I can. Anywhere in the world."

"But you can't commit to me forever just for when I happen to breeze through Kashmir. Or call you from Wyoming, Puerto Rico, or some other place."

"Of course not. Don't be silly. I won't be saving myself for you. Or yearning for your call. I'm poly, remember? I hope there are many loves in my future."

"If you can ever come out of the closet," Bobby said.

"Well, there's that problem, I grant you."

"Then I don't get it. I might be falling in love with you, but I honestly don't know if I can ever return this unconditional forever parttime love that you talk about. Love isn't something to be turned on and off like a spigot."

"Oh, you can turn it on like a spigot once you learn how. You just can't ever turn it off again. Love is an ability. And like all abilities, love takes practice. And I'm not talking about sex, I am talking about spiritual oneness, which we have. We both have it. It's just that I am the only one of us who is aware of it yet."

"Is this part of Buddhism?" Bobby asked. " You don't sound very Sikh."

"Buddhist? Why do you think that?"

"Maybe because you have baby Buddhas laying around your houseboat."

"Of course," Lucky said. "Like you, I was raised Sikh. My parents are very traditional. But I have left most of that behind me," Lucky continued, "Buddhist? Not really that either, but much of that faith I find compatible."

"All I can say Lucky, is that your idea of love is over my head."

"For the present it is," Lucky said. "But I can teach you. But only if you live long enough. So let's put this crazy idea of yours on hold for a couple of weeks while I teach you the mysteries. What do you say?"

***

Two days later Bobby was again driving up the mountain road to Oblivion for some milk. Dalha was at his side, her face inscrutable as she approached her home country. Tucked in the back seat wedged between mountains of hiking and camp gear was a very unhappy Lucky. They finally pulled up at the end of the road. It had been a silent drive. Everything had been said before they left. With Dalha as his guide and companion, Bobby would at least be accepted by the locals. He just had to stay hidden from the authorities.

As before, Dalha's dads appeared out of nowhere. The family greeting was understated to say the least. All were ready to move without any ceremony. Bobby looked at Lucky who threw herself into his arms, giving him a long kiss.

"To remember me by?" Bobby asked when they pulled up for air. She just nodded Indian style with tears in her eyes. Lucky then gave a hard look to Dalha. Unspoken orders. The taller girl replied with a slight bow. The two men set out. Dalha followed. With one last look and a small hand wave, Bobby was off, leaving an unhappy Lucky alone amidst a desolate landscape. Pulling her collar tighter against the wind, she watched the place where they had disappeared into the woods, hoping for a surprise return. Then sadly she returned to the car.

CHAPTER 50

NIKIAS

"I had long assumed that you and the rest of the platoon died that day defending the pass," Agi opened. The two men were finally alone sitting on a log in the dark not far from the cabin.

"How is it that you are not still a soldier of Sparta?" Nikias asked.

"Look at me, Nikias. I'm a cripple."

"I mean, how came you to be here?"

"What do you remember of that day?" Agi asked.

"We sent you back down the road for reinforcements. You never came back. The Corinthians attacked. We fought. I fell. There isn't much more I can tell of the battle itself."

"We came back, Nikias. We came back. You must have already fallen, but there was still a small remnant fighting when we reached the pass." Agi paused for a moment, thinking back. "It was hopeless. Two companies supporting a collapsing platoon against thousands. The rampart had already been overrun, but you know Spartan officers, we charged in anyway. Javelins were raining down on us. Like you, that's all I remember of the battle."

"So you did come back. A relief column came. Somebody did try. That's nice to know." Nikias thought for a bit before continuing, "You know it isn't easy to stand and fight when hopelessly outnumbered."

"Easier than running I guess."

"Was it?"

"I came back, Nikias. Sure, I didn't want to. Who would? But I did. We saw it was hopeless when we got to the pass. And still we came on."

"I hear you, Agi. I don't judge anyone anymore. What's the point?" Agi said nothing.

"These girls think the world of you, Agi. How long has it been? Six years? You can't fake that. You're the real deal."

"I…I knew you saw through me, Nikias. The girls don't know what I was."

"Well, the way I see it, doesn't matter what you were, just what you are."

"And you, a servant of Aphrodite." Agi grunted a laugh. "An odd end for a Spartan."

"You'll see why tomorrow, my friend."

"Am I? Your friend?" asked Agi.

Nikias considered the question. "Agi, I wouldn't go back to Sparta for a brick of gold. I love my life. And I can tell you love yours too. But, it is nice to have someone around who knows what it is to have been a Spartan soldier." He threw his arm over Agi's shoulder. "Doesn't matter how good a soldier we were. It is something just to have been one."

"We've sure tasted the same dust," Agi agreed.

"Ooh, Rah."

***

The next day, Nikias led the two sisters and Agi back to the fountain, arriving late afternoon. Agi limped in painfully after the long journey. They had set out early that morning knowing it would be slow going for him. The Arcadian mountains are tough terrain for a disabled person. Now sitting and listening to the chatter around the campfire with everyone, Nikias reflected on how Daphne and Lorae had fussed over him incessantly, which Agi accepted with good humor and humble gratitude. How an enthusiastic Helen had flown into his laughing embrace upon arrival. Definitely not the Agi he had known in the army. When they had reached particularly steep inclines or declines during their long day of travel, Nikias had lent his strength to help Agi out as well, but for the most part he wasn't needed. The two little sisters knew just how to support the big man and he knew just how much they were capable of. Everything he could do himself, he did. No boasting, no slacking. A new Agi.

Now Nikias watched in astonishment mixed with admiration as Delia talked with Agi and the three sisters. They were eagerly pouring out everything about their lives together seemingly without prompting, like children excitedly recounting their adventures to their mother at the end of the day. Interrupting, adding, arguing, but always laughing. This showed a new side to his lady. The girls and Agi were somehow just drawn to her. As was he. To Nikias, she was always a perfect blend of passive contentment and erotic passion. Two sides of love. The five of them suddenly erupted together in laughter, drawing Nikias out of his reverie.

"Well," Delia said when all had finally subsided. She rose. "Welcome my new friends to the fountain of Aphrodite. This is a joyful meeting at a joyous place, a loving place, and a place of safety. We are all under the loving protection of our goddess. Tomorrow we will perform a healing ritual for our Helen. We have prepared, she and I. Now for Helen's beloved. Daphne, stand before me."

The girl did as she was told. Delia placed her hands on Daphne's shoulders and looked serenely down into Daphne's eyes who stared back wide-eyed, intently, then suddenly blushed and turned away. Delia gently stopped her, held her eyes again with a loving smile, then kissed her forehead before sending her back to her seat.

"Lorae, stand before me." The youngest sister gazed up openly at Delia. The two women melded eye to eye for a long silence as all watched. Finally, Delia gave her a nod and a grin, releasing the girl from her gaze.

"Agi, stand before me." The big man stumbled as he stood, stiff from the long journey. He waved off the three girls who leapt to their feet in support. Agi caught himself and squared off with the priestess, nose to nose with the tall lady. They stared openly into each other for a long time. Finally, Agi's head dropped in seeming sorrow. Delia kissed his hair as she embraced him for a long time. Agi returned to his seat.

"You have all committed, my friends. Tomorrow afternoon we will perform the healing ritual. For tonight, sleep in peace, and sleep late. You must all be strong for the trial before you."

CHAPTER 51

COMING BACK

"Stop the car!" Tina shouted. "Pull over, please!" The car skidded through rock and dust as Pally swerved off the road and broke. Tina had the door open before they had completely stopped. She ran a few yards then stopped. Looking southwest. Pally spilled out after her.

"Tina, what? Are you okay?" Tina turned back to the rocky summit that overlooked the road. "Here. Here. I know it. Feel it in my bones like never before."

"What? Tell me."

"Oh, Pally. They were too many. Too many. We didn't stand a chance."

"Too many? Who"

"So many. The Corinthians, Pally. I can practically see them marching up the road we just drove over. Only there was no pavement. Dust. Dust in my nose from a thousand footsteps carried on the wind." Tina fell to her knees, then hands by the side of the road, weeping. A car slowly topped the summit, continuing down toward the distant plains to the south.

"Tina, you're scaring me." Pally squatted beside her, hugging Tina and pressing her cheek on Tina's back, sweaty in the sun. She felt ribs under her hands and the start of soft flesh on the back of her thumb. Pally rose as she felt Tina straighten, then rise. Pally took her hand. Tina looked down at it, then released it.

"It didn't last long. A bitter fight, but brief. We stood no chance."

"Did you, did you die here, Tina?"

"I fell for sure. But no, I don't think so. We need to go that way," she said, pointing down a slope to the right of the road. "It's somewhere down there."

"What?" Pally asked. Tina didn't answer, just started walking.

***

Ajita pulled over as soon as she was out of sight of the other car. She waited, looking in her rearview mirror. Nothing. She got out and fetched the lunch basket Stavros had given her. Feta, bread, olives, and an orange. Plus a small bottle of Metaxa. Ajita couldn't help but smile. The Greek brandy really did get the taste out of her mouth, just as Stavros had promised.

Stavros. The man was clearly smitten. Here he had bartered food and a roof for sex, then had courted her at the same time. Ajita didn't mind. The airport had been a shock, but three days of physical contact with Stavros, hours each day, had gotten somehow comfortable. Even intimate. The first real intimacy of any kind she had known since Rohit had died and the first physical intimacy ever. Ajita enjoyed her lunch on the side of the road, and the peace of solitude, something she'd known little of in her city life. Solitude wasn't bad if you weren't really alone.

Still nothing in the rear view mirror. Another car drove by, but it wasn't them. Ajita slowly reversed back up the side of the road until the other car was in sight. She stopped and watched. No movement. She got out, looking around. Nothing on either side of the road. Then she caught the movement out of the side of her eye to the left. Two women walking downhill into the trees and brush.

***

Pally and Tina came across a stone house at the bottom of the hill a couple of miles from the road, skirting wide of it they came into a grove of citrus trees, lemons and limes. The scent was all about them as they wandered through in wonder. A goat bleated somewhere nearby. Tina kept looking back at the house.

"I was here too, I know it."

"Same as on the road?"

"No," Tina shook her head. "A completely different feel. These were good times." She looked back at the house again. She could faintly hear music on the air from the house. They continued slowly through the grove still slightly downhill to the far side of the meadow. Tina took Pally's hand in hers, smiling.

"I lived and loved here, Pally. Had a good life here." Pally squeezed her hand.

They strolled on in silence. Tina was suddenly drawn to her left. There was a large low stone at the far end of the grove. Tina moved toward it, she released Pally's hand as she rested her hands on the stone.

"*Zeus no*," she whispered in Greek.

Tina draped herself across the stone, then rolled on her back, moaning. Pally couldn't tell if she was in agony or ecstasy. Like at the hospital that first day when Tina had been strapped down. Pally glanced back in the direction of the house. No sign of movement. Tina spread her legs, knees up, still groaning and murmuring words Pally couldn't understand. With one last look over her shoulder, Pally gently and slowly slid Tina's shorts and panties off, feeling her own anticipation build, watching Tina's face for a sign to stop. But Tina appeared oblivious, eyes closed, her hands caressing herself. Pally gasped as she gazed down between those pale thighs, what a lovely sight. Tina had already blossomed. Pally rested her hands on Tina's outspread knees, spellbound. Her heart was pounding as she let her hands slowly inch down the soft skin of Tina's inner thighs, still watching Tina's face for awareness. Her fingers touched dark blonde pubic hair. Pally stopped, hardly daring to breath. Aroused adrenaline rushed through her. Pally leaned closer in. Still watching Tina's face, Pally touched Tina's open sex, but held her fingers still. A jolt went through her own sex as moisture from Tina's juices was on Pally's fingertips. Tina moaned with a slight pelvic thrust. Pally lost control as she emitted a slow purr herself. She dipped her fingers into Tina's well, smearing both openings and the blonde peachfuzzed stretch in between. She gazed down between Tina's thighs, the slender lines of her firm muscles, then Pally's tongue went to Tina's firm spot as her fingers dipped deeper, her thumb massaged Tina's other opening. Pally took her time, reveling in that dizzy feeling, then her other hand went down her own shorts. Tina moved to her rhythm.

Gradually, Tina's groans grew louder. And she was speaking clear words now, just a few at a time in cadence with her panting. Pally knew they weren't in English. Should she stop? She knew she couldn't. She removed her hand from her own pleasure to slip- slide it up Tina's belly. Taut. She was close. Pally's tongue quickened. Soon Tina convulsed. Ecstasy, not agony. Pally slid her thumb deep up Tina's anus. As deep as she could to accent her own orgasm erupting within her. Tina sat up suddenly with a roar. The thumb slipped out as her thighs locked tight around Pally's neck in a figure-four wrestling hold. Tina launched a right cross through Pally's left cheekbone then rolled to her left off the stone to the ground. Pally was forced to follow the roll, her neck and head more a part of Tina then Pally. Numbed by the punch and the crushing force of those thighs, once alluring now lethal, Pally was helpless. Her orgasm was still shivering through her all the while. Now sitting on the ground as she had been on the stone, Tina pulled back her open palm for the kill.

"*Die, Corinthian scum,*" she hissed in Greek. Pally could only stare at that still lovely face full of hate. The intense baby blue eyes of the American locked onto the Indian's bewildered big browns. Pally's eyes were practically bulging from her head from the pressure on her neck, but she couldn't open her mouth to speak. She tasted iron as the cut on her cheek trickled over her lip.

The club struck the back of Tina's head before she could deliver the death blow. Pally panted as the lock on her neck slackened. But she didn't move. Just lay there panting, shocked and exhausted. She and Tina lay prostrate on their sides now. Pally's nose resting in Tina's pubic hair, the scent of her sex, surreal. Then she fainted out of full consciousness.

***

Ajita was standing over the Indian police detective. She was starting to stir a bit, trying to get her head out from between the American's legs. Ajita took a fist full of shirt and pulled the Indian woman to a sitting position. Then she hit her on the back of the head with her tree branch as she had done to the American. Letting her drop, Ajita took a breath, still stunned herself by the strange scene she had witnessed, then joined. She looked down at her handy work. The two women didn't even twitch. She had never knocked a person out before, so didn't know how hard to hit. She had hit hard. Very hard. She checked pulses and was relieved to find that both were still alive.

CHAPTER 52

AGI

Agi was aware of a fierce pounding in his head. He tried to get his bearings, but when he opened his one good eye he still couldn't see. His hand went instinctively to his face. Or tried, but couldn't. His hands were bound behind his back. Frustrated, he struggled to free his hands, but still couldn't. Then it struck him like a lightning bolt from Zeus. He couldn't free his hands. He had two of them. He clasped his hands together behind his back. What miracle was this that he had his long lost hand returned? What bitter irony that it was bound. With all his strength he twisted and pulled on the chords that bound him. They started to give and loosen.

His blindfold was torn off. Agi blinked in the sunlight. Strange words were spoken. A woman's voice, but he didn't understand. And yet? His head pounded even harder as he closed his eyes against the brightness. His eyes! He looked down at the ground away from the sun and immediately saw the stone. That horrific altar where it had all happened. He had lived near it with his girls for all those years, but had always stayed away from that stone. Now it was right next to him. Compounding the pain already in his head, it was all flooding back, the fear, the helplessness, the humiliation, finally the mutilation. And worst of all, worse even than the pain, was the memory of ecstasy. They had all laughed every time he had spouted his seed, even as they raped him.

There was movement. He looked toward it dully, trying to sift through the pain, past and present. A dark woman stood there. Long limbed with long jet black hair. He knew her. Had seen her before somewhere. The Nubian spoke, but the sounds had no meaning to Agi. He suddenly remembered the chords binding his hands and with a wild pull his hands slipped apart. He saw the tree branch coming before his hands could rise to block the blow.

***

Ajita didn't know what to do. She had knocked the American out again, but this time her head was bleeding. She hadn't meant to have to hit her a second time, but she had just seen what she did to the policewoman. And her own lover too. Ajita remembered the episode in the hospital all too well. And Rohit's death. The big sister of the dead little brother started to sob. She looked at her stick. She could pound the life out of the unconscious blonde woman here and now. Looking down at her now, she saw a frailness in the limp figure. Saw age and maybe a sign of her own suffering. It just wasn't in her. Revenge, if it was to be revenge, couldn't be blind. She needed to talk to this woman. Confront her. Tell her the depth of her own loss. And the value of Rohit's life. Understand who and what she was before rendering a final verdict. The policewoman was stirring. She would know what to do with the American. Frustrated at being so close, Ajita fled into the woods at the edge of the meadow to again watch and wait.

CHAPTER 53

THE CHASE

The warm wet tongue across the stubble of his jowl brought a groan out of the man. Hercules licked his chops loudly and attempted once more to rouse his master with a lick on the ear. Homedes groaned again, struggling stiffly to sit up, still feeling the root that had slept against his spine. Hercules muzzled his head against his master's neck, Homedes scratched the hound under his chin.

"I'm awake, boy, I'm awake," he said hoarsely, rubbing the crust out of his eyes with his free hand.

He opened his eyes fully now to look around. There was a hint of dawn in the cold wet air. Everything was dripping, but at least it hadn't rained. One of his soldiers, Dicus, was stoking the embers back to life. Everyone was on the move, albeit slowly. Homedes roused himself to his feet. A soldier returning from the trees nodded in silence as he passed his leader. Homedes went a bit further to find his own tree. Every part of him ached. Regular exercise was one thing, but living on the march had a way of discovering new muscles to torment.

They had been four days marching in an attempt to pick up Aristol's trail. Nothing so far. Homedes knelt at the trickle of a stream to drink and wash away the night. He felt his stubble with dissatisfaction. No niceties on the trail. Back to his feet he stretched his arms over his head, moving to work out the kinks. Yes, he could still campaign. He wasn't an old man yet. He broke his fast on a bit of biscuit and hot tea. They'd provisioned at the last likely village they were going to find yesterday morning. Just carrying what they could on their backs and relying on the mountains for water, Homedes reckoned they had a meager week of supplies with them. That meant there and back again.

They had camped on the edge of a laurel grove mixed with ash running uphill from the stream. Looking around in the growing light, the place had a pleasant look to it. And feel. Homedes had only been in this area for war, but Arcadia was different somehow. In an unsettling, but not bad, way. There was no government here. That was it. Still a no man's land between the powers,

Arcadia belonged to Pan more than anyone else. And the few folk who lived here were rustics, little better than the animals they husbanded, but they were fiercely independent. Not just from the city-states, but from each other. There was no order in the Arcadian mountains. Unsettling indeed.

The soldier, Dicus, was feeling the same way. Unsettled. He too had only been in Arcadia for war. He had deserted into this area after a battle with the Spartans and after a few years of wandering had lucked into this gig with Homedes after he had fired one of his soldiers for abusing a slave. Dicus never abused a slave. But he remembered all too well, and with guilty pleasure, a past time when he hadn't been so gentle. In Arcadia. But that was years ago.

Homedes was only guessing that Aristol would come this way. It was a long shot, but he had to try. The runaways could have gone north up the lake, then punched their way through the mountain range down to the Gulf of Corinth and the sea. The world opened up by way of the sea. But Aristol was no sailor. Homedes didn't think he would take that path. On top of that, once out of the mountains the coast is quite populated. No place for runaway slaves. Still, it was the easiest path of escape. Homedes had a squad of soldiers pursuing that very course.

They wouldn't have gone east, deeper into the heart of Corinthian territory and the most populated parts as well. West to Achaea? Possible, but it was no better than Corinthia. Relations were pretty good between the two right now. In fact, the Peloponnese had been fairly peaceful the last few years since Sparta took a licking in that sea battle off Pylos against a combined fleet of Corinth, Athens, and Achaea. That had settled the Spartans down a bit, who were always the ones stirring up trouble. No peaceful pastimes, that was their problem, Homedes had always thought. But the Spartans weren't navy creatures and had bit off more than they could chew on the Ionian Sea. Now there was only the occasional skirmish, pointless encounters resolving nothing, like the one that had taken his son so many years ago during the days of open war, Homedes thought bitterly. His son. Sons. He had to find the one he still had. Aristol.

No, his boy would head south. Homedes felt it in his bones. Not to return to Sparta, there was nothing for him there. But to lose himself in these Arcadian mountains. Forever. It would be the perfect place for his band of misfits. Rugged, empty, owned by no power. Except the gods themselves.

Glancing deeper into the laurel grove at the edge of their camp, he felt a wholesome tingle run through him. He had allowed no living wood to be cut from its trees. Not that his men needed the order. The grove had a sacred feel to it. Homedes had felt that they could pass the night peacefully under its eaves, and so they had. He quietly thanked the gods and returned to the campfire. Now it was time to move on. Hoping that Hercules would pick up the scent. He'd give it three days. If no luck by then, they'd head home. His men deserved better than to follow a fool, so he wouldn't play one. Three days, no more.

***

The cold camp of his prey was a mere day's march deeper into the Arcadian mountains. The runaways had seen little sign of other people. More animal trails than anything else. They weren't really going anywhere further, but rather scouting around for a likely site to build their new home. The push to get away and free had slowed once they had reached their destination. Now while still on the move, they were focused as much on foraging for food than anything else. They had few tools with them, but fortunately, with the advent of spring, the land was generous. Still, belts were pulled tight and the pinch of hunger was ever present.

Aristol's Spartan survival training was keeping them alive, but not much more. He had found a likely branch of ash and was working it into a spear with the one tool they had taken from home, a knife. He had no means of fashioning a metal or even stone tip and Ife wouldn't permit a fire, even at night, to harden the wooden point. There had been little argument. The others had each found a long stout walking stick from the occasional fallen branches scattered about. Having heard wolves howling last night, nobody wanted to be empty handed. On top of that, they all sensed that they had not seen the last of Homedes and the scent of wood smoke could carry some distance. Hiding from other people as they had skirted estates and villages, stealing food when the opportunity arose, had been slow going, but they had managed it.

Now they were into Arcadia, home, but Aristol knew that Homedes must have made up for lost time as they themselves had moved so slowly. The mountains were not a source of safety yet. They had to go deeper in, Aristol decided. He was their leader, but he had yet to come across any spot that seemed familiar. After all, he had entered Arcadia from the south by way of the main trail to the summit where he had fallen in battle six years ago. Aristol figured the trail pass summit was maybe a day east and a bit north of where they now were.

The nights had been cold indeed, but their shared body warmth had sufficed. Dani and Aria were already discussing plans of what they would need to build before the next winter, while Ife and Aristol focused on survival in the here and now. The morning sun hadn't cleared the nearest ridges, but they had daylight. Aristol saw Aria come out from behind a tree to rejoin the group. The last one.

"Time to move out. Start our day," Aristol said with as much encouragement as he could muster.

"It's a lovely land, Arcadia," Ife replied, looking around. "Thank you, Aristol for leading us here." She hugged him just as Aria arrived to join in. Ife's cheek to the thin blonde growth of his, Aria's head nuzzled between her bosom and his hard chest. Dani enveloped the girls from behind, his hands on Aristol's shoulders. Their eyes met.

"You've done it, my brother," Dani said softly. Aristol said nothing, but his eyes moistened in response. They held their group hug in silence. It had become a ritual at the start and end of each day. As if on cue, like a flock of birds changing course, they broke up and started up the next hill. The morning sun glanced over their left shoulders as they hiked the steep incline. Aria found the trace of a deer trail heading up so she followed it. The others fell in line.

CHAPTER 54

TINA

Tina rested on a rock at the summit of the next hilly range, feeling the sweat trickling. It had been a few hours since the episode in the meadow. Her head was hurting again.

"Let's stop here for a bit. Truth be told, I'm not young anymore." She looked down their back trail, but couldn't see a sign of anyone. Somebody had hit them, but neither of them knew who it could have been. Or why.

"We should have gone back to the car. I could use some more water," Pally said. "And my head still hurts."

"Mine too. I told you to go back, Pally. I don't want you getting hurt."

"I have an assignment, remember? I can't arrest you, but I can't leave you either. And we might be followed."

"I'm just an assignment again. I can't blame you."

"Hey, I love you. I'm the girl who asked you to marry her. Who is still waiting for an answer, by the way."

"Well, you have every right to withdraw your offer. I'm schizoid."

"You're not sick. You just have one body, two souls, and two minds."

"That sounds schizoid to me."

"Tina, if you ask me, your Spartan just needs to find some peace. And I will help him find it. But not right now. We're both injured. We should go back, rest up, and return in a couple of days."

"I hear you, youngling, but I can't. I mean, my head hurts too. My feet hurt. My knees? They're killing me. I haven't hiked like this for years. I'm feeling my age, Pally. But we're close. So close. And he is still with me like never before. I'm remembering things. Just bits and pieces, but some. Images more than memories really."

"Well, I could still use water."

"Me too. There is a creek at the bottom of this hill. There was a creek at the bottom of the last one and there's water at the bottom of this one. I know that."

"I hear you. And this is friendly terrain for survival, but wandering so deep into the wilderness without even a canteen goes against common sense, let alone my training."

"This isn't exactly wilderness, Pally. People live out here, few and far between I admit, but we have seen orchards, even a couple houses in the distance."

"So we're trespassing."

"Oh, come on. We're close, Pally. I feel it."

"I know. And I fear it," Pally paused before continuing, "I fear you. What you'll become when you get to where you are going." She was still standing apart from the rock Tina was perched on. Tina opened her arms to Pally.

"I'm so sorry, youngling. I never wanted to hurt you. I love you."
Pally relented, going into her embrace. She let out a deep sigh, trying to chase away the fear. She pulled back a bit to look at Tina.

"I know you would never hurt me, Tina. But him? We know what he can do. I've been trained to fight. Maybe I can defend myself against you, against him, if I am on my guard, but I doubt it. I'm scared, Tina. And it's tearing me up inside."

"I know, Pally and I don't blame you. But I've been thinking. Thinking of the events when he came: the bank, the hospital twice, and now here."

"Well?"

"So don't scare me, don't tie me down, and keep your thumb out of my ass."

Pally laughed in spite of herself. They were silent for a while. They took in the scenery of the next ridge about a mile away. A bird piped a tune nearby.

"Can we talk, Tina? I mean, I know you're dealing with a lot right now, we both are, but we have another situation here too. And I've been trying to summon the courage to talk about it."

"I know."

"I'm scared. You know that. But what I'm most scared of is that you'll say no. You haven't said yes, that's for sure."

"If I say yes, then you'll really need courage. But please Pally, I know it's hard. Let's get through this, whatever it is, first."

"I don't get it. If you love me…"

"And I don't get who loves you," Tina interrupted, "Me? Or him? Did Tina Marin suddenly turn lesbian at the ripe old age of 51? Or is my Spartan warrior simply being a man?"

"I've been a lesbian my entire life," Pally replied. Then she sighed. "God, I don't think I've ever even said that word out loud until right now."

"Neither have I, at least not applied to myself," Tina said.

"And in truth I haven't been. I've only wanted to be." Pally chuckled grimly. "A virgin until 32. How pathetic is that? Until you."

"Thank you for waiting, but that's another thing. An incredible burden. Am I to be your only love experience? That doesn't seem right to me."

"It does to me."

"Now Pally, now. But time marches on. And don't forget I am almost 20 years older, youngling."

"You're beautiful, Tina."

"What you call beauty will soon fade away. It's already started. I'm okay with that. But will you be five years from now? Should you be? I don't know."

"So I should find a good Catholic boy like my parents want, is that it?"

"Just follow your feelings, Pally. That's all any of us can do, I guess. Are they really just for me? Or am I just available?"

"I love you, Tina. Truly I do. Who else could I have this conversation with? This intimacy? But,"

"But what?"

"I'm still interested in men too. Well, not interested in, but attracted to. I mean, mostly girls. I guess that's why I've never pursued any of the boys my parents rolled at me. Why I became a cop maybe. To hide behind a career that discourages men."

"Shouldn't you at least try a man before settling for little old me for the rest of your life? They're not bad, let me tell you. I've had plenty."

"So that's it." Pally looked to the ground. "Huh." The breeze spoke through the trees, rustling the leaves, but the women were silent.

Finally Tina said, "Look, I don't know where it is coming from in me, but it appears we are both bisexual. At least right now. How can we be married, monogamous, when that goes against our very nature?"

"Bisexual. I'm bisexual," Pally repeated. Another chuckle. "I've never said that word out loud either."

"Well, it's a new idea to me too. A bit of a shock."

"You seem to take to it quick enough," Pally offered. Tina laughed.

"So I did and that is all me, Tina Marin. When I want something, I go for it. And I wanted you, I still do."

"Well, we're here all alone in the middle of nowhere," Pally suggested. "We haven't seen a soul in the last two hours."

Tina couldn't resist, headache or no. She slid her hands under Pally's T-shirt. Her belly was slick with sweat. So sexy. Tina flipped Pally's bra up and over, setting her free. She dove into Pally's ripe breasts, one in hand, one in mouth. Pally's hands went through Tina's hair as her own head went back and she arched.

***

Ajita watched their love making from not far away. Just like before. She had made her approach as they spoke. She laid her stick quietly to the ground. She wouldn't risk hitting them again. There had to be another way. So she waited. Wishing she could join them, as she watched, her hands went to her own breasts. Thinking of the hospital. Of Stavros. She was soon naked to the waist, enthralled, witnessing the two lovers. Her own sweat oiled nipples slid softly under her fingertips. They hardened, sending tingles down under. Ajita leaned back against a tree and widened her stance as her hands slid down to her belt buckle.

Her pants were half down as she slipped to her knees, Ajita wasn't hiding anymore. The women were laying on the rock a mere fifty feet away, both nude now, they were laying on their sides facing each other, kissing and caressing. Dreaming she was between them, Ajita slid one hand down her belly and the other down her back. Soaked with sweat, it was a wet finger that pressed gently into her rear. A moan escaped her lips as she closed her eyes. In sync at both ends, her thighs began to flex, melding to the two imaginary partners, one blonde, one brown. So good, so pure, her pleasure began to build, then peaked with a startled cry as she convulsed over and over again. Spent, Ajita's panting subsided to sighs, sitting back on her heels. She opened her eyes to see Tina and Pally standing before her. Pally had the stick in her hand.

"There's dried blood on this stick," Pally stated. Ajita said nothing, trying to adjust to the sudden situational change. "And it's no coincidence that I am meeting a fellow Indian here in Greece in the middle of nowhere." Still silence from Ajita.

"Let me try," Tina offered, "Why are you here? Why have you followed us?"

Ajita glared at her. "You really don't know, do you? You don't know who I am."

"Well, who are you?" Tina asked.

"We've met before. My name is Ajita Kaur. You killed my brother."

"Revenge," Pally said.

"No!" said Ajita quickly. "At least…I'm not sure." Her chin fell to her chest. "I don't know. I just don't know."

"Sit down and put your hands on your head," Pally ordered. "Tina, go through her bag." Tina looked hesitantly at Pally, saw her professional look, then did as ordered. Pally stood there studying the other Indian woman, tapping the thick stick onto her palm. This Ajita was slender, like Tina, Pally was thinking. Only younger, darker and fuller in the breasts. Much fuller. What would it be like to stroke them? Ever so gently. How would she react? Ajita was still undressed with her shorts around her ankles, her knees wide as she sat with those elegant ankles crossed. That black tangle between her thighs looked so inviting. Pally was suddenly aware that Tina was looking at her. She had some rope in her hand from Ajita's backpack.

"What are we going to do with her?" Tina asked.

"Well we can't turn her loose. We either turn back and take her to the local police, or take her with us."

"I can't turn back now," said Tina.

"And I can't leave you to go on alone," Pally replied.

"That's it then. Now we are three."

"Put your hands behind your back," Pally ordered Ajita, taking the rope from Tina. She handed the stick to Tina. "If she so much as twitches, you jam this stick right here. As hard as you can." Her finger touched lightly on Ajita's solar plexus. Ever so close. "Got that, Tina?" Tina nodded, gripping the stick in both hands. Pally bound Ajita's hands securely behind her back. Satisfied that Ajita was helpless, Pally relaxed. "Now up you go," she said, hoisting Ajita to her feet from behind under her arms. Hair and sweat on her fingers. She wiped them on her own bare belly.

"What a strange circumstance," Tina said. "Three naked women out in the middle of nowhere in the Greek mountains. None of us are from here. And none of us know where we are going. Or really why."

"I know why I'm here," Ajita said sullenly

"We know why you're here too," Pally said flatly.

"But why are you here?" blurted Ajita.

After a moment, Tina spoke. "Because I didn't kill your brother. We're trying to find out who did."

CHAPTER 55

THE SCENT

The full-throated barks of Hercules thundered back to them from ahead. Maybe he'd found something. Homedes and his squad of five soldiers picked up their pace to join the big hound. They had topped another ridge by midday. After rest and a meager meal, Homedes had decided to turn left to follow the ridgeline instead of downhill deeper into Arcadia. The hope was to cut Aristol's trail so Hercules could catch their scent. It was a risk, of course. Had the runaways crossed this ridge to the left of their position or to the right? Or perhaps not at all, but they had to try something. Now Hercules was excited, Homedes hopeful. His men were talking back and forth to each other as they approached the hound. A good sign, thought Homedes. Silent soldiers were not happy soldiers. Another single signal bark from the big dog for guidance. They found Hercules holding his place on the ridge, his tail wagging wildly.

"What is it, boy?" Homedes asked, rubbing the dog's head. He pulled out the pieces of garments that had belonged to each of the runaways and let the dog sniff them again, as he had done every morning. Hercules let out a bark and plunged down from the ridge to their right, his nose to the ground.

"He's found them," Dicus shouted. They all cheered, including Homedes.

"You are all doing great," Homedes said to his men. "After all our years of easy living, I'm proud of how you have all handled this journey. Now we'll find them, men. Then head straight home. I, for one, could use a bit of easy living again." His men laughed and guffawed in response.

"Once we find them, sir. If you order us to run all the way home you'll get no complaints from us," a corporal said, echoed with harrumphs from the men.

***

The runaways were working their way down the far side of yet another ridge. It was late in the day and Dani was on point now. He stopped suddenly and signaled a general halt. Aristol came up quietly behind him.

"I see a cabin ahead," Dani whispered. "See? Past that big tree to the left. We're already closer than I'd want to be. Sorry."

Aristol patted Dani's shoulder in response. "Let's work around it to the right. Slow and silent."

They all moved as quietly as possible keeping their eyes on the house. Ife tripped on a branch underfoot which cracked loud enough to wake the dead. Everyone froze except a few nearby crows who flapped into flight. No sign from the cabin. They moved on again.

"I don't think anybody lives there," Aria whispered in Aristol's ear. "There's no smoke from the chimney. And that little corral looks likely for sheep. But there's no livestock. Wouldn't they be home from feeding by now?"

"Maybe," Aristol replied, not well versed in caring for farm animals. "What do you suggest?"

"Let's go say hello," Aria replied.

"With our collars on?" asked Dani.

"Sure, why not?" said Aria. "We aren't in Corinthia anymore. Will they care? What would they do anyway? That cabin can't hold a large family. No bigger than the four of us."

"I agree," Ife chimed in.

"Alright all," Aristol said loudly. A bit louder than necessary. "Let's loop wide around the house then call our hellos to the front door." They all watched the cabin as they walked, but saw no sign of life. They crossed a small stream, more of a rivulet but enough water to support such a small homestead. They drank their fill and washed the walk of the day off.

"Might as well look presentable to meet our hosts," Aristol said, but he too was starting to think the place was abandoned.

It wasn't long before they were inside the empty cabin and had a fire going. They found a bit of bread and jam, some dried mutton, but also a fair portion of pine nuts and honey. After days of short rations, it seemed a feast

"I don't feel good about this," Ife said as she finished her last bite. "This place looks lived in and we just ate all their food."

"I agree," said Dani, "but we are in need. If they come back, we'll help them find more. Meanwhile, I'll bet that bed will hold all four of us. It looks mighty comfortable after all these nights on mother Earth."

"Let's see," Aria purred into Ife's ear, whose reluctance vanished. She swept Aria into her arms, kissing her deeply as she laid her gently under her. The boys joined from either side and were soon each suckling on a small Persian breast. Aria gasped in delight as Ife released her lips and slid down to position her face between Aria's quivering thighs.

"I love you guys," Aria panted.

The four of them slept past dawn for the first time since they had left the estate. And even then, they woke up to some morning loving. But eventually there was nothing to keep them there. It was not their home, and they all felt someone would return.

"We should stay another day, to see if they return," Dani said. "We should thank them."

Aria disagreed. "No, let's push on, but I feel we are close to home. This is good country."

"Just a few more hills deeper into the mountains," Ife said. "We'll find a place within a day's walk from here and then come back to repay them when we are settled."

"I wish I could leave a letter," said Aristol.

"Do you think they could read it?" Aria asked.

"You never know," Aristol replied. "Look at us. Between the four of us we can read three different languages."

"Then I'll scratch a 'thank you' in runic, Persian of course." Aria dug the brief symbols into the stone of the chimney with the knife. "It may not mean anything, but it might be a starting point of contact when we return."

"Let's at least gather a load of fresh wood for the fire before we go," Dani said.

After gathering the wood and cleaning up the place, they were soon out of the woods, across a small pasture and heading down to the bottom into a gully. It was a lovely cool spring morning, and while they made good time, they enjoyed the colorings of rebirth all about them. The soft green hues of new leaves against the backdrop of the grayer evergreens. And everywhere there were clusters of ground flowers, red, white and purple sprinkled across the landscape. Gentle breezes intermixed with shafts of sunlight through the foliage made for a comfortable stroll. At the bottom of the gully was a trickle of a stream. Just enough for drinking, washing, and splashing with loving laughter. The sense of escape ran away from arrival. This land was their home. And onward they climbed up to the next ridge, marveling at the ever increasing beauty about them.

"Demeter herself has blessed this land," Aristol whispered to himself and gave a silent prayer of thanks to the goddess.

And so they continued through the day, falling deeper in love the further they penetrated Arcadia. Down a hill, up another then down yet again until at the bottom they arrived at a fast flowing stream, cold, wide, and deep.

"We're here," said Ife, "this is it. Home." They all looked around, feeling her truth. Aristol let out a deep sigh, releasing a long carried burden.

Dani gave him a deep hug, kissing his lips, cheek and neck. "Brother," was all he said. Aristol broke into a broad smile.

"I remember that happy boy," Ife said, smiling. "Welcome home, soldier. A soldier no more."

Aria hugged the Spartan from behind. A wave of contentment was within them. Then they all stiffened as two thunderous barks reverberated through the woods.

"I know that bark," Aristol said, grim again.

"Hercules," said Ife.

CHAPTER 56

TINA

Looking back briefly, Tina could see that Pally was really struggling as the three of them half hiked, half slid down the hill. But Tina couldn't stop. Pally kept a hand through one of Ajita's arms to help their captive keep her balance on the uneven terrain. Tina was ahead of them, moving with an eagerness that in the back of her mind she knew was uncanny. She suddenly slipped on some loose ground, landed on her butt with a thud then slid a few feet to a halt.

"That's it," Pally ordered. "It's time for a rest break."

"What?" Tina was back on her feet facing up the hill at her two slower companions. "We can't stop now. We're almost there."

"We stop now," Pally said, planting herself onto a stone and pulling Ajita down next to her.

"Pally," Tina started.

"No Tina," Pally broke in. "I'm tired and my head hurts. Go ahead alone if you must, we'll catch you up."

Pacing a few steps Tina looked with yearning down the hill. What with the foliage, she couldn't see the bottom. Then she looked back up at Pally and Ajita. Pally's eyes were closed. Ajita watched her warily.

"Five minutes!" Tina shouted. "That's it!" But she couldn't sit herself. Her mind was racing and her body felt a rush running through her as well. In the back of her mind, she knew her body was aching, feet, knees, and shoulders. Images flashed through her mind, scents, feeling warm mist on her face, but the day was dry.

Tina took three slow deep breaths through her nose and out through her mouth, trying to compose herself. To get control. She looked back up at Pally and at the woman sitting next to her. Noticing them, she suddenly realized she was seeing them through a man's eyes. With what must be a man's appreciation for their features of face and frame. It was a frustrating self-awareness. Was she, Tina Marin, really attracted to Pally? Did she really love her? Tina thought through their recent intimate moments and realized she did. She remembered it all vividly. Maybe this man inside had led her to the water, but it was Tina who drank. And drank deeply. Making love to Pally, another woman, was a memory she would never erase. She didn't want to. And she wanted it more. Her body responded to her thoughts.

"Bisexual," she muttered to herself. "I really am bisexual," truly accepting it now in her own mind. Embracing it. She looked downhill toward her future. And her past. *Who was he? Who was I? Who am I now?* Her sudden, recent pull toward young Bobby leapt into her mind. Where had that come from? Bobby was always adorable, but this urge was new. She had wanted to take him. Imagining the young man right now in her mind's eye, his lean lines, his dark eyes, that wide white smile framed by black beard. Yes, she would take him right now if he magically appeared. Tina looked around, just in case. Another thought came to her. Was the man inside her gay? Is that where her change toward Bobby was coming from? No, he is bisexual too, Tina realized, remembering Pally. And Ajita. And the young mother on the beach the other day. *Well, alright then.* Tina arched her back, stretching her hands over her head, trying to get the kinks out. Then she bent over touching her toes, feeling the resistance in her calves, hamstrings, and glutes. She held the pose as the tension lessened somewhat. Then she stood upright with a deep breath.

"Time to move out," she called to the others. The two Indian women stood in response without a word. Tina looked back up at them with a smile. Pally sighed and gave a weak smile in return. Tina turned, marching down the hill. The rush ran through her again with each step. Soon.

CHAPTER 57

HELEN

Delia called them all to the base of the fountain stone. It towered more than twice her height above her with the perpetual plume bubbling even higher up and over into the pool. She bowed to the fountain then turned her back to the stone to face the gathering. The eternal rush of water pervaded the place. Delia beckoned with her arms. The others walked through warm mist as they approached the priestess. Before Delia, stood a wide shallow stone basin resting on an unadorned stone pedestal, waist high.

"For this ritual we must all remove our masks," Delia spoke in her strong clear voice, "that which hides our shame from others. And from ourselves."

Delia slipped her gown off her shoulder, let it slide to her ankles and stepped out, now clad only in a slender silver necklace with a pearl upon it on her breast. The others followed suit, disrobing in various levels of discomfort. Agi worried that they noted his lack of balls and hoped his crotch hair and penis, which had been spared, hid his shame. *"Let him keep it," he had laughed, "it will never stand again anyway. An ever limp reminder."* And so it was.

Delia took a large urn and stepped down into the water wading out to where the fountain's water pounded down into the pool. Standing in water up to her shoulders, she took a moment to embrace the fountain's flow on her head, neck and back. She dipped her head under the surface so her streaming white mane fell slick down her bare back as she rose out of the water, just like Aphrodite herself in the dawn of time. Then holding the urn high, Delia filled the urn with splashing fountain water. She returned to the stone basin and placed the urn in it.

"We have all removed our physical masks, but there can be masks covering the heart and mind as well. This ritual of our goddess Aphrodite will return the love of Helen by removing her masks," Delia said to the group, but her eyes rested for a moment on Agi. He lowered his head. "We all know Helen to be a person of love," Delia continued. "She loves her family. Truly, but not fully. Not to the infinite extent of which she is capable. Because my friends, Helen does not love herself. One can never truly love others without first loving within. There is fear within her, blocking her love. She hides herself in shame, that part of her she won't accept, won't share, and will not love. Helen must take off that mask, and fully share herself with those she loves."

Delia took Helen by the hand and led her to the stone basin. Standing behind the smaller woman, Delia unbraided her long hair, then stood back against the fountain stone. Helen emptied the urn slowly into the basin, then took a step back. A light steam rose off the water in the basin. Delia came forward and leaned over the basin, three times she took in the steam and breathed upon the water. The steam subsided and the water in the basin stilled. All were silent within the group as the fountain continued its eternal roar, mingling with the softer sound of the waterfall a bit further away. The warm mist permeated them. Delia nodded to Helen, who stepped up to the basin and bent over the basin to look upon it.

"Look into the mirror of the fountain, Helen. See your image and speak."

"I see the scar above my eye from when I fell running from a wolf."

"Speak louder Helen," Delia called, "So our goddess Aphrodite will notice you over the roar of her fountain."

With an effort, Helen's usually soft voice sailed over the water's sound. She repeated her first words, then, "I see my face, my thin lips and small mouth. And my bushy brow, my yellow skin."

"Lean further over the mirror, Helen," Delia commanded.

"I see my bony breast."

"Others don't see you as you see yourself. Go back to a time when men looked upon you differently. Tell us," Delia commanded. Helen choked as she first tried to speak.

"I'm scared. He tells me not to fight him, so I don't."

"Louder Helen!"

"He tells me not to fight, so I don't!"

"What else?"

"He, he puts his mouth to my breasts."

"How do you feel, Helen?" Delia asked. Muffled sobs erupted from the petite woman.

"How does it feel, Helen?" Delia pushed.

"Help me, it feels so good! I feel worshiped, like a goddess," Helen wailed. "I don't want him to stop!" The girl was heaving and sobbing openly now. The others leaned toward her in support, but a hard look from Delia kept them in place. Only Nikias remained impassive, riveted on his priestess, not Helen.

"What's happening now, Helen?"

"He's sliding slowly inside me. Gentle, as he promised. It hurts a bit, but fits. Like I am splitting in two to become one. I am filled with warmth inside. Weight is on my belly and thighs. But not a burden, It's part of me. I am made for it. I don't understand! I know it's wrong!" tears were streaming down her cheeks now. "I don't want us to ever stop!"

"Then what is your fear, Helen?"

"I should fight him! My mother always told me to run. My father always said, if running fails, fight. Always fight! At first I am afraid, but then he touches me and there is more than fear. More powerful than fear. Why am I not fighting as father said?"

"Answer your own question, Helen," Delia persisted. "Why are you not fighting him?"

"I don't fight because I don't want him to stop. I hear the others laughing as they hold me down. They don't know that I would embrace him with my limbs, my being if they only let me go. I am foul. So foul. My family. My sisters." Helen sobbed uncontrollably. Unable to speak further.

"What else, Helen?" persists Delia. "Speak," she commands, "What is happening now?"

"Crushing pain in my chest," Helen gasped. "I can't breathe. And, and he is gone. There's noise all around me, but I am so alone. Dying. But I can't go to my parents like this. Can't face them. Can't die. The fullness that was within me, my oneness, is gone forever. Can't live."

Delia took her gently by the shoulders. "Helen, come back to the now," said the priestess. "How do you feel now?" Helen sobbed, unable to go on. The others waited in silence.

"I…I wish Agi hadn't come when he did. I wish I was still with Him. I wish I was his woman. By the gods, I need to die!" She suddenly sprang away, racing for the pool, but Delia was ready, tackling her to the ground before she reached the water. The rest of them followed.

"Make a circle around our beloved Helen," Delia commanded. "Don't hold her, but don't let her out."

"Let me go, let me die! Or better yet, kill me!" Helen cried, panting, pivoting inside the circle like the trapped animal she was.

"Kill me!" she screamed. "Agi, you should have killed me that day, not him! Daphne, Lorae, you should never have healed me. You should have left me to rot in the dirt. I am dirt." She charged at her two sisters, who fell back before her wrath, but the others restrained her."

"Hold her firmly!" Delia ordered. "Helen, let it out, girl. Let it out!"

Helen thrashed and screamed. She rained obscenities and curses upon everyone, such words as Agi and her sisters had never heard from her lips, but mostly she cursed herself.

"Keep fighting, Helen," Delia encouraged. "You're not done yet. Not free. Fight harder. For your father!"

Helen strained to free herself from the many arms that held her, snarling, thrashing and flailing. For a moment her left arm slithered free and she smashed her fist into Agi's face. He just hugged her, tears in his eyes. It was Daphne that grabbed her arm to stop a second blow.

"We see you, we hear you, we know you, we love you," Delia began the chant. The others took it up as Helen struggled on. She let out a high pitched, bloodcurdling screech that went on forever.

"We see you, we hear you, we know you, we love you."

And so it went on. Only feral noises now came from the slavering mouth of the captive girl, no words. Spittal and snot flew. Snakelike, Helen writhed, twisted, and turned, grunting and panting to exhaustion. The others lessened their grips sensing she was done, then she lashed out again. Nikias caught a kick inside his thigh. That was close!

"We see you, we hear you, we know you, we love you."

Eventually Helen subsided to soft sobs, utterly spent. With a silent command from Delia, they released her to lay on the grass, crying it out. When her crying settled, Delia raised Helen up to her feet. Helen's legs were shaky. With a nod to Daphne and Lorae, Delia stepped back and the sisters hugged Helen.

"Oh Helen," said Daphne, "father didn't mean to hurt you, just wanted to protect you, but he would never judge you. And we are so sorry you have carried this burden alone for so long. We love you all the more now that we know."

"Silly girl," Lorae said through her own tears, "to think that I could ever be anything but proud of my big sister."

"Big sister, eh?" Helen laughed out a sob. "You're taller, remember?" And the three of them laughed through their tears together in their group hug. Agi held back, looking upon the girls with longing. Delia caught his eye for a moment. Your time will come, the pale eyes of the priestess said.

"Agi," Helen called, and their circle opened to let him in.

CHAPTER 58

MILLER AND KHERA

Special agent Dorothy Miller of the FBI drummed her fingers on the steering wheel. She saw Khera approaching on foot. She didn't like to be kept waiting.

Khera opened the passenger side door and got in without ceremony. "What is so urgent? And why not just a phone call? Don't you trust our security?"

"No, I don't. And as for the urgency," Miller began.

"I'm not at your beck and call you know," Khera interrupted. "This is my country. I don't work for you."

Miller took a deep breath to restrain from throttling the man then and there. "The urgency is for your country's security, not mine. So when I am doing you a favor I expect at least some civility."

Khera flushed, but his voice was measured. "You have my attention," he said.

"Bobby Singh, Marin's replacement, has been snooping around Kashmir."

"I know that. What of it?"

"He has been reporting to me daily," Miller said. "I don't think he has been telling me everything, but he has made contact with two women pertaining to the independent Kashmir movement."

That raised Khera's eyebrows. "Names."

"We'll get to that in a moment. Bobby has gone dark. You need to find him. As you said, this is your country. I can't investigate here."

"I'm on it," Khera said. "But just remember I don't work for you."

"Of course not, but I'm getting the feeling that Bobby may have stumbled across the trail of your mystery woman."

"You think she is one of the women he is meeting?" Khera asked.

"I don't know but you had better look into it. If she is, that kid might be in real trouble."

"That kid might be dead," Khera said. "Like I said, I'm on it."

"Thank you. Keep me posted," Miller said.

"You just come clean with everything you have. Everything. Now let's start with the names of these women," Khera ordered.

***

Miller was still in a foul mood from her interview with "that asshole" Khera when she hit the gym at the American Embassy school. It was late in the day, the school was long closed, so there were only a few embassy staff on the floor when she arrived. A few servicemen, enlisted kids most likely, were shooting around on the basketball court. But somebody was already on the big bag in the corner. That was the workout she wanted, beating up that bag, pretending it was Khera. She was about to work on a rowing machine until the bag was available when an errant basketball rolled her way. A young man expected her to toss it to him, but instead Miller dribbled in then pulled up for a 25 footer. Swish!

"Would you care to join us?" one of the young crewcuts asked. Probably a marine. "We could use a fourth for two on two."

"Sure," Miller said, "why not."

Without further ado, Miller found herself squaring off against a redheaded kid who looked like he could still be in school here. Her partner took the check, Miller cut across the paint taking a bounce pass then popped a fadeaway 12 foot jumper. Swish! The redhead flushed as the other two hooted. He was paying more attention now, covering her closely. Miller took a pass, couldn't break free, passed it off. Her partner took a jumper that rolled off the rim. The redhead beat her to the rebound. He was a bit taller and longer than she was. And quick on his feet.

After a few passes he got the ball back at the point, faked right and drove left. Miller was all over him but he just managed to beat her to the rim for a layup. Miller had his full attention now too. The game was on.

The intensity between Miller and the redhead kid was obvious so the other two players were feeding them, and weren't shy in their commentary either. Clearly the redheaded serviceman didn't want to get beat by a woman. And he didn't. Every time he drove to the hoop he was just that little bit faster. Even when she saw it coming. He wasn't even trying to fake her out anymore. Miller was all over him pushing with her body, in the air with him as he released his shot, the tips of her fingers just an inch from touching the ball, but it careened cleanly off the backboard into the net again and again.

It was finally game point and Miller was determined to stop him. She gave it all she got, fouling him in the process. The redhead kid went to the floor hard, but the ball went through the hoop nonetheless.

Miller gave him a hand to his feet. "Good game," she told him, then a nod to the other two, "Gentlemen." With that she walked over to the now vacant big punching bag in the corner.

"Yo Liam, shoot the ball or give it up."

In response, the young redheaded USAF airman turned his eyes and mind from the big black woman he had just been battling. And beaten. A few minutes later they were still shooting around.

"Check it out," a marine said, nodding to the corner. Miller was pummeling the bag with a relentless series of punches, knees, and kicks. "I'm guessing that punching bag has red hair."

"You beat her on the court, Liam but don't get into the ring with that lady."

"I'd never hit a girl anyway," Liam said as he watched her work on that bag.

"Bro, you'd never get a chance to hit her. The only thing you'd hit is the deck, with your face."

"You work security," Liam said, "who is she?"

"She's big brass. FBI Special Agent in Charge, Dorothy Miller. And you do not want to get on her bad side."

"Too late for that!"

***

Later that night, settled in his bunk, Liam was reliving the game covering the woman. She was strong. He had been all over her on defense. Her sweaty skin rubbing against his. She hadn't dressed to play ball, with her tight black two piece outfit he remembered their close quarters contact. He had been distracted and she had scored some points because of it. Liam wondered if she had done that on purpose. And he could still feel her boobs pressing against his back and shoulders. The heat of her. Liam had never played any sport against a girl and didn't even know any black girls. Back in Iowa there were only a few of them in his high school while he was shy around any girl. Usually he fell asleep thinking of a particular girl back home. A lanky blonde with a pert freckled nose. But tonight his thoughts were on a woman, big and black. As his shorts filled, his hand slipped under the elastic band.

CHAPTER 59

AGI AND TINA

"I told you there would be a stream down at the bottom of this hill," Tina said with excitement, *"We're almost there!"* The two Indian women stopped and stared at her.

"What?" Tina asked in response to their expressions.

"If I'm not mistaken, you just spoke Greek," Pally answered

"You're not mistaken," Ajita said.

"When? What did I say?"

"How would we know?" Ajita asked. "You tell us what you said."

"Well, I think the last thing I said was, 'we're almost there'."

"Well, you said it in Greek," put in Pally. "See if you can say something else."

Tina thought about it for a moment. "I can't. I don't know Greek any more than you do."

Ajita turned and kicked Tina hard in the knee. As Tina buckled with a grunt, Ajita kicked her again in the gut. Pally knocked Ajita to the ground before she could kick Tina again.

"Remember Greek now?" snarled Ajita from the ground.

"What's that matter with you? Are you insane?" Pally yelled at Ajita. Ajita went wide-eyed, but she was looking past Pally to Tina.

"You dare defile this sacred soil with violence?" Tina, or Agi rather in Tina's body, glared intently at Ajita, whose hands were still bound behind her back, but she had managed to work her way up to her knees. Tina stepped into a sidekick to Ajita's head, but Pally saw it coming, just in time. She pushed Tina as she was balanced on her back foot. Tina went down, but bounced back off the ground to her feet instantly. Pally put up her guard, standing between Ajita and Tina. She was shaking.

"Tina, my love. It's me, Pally. Come back to me, please."

Agi just growled as he squared off against this new enemy. He remembered her now. *The rape at the rock. And the other Nubian, had come to him when he was strapped down in that strange building. She had threatened him with a knife.*

They were in league together, the two of them. And yet so lovely. Where were the others? His girls? Why was he so alone so close to the fountain?

"Daphne, Helen, Lorae!" he roared at the top of his lungs. Pally flinched at the shout. *This one is afraid. She won't attack. Yet she stands ready like a soldier. Like I taught my girls. "Stand down. I will not defile the fountain without need. And I no longer wage war on women,"* Agi said. He took two steps back and lowered his guard. Pally too took a small step back. She could feel Ajita against the back of her legs.

"Are you okay?" she asked over her shoulder.

"Yes, thank you. What do we do now?"

"Make no move. Wait for Tina to come back."

"But I need to know why she killed Rohit," Ajita cried. She sank onto her side in the soil, sobbing.

CHAPTER 60

ARISTOL

Hercules kept barking. Louder and nearer.

"Double time now, everyone downstream!" Aristol ordered. "Spartan style. Fifty steps running, fifty walking. March!"

Aristol led the way, Dani in the rear with the girls in the middle. Hercules barked again as he came into view and saw them running away. Why were his friends not welcoming him? It's a game! He bounded in joyful pursuit, barking again. The four runaways heard men shouting now. They weren't far behind. Only the innocence of Hercules had prevented an easy capture.

"Do you think we'll outrun them?," Dani asked. "They're on our trail now. We can't stop anywhere, Aristol."

"There's a lot of Arcadia still. We'll stay ahead of them until we find a crossing," Aristol replied.

"We're younger and stronger than he is too," Ife saide. "And we want it more. Hercules may catch up with us, and he'll be welcome, but he won't hinder us. We'll outlast the rest of them."

They hadn't gone far when the stream widened suddenly into rocky rapids, but it was very shallow. Aristol veered sharply into the water, gasping as the cold swirled around his calves. Half way across, the big dog bounded among them, snorting and shaking with joy at having found his friends. Aria hugged the hound around his thick neck as she slogged through the deepest part just above her knees.

"Now that you found us boy, help me out," she said. And the dog responded by thrusting to the far bank, pulling the small woman out of a hole.

As they reached dry land, Homedes and his soldiers were just coming off the hill and to the narrow stretch of level ground before reaching the water. Hercules turned, barking proudly to his master.

"Well done, Hercules," they could faintly hear Homedes shout. They turned to see him waving to them.

"Quick, further downstream. Ife, take the lead," Aristol urged.

They sprinted away with Hercules bounding alongside, enjoying the fun. Aristol stayed to the rear, determined to have it out with Homedes so the others could escape, especially Ife. But now he heard shouts and commotion ahead of him too. He clearly heard Aria's voice calling his name. Torn, he looked over his shoulder in the direction of his friends, they were out of sight around a massive stone, but he could clearly hear unfamiliar voices, some female, and dogs barking, amidst the roar of churning water. He turned to the river to see Homedes leading his soldiers through the water. They could see him waiting for them. Homedes was still waving as he waded across. They would soon be ashore.

"Aristol!" both Ife and Aria shouted now.

He turned and bolted to the call of his friends. Aristol came around the stone to the strangest sight he had ever seen. A picturesque garden lay before him, but the people there distracted him from the scenery. His three friends were hemmed in at spear point by five naked warriors, the three in the center were small young women, as like in stature to Aria as if they were kindred, flanked on either end by two equally naked, but much larger male warriors. All five held their spears at the ready, pointed against his friends. The strange girls, he couldn't help but notice were cute, wore slender chain girdles on their hips each with a single pearl suspended from the chain below the navel. The two men were also naked, wearing only a single slender chain around their necks with a pearl upon their chests.

"Aristol!" the two men shouted in sudden recognition, linking the name to the man. Baffled, Aristol looked at the bigger of the two, he had a badly mauled face, but seemed familiar.

"Aristol!" shouted the other man now, "Well met. We thought you long dead."

"Nikias?" Aristol looked back at the other man, "And Agi. I don't believe it. How..."

"Aristol!" Homedes shouted as he rounded the corner of the stone with his soldiers at his back.

Ife shrieked in horror at the sight of him. Spurred to action by Ife's cry, Aristol wheeled around and charged, lunging his spear at Homedes' diaphragm, who was just slowing up. He tried to block the point with a downward left arm, but only managed to divert the point to pierce him just above his left hip. The spear went clean through and as their eyes met, Aristol released his spear in horror at his own actions. Homedes collapsed to his back as his knees buckled. Both his hands gripped the bloody shaft that impaled him. Still holding Aristol's eyes as he grimaced, fighting back a cry.

The two Spartans sprang at the startled Corinthian soldiers, who while they had spears in hand, hadn't been expecting a fight. Their shields were still slung on their backs and their swords in their scabbards. The three girls leapt to Agi's support.

"Who dares violate the sacred fountain of Aphrodite?" a voice thundered from above. There astride the top of the fountain stone stood Delia. But not Delia.

"I am the priestess of Aphrodite's fountain, but now we speak with one voice!" she thundered again, "I am Aphrodite!" Everyone stood still. "Drop your weapons! On your knees to me or taste my wrath!"

Awed, men, women, and hounds looked up at the tall white naked lady towering over them, hands emptied spears as they dropped to their knees. Some gazed up at the lady, mesmerized, others looked to the ground in dread. Even the dogs whined and whimpered, with tails between their legs.

"In the name of love, I beg thee lady, spare this man. I love him," Aristol cried, "Say not that I have slain him!"

Delia leapt down from the fountain stone to examine the wounded Homedes.

"Nikias, go fetch my healing box," Delia shouted, Aphrodite no longer. "Agi, fetch my gown over there."

Agi complied, bringing it back to her. She wrapped the cloth tightly around the spear and wounds on both sides of the man's hip to staunch the bleeding. The white gown soaked to dark red quickly. All were gathered around the fallen Homedes now with the priestess tending to him.

Dicus noticed Agi as he limped to the command of the priestess. He was stunned at the sight of him, but there could be no mistaking him for any other than the Spartan he and others had raped and mutilated those five odd years before. Agi felt his stare and saw the Corinthian soldier. Recognition was instant.

With a roar Agi was on him, his stump where his right hand had been, struck deep into the gut of Dicus, knocking the wind out of him as Agi throttled Dicus with his left, bearing down on him driving the soldier to his knees. Dicus tried to break the iron grip around his throat, but couldn't. The pain was excruciating. So in desperation, Dicus pulled his knife and drove it up into Agi's groin. Into the same wound where they had castrated the man years before. He drove the knife deeper with renewed vigor as Agi's grip on his throat lost its strength. A strangled cry escaped from the twice wounded man as his life gushed down his thighs. Coming up off his knees, Dicus pulled out his bloody knife and drove it up under Agi's ribs, up to the hilts. He twisted his knife as the blade reached Agi's heart and the big man collapsed in a heap. Agi twitched a few times then was still.

The whole fight had lasted only seconds. The others were rooted in shock and horror. It was Lorae who broke the silence, with a feral scream she kicked Dicus in the neck as Agi had taught her. He went down, stunned. The other four soldiers were aroused now, drawing their swords as Daphne and Helen gripped their spears, ready. The soldier nearest to the unarmed Lorae raised his sword to behead the girl. It was Ife who sprang on his back with a grunt, biting the man's neck as her weight made him stagger, trying to keep his feet. Aristol grabbed Lorae's spear and the other two girls squared off with the other soldiers. A hoarse cry was heard over the clash of combat.

"Stand down!" cried Homedes, "Stand down," he said again, though the second time was barely a croak.

He was nearly spent with the effort. The soldiers withdrew with their backs to the supine Homedes, but still facing the others. Dani and Aria pulled Ife off the one soldier. She was not inclined to ever obey another command from Homedes again. The soldier rejoined his fellows defensively around Homedes.

"They attacked Dicus," the corporal called over his shoulder to Homedes.

"He murdered Agi," Aristol cried. The three sisters then lost all thought of combat as they clustered around their fallen man, sobbing and wailing.

"Put your weapons down, all of you, or I will recall Aphrodite," Delia commanded. "You five go over there and sit down. Do nothing until I tell you to." The soldiers obeyed, having no desire to see the return of the angry goddess.

Nikias came sprinting back to the garden, pulling up as he took in the scene. He gave Delia her healing box, then went over to the girls mourning over Agi. Delia knelt by the weakening Homedes and motioned Aristol to his side.

"It is too late for me," gasped Homedes to Delia.

The priestess nodded in response. "You have only a moment. Use well the time."

"Aristol, children. Forgive me. Forgive," Homedes was gasping with each word now. Ife, Dani, and Aria gathered round the dying man. "Never wrong to love, but it must be equal. See that now. I grant what you have already taken. Free. You are free. Ife, not my equal. Better. Better."

"Spare your strength," Aristol begged, holding his hand. Homedes managed a weak smile. Aristol kissed him on the lips as the man breathed his last.

***

Delia scanned the solemn faces of her companions. Her children. The funeral rites of the past few days were over and the bodies of Agi and Homedes were in the ground.. The soldiers of Homedes had departed with Delia's command never to return or reveal this place. She knew that they would not. The three sisters and the four newcomers were watching her. Nikias too.

"Come children. To the fountain all," Delia told them. "It is time to cast aside your sorrow. The lives of our loved ones live on in our love. So let us all love."

She watched them file to the fountain steps, disrobe, and descend into the churning foam in silence. There would soon be laughter and frolic. Eight of them in all, five women and three men. Her new flock. She would teach them all the sacred rites of Aphrodite. The freedom from pride and shame. The humble, joyful sharing of body, mind, and spirit. These, her children, would have children. And Delia would finally grow old. She would pass her leadership to one of these women. The next priestess of the fountain. Love would flow through the ages as does the fountain itself. Nikias caught her eye, smiling at her. He knew. A booming laugh welled out of her. Hearing her, everyone turned. With a shout and a few swift strides, Delia was airborne, diving into the frothing pool. She broke the surface rejuvenated by the warm waters. Surrounded by her family.

PART TWO

JOININGS

CHAPTER 1

AGI

Agi, in Tina's body, turned his back on the Nubians, walking in the direction of the fountain. After a moment, he could hear its music, exciting yet so soothing. Aphrodite had healed his Helen in the fountain and now he hoped it was his turn. Pally helped Ajita to her feet.

"Untie me," Ajita hissed. Pally just glared at her, pushing Ajita ahead of her. They followed Tina in silence, keeping their distance.

There it was on the other side of the stream! There were people there, some were in the water, one was even swimming under the icy waters of the waterfall. Who were they? He didn't recognize any of them. Where were his girls?

Focused on the fountain across the creek as he walked, Agi tripped on a stone falling to his hands and knees. He noticed his hands before his eyes relishing in the sight of his lost right hand. And he was seeing it with two eyes. *Oh, the power of Aphrodite, granted through the grace of his Lady Delia.* He studied his right hand, then his left as he rose off his hands. So pale and slender, but his hands used to be hairy, coarse and strong. His lost hand went up to touch his lost right ear. It was there! Between thumb and forefinger he stroked its length down to his lobe. *What had happened?* He rose to his feet and ran upstream to get to the ford. The length and strength of his right hamstring was evident in his long gait. *I am no longer a cripple!*

He needed to get to the fountain. He would beg the lady to look into the basin. Perhaps he could see his image. Then maybe he would see the extent of the metamorphosis Aphrodite had wrought upon him. To save her from Apollo, Daphne's father had transformed the nymph into a Laurel tree. *What have I become?*

Turning left into the ford, he splashed as quickly as he could across the stream. The rush of the rapids around his legs blended with the more distant roars of the falls and fountain. The chill of the water shivered up through his chest.

***

Pally and Ajita stopped at the water's edge, watching Tina pushing through the rapids, now up to her thighs.

"Get in there," Pally told her captive, pushing her forward.

Ajita took a single step in the icy flow and stopped. Pally pushed hard on her back and Ajita staggered forward several steps deeper in, struggling to keep her balance between the fast flow and the uneven rocky streambed.

"This is crazy!" cried Ajita. "Untie my hands!"

"Like hell I will," came the reply as Pally pushed her forward again.

Ajita staggered forward again, stepped into a hole and fell sideways fully into the stream. Her legs were flailing to find solid footing. Pally yanked her up by the back of her shirt. Ajita sputtered as her head broke the surface.

"You're trying to kill me! Untie my hands!"

Pally looked at her shivering soaked to the skin countrywoman, suddenly finding her wildly attractive despite the chill surging through her own nethers. Then she looked at Tina who was nearing the other shore. Swearing, she untied Ajita's hands.

"Get going and stay ahead of me or by God I will drown you," Pally snarled.

She could see Tina on the water's edge. Without a look back, Tina broke into a run downstream toward the huge stone with the fountain bubbling out of it. Ajita stepped in another hole and went in up to her shoulders splashing and sputtering. Pally went all the way in as well trying to drag her back up. They found firmer footing again and laboring across finally reached the other side both soaked to the skin and shivering.

"This is crazy," Ajita said.

"It wouldn't have happened if you hadn't attacked her."

"She's crazy. This whole business is crazy."

"Shut up and get moving. Where has Tina gotten to?"

"She must be behind that big rock."

They both broke into a trot. In a short while, they rounded the fountain stone to the garden. A half dozen people were there, gathered around Tina. An animated discussion was underway with everyone gesturing and speaking in Greek at the same time, including Tina. The locals, for that is who they were, stopped talking at the sight of Pally and Ajita. Tina had been in the process of undressing despite the apparent protests of the already nude locals when the Indian girls arrived.

"Ajita!" one of the men shouted. It was Stavros from the motel. "What are you doing here? How did you even know about this place?" And then with a grin, "Had I known you were coming, I could have given you a ride." Then seeing Pally, he recognized Tina for who she was. "Of course, the American." All the other Greeks began speaking again at once, including Tina.

"Can you all please speak English!" Pally shouted over all the noise.

"Who are you?" a woman challenged her in English. "This is our land. We don't speak your English at your command. You are trespassing."

"It isn't my English, but I doubt any of you speak Hindi," Pally said.

Tina interrupted with a rapid barrage of Greek at the Greek woman while gesturing at Pally and Ajita. The woman spoke back in Greek and Tina subsided, but with a very concerned look on her face. Then, in seeming defiance, Tina finished stripping, strode boldly to the fountain pool and dove in. She surfaced and breast stroked slowly around the churning pool.

"Who are you people?" the woman demanded again, "and who is that mad woman that speaks Greek like from the days of Socrates?" she asked Pally, gesturing to Tina gliding about in the pool.

"They stayed at the motel," Stavros put in.

"And you invited them here? Without asking me?"

"No, Thea. I didn't know they were coming."

"Then how did they get here?" Thea demanded. Then to Pally and Ajita, "How did you find this place? Who told you about it?"

"Nobody told us. Look, it's a long story, but Tina led us here," Pally replied.

"Tina?"

"The mad woman," put in Ajita, still shivering.

"Well, mad she may be, but she knows better than you two," said Thea. "The pool is warm. Now that you are here, get out of those cold clothes and warm yourselves." With that, she turned to Stavros and the others. A rapid exchange of Greek ensued.

The two women exchanged a look, Pally shrugged so they both went to the water's edge, their shoes squishing with each step. The shoes were the first thing off, but then the two Indian women were immediately self-conscious about proceeding further. They looked at each other, both hesitant. Finally, Pally started to unbutton her blouse, so Ajita pulled her T-shirt over her head. They pulled their shorts down at the same time. Suddenly reckless, Pally openly admired Ajita's long lean frame with a beaming smile. Ajita smiled tentatively back. They took the few steps to the stone rimmed edge of the pool.

"Stop," Thea barked from behind them. "You have ruined our ritual already, but you will not desecrate the fountain of Aphrodite." The two Indians looked at her bewildered.

"You just told us to get in," said Ajita.

"No clothing," Thea ordered. "This is the cleansing fountain of Aphrodite. You must not hide your shame here."

The two Indians stared at the Greek woman naked before them, as were all the others. Indeed there was no shame on her weathered face. Pally figured she was about Tina's age, but showing it more than Tina. She was a short woman who had once been lithe, but now carried a few extra pounds all around her, showing mostly in her soft belly and hips. Only her tiny pale breasts hadn't accumulated any fat, retaining the small size of her youth. In any case, she was clearly shameless, and very much in command. Looking at each other again, the two Indians removed their bras, still covering themselves with their hands.

"Hands on hips, so," said Thea, "stand straight. You are accepted here as you are." Slowly the Indian women complied, looking at each other.

"You like," laughed Thea, her stern face transformed with a smile. "Nice. Now the bottoms."

They were soon in the pool, sitting with their bare backs and bottoms on the smooth stones around the edge. The chill ran away from their bones. Both women dipped their heads underwater several times. Tina continued to stroke slowly around the pool. Sometimes she bobbed on her toes under the falling fountain. She spoke to them once in Greek, but they didn't respond.

Ajita sighed, "I feel better than I have for a long time."

"Me too, this is crazy, but I am happy we are here."

"It is very strange, but I just realized what I am feeling now because I hadn't known it was missing."

"What?" Pally asked her.

"Hope. I'd been missing hope," Ajita said. "Ever since Rohit died."

"What about love?"

"For me? I haven't been missing it because I've never had it," Ajita confessed. Thea and Stavros joined them sitting in the pool.

"You feel better. Now tell us your story," Thea ordered. "And hers."

"It's a rather long story," Pally replied.

"Then I ask questions, you answer. How did you find this place?"

"Tina led us here," Pally said. "But she didn't really know where she was going. We think she was a Spartan soldier in a past life. From a long time ago. He knew where to go."

"So that's why she speaks such crazy Greek," Thea exclaimed. "Like the ancients, but also uneducated. She is difficult to understand. I can only make her out because I studied at university. Who is she really?"

"Her name is Tina Marin. She is an American news reporter," Pally said.

"She killed my brother," put in Ajita.

"We think she did that when she was the Spartan soldier," Pally added.

"This woman killed your brother recently? Here in Greece?" Thea asked with alarm.

"No, in New Delhi," Pally explained. "In India. But it was self-defense. I am a police officer in India."

"Rohit, couldn't hurt anyone," Ajita protested. "I've told you, he was trying to help her."

"I believe you, Ajita. And so does Tina. But it doesn't change the facts. Your brother was part of the group engaged in a crime. Tina was under assault and she acted to defend herself."

"And she fights like an ancient Spartan soldier?" Thea asked, pointing at Tina.

"Oh, she fights alright," Pally said.

"And she thinks she is that Spartan soldier right now?" Thea asked. "Swimming twenty feet away from us?"

"We hope Tina will come back soon. But if she is speaking Greek, she is the soldier," Pally said. "She doesn't understand English."

"She hardly understands us either. Only I can speak to her because I studied the ancient language. She keeps asking about people we don't know. Maybe people from the past. And she wants to look in the reflecting bowl. She kept asking for that, but we have no such thing. And she wants to be cleansed by Aphrodite although exactly what she means by that isn't clear."

"You said we have ruined your ritual. Could that cleanse Tina?" Ajita asked.

"This is the fountain of Aphrodite," said Thea. "Our family has tended the fountain forever. Even when the Turks were here and used it as one of their baths, we tended it. Now it is ours again. This is private. The property of our family. We don't want others."

"If she is as dangerous as you say," Stavros put in, "how do we get her out of here?"

"We need to get her back to being Tina," said Pally.

"Let her see herself," suggested Ajita. "Bring her a mirror. Maybe if the Spartan warrior sees that he is really a woman then the woman will come back."

"Go get a mirror," Thea ordered Stavros. "The biggest you can find in a hurry."

"There is a full length mirror back at the house."

"Get it."

"It will take about ten minutes," Stavros said as he got out of the pool waving to a cousin to help.

"Meanwhile," Thea said, "we leave that one alone. Don't talk to her," Thea told the two Indians. "We three will stay here in the pool with her until Stavros returns."

But Tina approached them before Stavros returned. "Where is the priestess? The Lady Delia? I need to talk to her. She said that my turn would come."

"I am the priestess Amalthea," replied Thea, "What is your name? Where are you from? And how can I help you, my child?"

"I am called Agi, once of Sparta, but now of Arcadia. We live just a day away from here. I wish to see the gifts that Aphrodite has granted me."

"Tell me, Agi. What gifts are these?"

"Aphrodite has restored that which was taken, my right eye," Tina touched her eye, "my ear," again a touch, "my right hand. And I am no longer a cripple."

"If you have been given all these things, Aphrodite is indeed generous," Thea said, "What more do you seek? What more would you ask of the goddess?"

"She restored me, by changing me somehow. I…I think I am a woman now, strange as that may sound. I am not as I was."

"The gods often bestow their gifts through metamorphosis," Thea said, "so it may be with you. I have called for a reflecting wall, so that you may see your own countenance."

"Thank you, my lady."

"My servants come with the reflecting wall now. Let us go to them, my child."

Thea took Tina by the hand and met Stavros and another carrying a full length mirror with a blanket over it. Pally and Ajita followed in silence, exchanging glances, having no understanding of what had transpired in ancient Greek between Tina and Thea. Thea directed the men where to station the mirror and to hold it on either side. She guided Tina to stand before it.

"Here now Agi of Arcadia, behold the bounty of Aphrodite," Thea declared in a strong voice as she removed the blanket. Tina gaped at her image in wonder. She reached to her image in the mirror.

"Do not touch the reflecting wall," Thea commanded, and Tina stepped back. She touched herself slowly everywhere, watching her reflection confirm what she was feeling.

"Oh Lady Amalthea, this is wondrous indeed. I am whole. And I am not ungrateful, but inside I am still very much a man and I still carry my wounds in my heart. That is what the Lady Delia promised to cleanse. So that I could be whole in body, mind, and spirit."

"Truly my child," Thea replied, "even the gifts of the gods come at cost. Yours may be to learn, to live, what it is to be a woman. Perhaps you have not always treated women with the reverence that is their due."

Tina cast her eyes to the ground. "Truly, my lady, you see my heart as clearly as does Lady Delia. But I had already changed in my heart, towards my precious girls, before this gift was granted. They don't know my secrets though. Only the Lady Delia read my heart and saw my secrets, and now you, my lady." Thea was silent now. Uncertain in what direction to turn this situation.

"Please Thea," Pally said softly. "What is happening? We need to get Tina back."

"The Nubians!" Tina growled, turning to Pally and Ajita. "Why do you pursue me? What have you done with my precious girls?"

"They are here at my command, Agi," Thea declared. "They are my servants." Then in English to Pally and Ajita, "Bow to me, then return to the fountain pool until I call you." She pointed to the pool, and Tina watched the Indian women bow and back away to the pool.

"They are lovely," Tina said to Thea, "Yet wily and dangerous I deem."

"Pay them no mind, Agi. Tell me about your girls."

"The sisters, Daphne, Helen, and Lorae. I expected to find them here. Please tell me where they are."

CHAPTER 2

SHE

She was strolling through the gardens near the lake in Srinagar. Enjoying the crispness in the air and the view of the distant mountains. The ever present background noise of traffic, marring the experience, annoyed her. She preferred perfection. So the American kid was going over the top into the Siachen Glacier country. That was bad news. What was he expecting to find? Was he tracing her backtrail just by accident? She doubted that, but this was a risk that had to be eliminated before it became an event. And the kid had Dalha as a guide so she couldn't count on him just freezing to death along the way as most people would. He must be pretty good to have found Dalha so quickly. And he must be very good to have gotten her cooperation. Dalha was a suspicious slut, trusting nobody after what She did to her. So how did he get to Dalha? Then she smiled to herself. Of course. Suspicious Dalha may be, but still a slut first and foremost. He's got her thinking between her thighs just like She did. That American kid must be good. Very good.

Now She had to drop everything here to go north after them. Bobby Singh had to die. Preferably before he discovers anything, but definitely before he can get south again into telecommunication range. So it would be done in the high country. Dalha? She'd rather not if it could be avoided. She rather liked Dalha. Yes, if she can eliminate Singh before he actually learns anything then he'll just have an accident. Dangerous country up there. Anything can happen.

But if he learns anything then Dalha will have to go too. The Singh kid might be good, but he too is thinking between his thighs. Dalha will see to that. He'll tell Dalha everything. Silencing Dalha will be a stickier wicket to play. Two accidents will raise suspicions with the locals. An accident of nature ending Dalha will be less plausible being so obviously from the high country herself. Then, She still needed to get back south again after the deed was done. That required trusting a sherpa. No doubt about it, this whole trek north and back again was going to be a delicate play. She smiled again. She was looking forward to it.

CHAPTER 3

LIAM

USAF airman Liam Miller knocked lightly on the door of the Assistant Air Force Attache's office. Then he entered with a pot of coffee in hand. He was expected. The assistant attache had two other officers with her. Their conversation stopped as Liam placed the pot on a side table.

"Thank you, Miller," she said, "That will be all."

Then Liam was back out of that inner sanctum as fast as he could without running. On his first deployment, Liam had been in India for several months. He was a small town boy so the big foreign city of New Delhi was overwhelming. And Liam was feeling home sick, totally out of his element. The embassy complex where he worked, almost 30 acres in size, was American enough but outside on the city streets was a whole different world. And inside the embassy, Liam was at the lowest level of the enlisted service personnel. He was a gofer.

As a naturally humble young man, Liam was content with his role. He had wanted to get away from home after graduating high school and boy he got it in spades. So he usually spent his after hours at the gym playing basketball with other enlisted men.

He had never seen Special Agent Dorothy Miller while working on the huge embassy grounds but since that basketball game they occasionally overlapped at the gym. The FBI lady never played another basketball game there that he knew of but sometimes he would see her banging on the big bag or over at the rowing machines.

Making a point of never making eye contact or approaching her, Liam was nonetheless always aware of her presence. Sitting out because they had an odd number of players, he one day wandered away from the game to watch Dorothy working her martial arts on the big bag in the corner. He kept what he thought was a respectable distance away from her when she suddenly stopped to stare at him. Liam took an instinctive step back, but she waved him over.

"This isn't a spectator sport, young man," Dorothy said.

Liam blushed. "I, uh…"

"What do you want?"

"I was just kinda wondering if you could, uh, show me how to do it," Liam said. "You know, teach me."

Her hard stare softened somewhat. "I haven't the time," Dorothy said. She gave one more wicked left to the bag then walked off toward the locker room.

CHAPTER 4

RITUAL

The local Greek party at the fountain, along with Tina, Pally, and Ajita had finished a light al fresco meal. Thea had sent Tina back into the pool.

"The mirror didn't bring your American friend back," Thea said. "Agi is here for his cleansing ceremony and will stay until he gets it. We will hold the ritual in one hour."

"But do you know what to do?" Pally asked.

"Of course," Thea replied. "The women of my family have tended this fountain for centuries. We don't call ourselves priestess anymore, but I lead all rituals."

"But I thought you don't have a cleansing ritual," said Ajita.

"We will have a ritual."

"You'll make something up right out of your head?" Ajita asked, skeptically.

"Not just out of my head. Out of my heart, out of my soul. Your souls too. There are ten of us here, plus the American, all will play a part. Only I will speak unless I tell you to. I will conduct the ritual in ancient Greek."

"Then we won't fully understand," put in Stavros.

"When I need to give you instructions, I will use English." Thea laughed, "That is the language of the gods that Agi can't understand. I have already told him so."

"And she believed that?" asked Ajita.

"Of course," Thea answered, "I am a priestess of the fountain. You two, you also need to believe in our rituals. We all here believe. Ritual requires an open body, mind, and soul. Faith. Prepare yourselves. You may meet your own demons soon."

They all entered the pool by the edge in waist high water. The soothing warmth was a balm to all. The splash of the fountain pounding into the pool filled their senses. Thea beckoned Tina to her. Then Pally and Ajita. With Agi facing the priestess and the Indian women facing each other, the four of them formed a tight square, shoulder to shoulder, hip to hip. By Thea's order, the four of them locked their arms at the elbow with each person on either side and clasped hands with interlaced fingers holding their hands before them into the center of the square at the waterline. The formation was so tight that all hands touched in the middle. Thea had Stavros and the rest of her companions form a wider circle hand in hand tight around the inner four. Ajita felt Stavros' familiar thigh against her bare butt and couldn't help but smile. She leaned her head back onto his shoulder.

"Do not ever break contact until I say when the ritual has ended no matter what happens," Thea called in English, then repeated the instructions to Agi in ancient Greek. Thea hoped that her orders and the tight formation would serve to restrain the Spartan warrior, if necessary.

"This is the cleansing circle of atonement and forgiveness," said Thea in ancient Greek. "Agi of Arcadia is here to share his secrets of shame at last, to atone for his wrongs, to be forgiven, loved, and to love in return."

"But my three girls, the sisters should be here," Tina protested.

"They are with us. I can feel them," Thea told him, "and when you next see them they will already know everything that you tell us today. Now tell me, this company, Mother Earth Gaea, and Aphrodite of your shame. Then be accepted and loved."

Then Tina began to speak slowly, hesitantly at first. Pally and Ajita watched and heard the strange words coming out of the familiar face so close to theirs. But Tina's eyes were locked onto Thea's. Occasionally Thea spoke in ancient Greek if Tina stopped talking, presumably prompting her on. Tina began to sob and sway as she spoke. Thea cried with her. Then suddenly, Tina threw her head back and let out a full-throated bellow to the sky that thundered over the white noise of water. Thea threw her head back, joining Tina with the same cry. They both drew breath to sustain the cry over and over again until it finally subsided into a dying wail.

"Everyone," Thea called out in English, "Repeat this mantra after me and continue until I tell you to stop: Forgiveness, acceptance, we love you, as one."

"Close your eyes. Listen to the language of the gods," Thea said to Tina, "Take up the chant though you know not the words. Let them enter your soul and you will understand their meaning."

Agi began to join the English chant, awkwardly at first, then clearer and stronger. Over and over, the chant went on. Forgiveness, acceptance, we love you, as one. It went on and on as the minutes went by. Then Tina's eyes opened wildly, she looked side to side at Pally and Ajita who were chanting the mantra with the others. Then she locked shocked eyes with Thea again. Tina's knees buckled, but the tight formation kept her upright.

"Two thousand years!" Tina cried in English. "My girls! Daphne, Helen, Lorae! Gone! Gone for so long! Over two thousand years!"

"The cleansing is complete," Thea shouted over the chanting. "The ritual is over!"

The Greeks in the outer circle clapped and cheered, exchanging hugs. Tina threw herself into Thea's arms, sobbing.

"I know it is a shock, my child, but there is no reason to believe that your loved ones of long ago didn't live out full lives," Thea spoke in Tina's ear still holding her hug. "Cherish their memory without bitterness. Remember, this is the gift of Aphrodite, not to be scorned. Now, to whom do I have the pleasure of embracing?" Thea asked in ancient Greek.

"My name is Tina Marin of America," Tina replied in ancient Greek. "And Agi of Arcadia," she added in English, pulling back to wipe away tears.

"Nice," Thea replied with her broad smile as they separated. "Now you two should greet your companions." Tina turned to find Pally and Ajita in a deep embrace crying together. They opened their hug to allow Tina in.

"We are so sorry," Tina said to Ajita.

Ajita sobbed out a reply, "You couldn't help it. But Rohit."

"I know. I know. So sorry. Later, I will want you to tell us all about him." Tina and Pally then embraced while Stavros was waiting for Ajita.

"Malakas. I'm a dick." Stavros told her. "You should hate me. I hate myself."

"No you don't. And you shouldn't. Yes, you are Malakas, a dick. That was so wrong taking advantage of me like that. But even so, there was never any hate in your heart. No fear. Just love. That is how it worked. That is how you won my heart," explained Ajita. Stavros scooped her up in his arms.

"I'm the luckiest man in the world!" he shouted to the sky as Ajita laughed for joy. Everyone cheered. After a while, all had departed the pool, except Tina and Pally, who sat together at the edge.

"So both of you are in there, conscious at the same time?" Pally asked.

"Yes, it's a bit crowded," Tina replied with a grim chuckle. "Over two thousand years! I still can't get past where I am, or when I am rather. Over two thousand years." Tina began to cry.

"Agi?" Pally asked, "Do you think you could learn to love me? Like Tina does? If she still does."

"Good lord, youngling. It doesn't work like that. You don't have to address us separately. We aren't separate at all. We are one. I suppose there isn't a Tina anymore. Or an Agi." She laughed.

"But whose personality is it?"

"Both. Blended a bit I guess. Maybe depending on the circumstances. You know Pally, we may need to back off a bit. Our relationship, I mean. You have no idea who you are dealing with. The things I've done. The way I think and feel about things. It's different now."

"You, you don't love me anymore?"

"I do, Pally. I do. Now more than ever. But love and relationships are two different things. And I find you wildly attractive, Pally. In fact, I wish I had a phallus right now. But I've been wishing that for quite a while," she chuckled sadly, "for over two thousand years. Sure wish I could see the girls again. I miss them like it was yesterday. Two thousand years." Tina stared into the swirling waters of the pool, lost in thought. Teary eyed, Pally slid out of the water and walked away.

"How is your friend?" Thea asked. Pally just stared at her, then burst into tears throwing herself into Thea's arms, soaking the woman's recently donned clothing with her wet nudity. Thea took her in.

"It's all right," Thea hummed in her ear.

"I don't know who she is anymore. Finally I find someone, and now I'm alone again."

"You are never alone," Thea said with passion, pulling her head back just far enough to look into Pally's brown eyes. "None of us are. We are all connected. As one."

"Through God, you mean. I don't think religion will solve my problem."

"Religion," Thea scoffed. "God or gods. What are they but extensions of our collective selves? And we of their collective divine selves." Thea took her by the hand, leading her into the woods. "Come, I will show you. We are at the temple of Aphrodite. We will channel the divine Aphrodite within us." Thea beamed a broad smile to her. "You see. You like."

CHAPTER 5

AJITA AND STAVROS

Stavros and Ajita strolled hand in hand along the stream on the far side of the fountain stone, savoring the sounds, scents, and sights.

"What an incredible place. The feel of it all," Ajita said.

"Yes, sometimes I feel it truly is touched by the gods. By Aphrodite."

"So you still believe, all of you here, in your gods of old?"

"If you mean as a god to pray to for help or for divine intervention, then I would say no. If you mean as a force to channel our own spiritual selves, our own Aphrodite, then I would say yes."

"You're a philosopher. That is so over my head," Ajita said.

"I'm Greek," said Stavros. "We are all philosophers. We started it, you know."

Ajita chuckled, thinking of India's ancient history. "You Greeks just keep telling yourselves that." They strolled in silence. "Such a paradise here," Ajita said, "so secluded. Who owns it?"

"We do. It's a family place. Thea actually holds the title."

"And you're related?"

"She is my second cousin, no third."

"And the rest of you?"

"We aren't all related, but anyone who isn't was brought in by a family member at some point in the past. And then that family becomes a multi-generational branch. And then you know how things happen, and the families blend."

"The ritual we ruined earlier when we arrived. What was it?"

"Our monthly event. We all get together in a circle, channel Aphrodite, disrobe each other, greet each other in the three realities; body, mind, spirit. Really merge and meld, you know." Stavros laughed. "Then we orgy our brains out. You interrupted us right at the greeting ceremony." Ajita didn't know what to say to this information, so she said nothing. "Are you shocked?" Stavros asked.

"I don't know what I am. I guess I'm sorry I spoiled your fun."

Stavros laughed. "It is fun, but it is so much more than just sexual fun. And don't get me wrong, sex really is fun, But mainly it completes our connections of body, mind, and spirit."

"You don't have to tell me how much you enjoy sex, remember?"

"I do indeed. I learned that here. Our ritual orgies are joyful. We laugh so much."

"While having sex?"

"Sure. We laugh for joy. But at the same time, here, it is our physical consummation of our spiritual love. The many become one. I…I can't really describe it better than that. Thea says it is a recurring theme. In philosophy, I mean."

"I'm not sure I understand what you mean. But I felt it, sort of, in Tina's cleansing ritual."

"Yes, wasn't that powerful? It's like…I shouldn't say more, I would only be parroting Thea." Stavros paused for a moment. "But this much I will say, I can't explain it to you or others, I haven't that skill, but I know it, with certainty. Thea says having certainty is wisdom."

Or folly, thought Ajita. She said, "Well, I am sorry we ruined it for you and the others."

"You didn't. We'll simply adjust our schedule. Today is Saturday. We'll start fresh and early tomorrow morning."

Ajita didn't say anything to that, wondering suddenly where she would sleep tonight. It was a long hike back to her car. She wouldn't make it before dark. Stavros must have been reading her mind.

"Of course the three of you can stay with us tonight," he said. "Not everyone showed up, we rarely get everyone, so there are spare beds." Ajita smiled her thanks. They approached a small grove of laurel trees.

"What a lovely spot," Ajita said.

"A special place. I brought you here for a purpose. For us to become one."

"It seems to me we did that back at the motel."

"Not like this. Sure, I was channeling my love to you, and you sensed that and accepted me, despite my bad behavior. But this ritual is first spiritual oneness then physical intimacy to consummate that oneness." Stavros dropped on one knee. "Will you become one with me, Ajita?"

"Is this a marriage proposal?" Ajita asked, totally taken aback.

"Well," stalled Stavros, surprised at the question. "It is now. Yes, sweet Ajita, yes!"

"And tomorrow you'll participate in this orgy?"

"I see what you mean. Look, maybe you can join us too."

"No, you look," Ajita replied, suddenly angry. "My first sexual experience of my life was just a little over a week ago when I gave your cousin a blowjob at the airport. Out of desperation. A less than pleasant experience, but as it wasn't physically painful, I could handle it. Keep it in perspective."

"Ajita…"

"No, let me finish," she continued, "then you came along and I submitted myself to you, also out of desperation. Out of sheer hunger." Stavros hung his head. She lifted his chin. "Somehow that transformed into something beautiful that I still can't understand. You are in me, that is for sure. Part of me."

"Well, then?" Stavros beamed.

"I'm not going to marry you then have sex with everyone at the wedding reception. Sorry. That is way over the top."

"It's not like that."

"No matter what it's like, it's not going to happen," Ajita declared. "Now do you want to marry me? And live with me? And be only with me?"

Stavros held her eye. "I love you, Ajita. But I love others too. I won't disavow them. That would be wrong. It would be unnatural. And I can't be other than I am." Ajita said nothing, turning away looking into the trees. "What now, Ajita? You were chasing Tina and Pally. For a reckoning. Well, you've had that, haven't you? For Rohit, who is gone. What now?" He saw a shiver run through the girl as she cried. He hugged her gently from behind. "We don't have to get married if you don't want to. At least not now," Stavros continued. He turned her around to face him and looked into her eyes. "I open my heart to you Ajita, for now and forever. To live and let live. To be together, and be apart. To come and go. To call when in need, and to help when called. To accept you as you are, now and forever." Stavros closed his eyes and prayed in silence for a moment. He opened his eyes. Ajita's wet eyes were closed too. "It is done," Stavros said, a ridiculous grin across his face.

Ajita opened her eyes feeling a rush of euphoria surging from her chest and forehead through her entire body. "For me to," she whispered. "It is done. For now and forever." She laughed for joy. They hugged head to toe. One.

CHAPTER 6

PLANS

The weather that Sunday morning was perfect. Some dozen people were crowded in the kitchen/dining room in the house, hidden in the trees, a good five minute walk from the fountain. A light breakfast was underway, chaotic and synchronized at the same time as people puttered about the room, reaching for bread here or eating fruit there.

"Everyone be clean and ready in an hour," Thea called over the conversations. The room began to empty as people went about their business amid much talking and laughing.

"And you three," Thea said to Tina, Pally, and Ajita. "Much was felt and said yesterday and into the night. You have made your decisions." The three women looked at each other.

Pally spoke first. "I will stay here for a few days as you have offered, Thea. Then I need to return to India and report."

"You say nothing of this location," Thea ordered.

"I won't," promised Pally.

"Good," said Thea, smiling. "Clear your mind and heart when we others have left. And you'll have the fountain all to yourself. I will return Wednesday from Athens. I have business that can't wait or I would stay now," she kissed Pally on the forehead and then softly on the lips.

"Thank you, Thea."

"I will leave with Stavros tonight after dinner," Ajita said. "He needs help with the motel for a while." She shrugged, "We'll see."

"I can believe that," Thea replied, "I understand he neglected many chores that needed attending while you ladies were visiting the beach." Ajita blushed as the others smiled. "It is a good place that Stavros has by the sea. A good life."

"We'll see," Ajita said again, but she too was smiling now.

"And what about you two?" Thea asked Tina. Everyone chuckled

"WE have to get back to work," Tina said. "To the assignment that brought me to India in the first place. I have a young colleague who should be in Kashmir already working on it. But after this assignment I will come back to each of you wherever you are." She looked pointedly at Pally. "This isn't goodbye."

"I can drive you into Athens," Thea told her.

"Honored, my lady," Tina replied. Thea ignored the formality.

"You are all welcome here anytime, my friends," Thea said. "What we shared yesterday connects us wherever we may go. But you must keep its secrets. You may not participate in today's ritual. This orgy as you call it. Orgia in ancient Greek, it is a beautiful and fulfilling experience that goes far beyond the physical sex. English is such a crude language. Too few words, too few."

"We'll stay clear of the holy fountain," Tina said, "we have much to talk about, the three of us."

"You mean four," Ajita said with a laugh. Pally smiled sadly at Tina.

"So. I must clean up," Thea said, "And prepare for the ritual. Someday you may wish to join our body. There is a ritual for that as well if that be your path. Meanwhile, enjoy the house and the grounds. There is a path behind the house that leads up to the ridge if you wish to hike."

"Thank you, Thea," they all said as she left the room. The house was buzzing with activity all around them, but the three women were alone around the kitchen table holding hands. They looked at each other, but nobody spoke.

CHAPTER 7

GETTING TO KNOW YOU

"Ajita, this spot is lovely," Pally declared. Looking around as the three of them strolled together through the broad laurel trees.

"Yes it is," Ajita replied. "Stavros brought me here yesterday."

"It has a feel about it," Tina said. "The gods are definitely with us here. Now."

The Indian women looked at their American friend quizzically. "Which gods, Tina? Do you really believe in them?"

"I've believed in them all my life, but have never felt them before so acutely as now. Except at the fountain." Tina looked at the other two. "You don't believe me. Look, I watched the Lady Delia transform into the goddess Aphrodite. Right before my eyes. Her sheer power permeated my body. I was paralyzed." Ajita and Pally said nothing in reply. "You don't believe me. But then you wouldn't. Your gods are so remote. Subordinated to science as they are."

"Don't you believe in science anymore, Tina?" Pally asked

"I do, Pally. I do. But I also know what I know. Know what happened before my eyes. To me. And let's face it, my metamorphosis is not the work of Jesus, is it?"

"She's got you there, Pally," Ajita said with a soft smile. She placed her hand on the broad branch of a tree leaning over the path, suddenly sensing the life of the tree touching her. There was moss on the bark under her fingers. "There is something special about this place."

"Yes. I'm not sure I would have felt it before as I do now," said Tina.

"What do you mean?" asked Pally.

"I'm saying that Agi is more spiritually aware than Tina," Tina replied. "The sheer sensory physicality of life is so, was so…in your face than now in this modern world. Death was a daily reality. Pain. Rapine. Killing. Dying," Tina suddenly doubled over, gagging.

"What is it, are you alright?" The younger women guided her carefully to the ground. Tina was on her knees panting until she regained some control.

"I'm alright. Okay," Tina sighed. "I just recalled my own death." Pally's and Ajita's eyes met, but they said nothing. Tina rose back to her feet, with help on either arm. "I'm okay now, thank you ladies. Wow, that was a shock. It was like the knife went through my groin all over again. Right now. I didn't know the memory of pain could be pain itself."

"It can be," Ajita agreed rather grimly.

"Let's get you back to the house," Pally urged.

"No, I'm okay. It's nice out here. Wholesome. Maybe this is part of the process. There's a bit of grass in the sun over there. Between those trees. Let's sit for a bit. My head is hurting again." The three of them were soon sitting side by side, facing the spring midday sun with eyes closed. "What are you guys thinking?" Tina asked.

"Well," replied Ajita, "if you must know, I am wondering who Stavros happens to be having sex with at this particular moment."

"Nice," Pally laughed. "But try not to think of it like that. I don't completely understand it, but Thea introduced me to some of the mysteries yesterday. I'm not sure what it is yet, but it is more than just sex. Much more."

"I'm so happy for you, Pally," Tina said.

"Don't get ahead of yourself, Tina. I love you very much. That isn't going to change. And I want to spend my life with you. My marriage proposal still stands and I am hoping, praying, for you to say yes."

"Then what was yesterday? With the Lady Amalthea?"

"Perspective. It was lovely. And Thea is lovely. A bit bossy perhaps, but so loving," Pally said softly with the smile of memory. "I have a perspective now that I didn't have before. That there is more of love than just you and me, Tina."

"Encouraging," said Tina. "I feel less pressure now."

"I feel I have that too," added Ajita. "A new perspective, I mean. On life. Thanks to the cleansing ritual. It touched me deeply. I felt I was being accepted too."

"You are," Tina and Pally said together. The three of them went silent. Each absorbing what had been shared.

"Tomorrow morning early," Tina said, "I drive back to Athens with the Lady Amalthea. She'll drop me at the airport. We three will go our separate ways, but only for a while. So before we part, Ajita, tell us about your brother, Rohit."

PART THREE

THE HUNT

CHAPTER 1

BOBBY AND DALHA

Bobby had never felt so cold, but the chill had at least reached an uncomfortable equilibrium. Panting hard as he trudged through the Himalayas, the young man looked at his hiking companion ahead of him, both quiet and complacent. Then back at Dalha leading from the rear, looking big and bulky in her heavy clothing. Used to it. Both of them. Bobby stopped without a word. Noticing his fatigue, the others waited patiently. They were above the timberline now. A steep stony landscape laced with white satin. Bobby looked up all around him at the impossibly high peaks, feeling helpless in the loneliest place on the planet. If this was China, it was Bobby's first visit to the second most populated nation in the world. He felt he was at the top of the world and still looking up. Emptiness. Complete and utter. But not as empty as it appeared.

"Just a little bit further for today, Bobby," Dalha said. "Hang in there."

***

It was more of a box than a hut. You couldn't stand up in it. Bobby could barely sit upright. And hidden by snow high in the Himalayas, Bobby would have walked right by it without even knowing it was there. But it was shelter for the night and well insulated on the inside, lined with furs. The place was rounded, with maybe an eight foot diameter, and domed with a little entry vestibule, big enough only for one person at a time, for removing boots and outer garments so as not to bring moisture inside. Similar to the Eskimo igloo design, but made of wood and hides covered in a perpetual covering of snow.

Once inside with the door closed, the darkness was complete and utter. Even the keenest eye needs some light to work with for vision. There was none. Bobby sat miserably hunched over with his arms wrapped around his legs. His knees were under his chin. He could hear the quiet breathing of the other two bodies so close to him. Bobby was panting and shivering.

"What do we do now?" Bobby asked softly, knowing only one of his companions, Dalha, understood Hindi.

"We rest. We sleep. Tomorrow will be longer than today."

"Got it," Bobby replied, not wanting to complain, but totally miserable. He shivered again. A brief shuffling of movement told Bobby that their guide, one of Dalha's fathers, had gone horizontal. In no time, Bobby heard the soft steady breathing of sleep. Dalha was on Bobby's other side. Not wanting to disturb Dad, Bobby said nothing. He was thoroughly wretched. This first day had been as tough as any in his experience. Most of it was just uphill or even horizontal walking, bad enough at this altitude. But then there were stretches so steep that they needed ice axes in each hand and spikes attached to the bottoms of their boots. Unfamiliar as he was to using these tools, Bobby was less than efficient to say the least. Then there came one point that was completely vertical over 100 feet up. Dalha's dad climbed up like he had done it before, then a line came down and Bobby was hoisted up like a sack of potatoes. He tried to help when he could find a hand or foot hold, but for the most part he was simply frightened and useless. After Bobby was up, he was at least able to help haul Dalha up. She was clearly no novice to climbing, but wasn't a patch on her old man. Not for the first time, Bobby asked himself what the hell he was doing here? Then he remembered, we do it for the stories we can tell.

In the blackness of the hut, Dalha leaned into him. Bobby leaned forward too. He could feel her warm breath on his cold nose, somehow reassuring. Her long arms were around him now as she slowly guided him onto his side next to her, a crescent half around his inner circle he was facing into her. Bobby's butt vaguely felt the contour of Dad against him on the other side.

"On your back, Bobby," Dalha whispered in his ear. "Relax. You need rest. Sleep."

Huddled as he was in the fetal position, Bobby didn't comply. "I fear if I fall asleep I won't wake up," he whispered back earnestly.

His shivering was audible. This was no joke. Something hard was placed into Bobby's mittened paw. "Chew," Dahla whispered. "Eat. You need calories." Bobby took a bite and munched away. It was a jerky. Of what animal he had no idea but the flavor was strong and savory, his mouth filled with saliva in response as Bobby worked the meat. He swallowed and took another bite. Maybe he would live after all.

"Take your time," whispered Dalha. "We have all night."

It was a long stick of jerky and Bobby did as he was told. He took a sip of water from his bottle, but only a sip. There would be no more piss breaks until sunrise. He couldn't imagine going back out into the night air to pee. Bobby emitted a shivering sigh as the last bite of jerky went down. "Thanks Dalha," he whispered, "I feel a bit better now. Good night." A hand was against his bearded cheek, its warmth a shock. "How could you possibly have warm hands?" he hissed.

"They've been between my thighs," she replied. Bobby imagined her wide smile. "Now give me yours."

Facing each other on their sides, they were touching nose to nose, breathing into each other. Dad shifted a bit in his sleep, his butt now more firmly against Bobby's. Startled, the young man froze. Dalha removed one of his mittens. His hand was stiff, and not only from the cold.

"Relax, Bobby. Loosen up or you really will freeze to death." She rubbed his cold hand between hers vigorously, shaking and flexing his forearm as well. Then she pulled his hand inside her coat and under her many layers of clothing to place his hand against her bare belly. It felt luxuriously warm on his tingling fingertips. Her two hands pressed the back of his hand against her. Bobby could feel the thin layer of belly fat, soft and loose, as well as her abdomen muscles under, supple yet strong to his touch. They stayed that way, motionless until his hand warmth reached equilibrium with her body. She pressed her hands on his as a signal to keep his hand in place. Then she took the mitten off his other hand and repeated the process to warm it, sliding it inside her coat and clothing under and around her waist to rest on the small of her back. Her right hand went back to covering his left on her belly while she reached behind to place her left over his hand on her back. Minutes passed as they lay nose to nose, breathing soothingly in sync. The warmth from Bobby's hands slowly spread throughout his body. "That's better," Dalha whispered.

Leaving Bobby's hand on her back to its own devices, Dalha slid his belly hand in hers, with agonizingly slowness, up her torso to rest on her breastplate. She was flat chested for the most part, the bone of her sternum starkly clear in his mind's eye. She guided his hand down over one breast. Bobby could feel a large soft areola over a small warm mound of flesh. Bobby let out a sigh, picturing her beauty in the darkness. One of her hands moved off his to her other breast. He caressed her gently, sensing that Dalha was stroking herself as well. With his other hand, he softly circled the small of her back. Palm and fingertips only. Dalha shivered, but not from cold. Bobby was feeling warm enough for two now. She guided his hand from her breast slowly back down her body. Just an aching inch of movement, then a stop. Time passed. Bobby thought she had fallen asleep while he was so sensually alert to her touch. Then her hand moved his hand another inch again only to stop again. Was that intentional or just the motion of sleep?

His touch grazed over the hole of her bellybutton. Another stop. He wished he could kiss her there, taste her there, explore her with his tongue. The darkness, the sensory dependence on hand touch, aroused him like never before. While no longer cold, the pressure of her father's body against his backside, the awareness of his presence, froze Bobby in place, lest his movement break the magic and end this most excellent agony. Miles of slow motion and his hand stopped, the very ends of his fingertips feeling hair. Bobby pictured a thick bushy black triangle. He knew they were close. He paused waiting for a signal to proceed, but Dalha's hand left his as she went back to her untended breast. Bobby was on his own now. How far did she want him to go? What if this was just still part of her warming process? It had certainly worked.

***

Dalha's nipples were erect under her own touch, reveling in his. Anticipating more. He was torturing her now, his hand still, so close and yet so far. She felt fire from his fingertips and still he didn't move. He was paying her back for her own slow motion. After an eternity, she felt his fingers begin to crawl, at a snail's pace, entering her rich black forest, his fingers entwining through her thick hair approaching her pubic mound. She felt his other hand inching down her back, his middle finger stopping to rest at the start of her crack. His patience was driving her crazy. His fear of presuming too much, slowing him down.

Bobby gasped as his finger felt moisture. Dalha held her breath. A hum connecting her fingers at her breasts to his on the verge of her swollen sex vibrated through her. He stopped again, waiting for her response. Dad began to snore. Dalha couldn't wait any longer. She undulated her hips moving her achingly open sex onto his hand. Bobby finally got the message loud and clear. He stayed slow, but steady, reveling in her response. His other hand slid down her bottom. Dalha raised her knee to clear the way as Bobby reached her warm wetness with both hands. One returned slick to her bottom, massaging and pressing gently. The other probed and plunged slowly but relentlessly deeper. When Dalha went into a silent, shivering convulsion, Bobby shocked himself as he exploded in his own pants. When she finally subsided, Dalha kissed him for the first time.

***

Daylight reflecting on fresh snowfall was blinding when they crawled out the next morning. Bobby was feeling uncomfortable in his soiled pants, and facing Dalha.

"Thanks for saving my life last night," Bobby said to her with embarrassment.

"Thank you too," Dalha replied with a wide smile and then a big kiss. Bobby pulled back uncertainly, looking at Dalha's dad who didn't seem to notice as he made off to attend to morning business. "What's the matter?" Dalha asked, suddenly unsure. Bobby looked away. "Look at me," she said harshly. "We're close to 5,000 meters high in the middle of nowhere, and you turn away from me? What, are you sorry it happened now?"

"I…I don't know what I feel," Bobby confessed. "I'm sorry, Dalha. I was with Lucky just yesterday. What does that make me? I guess I'm not very proud of myself."

"You're making me feel cheap, Bobby. Like a slut."

"No Dalha, you're not a slut."

"But you're sorry it happened."

"No. I…I just never did that before."

"Really? You were just with Lucky yesterday, remember?"

"Not that. Look, I'm embarrassed, okay?"

"For what?" she asked. Bobby fidgeted. "What?" she demanded.

"I came in my pants, okay? I came in my pants!"

Dalha laughed. "Well so did I if you didn't notice! There wasn't much more we could do under the circumstances."

"You don't think…I don't know, badly of me? I haven't felt this way since I was in high school."

"Badly? Are you crazy? You were magnificent last night. Merciless too."

"Really?"

"Really!" Bobby took a few steps to nowhere, still processing. "Look at me, Bobby." He did. She held his eye. "Are we okay? I mean, I know I am not beautiful like Lucky."

"You are."

"What?"

"Beautiful. You're beautiful."

"Stop it. I'm not. I know I'm not. You know it too."

"Okay, you don't look like Lucky."

"A classic beauty."

"Yes, she's a classic beauty. But beauty comes in many shapes and sizes."

"Like skinny with a flat chest and a flat face as round as a plate?"

"Like tall and athletic with a face all smile and eyes. Cute pug nose too. You're a very pretty girl, Dalha. So pretty in fact that I can't believe we are having this conversation."

"Really? Most men don't like me, Bobby. That's the simple truth."

"They're probably intimidated by you. You look down on most men. Tall and strong as you are. I know that view myself. And beautiful on top of that. Of course they're scared of you."

"Do I intimidate you?"

"Let's see, I'd die out here without you. But no. I'm not intimidated, but you are impressive, Dalha. A very impressive physical specimen."

"Cut it out, Bobby. Do you like me?"

"Of course I like you!"

"You know what I mean Bobby. Do you…do you want to have a romantic relationship with me?" It was Dalha who now fidgeted. "There, I said it," she added, more to herself.

Bobby chuckled. "Dalha, your insecurity is adorable. Because it is so misplaced."

"Well?" Dalha was close to angry.

Bobby put his hands on her shoulders, looking in her eyes. "I am at risk of falling in love with you, Dalha." He paused. "No, I need to be totally honest and now I'm scared. I am in love with you. That's the truth of it."

Dalha smiled. "I like that. You being scared. Hey, but what about Lucky?"

"Well, I'm falling in love with her as well. Strange as that seems."

"Not so strange I guess. My mum loves all of my dads." She took a few steps away. "We'll need to get moving soon. Any business you need to attend to, now is the time. Dad will be back soon and he doesn't like to wait."

"That's it? Really? My heart is in the snow at your feet!"

Dalha turned back to him, her face radiating joy. She threw herself into his arms. "You're an idiot Bobby Singh."

"I love you."

"You have a hell of a way of showing it."

"I was unsure about my performance last night. I mean, soiling your own pants is embarrassing."

"We shared that together. It was beautiful, Bobby. And you were wonderful."

"Really?"

"Really. Are you that insecure? You? Were you like that with Lucky?"

"Of course I'm insecure. You are, why can't I be? And Lucky? She has a way of taking control of a situation. Making her intentions clear."

"And I didn't?"

"You were warming me up. I just wasn't sure."

Dalha laughed. "Just kiss me, you fool."

CHAPTER 2

TINA

Dancing on her toes, Tina quickly set her stance, throwing a wicked left upper cut into the solar plexus of her taller adversary, followed by a right cross to the slack jaw leaning into her from the impact of the first blow. The imaginary enemy went down, out cold. A cell phone pinged. Tina grabbed her sweat towel as she went to retrieve her phone from the end table. A text from Tom, her editor. Later. Where was Bobby? That was the text she wanted. Needed. Wherever he was, somewhere north and east of her she suspected, maybe just a few hundred miles away, he must be off the grid. Or dead maybe.

Tina looked out the hotel window. Srinagar. She wished she could see the water from here, but the mountains were impressive. Tina wasn't in town as a tourist. Bobby had stayed here. The young fool should have waited for her. But she knew she wouldn't have at his age. Tina worked her left shoulder a bit, sore from the shadow boxing workout. She didn't remember feeling this sore after pankration practice before. Of course, that was over 2,000 years ago, when she was 20 years younger.

Looking down on the traffic moving through Srinagar, the old Kashmiri capital, part of her still couldn't get over the here and now that was the 21st century. And that those were the ice capped Himalayas she saw in the distance on this sunny spring day. The jagged peaks looked intimidating compared to the familiar slopes of Arcadia in Greece. She wished she could open the window, get some fresh air into the hotel room, but this was a newer building, like you'd find in America. You could never open windows in modern hotels.

It was the scents that bothered Tina the most, here in the 21st century, more so than the sights. The olfactory assault of the combustion engine. It permeated everything. Scent had been so different in that earlier life in ancient Greece. More animalistic in his city, Sparta, or on the march with the army. The musky smell of sweaty men, pungent, but somehow reassuring. Alluring even.

Tina remembered his first time. When she was a he, named Agi. The boy had been the same age as he was, but smaller. Most of them were. The two of them were on a teamwork training exercise, which had taken them far into the field. Growing grain had stood tall around them. They took a rest break although he hadn't really needed one yet. The other boy was weaker. Again, most of them were. Agi had been bored, then suddenly aroused looking at the smooth slender boy body with the sprouting pubic growth on the otherwise hair free skin. Agi had rubbed the boy's curly head vigorously first, then let his hand run down the sweat slicked back of his companion. He pushed the boy over on his belly as his own member sprang to attention. The boy didn't want to, tried to rise telling him to get off, time to get moving again. Agi punched him in the gut and, with the boy doubled over on his knees in shock and pain, had forced entry. Musing back, that first time, Agi had been surprised at the initial discomfort of entry, breaking through the resistance. Worse than uncomfortable for the other boy, as Agi would learn later from his own experience. But once in, it was awesome both physically and spiritually. So empowering. Yet so humiliating to be on the receiving end, which Agi knew now all too well. The shame of arousal, and ultimately orgasm, even against your will. And they had known it, had laughed at him because of it. Still, that first time, one always remembers that first time, pounding into that boy, the resistance gone out of him succumbing to acceptance, and yes, arousal. He couldn't even remember that other boy's name, but that first time had been especially sweet. The scent of the grain all around them. The smell of the sweat, and shame from the boy. He'd owned that boy from then on. Him and many others.

Those teen years had been good years to Agi. His training years when he learned to be a warrior. A soldier. A hunter. To measure himself against others and know that he was better than almost all, equal to the rest. Apex predators like himself. Together in a small group, single minded in purpose, they were truly a terrifying lot. Gangbanging had been fun back then. Unless you got caught. Or until it happened to you.

Tina shook herself out of these memories. Back into the hotel room. What a monster. But was he? Was I? That was a different world, over 300 years B.C. Before Christ. Who the hell was Christ to a Spartan warrior? We hadn't measured time that way back then. And all the confining morality that had come with this Jesus? Oh, the spiritual love philosophy rang true to Agi's ancient mind, putting aside the deification bullshit, but how and why had this Christian cult somehow tied itself into knots to restrict the physicality, the sensuality, the sexuality of life? Without that, what's the point of living? You are only in this body once, shouted the long dead warrior silently. Use well the time, for it is fleeting.

Heading to the bathroom for a shower, Tina caught herself in the mirror. Stopped to study herself. Fascinated by her own image. Still new to the ancient warrior. Familiar to the modern journalist. Borderline old, saw the critical eye of the journalist. What a metamorphosis from a big strong shaggy mutilated man to a slender pale blonde beauty, saw the warrior. She was almost twenty years older than he was when he had died, but still a beauty to the Spartan. To be immortalized in marble. Tina slid her hands, his hands, slowly from her hips to up under her small breasts. Cupping them high before releasing as the back of her fingers grazed over each nipple. She looked hard in the mirror. Who are you anymore? Tina moved on toward the shower. There was work to do.

CHAPTER 3

TINA AND LUCKY

"I know who you are," Lucky said, seeing the blonde woman on her doorstep. "But how did you find me?"

"Bobby," Tina replied. "We reporters leave notes, you know. He reported to our editor, then Tom shared them with me. So here I am."

"Here you are. Well, I suppose you should come in now that you are," Lucky said warily, stepping aside to allow Tina to enter her houseboat. She hadn't thought that Bobby would report on her, but it made sense. Thinking of their lovemaking, she wondered how much detail Bobby had provided. Lucky suddenly realized with a start that Tina hadn't moved, but was studying her face.

"Am I really welcome?" Tina asked.

"Yes, of course," Lucky said, relenting in her own mind as she took her guest by the hand and guided her inside. "Please come in." Tina noted the contrast between the drab loose attire of her hostess and the cushioned red opulent décor of the floating efficiency apartment. "Rest yourself here," Lucky said, offering her guest a spot on a plush burgundy settee.

Tina sat erect on the edge of the furniture, her weight still firmly on her feet so she wouldn't sink into the deep seating. Bobby clearly trusted this woman, but he was young and naïve. This was a beautiful woman trying not to appear so. And doing a pretty good job of it. What was she trying to hide? Lucky plopped herself unceremoniously into the other half of the settee, her baggy trousered leg resting against Tina's khakis. Tina recognized the intentional intrusion into her personal space, and deciding not to move, allowed it. Intimidation or a come on? Tina wasn't sure which, but neither would work.

"So what can I do for you?"

"Tell me where to find Bobby, of course. He's checked out of his hotel. I had hoped to find him here, although I didn't really expect it."

"He's too stubborn to have come back so quickly, on his own." The worry in Lucky's voice was obvious.

"I know," Tina said softly. "Either he'll get the story or die trying."

"So you know. There is nothing we can do, but wait."

"Well there is a lot more I can do. I'm going after him."

Lucky stared at her aghast. "You Americans! Do you think you're immortal?"

"Something like that," Tina laughed. Agi was laughing with her on the inside.

"Really? Bobby was bad enough, but at least he is Indian. A blonde woman in the Himalayas? You must be mad!"

"What I must do is help Bobby. We have a job to do, he and I. We're professionals."

"This won't be quite like interviewing some senator in Washington. I've looked you up."

"If you researched me properly you'll know I've reported from some wild places. Sub-Saharan Africa. The Arctic circle."

"Oh I did. Those were man against nature assignments," Lucky replied. "This will be very much man against man, or woman I should say, and with a mean Mother Nature in the mix to boot."

"I can handle man," Tina growled.

"Oh I know you killed those two terrorists in the bank a few weeks ago. You were big news for a bit. Although Bobby didn't say much about that."

"He doesn't know much about that."

"But you are one person walking into a brewing three sided war," Lucky went on. "And everyone will know that you aren't on their side. Nobody will have your back."

"Reporters don't choose sides. That is our protection."

"Sure. Where such rules of decency hold. You'll be going into places where hair like yours, a complexion like yours, has never been seen. You'll be like a creature from another world. And you won't likely get a chance to explain your impartiality. And nobody will understand your English anyway even if they were inclined to listen."

"That's why you're coming with me," Tina told her. "You'll be my interpreter. My cultural liaison."

Lucky stared at the American, big eyed.

"Look, I know you care about Bobby," Tina said in a softer voice.

"So he told you."

"No. Bobby is a gentleman. But I can tell."

"I tried to stop him, but he wouldn't listen," Lucky said, fighting back a sob. A tear rolled down her soft cheek.

"You couldn't stop him," Tina said, taking Lucky's hands in hers. "But you can still help him. He is going to need it." Lucky sagged onto Tina's shoulder crying openly now. Tina took her in, feeling her curves under the oversized sweater.

***

Outside, the Intelligence Bureau agent waited patiently in his car, watching the barge that Tina Marin had entered. It was the residence of one Khatri Singh, aged 37, but owned by her father. The agent had been tailing the Marin woman since she entered India two days ago. His boss, Inspector Khera, had expected Marin to return from Greece so the IB had been monitoring all incoming flights. The agent remembered the recent event at the bank and the subsequent celebrity of the American reporter for killing the two terrorists. Khera had briefed him that he was to observe and report only, to intervene only if there was a violent incident. So far so good, but the IB considered this woman very dangerous. Despite the woman's harmless appearance, the IB agent took the assignment seriously. He would keep his distance, but remain vigilant. It would mean his job if she gave him the slip.

CHAPTER 4

PALLY

Sub-inspector Pallavi "Pally" Agarwal of the New Delhi Police Department tried to relax as the jet took off from Athens to New Delhi. Heading home. She hoped that the weather report, announcing a smooth flight, would prove correct. The flight to Greece a couple weeks ago had been terrifying. She had almost completely lost her cool. If it hadn't been for Tina, she would have. And if it hadn't been for her fear, their feelings, Tina's and hers, wouldn't have come out in the open. That first kiss as the plane dropped and lurched to a landing, desire mixed with despair of dying, had been wildly erotic.

Tina. She was about a week ahead of her. Funny how it was. Pally hadn't thought of Tina since Thea had returned to the fountain retreat three days ago. Until Thea had dropped her off at the airport this morning to fly home to India. Thea had chased Tina from her mind. But now Pally was chasing Tina. It was like Tina invaded as soon as Thea's Audi was lost from view in the airport traffic. Pally wasn't alone for even a moment. And maybe that was a good thing.

Then there was Khera. She had phoned the angry IB inspector, her temporary boss, before getting on the flight. Seconded to the Intelligence Bureau to "escort" Tina safely out of India, Khera had been expecting daily reports on all activities in Greece, but Pally had gone dark the entire time. Falling in love can do that to a girl. She had expected Khera to be done with her, to release her back to her job on the New Delhi force, but he hadn't. She had one chance to redeem herself, Khera had told her. If she did well there might even be a permanent post as an IB agent. That would be a big step forward for Pally's career. Something she had always wanted, but thought beyond her reach. Now she wasn't sure she really cared.

The mystery and magic of Tina had burst into Pally's suppressed sexuality when she had been assigned to investigate the failed terrorist attack. Tina had explored her own dual identity with Pally, not knowing where it had come from or where it was going. Even now, Tina didn't know if it was the inner man, Agi, who was attracted to Pally, a new found lesbianism long latent, or some blend of both. Despite her assurances of love, Tina had put the brakes on their relationship to grapple with the warrior within her. She needed to understand, and so be at peace, with who and what they were. Pally had been heartbroken, still was, and yet.

Thea was the reason Pally was a week behind Tina. Pally had stayed on at the fountain retreat house rather than continue in the company of Tina. Rejected as she felt, Pally couldn't bear to return to India with her despite Tina's concern for her and protestations of love. Thea was a healer. It was she who had led the ritual that brought the past life of Agi the Spartan warrior into the present consciousness of Tina the American journalist. And in doing so had ended Tina's relationship with Pally. For now anyway. So after everyone had left the retreat, Pally had a few days of contemplative respite alone in the warm pool of the cleansing fountain. If the waters alone couldn't cure, they were a soothing balm on her heart. Then Thea had returned as promised. They had talked, laughed, and cried together. Thea had gently led Pally through the ritual of oneness. Pally now understood that she was not alone, never had been, and never would be. In Thea, she found the certainty of eternal unconditional acceptance, love, and learned to return it in kind. Tina had never been out of Pally's heart the whole time she was with Thea, but she had been out of her mind, giving Pally time, under Thea's guidance, to explore and discover herself unencumbered. Now Tina was back on her mind, both personally and professionally, while Thea remained in her heart forever.

A bump of turbulence broke Pally's reverie with a jolt of adrenaline. The plane was smooth and steady again, streaking 30,000 feet over land and sea at 500 miles an hour. Pally tried to relax, focusing on her next steps. Her orders were to catch up with Tina and stick with her for as long as she remained in India. If she eventually chose to leave the country again, this time Pally was not to follow. Khera had called Pally a valuable data gathering tool, but of limited use. He didn't believe that the American actually trusted Pally, but just pretended to for her own as yet unknown purposes. Khera intended to find out what those purposes were. He suspected they were sinister to India's interests. Even if Pally was being fed a line of lies, her relationship placed her in a unique position to observe. As a first stop before catching up with Tina, Pally would meet Khera and a panel of experts to be debriefed. To glean information out of the police sub-inspector that she didn't even know she had. Fully believing in Tina's innocence of any malice toward India, Pally expected the debriefing to prove that Khera was mistaken.

***

"So you're still convinced that Marin is in touch with a past life from ancient Greece?" asked Khera, clearly not convinced himself.

"Yes, Inspector," replied Pally. "Now more than ever. If you had witnessed, been a part of the ritual, you would have no doubts."

"An interesting story you tell," put in another interrogator. "Tell us more about this place, and the ritual."

"I have already described it as thoroughly as I can and recounted the events in as much detail as I retained."

"You haven't given us the location of this fountain or the names of the people involved," said Khera sternly.

"Nor will I, Inspector," Pally shot back. "I gave my word and I assure you I will take that information to the grave. If that ends my career, so be it." Khera grunted.

"Let's go back to your relationship with Tina Marin," a psychologist ordered, the only woman on the interrogation team.

"I assure you, as I said before, Tina trusts me completely."

"Yes, but why is that I want to know. Why would a suspect trust a police sub-inspector assigned to keep her under surveillance?"

"Because I believed her from the beginning," Pally answered with suppressed exasperation. "I was the only one who did. And apparently I am still the only one who does. If any of you showed signs of believing me right now that would be the start of a trust relationship, don't you think doctor?" The psychologist sniffed.

"So she trusts you, I'll give you that," said another IB officer. "And you obviously trust Marin as well."

"So?"

"So, clearly your relationship is beyond professional. What exactly is it?" he demanded.

"It is the sub inspector's job to get as close to Ms. Marin as possible," Khera interjected, coming to Pally's defense. "By any means necessary as far as I am concerned. Let's keep perspective on what we are dealing with. Ms. Marin might be part of a malicious infiltration of India to undermine our culture and political stability apparently with a focus on undermining our hold on Kashmir. It's already a tinderbox."

"Then let's just deport her and be done with it," the IB officer said.

"Normally I would agree, but this is not a normal situation. We have Sub-inspector Agarwal on our side. And although she believes in Marin's innocence, she has a strong police record, is open minded, and remains our best asset. We are better off having Marin in India with Agarwal at her side than outside India stirring up trouble by other means. We have a chance to break this ring rather than just deport one link in a chain." Although the room wasn't convinced, it was Khera's call so nobody argued.

"And I will keep an eye out for any hint that Inspector Khera is correct and report accordingly," Pally said. "Meanwhile, if I am right about Tina, then she herself is an asset in India's cause. Her very assignment is to investigate the cause of the escalated unrest in Kashmir. And regardless of who she really is, her credentials as an investigative reporter are well documented and impressive."

"We're done here," Khera said, standing up. As the meeting broke up, he turned on Pally. "You call me daily from now on. Don't go dark on me again."

"If I don't call, Inspector, it will mean I'm in trouble. That will be a message in itself."

"It's a dangerous assignment," Khera said, somewhat mollified. "Now off you go to Srinagar to catch up with your quarry." As Pally left the room, Khera's voice followed her, "And take care of yourself."

CHAPTER 5

AGI AND TINA

Agi broke into the hut, smashing his shield against a frail door that didn't just break open, it burst asunder into so many fragments, it was no longer definable. Striding inside, victorious, his chest was heaving from recent exertion. Blood dripped down his sword arm, but it wasn't his. He took a moment to lick it off his wrist, lest it reach his palm and loosen his sword hand which was already slick enough with sweat. Still warm, the blood and sweat mix tasted good.

The rush of combat was slowly subsiding; the inherent confidence of the Spartan soldier, the professional concentration forged through years of training, and nagging in the not so remote back of his mind, his old friend Fear. Yes, Fear was his friend he often reminded himself. For it would keep him alive. It tempered his pride, lest he succumb to hubris, the infamous flaw of Odysseus, Agamemnon, and so many others. Friend Fear kept him secretly humble before the fight and during the fight. But now the fight was over and Fear demanded his due. An outlet.

Cowering on some animal skins in a corner, moaning and whimpering, were a woman and two children. They were tending to a fallen man. Or had been. His arm was practically severed just above the elbow and there must have been some other wound near the hip or thigh. There was blood everywhere, but it was no longer flowing for his stream of life was spent. Now his family was mourning. Agi saw it all in an instant. Wounded in the fight to protect his village, the man had limped back home and bled out.

A scrawny boy, maybe nine years old, sprang from his father's side and rushed at Agi in a rage. He swatted the boy aside with a shielded backhand launching the small body airborne against a wall. He let his shield slip from his hand and arm. He would need it no more this day. His short sword was still in his right hand, in case the woman too had any ideas. The little girl was just a toddler. Let her watch and wail. The woman rushed to her unconscious son with a cry.

He took the woman by her long disheveled black hair, dragging her away from the boy, but she clutched her inert son fiercely to her breast causing him to be dragging both mother and child to the low bed on the other side of the room. This wouldn't do. He jerked her head back hard, creating a gap between mother and child causing a cry to escape from the woman's soul. He placed the blade of his sword against the boy's throat and asked the woman a question with his eyes. She released her son and fell back with a sob. He dropped the boy and tossed the woman on the bed by her hair. The boy moaned, distracting him for a moment. The boy came to his hands and knees, shaking the cobwebs out of his head. Then he looked up at the invader with a hatred greater than his strength. *I'll not have this one growing up to track me down ten years hence for revenge.* As the boy sprang at the man with a shout, the woman screamed. Agi hacked wickedly into the thin neck of the boy, half severing his head. Blood spurted in pumps from the gurgling open throat of the fallen convulsing child. The woman screamed again rushing from the bed, but she was caught and thrown back. The sword was no longer needed. Fear had his own sword and he demanded his due. Now.

He was soon thrusting hard and deep. The sounds coming from the woman were of no consequence to him. She was limp beneath him, but she moistened up just the same. He thrusted away mindlessly. The present senses in his genitals chasing away all thought. This made it all worthwhile. Living with Fear. And feeding it with frenzy. That familiar welling in his groin never got old. Soon. He kept thrusting away into the woman in ecstasy, almost ready to explode. *Wait, what was that buzzing?*

Tina's pelvis was still raping her pillow when she came into consciousness in response to her cell phone buzzing on the nightstand. Awake, Tina collapsed limply face down onto the pillow. Her whole body was slick with sweat, except her groin. There it wasn't just sweat. She was close. Her cell kept buzzing. Her hands slid down to her sex. To hell with the phone, she had a dream to finish.

***

As Tina drove through the streets of Srinagar to Lucky's floating home, she was still trying to sort out that dream. It was very troubling, for while it had been a dream it was also a conglomeration of assorted memories. They had really happened. Numerous times. Killing kids. Raping women. Sometimes killing the women afterward if they showed too much fight. Sometimes raping kids if they were old enough, boys and girls. He had done those things. She had done those things. As she was driving wide awake in the here and now, Tina could recollect those experiences. Not only the events, but the sensations. The feelings while in the act. If she still had a penis, she'd be throbbing right now, swelling her pants at those memories. Horrified, Tina felt a moistening between her thighs. Good lord, this has to stop. She willed herself to do so.

The shame of Agi's past, their past, overwhelmed Tina. Those countless victims, every one of them were just the same as Agi's own precious girls. The three sisters who had rescued him in his need. Nurtured him back to health. Took them into their home and hearts. Loved him. Tina could picture them in her mind's eye from Agi's memory. Three little lithe women, dark of hair and hazel eyed. Olive complexioned. Lovely, each of them could have fallen prey to an Agi in another circumstance. Helen had actually been raped, but not by Agi.

Ashamed? No, Agi wasn't ashamed. He accepted his past. It couldn't be undone. What was the point of shame? Regret? Certainly, but there was no point wallowing in it. The past was the past. He was different now. Had already been different, a better man, before he died two thousand years ago. And it was the way of the world back then. Probably still is now. Human nature didn't really change. And he had been cleansed in a ritual led by the Priestess Amalthea at the Fountain of Aphrodite. So Agi reasoned.

It was Tina who was ashamed. Agi's redemption at the fountain had been Tina's awakening to her past life. They were both still grappling with it. And each other. One in body. Not so in mind and spirit. Not yet anyway. "We have to live with it," Tina said aloud, alone in the car. "With each other. Sooner or later we need to be of one mind." No answer.

It took Tina a while to find a place to park along the lake where Lucky lived, but she finally found a spot. She sighed as she unbuckled her seatbelt and unlocked the car door. But then, the passenger door surprised her by opening and Pally slid into the car. Tina gasped.

"Hello Tina," Pally said cheerfully.

"Pally. What are you doing here?"

Pally laughed. "Still on the job, Tina. Glad to see me?"

Tina frowned. "Honestly? I don't know what I feel. Wait. How…"

"Your old friend, IS Inspector Khera," Pally interrupted. "Remember him? Loves your ass, but doesn't trust the rest of you an inch? He's still my boss and I'm still assigned to keep you company during your stay here in India."

"Pally, we can't start this all over again. What I told you at the fountain still stands. I can't get into a relationship with you. Certainly not now, maybe not ever. I'm just too screwed up in the head. I'm sorry."

The Indian cop absorbed this news. In fact, she had been expecting it. Tina saw a sad smile as Pally focused the face of Thea in her mind. She was looking at the lovely lean blonde who had made such passionate love to her only a few weeks ago while picturing the wizened smile of the priestess of Aphrodite who had counseled her after Tina left. Funny, she thought. Both Thea and Tina were about the same age, almost twenty years older than she was. But Thea seemed older, and much wiser.

"Look, Tina," Pally explained. "I can't pretend that I'm not still crazy in love with you. I am. But thanks to Thea, I have some perspective on what love is. And what we are."

"The Lady Amalthea, you mean. She is a priestess of great power and wisdom. What is her counsel?"

"That it is right to love a person, all people in fact. But we must live and let live with complete acceptance of each other as we are. Without any expectations. Without any rights of ownership. We can always offer, but never demand."

"And what do you offer? Do you still offer marriage and a life together in America?"

"Is that what you want?"

"It doesn't matter what I want, what do you offer?"

Pally paused for a moment, then sighed. "If I may do so without dishonor, I think it best I withdraw my offer of marriage, Tina. Not because of you, but because of me."

Tina smiled. "Because of me too. We are both beginning new lives. Exploring who and what we are. I accept your withdrawal, Pally. I think that is for the best."

"Can I still be your youngling?" Pally asked.

"You will always be my youngling."

"I love you, Tina," the younger woman said softly.

"I love you too, Pally," came the reply.

They leaned into each other across the front seat, lips touching gently, then opening for a long, lingering exchange. As it ended, their foreheads and noses came together. Tina's hand was on Pally's breast before either of them knew it. Pally gasped.

"Stop it!" Tina barked.

"Tina?"

"Not you Pally, me. Or us rather."

"Agi?"

"I can't blame it on him. It isn't even honest to refer to Agi in the third person any more than it is right to refer to Tina in the first person. We are both me."

Pally rested back into the passenger seat with a sigh, adjusting her bra. "It sounds busy in there."

"It's chaos. But the Spartan soldier and the American reporter have one thing in common at least. A singular sense of duty. There are no battles to fight, not yet anyway, but there is a story to uncover, write, and tell to the world. And there is a young reporter out there somewhere who likely needs a wingman."

"And maybe the wingman could use a wingman too," suggested Pally.

Tina took a deep breath. "I accept whatever help you can offer, Pally. But your mission is different from mine. Maybe we can be on the same path together for a while."

"It may not be so different. I still believe in you, Tina."

"Thanks. I know you do, Pally."

CHAPTER 6

LIAM

"Dorothy. Call me Dorothy."

"Uh, yes Ma'am. Uh, Dorothy," a pause, "Ma'am."

Special agent Miller, Dorothy Miller, of the FBI sighed. She'd spent a lifetime building a persona to intimidate, to protect herself. Was it so difficult to put it aside when convenient? To relax? Allow others to relax around her? Strong walls she had built. Hair thin veneer is what it felt like to her now. Why? This place. It must be this place. Couldn't possibly be her. Miller's backpack still in his hand, the Air Force enlisted man continued his duties moving to her bed.

"Just toss it on the bed." She sighed again, staring at the unadorned wall of her room. As if she couldn't carry her own gear. For the most part, Dorothy didn't mind the trappings of authority that she had worked so hard to earn. Why was it bothering her now? She'd been stationed in India for almost six months now, a male dominated culture for sure. Patriarchal as fuck. Now she was in Pakistan. Just as bad, maybe worse. Was that it? She was too experienced an operator for that to be it. Adapt to the terrain, and the people, as needed to complete the mission. Her mission right now was to find an American citizen. To find out what the fuck was going on. To determine if American interests were being compromised, or even at risk."

"Uh, ma'am? Dorothy?"

"Come back for me at 1700," she barked. "Dismissed."

"Uh, yes, uh Dorothy."

Having this pimpled kid along with her, as her driver, her escort, her "protector" was bothering her. That was it. She could legally travel solo in this country, but she'd probably have to bust a few heads along the way. She wasn't here to bust heads, not yet anyway. That would just slow her down. Hence the escort, courtesy of the USAF from the US embassy in New Delhi. We're guests. And as guests we respect the customs of the country.

"And return appropriately dressed," Miller added as the airman went to leave.

The young man froze at the door. "Ma'am?"

"Dorothy."

"How do you want me to dress? Dorothy."

"In a salwar kameez. The outfits I just bought for us." Although he had handled the transaction. The man. "I'll be wearing one too. Dismissed. No wait. Sit down, airman." Feeling awkward, he looked around the sparse room, Dorothy was standing right next to the only chair. She sat down. "You can sit on the bed, airman."

"Yes ma'am." He perched himself on the edge of the bed, erect, sitting at attention.

This was ridiculous. Dorothy launched out of her chair, shoved him hard on his shoulders, knocking him back on the bed. "At ease, airman," she growled as she prowled around the small room. "What's your name, airman?"

He was sitting up again, but deeper on the bed. "Liam?"

"Liam. Have a last name, Liam?"

"Uh, Miller, ma'am. Uh, Dorothy."

"A long lost cousin. Wonderful." She was still prowling around. Feeling caged. He dared not get off the bed. A seeming sanctuary. Dorothy squared off in front of him. Towering. "How old are you, Liam?"

"Uh, I'll be twenty next month."

"Perfect. And where are you from?"

"Iowa. Well, daddy grew up in South Carolina, we spent a lot of time there too. You know, vacations. Visiting grandma and granddad."

"Really? My people are from South Carolina. Maybe we really are cousins." The ginger kid looked nervous. Good. And there were only just a few pimples along his jaw. Not so bad. "Now listen up, Cousin Liam. You've been seconded to me for as long as I need you. I wanted a strong young man and you fit the bill, but the attache's office has a helluva sense of humor giving me an Iowa boy. I specifically asked for somebody with mountain experience and he sent me a flatlander."

"But I love mountains," Liam said. "I volunteered."

"You volunteered? What, did they run a raffle?"

"Well, none of the marines at the embassy had mountain experience or couldn't be spared maybe, so they reached out to other service personnel. And I volunteered."

"I wonder if you'll still love the mountains once you've hiked over them."

"I will. I mean, I know I'm from Iowa, but I've been to Philmont twice."

"Philmont?" Dorothy asked.

"Scout camp. It's in the Rockies. Northern New Mexico. Beautiful. Like here."

Dorothy laughed, sitting down next to him on the bed. "A boy scout, perfect. Eagle scout, I assume?"

"Nah, I just made Star. Eagle's for nerds. I'm more into camping and hiking than gathering merit badges."

"Well, you'll earn a few before I'm done with you. We'll be going up the creek and over the mountain on this jaunt."

"Where?" Liam asked.

Dorothy gave the lad a long hard stare. He didn't quite wilt under it, but he blushed. "Siachen glacier country. Know of it?"

"Sure. It's what they all fight about, isn't it?"

The boy had a brain. Dorothy smiled for the first time. The change was so radical, so complete to Liam. Within the formidable black woman, he suddenly saw a girl. And he was smitten. His blush deepened.

"You okay? You look like you're going to blow that carrot top of yours right off your shoulders."

"I, I, nothing."

"Well that won't do. We're going to be spending a lot of time together. Take a few breaths and tell me." Liam remained mute. "That's an order." But her usual hard tone hadn't completely returned.

"I, I, I kinda like you. Okay? I have since, since that ball game. Remember?" Liam said.

"I remember." Dorothy felt a surge of compassion for the awkward kid. A cherry. Definitely a cherry. Still a boy scout. "Okay," she said, then whispered loudly, "I kinda like you too." She slapped his knee. "Now go get your salwar kameez on and come back in five. You're taking me out to dinner."

Liam grinned, "Yes, ma'am," he replied enthusiastically as he vaulted off the bed.

***

Dinner was a quiet affair. Nothing formal. Local fare and very good. Not generally a social diner, Dorothy focused on the task at hand. Enjoying it, but only commenting occasionally on the cuisine or the aromas. Liam watched her discreetly through dinner. The strength of her hands. The contrast between the dark shade on the back of her hands and the pink of her palms. The line of her square jaw, pronounced by the taut smoothness of her skin, the same dark hue of her hands. He suddenly realized that he couldn't tell her age. Not just by looking. She could be thirty or sixty, he wouldn't know. Only the fact that she was a special agent of the FBI, and that the military attaches treated her as a senior officer, plus her innate authority, led him to assume that she was older. They had both almost finished when Liam summoned his courage.

"So Dorothy," Liam began, still feeling bold using her first name. "How old are you?"

"Didn't your mother ever tell you not to ask a lady's age?"

"Yes, but well, the girls I know all brag about it the older they get. You know the big ones, 18. 21."

"21, huh? Well, I'm a bit older than 21."

"Sorry."

"Don't be. It's a silly rule. Nothing to be ashamed of. Actually, I'm not 21, I'm 43. What do you think of that?"

Liam took a deep breath. "I think that's…old," he said with a chuckle.

"Positively ancient. But I still have a spring in my step. Since my story will be a long one, seeing as I am practically a senior citizen, we'll start with you. Tell me about your short life."

"Not much to tell really. I enlisted in the Air Force after high school and ended up here."

"Clearly there wasn't a girl back home to hold you. Or was there? Were you running from a breakup? You wouldn't be the first, you know." Liam blushed, but said nothing. "You're no poker face, my boy."

He hesitated. She waited. "Lilly. Her name is Lilly. Adams. And I've loved her forever."

"Let me guess, Lilly is a big old black woman like me."

That at least took the seriousness off his face. "No. Nothing like that."

"Ah, you two were the prom king and queen, but she went off to college where you couldn't follow so you ran away from home to hide your shame."

"No, not that either," he replied with a laugh.

"What then?"

"It really wasn't anything that spectacular. Really wasn't anything at all. We were just friends, sorta."

"Friends sorta. You never told her. Jesus, Liam, you never told her that you loved her? Even liked her?" He blushed, but said nothing, his shoulders drooped and his head hung. "Look at me, Liam. Look at me." He reluctantly met her eyes. "You were able to tell me. That you like me. But never her?"

"She was always so, I don't know, way out of my league."

Dorothy laughed at that. "And I am not, is that it?"

"I didn't mean it that way," Liam rushed. "It's just that well, you ordered me to tell you, and suddenly I could."

"But you're still head over heels in love with your Lilly?"

"I know I sound like a fool, but I do love her still. And I always will. So I figured if I'm destined to go through the world alone, I might as well see some of it. And here I am."

Dorothy smiled. "So tragic. And at such a young age."

"Don't laugh. This is serious. And now I'm feeling guilty."

"About what?"

"Being here with you. Having a good time. Liking another girl."

"Don't be silly. You owe that girl nothing. Nothing. Love her all you want, for as long as you want, but don't let her break your stride." Dorothy paused, then changed course, "You're a big strong young man. Fit. What sports did you play in high school? Other than basketball."

"I didn't play basketball in school. Didn't make the cut."

"You were certainly good enough to take me to the hoop whenever you wanted."

"Yeah, but you're…" Liam didn't complete his thought.

"But I'm a woman. And an old one at that."

"No, you were tough. Tougher than I would have thought."

"But just too slow. 20 years ago it might have been different."

"I'm sorry," Liam blurted. "For taking advantage."

"Nonsense. You played to win. Let me tell you something, boy. If you hadn't played your best I would have known it. And then I would have been really pissed off."

"You seemed pretty pissed as it was," Liam said.

Dorothy sighed. "So changing the subject," she said, "Did you play any sports in high school?"

"Baseball is my main sport. But I played football too."

"You have the build of a pitcher. Long armed and lanky. What are you, six foot or so? 175?"

"A little over six one, but you nailed it on my weight. But I'm no pitcher. I played center field."

"Center, eh? Then you must have some wheels. And a gun. What about football?"

"Receiver on offense, safety on D."

"Which do you prefer?"

"Receiver. Definitely receiver. How about you? What are your sports?

"These days? Tennis is my game, when I get the chance."

"I never played. Just tennis?"

"For play, yes. For training, I focus on martial arts. Mostly boxing, and karate. As you saw in the gym."

"You have the look of a boxer."

"Now what the hell does that mean?"

"It's not bad," he rushed. "It's just that you look, well, powerful. And I saw how you can throw a punch. No offense."

"Relax. None taken. And I know that I am not exactly feminine in appearance."

"No, you're just a big girl, that's all. Five foot ten or so, right? Maybe 135?" She appreciated that he said girl rather than woman.

"I'm an inch taller and ten pounds heavier. And you know it. But thanks for trying."

"Well, you're very fit, that's for sure."

"Enough of this," Dorothy said with a pleasant growl. The boy had found his feet. That was the main thing. "We have a long day ahead of us tomorrow," she continued, "Let's shove off."

***

Dorothy worked her left shoulder, feeling sore after a long, tedious day of provisioning, packing, then moving to a hotel in Shogran not far from the Chinese border. Tomorrow they would drive into the mountains, go hiking, and not return. How their embassy in Pakistan worked it out with Pakistani security, Dorothy didn't know. She tried to get the low down, but was stonewalled. It bothered her, being dependent on a deal she wasn't a part of. How reliable was it? Just a local deal with one corrupt official or sanctioned by the government? Either way, at what point, in what situation, might the cooperation collapse?

"Where are we going?" Liam asked. They were both sitting together with all of their gear in Dorothy's room.

"China."

CHAPTER 7

DALHA AND BOBBY

Dalha and Bobby, led by Dad, slowly descended out of the snowy mountains into a small high mesa, a few miles in diameter, surrounded by more snowy peaks. To their right the clear sun was still peeking over the western slopes, but it wouldn't be long before a brief twilight led to dark. Brown grasses forced their way through patches of snow on the plain feeding various livestock casually tended by a sparse scattering of herders. A few nomadic encampments of four or five structures each were visible on the level ground nearest to the threesome working their way down to the flatland.

They met the four-footed residents before any bipeds, but it was easy for the travelers to work their way through. Bobby soon saw that they were passing between a quarter mile gap between two of the camps to forge deeper into the plain. Campfires were starting to flare up on either side of them and Bobby could see distant flickers before them. A faint yet pungent aroma, unpleasantly familiar, struck Bobby's senses.

"Is that smell from the wood fires?"

"From the dung fires, Bobby. See many trees around?"

A half hour later it was clear to Bobby which fire they were heading for. With a nod to Dalha, who responded with a soft smile, Dad veered off and, silent as ever, was soon swallowed into the early evening dark. A wind gust struck them full on the face and Bobby stopped, doubled over to avert the death of chill. Dalha removed a mitten from her hand, then took one of Bobby's, she thrust his hand with her strong grip into her pocket. A thrill ran through Bobby at her touch and for a moment he was oblivious of all else until he stumbled in the dark, almost falling to his knees before catching himself, with Dalha's help.

"You all right, Bobby? Good thing I had your hand."

"It was your hand that threw me. Or your touch, I should say."

"Well, well. Glad I haven't lost my touch."

"Oh, you haven't. Not with me. But hang on to me, despite your dizzying effect. I don't want to lose my way in the dark."

"No worries, I've got you. It's not far."

"Where are we going?"

"To meet my mum," Dalha said. Bobby staggered again and Dalha laughed. "You really had no idea just how dangerous this assignment would be, did you?"

"Why didn't you tell me for god's sake? And why isn't your dad coming with us then?"

"Oh, it's not his day of the week. I have more than one dad, remember?" Dalha said. Bobby was speechless and they walked on for a bit. "I'm kidding," Dalha said.

"Glad to hear it, but to be honest I wasn't quite sure."

"Of course they don't have separate days. They all live together and everytime they make love each of my dads copulates with mum. It's a rule, I think. Or perhaps just a family tradition."

"Really?"

"No, not really."

"Well how would I know?" Bobby took a couple more steps then pulled up, bringing Dalha to a halt as well. "Jeezuz Dalha, your mother? What should I say? How do I greet her?"

"You can't say anything because she won't understand you. Just stand right before her, respectfully look her in the eye, then gently touch her forehead to forehead, nose to nose."

"Okay, I can do that. I think," Bobby said, nodding his head.

"Then firmly, but ever so gently with both hands at the exact same time, you squeeze her tits."

"Funny. You're not helping you know. Is the forehead thing even real?"

"Nope. I just couldn't resist."

"That's it. Let's go back. To hell with the story. I'd rather be a plumber."

Dalha pulled Bobby back as he made to turn back to the mountains. "Relax, Bobby. No BS now. Just keep holding my hand, and let me do the talking."

"That sounds better. And much more normal."

Dalha started walking again, leading Bobby by the hand to the nearest fire with a vague shape of a structure behind it. "Just be your wholesome, handsome, charming self and if I know mum the three of us will be in the sack together before dinner."

"Will you stop? I'm really nervous here."

"Relax Bobby. You'll love it. I mean her. My mum."

"You've really got a mean streak. You know that, don't you?"

***

Dalha pulled a deep first drag on her cigarette. It felt good to smoke again after a week of abstinence. Bobby leaned into her as she held the lighter for him, his face a study. Dalha saw the frown on his brow, not from anger she knew, but he must still be processing all he had just heard. Across from her on the animal skin rug sat her mum. Patient, silent, stoic. She hadn't seen her mum for some years, but she hadn't changed much since from her earliest memories. Tall, strong, of the Earth, a part of it, weathered by the seasons, but indestructible as the mountains themselves.

Mum had finished telling her story, her life story for she deviated often from answering Bobby's questions, sharing so much with her long absent daughter. Dalha had translated every word and even though she saw the total lack of context of some of what she told Bobby and knew he had questions, the young man had listened only. Now the long talk was over and she was enjoying this cigarette. She took another sip of her drink from the same worn ceramic bowl her mum had served them stew. Now for the after dinner digestive with smoke. The Macallan 18 year old was a silky swallow.

"How much did you already know of what your mother has been saying?" Bobby asked.

"Me? Almost none of it. I left home as soon as I was able to hike on my own two feet over the mountains. I was twelve, maybe? Not sure. Only been back twice for visits. None of this was happening."

"Well, I'm glad it wasn't an unnecessary trip because I think I am beginning to see the picture."

"Believe me Bobby, I couldn't have saved you the trouble. This is all news to me. What do you make of it?"

"It sounds like somebody has infiltrated India without detection and they are using your people to help them. The question is why. And who? I came out here on a tip that we might be behind it all."

"We?"

"We, as in the USA. That is the story I need to uncover."

"Bobby, whoever is using this route is going to great pains to remain undetected. We've got to be careful. I've told you before. You stand out."

"Yes, and that strikes me as odd. There must be lots of ways to sneak in and out of India. Big country. Huge population. Thousands of miles of border and coastline. Why enter via the most difficult way possible?"

"It is the least populated area and, despite that it is highly militarized, there is a great deal of ambiguity regarding who owns what. Where the borders are. If caught, there is plausible deniability."

"And it is close to where they want to operate. After all, they didn't come in this way to infiltrate Madras."

"But there is something else. There must be. The key that makes it all fit," said Bobby, "That is the why. First we'll need to find out who."

Dalha took Bobby by the hand, "your hand is warm. You've got the chill out of your bones?" She noticed her mum watching.

"Yes, it is comfortable inside. Nice to be out of that heavy coat for the first time in a week." Bobby yawned. "I could sleep for a week."

With a wink to Dalha, her mum got up, threw on a coat and cape, then left the small home without a word.

"Wouldn't you like to clean up first? I know I would."

"You kidding? I'd kill to be clean. I smell so bad, I offend myself."

"Not so bad, noticeable, but I like it. Yours is a unique scent. I could recognize you in the dark. But come." Dalha led him to a curtained off stretch of wall near the cast iron stove. Two wide shallow vats, one filled over ankle deep with water, awaited them. "Here, I will help you undress."

"I can manage, Dalha. And you should go first anyway. There's not much water here."

"We have all the snows of the Himalayas for water, Bobby. Guests first."

"Well, I was taught Ladies First, but as you wish." He looked around for where to start, but Dalha pulled up a low stool and sat Bobby down. She pulled off his heavy boots, then his socks."

"Better burn those," said Bobby. "Now I really can manage the rest of the way."

"It is the custom here to bathe our guests when they first arrive."

"Wow! Really?"

"No, not really. You're too easy. At least I hope so. Just let me seduce you in my own way, ok?"

"Okay."

"No more talking," Dalha ordered softly. She stood him barefoot in the empty vat.

CHAPTER 8

SHE

She recited the coded answers in Kashmiri that got her a sherpa to guide her through the highest portions of the contested Siachen Glacier region from Indian control into what only nominally was Chinese controlled. There was a secluded and small high altitude valley cut off from any access but on foot that She needed to reach. It was the southernmost of a series of adjacent small valleys connected only by steep animal traces that the locals knew but seldom used. Useless for commerce other than what could be worn on one's back. That had been her secret path into India and it would be her path out. There were a few well known high altitude passes through the mountains into Indian Kashmir from Pakistani and Chinese territory, but they were never an option. It had taken her a long time to find this trail, used by just a few of her operatives since She first trekked into India some years back. Now She was heading out for the first time, but hopefully only to that first southernmost valley. And it would be a short stay. Get there, find Bobby Singh, kill Bobby Singh, then back to India.

That Dalha had gone with him was a surprising and troubling complication. She thought Dalha was from the Ladakh region and would be a handy cultural guide for the American, but hadn't thought she would know how to get north of the Siachen Glacier. A young, idealistic Dalha had been her first contact when She came to Kashmir. Dalha dreamed of an independent Kashmir of the old borders including not just Indian, but current Chinese and Pakistani territory. They had met at a student independence meeting. She needed the grass roots lay of the land, and had expertly plucked the naive Dalha out of the pack where most were more interested in socializing than politics. Even though Dalha had a cute boy buzzing around her like a fly, She had seduced Dalha with experienced ease. A few weeks into an intensely physical relationship, She brought the boyfriend in, who had still been hanging around Dalha, to make it a threesome. After some months, when She had learned all she could from those two, She dropped Dalha, presumably over a policy rift arguing that the focus should be on Indian

Kashmir first. She founded her own little independence group, starting by stealing Dalha's cute boy from her. But the group was just a cover for other activities and a means to find the type of people that She would find useful. It had been a couple of years since She had seen Dalha, although She kept track of her activities. Now it seemed She might have to kill Dalha too when she took out the Singh kid, if Dalha got in the way. She accepted that likelihood with a sigh of regret remembering Dalha's long body against hers. A nearby cough brought her back to the here and now. The sherpa set out. She hoisted her pack filled with her mountaineering gear. She followed step for step with her trusty ice ax in hand. Both a tool and a weapon.

CHAPTER 9

DALHA

Dalha nestled deeper into Bobby under heavy blankets. A soft purr coming from his sleeping lips. I put him to sleep, she thought with satisfaction. Still, Dalha was tired too. Physically satisfied herself from wonderful love making yet worried for a number of reasons. It had been a grueling journey, tougher than she remembered, but of course it had been several years. Still, at only 23 years old, Dalha shouldn't be feeling it like she was. After all, her fathers made the trek on a regular basis. But like her mom, her dads were immortal to Dalha.

Bobby and Dalha fit like a glove to hand. Both long and lean, both the same age, both Kashmiri. And they were in love. Sure it had happened fast, but that's how it goes sometimes. But then there was Lucky. Dalha had mixed feelings about Lucky. The thought of her lovely hourglass figure excited Dalha even now in her exhausted yet satisfied state. In a word, Lucky was gorgeous by anyone's standards. While they hadn't yet talked about it, Dalha knew that Lucky was entrusting Bobby to her care to be returned safely to Lucky. Was it just imagination that hoped for a triad with Bobby and Lucky together? What if Bobby and Lucky chose to be a couple leaving Dalha out in the cold? It had happened to Dalha a few years ago, her last relationship in fact. Dalha had been in an exciting relationship with a college boy. Through the Independence movement they had met a more mature woman. They suddenly found themselves in a wildly erotic threesome for a few months. Then just as quickly as it began, the young man and older woman had cut Dalha out without explanation, leaving Dalha wounded and insecure. Now here comes Bobby, the first man she has been interested in since, and he comes with an older woman far more beautiful than the last one. How could her bony frame compete with the luscious Lucky?

Although tired, Dalha wasn't sleepy. Too much on her mind. So she rested with her eyes closed against Bobby's long frame. Her thighs were aching, clearly out of shape for climbing atop mountains, and men. A slow hour passed of Bobby's soft snoring. Dalha gently removed herself from Bobby to stand over him looking down on his contented countenance in the dim light. The air was cool on her naked frame, but not uncomfortably so. She fetched the oil lamp from the other end of the room to hang it near the bed to cast clearer light on this young man who enamored her so. Without waking him, Dalha pulled extra bedding over her and Bobby, yet exposed his genitals to the light of the lamp. Everything between them so far had been in complete darkness or under blankets. She had felt him in her, which had been glorious, but had never seen him. Now she took a good long look at his flaccid member while he slept away. Dalha rubbed her hands together to make sure she wouldn't shock him with cold hands then she carefully cradled his scrotum. Bobby shifted slightly in his sleep. His foreskin lay like a silk sheet over him. Dalha couldn't decide whether to take him in her hand to watch him grow or feel him grow in her mouth. Saliva moistened her mouth making the decision. Lightly with her lips, Dalha lifted Bobby's limp member fully into her mouth surrounding him with warm wetness, drawing gently as on a straw. Dalha's head jerked back instinctively to avoid gagging as her mouth filled immediately beyond her ability to hold Bobby. Dalha didn't try, releasing him from her mouth, so her eyes were now a few inches from him. Still satiny sheer, his foreskin covered him fully but with no room to spare. Dalha sighed, never having seen such a beautiful sight.

"What's going on down there?" Bobby grunted.

"Shsh. Say nothing."

With a hand, Dalha slowly stroked down on Bobby releasing his shiny pink glans. She cooed softly at the sight. Then she began a slow full rhythmic stroke, watching and feeling his foreskin slide full length over him from bottom to top. Dalha was mesmerized.

"By the gods, you are beautiful."

WIth her hand holding his foreskin down, Dalha traced her soft tongue up to his top then she took him in as far as she could. He felt so alive inside her mouth, which was flooded with her juices.

Throwing the covers aside now, Dalha released him from her mouth keeping her mouth closed full of saliva. She was panting through her nose. She pushed his legs wide apart hiking his knees up too. She breathed his scent deeply through her nose as she traced south under his scrotum to find his anus. Pushing his cheeks wide apart, Dalha dumped a mouthful of fluids on his dark hair rimmed hole. Her tongue circled him causing Bobby to groan.

Dalha pressed the palm of her thumb against his opening as she rose up to take his erection deeply in her mouth. She pulled on him fast and hard. The pressure on his anus got stronger. Finally with a cry from Bobby, her thumb slipped fully in, just as he shot repeatedly into the back of Dalha's mouth. She drew back to the top of him so she could manage to swallow as Bobby's pulsating gradually subsided. Dalha slipped her thumb out of his butt.

"Ugh. My god, are you trying to kill me? What a way to wake up."

"I wanted to get to know you better. See you, smell you, touch you. Not just with my vagina."

"Well, I'd say you had a pretty good tour."

Dalha laughed. "For starters. I want to get to know your body. Intimate in all ways. And I want you to do the same with me. So that we know each other as we know ourselves. And accept each other completely."

CHAPTER 10

DOROTHY AND LIAM

Dorothy Miller, FBI, was angrily in pain. After driving east and north as deep as possible into the mountainous terrain of northeast Pakistan, she and her young Air Force Airman Liam Miller (no relation) had backpacked and climbed an additional few weeks. The young Liam had impressed Dorothy from the start, which had gradually grown to respect. He would go as hard and fast as Dorothy demanded without complaint and proved a canny hand at finding the best path in their general direction. The boy had sand, that was for sure. Then Dorothy had slipped working her way up a vertical rocky crevice, in the lead, sliding out of control back down onto the following Liam. His quick action and sheer strength had averted disaster and possibly even death for Dorothy. Nonetheless she had sprained an ankle and both her wrists trying to break her fall. The result was she couldn't move without Liam's support. They hadn't seen any people for a few days now but a couple miles back they had sighted a small abandoned homestead off their path. It was there that they had laboriously returned to for shelter and to regroup.

Dorothy was trying to think through how to deal with this delay. She would need to rest this ankle to heal enough just to walk. Meanwhile, they only had the supplies they had carried on their backs. Even if they could survive off the land, which was a full time job, they would accomplish nothing for their mission. Somewhere out there was the answer to who was trying to start a civil war for Kashmiri independence that nobody wanted. At least not China, India, and Pakistan. Or did they? Was this a Chinese power play? And what of Russia? Or deep in the back of her mind, how could the USA benefit? No point dwelling on that now, she was sidelined. With caring for their supplies, she calculated that they could hole up for a week to heal then manage to limp back to Pakistan in defeat. There was no other option.

Liam came in with a fresh supply of water for them. They were in a small single room building that appears to have functioned as either a smokehouse, sauna, or both. It was snug enough and there was ample supply of firewood for the intended duration of their stay.

"Liam, you have done very well, but it appears we have failed. Once I heal up enough, we'll turn back and you'll soon be back to your regular duties at the embassy."

"I'm sorry for that. This trip has been great."

"You have a strange idea of fun."

"Come on, Dorothy. Until yesterday, weren't you enjoying it too? I'd follow you anywhere."

"Well, you've made it easy. At first I was worried you'd slow me down, but hell there were times when I struggled to keep up with you. Then there is the small matter of you saving my life. I won't forget that. Ever. Plus my report to your CO will be stellar. And well deserved."

"I'm just glad I was there to break your fall. Wish I had done better so you weren't so banged up. How does it all feel? You must be hurting."

"I'll get used to the discomfort. You've wrapped me well with your first aid training. But it will be a long slow few days healing up. Meanwhile, I can't stand and I have two useless hands."

"We'll have to come up with ways to stay sane. Maybe we can sing some songs together or something like that."

Unfortunately, I have a more immediate need and I am sorry to say it will go above and beyond the call of duty for you and it won't be in my report."

"Anything. Just say the word. I can be your feet and hands."

"No beating around the bush. I need to take a crap. And I'll need your help to clean me up. Sorry."

Liam blushed a beet red, but said nothing.

"We'll need to share this wooden bucket left here and save our fold up one for gathering ice for drinking water. No lack of water supply anyway. Again, I apologize for this, but if I'm not cleaned I'll stink to high heaven."

"We could both use a good cleaning and now that we aren't going anywhere we might as well be comfortable. I'll need some, uh, instructions when the time comes."

"Sorry again, Liam but the time is now. And I can't poop in my pants lying here on the floor so start by getting my pants down to below my knees."

Liam got her belt loosened and her fly unzipped, but then Dorothy decided it would be better to get her standing before working her pants down. With some effort they finally had her leaning with her back against the wall standing on one foot with a bucket between her feet, her powerful useless arms akimbo.

"Okay, Liam now pull my pants down. Gently."

He did as instructed without seeing too much but the bulge under her tan color panties, the surrounding muscled belly and thighs were obvious. He felt a stir in his own pants.

"Now the panties. Get it done. And feel free to enjoy the view while you're at it. You'll pay the price at the other end cleaning my ass."

"Yes ma'am."

"Helluva time to get all formal again, airman."

Liam didn't respond, but slowly inched Dorothy's panties down revealing a dense black forest of pubic hair. He let out a sigh.

"What?" Dorothy demanded.

"I, uh, nothing. But, well, by god you're beautiful."

"Gee, thanks. Meanwhile, remember what we are doing here. Secure my panties as far down my legs as you can, now stand next to me against the wall on my bad foot side so I can lean on you. I'm going to slide down the wall a bit for better positioning. You stay put."

Without further ado, Dorothy promptly and thoroughly got both things done with Liam bracing her against the wall.

"Mission accomplished. You still okay, airman? I'm not exactly smelling like a rose."

Laim laughed, "After three weeks on the march I'm fairly ripe myself."

"Well, we have plenty of time for cleanup while I heal up and of course, with no working hands, I will need your help. For starters, get my T-shirt off. You're going to wipe my ass with it. Might as well get my bra off too." A pause and he followed instructions. "Good. Now, lay me down on the floor facedown, get rid of my crap outside, clean out the bucket, then put some water in it and report back to me with a bar of soap in hand."

"Yes, ma'am."

***

"All done down there? I feel squeaky clean." Dorothy said when Liam's cleaning efforts appeared to have wrapped up to her satisfaction.

"Almost."

"Liam, thank you. That really was above and beyond the call of duty."

"Just this one last step." He had been kneeling over her bottom between her spread out legs for his ministrations. Now he spread her cheeks and kissed her anus lightly, feeling his lips on her sparse surrounding black curls. The tip of his moist tongue gently touched her center. Dorothy giggled in surprise.

"Now that was a first in my life."

"Just demonstrating that I cleaned you so well I could eat off you," Liam said, laughing. "I'm going to get some more clean water and get more ice for melting, then give you a full bathing head to toe."

"Liam, listen to me. It was a chance encounter that brought us together, we are different in almost every way other than that we are clearly kindred spirits. I will be your friend forever, your mentor if you want, and your part-time lover as opportunity allows…"

"Like now?" Liam asked.

"Like now," Dorothy continued, "but I will never be your girlfriend, your spouse, or in any way your life partner other than in friendship. And we must, always, be discreet."

"I hear you loud and clear, Skipper. And I am so grateful, my lovely lady. Yours always to command. Maybe a day will come when it won't matter and we can be lifetime loving friends out in the open for all to see."

"Maybe, but probably not in my lifetime. Definitely not in my professional lifetime. Don't forget how much my career means to me."

A while later, Liam had melted ice into warm water.

"Ready for your bath Dorothy?"

"You bathe yourself first. And if you don't mind, I'll watch. Then you can bathe the rest of me."

The young man reddened, then with a big breath reluctantly disrobed.

"You don't have to Liam, if you are uncomfortable."

"I am nervous, but I want to. It's just something I've never done before."

Dorothy enjoyed watching Liam, then Liam's bathing of Dorothy was an incredibly sensual experience for both of them if not a sexual one. Dorothy, with both wrists and one ankle bound in crude splints, could do nothing but lay passively on her back. Accepting and embracing his touch with agonizing anticipation. When Liam ran the wet rag over her bare breasts, she quivered all over. When the wet soapy hands lathered up her nipples and she blossomed between her thighs. Liam started to bathe down her belly then stopped suddenly, standing up and turning his back to Dorothy.

"I'm sorry. I can't do this."

Dorothy rolled herself up onto her knees, right behind him. Her face inches away from his backside. "That's okay. I think I understand what you are going through. Put your hands on your head, close your eyes and keep them closed. Good. Now do an about face."

Liam obeyed and Dorothy had to lean back so that his erection didn't slapped her cheek. Dorothy paused to look at the pulsing member stretched taut, quivering before her. Ready to explode. Clear juice was already seeping out of his tip. Looked yummy. She knew he was really struggling to keep under control. Her mouth moistened but her lips were dry so she licked them once just before taking him quickly in. Liam came instantly with jolting convulsions amid primal grunts and groans. His hips were thrusting too, almost knocking Dorothy off balance. She held his thighs with her forearms as best she could while arching her head back to manage a swallow without choking.

"Oh, oh," Liam moaned as his orgasm subsided. "I gotta sit down," he said, as he collapsed clumsily to the floor with Dorothy still attached. She was on her belly now between his outspread legs, slowly sucking him dry. His erection subsided somewhat. Dorothy released him from her mouth resting her head against the inside of his thigh. It was covered with curly orange hair. Admiring his genitals inches away. Liam had a mass of rich red pubic hair the like of which Dorothy had never seen. His upper body hadn't much hair, more so from the waist down. Dorothy decided that she liked the look. They rested there in silence for a while.

"I'm sorry, Dorothy."

"Don't be silly. It's all good."

"No it's not. I…I came right away."

"Of course you did. That's natural. How could you not? After all, I doubt that you have had any release since we set out. Am I right?"

"Well, yeah."

"So in a little while we'll start again. And you won't come right away. And then there will be the next time and the time after that. Always getting better and better for both of us." Liam said nothing to that. "Just chill out," Dorothy continued. "My beautiful young man."

Dorthy dozed for a bit as Liam went into a deeper sleep. He was flaccid now almost disappearing into his hair. The transformation was startling to Dorothy. Beyond her limited experience. She thought back to William, her one big love relationship in her life when she was in college. He was a sweet boy and Dorothy had fallen so deeply the relationship had almost derailed her goals. Since high school Dorothy had been driven to success even though she hadn't an understanding of what success was. In her sophomore year at a career festival she had talked to an NSA representative then later to an FBI agent. When she learned that some agents worked overseas she was sold.

Since then she had been focused entirely on her career, acutely aware that one wrong step romantically could wreck everything. William, the son of a local businessman groomed to take his father's place, she had left in the rearview mirror with deep sorrow if not regret. Now he was a distant fantasy that visited her occasionally while she pleasured herself. And here she was alone, injured and physically dependent on this reliable young man. She moved against him and Liam awoke with a start.

"How do you feel?" she asked. He ran a hand through the tight curls of her head. She moved her head deeper into his hand in response.

"I feel good. Guess I was more tired than I thought."

"Well, we have no place to go and plenty of time, but do you think you are up to finishing my clean up? You only have one more part to do and I think you will find it the best one."

Under Dorothy's guidance, he gently cleaned up her genitals. He rose from his ministrations clearing the bucket and materials away. She saw that he was erect again, sorry that she had missed seeing how he grew from so small to....

***

Dorothy was still lying on her back trying to relax but not succeeding. Liam was sitting next to her near her head criss-cross apple applesauce, his penis rigidly standing at attention. Dorothy couldn't take her eyes off him. And she saw that his eyes were all over her as well. She was wishing she'd had an opportunity to trim her rather full pubic growth but that wasn't to be.

"So what should I do now?" Liam asked. "I mean I know what to do, but, well, how do you want me to do it?"

"Well, believe it or not, that was the first time I had ever done what we just did."

"What?"

"Taking a man in the mouth like that. I mean, I may be old but I am not all that experienced. Married to my career and all."

"So what was it like? Having me in your mouth? I mean it was incredible for me. And my first time too. Embarrassingly quick, of course."

"It was...I don't know, you were so alive in my mouth. It was exciting and yet natural. I'd like to do it again, that's for sure."

"I mean we can, and we will, but I'm thinking of something else first," Liam said.

***

Dorothy let out a slow deep breath, reveling in the easy weight of Liam's sleeping body on her belly. His cheek between her spread breasts. For almost a week now they had been living and loving together. Between the frequent lovemaking they'd had a number of intimate talks. Often with humor discovering their obviously different backgrounds. And Liam was the most nurturing caregiver for her injuries, which were beginning to feel much better. Tomorrow morning Dorothy would have him remove the splints from her hands and wrists. Her ankle was feeling better too judging by some non-loading bearing exercising she had been doing.

They would have to set out soon. Back to the real world. If they weren't running low on food, she would extend their stay in this paradise. All day and night, Liam had been driving into Dorothy's sex like a jackhammer as only a 20 year old athlete could. So satisfying, every older woman should have one if only for the physical satisfaction, and the fulfilling fatigue that seemingly endless sex can bring. And Liam was so sweet. It was going to be hard to let him go. Yesterday he had told Dorothy that he loved her and she had surprised herself how quickly and honestly she had replied in kind. Without reservation or hesitation.

On top of everything else, Liam had been shooting his seed into Dorothy countless times all week. That first time she had felt him release inside her, she had thought oh my God, but now it was more like que sera sera. She didn't care what the outcome might be. 43 wasn't too old to give birth. Borderline but not too late. So it was really now or never. What had she been thinking of being wedded to her career to the loss of love and the gift of bringing new life into the world? Perhaps she had been just waiting for the right partner. She would keep Liam's baby if it turned out she was pregnant. She still ovulated after all. And what a beautiful baby they would make. But she couldn't tie him down. Not at his young age. Sure he adored her now, perhaps always would, but Dorothy knew she was too old for him as a lifetime partner. No, if she became pregnant she would keep the baby. And he would be a part-time dad as much or as little as was good for him. Knowing his innate decency and honor, Liam would be an involved parent, but they could make that work with Dorothy being the primary parent.

Her career? Dorothy could resign and make it in the private sector, making more money too. So resignation, time off for childbirth, then find work as a working mom. She could do that. But with sadness Dorothy knew she could never tell her mother or any of the family. Mom certainly wouldn't understand. It would just hurt her. Until the world grows a generation further, it can sometimes still be selfish to come out. Liam roused from his slumber, latching onto the nearest breast.

"Hello baby," said Dorothy. By way of answer, Liam licked his way across to Dorothy's other breast.

Finally detaching himself, he said, "Ready or not, here I come!"

"Of course you're ready, and so am I, but still something else even before that."

"What?"

"Kiss me down under."

"Hey, we haven't done that yet. I mean, I nimble around the edges when I bathe you, but what a good idea."

***

Liam positioned himself quickly leaning on his elbows, utterly absorbed feasting his eyes on Dorothy's hairy black crotch, running his hands up and down the outside of her muscular thighs. They were quivering under his touch. He moved his hands under her taut hamstrings pushing her legs high and wide and he plunged in face first. He nuzzled her sex with his nose immersed in her scent. His mouth filled with saliva of its own accord which he emptied at the top of her anus to drip down. Then he licked slowly up to Dorothy's exposed clitoris.

"My god you're magnificent," he said before taking her pink protrusion into his mouth. Then he slipped two fingers deep into Dorothy's wetness while with his other hand he pressed the palm of his thumb on her anus. Dorothy responded to these triple sensations with undulating moans. Liam applied more pressure with his thumb on her ass while stroking back and forth to the rhythm of his tongue on her tip. He kept everything slow, taking his time. Suddenly Dorothy tightened around Liam's two fingers within her. Liam responded by sliding his thumb deep into her anal canal. Dorothy gasped and panted, moving her body to his touches until she erupted in ecstasy.

"I love you, Dorothy," Liam whispered as he disengaged.

"I love you too, Liam," Dorothy replied. Liam nuzzled into her moist pubic mound. They rested quietly on the floor together for a while.

"I'm glad you liked it. That was a first for us," Liam said.

"I got all lost in myself. You, my man, were a wizard. Hey, how are you doing down there? Let's get you taken care of."

"Aw, you need some rest."

"Nonsense. You must be ready to explode. What can I do for you?"

"Well, if you must ask."

"I must, I must."

"Hanging out down here as I am, I couldn't help but notice that your butt is beautiful. And it puckers when touched and responds to my caress."

"It does, does it?"

"It does."

"So what do you propose to do about it?"

"I thought maybe I could explore a bit deeper."

"Aha. Perhaps with something a bit bigger than your thumb? Something ready to explode?"

"Do you mind? Do you like it?"

"How would I know? I have never done that. I guess we can try. I pooped recently and you cleaned me up beautifully as always so I suppose it won't be too messy."

"And you are all still wet down here," Liam said, fondling Dorothy's nethers gently. "So?"

"So lay on, MacDuff," Dorothy said. "But slowly. Gently. This is new territory."

Liam came up to her, kissing Dorothy on the mouth long and slow. She crossed her legs around him above his hips. Liam dipped lingeringly once, twice deep into Dorothy's wet sex then withdrew.

"No," whined Dorothy.

"You want me to stay there?" Liam asked.

"Yes, always…but no. Let's explore."

Liam slid his penis down across her perineum, the sparse hair there slick. His tip rested on her asshole. It was wet, but tight. He held in place applying gentle pressure.

"Don't push," Dorothy gasped. "It feels great, but don't push but don't move either."

"I won't. I would never hurt you," Liam said.

"Just give me a minute," Dorothy said, breathing to try to relax her sphincter, enjoying the pressure from Liam's penis. A big breath out and she softened a bit. Liam's tip entered her anal canal then she tightened again.

"OMG," Liam gasped.

"Concur," panted Dorothy. Another big breath from Dorothy with a long slow exhale and Liam slid inside her until his tip was just to the inside edge of her canal.

"OMG again,"Liam said. "How do you feel?"

"I, I don't know yet. It's so different. Almost like I am pooping backwards," Dorothy said. Liam eased back out a bit in response. "Don't you dare leave me now," said Dorothy. "Just keep it slow. Long and slow. How does it feel for you?"

"Incredible. Tight like you can't imagine."

"I'm full like you can't imagine. Enough talk. Get 'er done, airman."

Liam pushed into his full length. His penis head feeling the openness at the inside end of her canal. Then he began a relaxing rhythm. Dorothy grunted in sync each time he entered. He looked into her eyes questioning, seeing her encouragement to continue.

"Get 'er done."

Liam increased his pace against his own volition, overwhelmed by the stimuli. He felt himself filling for the final surge, resisting his release until it was almost unbearable. He cried out holding for another two thrusts beyond all endurance then shot into Dorothy over and over, totally out of control.

"Oh my god, oh my god," Liam gasped. "Oh my god." Then getting hold of himself, still within her. "How are you, sweetheart?"

"I'm fine."

"But, no good, huh."

"I honestly don't know yet. It's just so different. We'll definitely have to try it again. If you're up for it."

"Oh, I'm in."

"You don't need to tell me," said Dorothy.

CHAPTER 11

LUCKY

Tina, Pally, and Lucky were back in her barge after a long, mostly silent drive back from a failed attempt to negotiate a sherpa needed to follow Bobby and Dalha. They hadn't bought all the gear needed, had just wanted to arrange passage, but the sherpa was adamant that he would not take them despite Lucky providing the password. With Lucky translating, the conversation had been awkward and broke down quickly. The sherpa had eyed Tina with overt suspicion when she suddenly pounced on the man, taking him to the snowy ground with a wicked choke hold growling threats in Greek that nobody understood. It was quite an effort for Pally and Lucky to drag Tina off of the sherpa. "Tell him I'll kill him if Bobby doesn't come back!" Tina had shouted in English. "I'll kill him!" Lucky had refused to translate despite her first terrifying glimpse of Agi, but no translation had been needed. The shaken sherpa got the gist of it and quickly disappeared into the trees.

"So what do we do now? Lucky opened as she plopped deep into her sofa.

"We need to find another way up there," Tina said, prowling around the small room.

"I'll report to Inspector Khera," Pally said, "Maybe he can help."

"Khera, that asshole? He's not going to help me."

"I'm afraid of you, Tina," Lucky said.

"Yeah, you've got to lighten up, old girl," said Pally, "You have me on edge too."

"I need action. To do something. We can't just sit here."

"One would think a Spartan soldier would have more discipline," Pally said.

"Discipline? Without a captain telling me what to do? I go my own way. And I don't see any captains here. That boy is out there and he needs my help."

"Look, I am going to step out to the car and call Khera," Pally said.

"Don't you dare leave me alone with him," Lucky said.

"Afraid of me?" Tina asked. "You should be. Don't want to flirt with me again like when we first met?"

"Just stay here, Pally," Lucky said.

"No, go call Khera. Good idea," Tina said. "Lucky and I will get better acquainted."

"Tina, get yourself under control."

"Or what, Pally? Or what? Go make your damned phone call."

"I am an officer of the law, Tina. And this isn't Sparta two thousand years ago. You leave her alone."

A quick left cross to Pally's jaw and she was out cold on her feet. Tina caught her to lay her gently onto the plush carpet. Using her belt and boot strings, Tina had the inert Pally bound wrists and ankles in short order while Lucky watched in horror.

"Well that's that," Tina said. "Are you going to take your clothes off or will I do it for you? It's all the same to me."

"No, please," Lucky whimpered, as Tina took her by the elbow and led her into the bedroom.

"Don't be silly, woman. You want this and you know it." Tina stood her at the foot of the big bed. "Stand there and don't move, don't talk. Now let's see what we can find," Tina said as she rummaged through Lucky's furniture. An assortment of dildos and lubricants were in the night stand. "Of course, these will do nicely." Then from the lower drawer off the nightstand Tina discovered a strap on belt. "Bingo!" Tina shouted. "I knew you'd have all the toys."

***

Lucky watched in fear and fascination as Tina quickly undressed and adjusted the belt to her waist.

"Use lubricant on yourself before strapping on," Lucky said. "No, the blue bottle."

"See, I knew it wouldn't be rape. More is the pity, with the mood I am in." Tina said as she followed Lucky's guidance and got herself harnessed in. Tina then lay on the bed propped on the many plush pillows, admiring the largest of the dildos protruding from her genitalia. Lucky focused on the wisps of blonde pubic hair sneaking out behind the big black phallus. Tina oiled her small pale breasts and began feathering herself.

"Now peel down, Lucky," Tina said. "Take your time."

With an undulating dance, Lucky found herself undressed quickly so eager was she to come to grips. To be taken by this masterful man/woman held her spell bound.

"I hope you like it rough, Lucky. Because I'm gonna be. Rough."

Lucky felt herself blossoming, seeing Tina's eyes riveted on her genitals.

"Oh my god, will you look at you, Lucky," Tina said, her eyes on Lucky's larger than usual pink protrusion. "Magnificent, Lucky. Truly magnificent. My clit is rather small, me being petite in all ways. I envy you."

The door burst open as Pally strode into the room.

"What the fuck, Tina. What's going on here?"

"Aptly put, Pally. Fuck. Because that is what is about to go on. I knew those bindings wouldn't hold you long. How's your jaw, sweetheart?"

"Sore godammit. Don't you ever cold cock me again. Remember, two can play that game."

"Promises, promises. And such language from you, a good catholic girl."

"Blow it out your ass, Tina," Pally told her, then seeing Lucky's erect clitoris, "Oh my god!"

"Yeah, that's just what I said," Tina told her.

Lucky felt herself blush with horror and pride at these two women spellbound by her beauty. Her large nipples on her full breasts also stood erect. With an effort she kept her hands empty at her sides, waiting for Tina's orders.

"Pretty impressive, isn't she Pally. Come girl, let bygones be bygones. Help me pleasure this lucky lady." Tina rolled off the bed to Lucky taking a breast in her mouth. As Pally latched on to her other breast, Lucky reeled. The two women helped her down on the bed, both keeping their mouths full. She felt four hands urgently exploring her nethers. Lucky was dizzy. She felt Tina detach from her breast and Pally also. Tina sprayed lubricant wildly across Lucky's chest.

"Come on, Pally," Tina said.

Tongues were moving down her belly quickly and all over her sex. Lucky's own hands were all over her breasts adding to the myriad sensual sensations erupting pell-mell across her body.

"She's ready, Pally," Lucky heard Tina say. Lucky found herself laying atop Pally now, belly on belly, with Pally's face in her crotch, Pally's lips and tongue hungrily all over her clit. Lucky was vaguely aware of her own face on Pally's pubic mound, but she was in no condition to do anything. She felt Tina pull her hips to get Lucky on her knees on either side of Pally's head.

"Here's a pillow for under your head, Pally so you don't have to strain your neck," Lucky heard Tina say. "And now let's do it," Tina shouted. Lucky could only gasp and grunt as Tina drove the big dildo all the way into her again and again. She had no sense of time. Finally Tina thrust deep in but did not withdraw.

"And now for the other one," she heard Tina say as Pally continued to suck on her swollen increasingly sensitive clit. Lucky felt warm moisture on her anus, then pressure from another dildo. Gently, slowly this time as her vagina remained full and clit teased incessantly. Lucky dumbly, vaguely, like a detached onlooker, wondered how there would be room for another dildo inside her. She groaned as it was suddenly deep inside her. Tina began thrusting again in and out of Lucky's vagina.

"Now, Pally, now!" she heard Tina shout. "Lay it on her."

Lucky felt Pally's tongue flickering faster along the length of her clit even as the sucking became rougher. Out of control, Lucky erupted then squirted uncontrollably into Pally's mouth who quickly detached, coughing and spitting, then rolling out from under Lucky. She felt Tina's arms wrapped tightly from behind as she humped Lucky uncontrollably until the blonde woman's own orgasm was spent.

"Now that's what I'm talking about," Lucky heard Tina say as she withdrew everything from the exhausted Lucky who just lay on her belly panting not sure where or who she was.

CHAPTER 12

AFTERMATH

Lucky woke to the aromatic scents of cooking. Trying to get her bearings. Gentle hands started caressing her head and hair.

"How do you feel, pretty lady?" Tina asked.

"Ugh. Like I have been trampled by an elephant," Lucky said. Tina laughed in response.

Lucky got her eyes in focus and lifting her head realized she had been sleeping on Tina's bare belly. She idly ran her fingers through Tina's small patch of public hair since that is where her hand was. "God, what time is it?" Her stomach growled loudly.

"It's tomorrow."

"What? It wasn't even dark when we, when we…"

"We all slept through the night. We were all pretty bushed, I guess. I think it's about 10am. Pally and I woke up about an hour ago. We figured you could use some extra rest."

"Ugh," was Lucky's response. "I'm sore all over."

"It was quite a ride, but surely you've been taken by a man before."

"Not like that. Gentlemen."

"Nobody ever accused me of being one of them," Tina said. "Come, let me help you out of bed."

She rolled out from under Lucky and took her by both hands to get her sitting up and then standing. Lucky was unsteady on her feet."

"You okay?" Tina asked her.

Lucky looked into Tina's big blue eyes seeing the pleasant American woman almost twenty years her senior. "Serious question," Lucky said, "Are you crazy?"

"Oh come on, it wasn't that bad, was it?"

"It was…surreal."

"Want to do it again?" the blue smiling eyes asked.

"Honestly? Not right now that is for sure. But yes. Just give me some more rest. Like a month's worth. I feel like I've been split in half twice over.

So yes but only after some slow lovemaking first. And some long girl talks. And lazy walks around the lake."

"Fair enough. That sounds good. You know, I am pooped too. And I am not the young man I was a couple of millennia ago."

"Thank god. You must have been downright lethal back in the day."

"You have no idea." Tina said, gently kissing Lucky on the lips. "But you will always be safe with me. Even if I do get a bit rough around the edges. Don't fear me. And you can always say no."

"And if I had said no yesterday?"

"Moot point. Had I stopped before we started, or anytime in between, you would have begged me to go on."

Lucky sighed. "You're right. Lord help me but you are right"

"Brunch is ready!" Pally called from the other room.

Pally was serving au natural. Lucky goggled at her getting a full view of the Sub-inspector naked for the first time.

"How are you feeling, Lucky?" Pally asked.

"Like I'll be walking bowlegged for a week."

"You got off easy. First time I went down on Tina she would have killed me if she hadn't been knocked on the noggin by another girl."

"Sweet."

"Which reminds me," Pally said as Tina and Lucky pulled their chairs out to sit. Pally hit Tina with a wicked punch to the solar plexus. Tina collapsed to her knees gasping for air. Lucky was shocked. Pally waited for Tina's lungs to refill then helped her into her chair. "Now we are even. And no more sucker punches."

"Okay," Tina gasped.

Without further ado the three of them waded into their brunch with gusto, filling three very empty bellies. Eventually the three of them pushed back from the table, content.

"Okay, first order of business," Pally said. "The bad news, Khera said that under no circumstances are we to sneak north across the border. I'm not saying you can't go, but I am following my boss's orders so I am out on that excursion."

"Well, that's no help," Tina said.

"But there is good news," Pally continued. "Remember special agent Miller of the FBI? She is infiltrating the area by way of Pakistan as we speak."

"Great, let's catch up with her."

"I don't think so, not sure if Khera actually knows where Miller is or how he got her intel but he is definitely not telling us. And Miller is already incommunicado. So we'll just have to wait."

"No good, we can't just wait here."

"I have an idea," Lucky said. "Let's take a long walk on the lake, think things through, then you two draw straws to see which of you goes first getting the same attentions you two gave me. You'll be sore, but I can guarantee you it will be worth it."

Tina and Pally both blushed.

CHAPTER 13

BOBBY

Bobby inhaled deeply on his cigarette knowing their supply of smokes were running low. There wasn't any kind of store in this valley to buy more when their packs ran out. Or anything else for that matter. No stores, no use of currency, no functional governance either. These people were tribal as they had been for thousands of years. Bobby took a small sip of the precious scotch as well. The liquor supply wouldn't be restocked, if ever, until the next stranger came through to barter for passage south into India.

It was just dark on their third evening at Mum's house. For the first time Bobby was alone, but feeling relaxed. The story was not going too well, but the lovemaking was wonderful. Bobby and Dalha had talked a lot too and had agreed that they would be life partners forever. Sure, it had been a wildly rapid romance, but they knew. In the back of Bobby's mind was Lucky, and he didn't forget Tina either. Lucky was Poly, and Dalha's Mum had multiple dads. Maybe she wouldn't mind. Hell, Dalha didn't even know or care which one of Mum's several husbands was her biological father. So maybe she would be open minded about Lucky. That would be a helluva threesome. Plenty of time to raise that subject later. After all, Dalha already knew about his relationship with Lucky. But right now Bobby just wanted to keep loving Dalha every day.

Now Dalha and her Mum were out visiting neighbors without Bobby along, hoping people would be more forthcoming with information. Bobby turned out to be something of a distraction and he became the subject of any conversation when he was present. So Dalha and Mum left him home alone this time.

Finishing his smoke, he got up to step out for a leak and suddenly froze with a cold pistol barrel behind his ear.

"This is a silencer you are feeling so I can kill you right now and nobody would be the wiser," She said. "Or you can talk to me and maybe live."

"What do you want to know?"

"Not here. Step outside and stay in front of me. I find that the pressure of a gun barrel provides clear direction."

"I need my coat."

"The cold won't kill you. It's not a long walk."

Bobby was shivering uncontrollably by the time they reached the abandoned hut almost an hour later.

"It's nice and warm inside. Just answer two questions and I will let you in," She said. "Why did you come here?"

The pistol was still at his ear and Bobby had yet to see his abductor. This gave him hope. It was the voice of a woman, but Bobby might yet survive this if he never sees her face. He needed to get warm or he would die for sure. And he didn't really know anything so the truth was his best hope.

Through chattering teeth, Bobby struggled to speak. "I think that some operatives from a foreign power are infiltrating Kashmir through here so I came here to ask around who it might be."

"Congratulations, the answer is me," She told him. "And what have you learned so far?"

"Nothing. Nobody will talk to me."

"So Dalha is asking questions without you. Smart girl that Dalha."

"Please let me inside. I'm freezing," Bobby begged.

"Well, you've answered my questions, and honestly too," She said. "So I am going to back away while you count quietly to yourself up to 60. Then I will whistle and when you hear that you can go inside and warm up. Bear in mind that I am an expert marksman so if you touch that door too soon I will silently drop you where you stand and Dalha won't find your corpse until tomorrow morning. Start counting."

The intense cold numbing him, Bobby could hardly stand as he began his count. He heard faint footsteps departing, but after a few seconds he couldn't hear anything but the wind. Time marched slowly. In all the wind he couldn't hear the whistle. Maybe She had already done it and he hadn't heard her whistle over the roar of the wind. Or maybe She was testing him, ready to blow his brains out if he moved too early. More time passed and still he heard nothing but the wind. He had to get inside or it wouldn't matter if She shot him or not. Bobby lunged for the door hoping to get inside quickly and dodge a bullet. But his lunge was just a stagger. His legs could hardly respond to his bewildered brain's commands. He fell to his knees before the door but managed to get both hands on the latch. Locked. At that moment, Bobby Singh knew She had killed him.

CHAPTER 14

DALHA

"Come Dalha," Mum whispered in her ear. The daughter came out of bad dreams slowly into the nightmare of reality.

"Your fathers have returned," Mum said. Dalha rose reluctantly to a sitting position with her Mum's help. She slowly focused on her surroundings, still engulfed in Mum's embrace as she had been for, what, two days maybe? Dalha wasn't sure. The four brothers, her Dads, were sitting in a semicircle on the floor around her and Mum. Dahla had been wrapped up with Mum since they had returned from finding Bobby frozen that horrible morning. Once there had been daylight they had tracked Bobby to where he died. Bobby had wandered out by himself in the dark that night without his coat on. It didn't make sense. Why would he do that?

"Come Dalha," Mum said. "Hear your fathers." Dalha looked in their stoic eyes seeing their love, their sorrow, but anger and determination too.

"At first it appeared that your man had walked off alone," one of the dads said. "But now we are sure that someone else followed in his footsteps step for step then backed away doing the same thing."

"In the dark? How? Who?" Mum asked.

"We know who. Not her name, but a woman," said one dad.

"It was hard to tell at first because her track is smaller than Bobby's," said another.

Dalha began to cry again.

"She came to us a few years ago from the north. I remember guiding her south from here and remember that she followed my footsteps, step for step all the way. I remember because I admired how good she was at doing it, saving her energy."

"Who is she?" Mum asked.

"I only know she is one of us. From one of the valleys further north. But nobody here had ever seen her before."

"Then I guided her here from the south. We arrived two days ago," said a dad.

"Where is she now?" Mum asked.

"Gone. She left following the same path we came in on. Using the exact same footsteps. But we could tell."

"Then she will die on the trail," Mum said.

"I don't think so. She knows the way now. And knows the ways of the mountains."

"Your fathers and I will pursue her at first light," one dad said.

"No," Dalha said. "She is too dangerous. She will kill you."

The fathers said nothing, unwilling to upset Dalha but determined to avenge this murder.

"Here me, my fathers," Dalha said. "This woman is who Bobby was looking for. Bobby thought that she was hired by foreigners to start a war. Now we know she is also an assassin. I know people south, professionals, who will track her down. And put an end to her."

The fathers still said nothing, reluctant to pass this duty to others..

"Hear your daughter," Mum said. "Dalha knows more of this matter than we. And it is Dalha who has been injured by this woman. It is her grievance. You will abide by her wisdom."

"Please take me south starting tomorrow," Dalha said to her fathers.

"Then so we shall. But we will take another path. That the woman does not know. It will take a day longer, but there will be no risk of ambush."

"What of Bobby?" Mum asked her daughter.

"Keep him safe here, Mum," Dahla said. "When all is done, I will return for him."

CHAPTER 15

TINA AND DALHA

With Lucky at the wheel, the three women pulled up to the rendezvous point as per Dalha's brief text that managed to get through the spotty coverage yesterday. They could see the tall girl standing alone in the clearing. Nobody else was in sight.

"They are going to take me back north, whether they like it or not," Tina said. She was the only one who had brought mountain climbing gear for the trek.

"Let's wait to hear what Dalha has to say first," Lucky said. "And let me do the talking. Dalha is an odd fish."

Tina was out of the car first, not waiting for Lucky and Pally. "Where's Bobby?" Tina demanded.

"He's dead," Dalha said.

Tina had known it all along, but hearing it was a bitter blow. She could hear Lucky sobbing behind her. The tall girl's face was expressionless, but her eyes were wet.

"Tell me," Tina said.

"A woman followed us north, kidnapped Bobby, then killed him."

"And where were you?" Tina asked. "And where is this woman now?"

"Dalha," Lucky cried. "You were supposed to take care of him."

Dalha broke down at that. "All I know is that I love him."

"Where is the woman now?" Tina shouted. She felt Pally's hand on her shoulder but jerked away from the touch.

"I don't know for sure, but she came back south ahead of me," Dalha said.

"Then you have no business in the north, Tina," Pally said. "There's nothing for us there. Back in the car everyone. Dalha, get in the car too." Nobody moved for a moment, until Pally opened her door, then they all followed slowly.

"This isn't about a news story anymore," Tina said.

***

There was silence in Lucky's plush red living room on her house barge. Dalha lay on her back, her long frame stretched across thick carpet between the settee, where Tina and Pally sat hand in hand. Lucky was in a chair from the small dining table. Dalha just stared at the strange red ceiling thinking nothing. Feeling miserable.

"Look," Tina finally broke the ice, "I know I haven't been myself lately" she began.

Dalha sat up suddenly. "Who are you people? And what do you have to do with my Bobby?"

"I am, was, Bobby's colleague and mentor," Tina said.

"Then why weren't you with him?" Dalha demanded. "Maybe he'd still be alive and you dead."

"If only that were true," Tina said. "I feel like I've lived too long already."

"Don't say that, Tina," Pally said. "Don't ever say that."

"You know I figured it out. I've spent 87 years alive on this Earth. In two bodies I grant you, but that is enough for anyone."

"What the fuck are you talking about?" Dalha shouted.

"Easy," Pally said.

"No, I want to know too," Lucky said.

"Relax, Pally," Tina said. "I won't go Greek on anyone. I still miss my beloved three girls - Daphne, Helen, and Lorae - very acutely so I understand how you feel, Dalha. And I am no stranger to death."

"What the fuck?" Dalha repeated.

"That's it, be angry. Pour it all out of you on me," Tina said.

"You got it," Dalha cried, on her feet now standing tall.

"You want to hit me, Dalha? Go ahead, I deserve it."

Dalha lashed out with a wild punch to Tina's cheek where she sat. Her hand hurt with the impact.

Tina stood up. "Hit me again."

Instead, Dalha drove the smaller woman back into her seat with both hands on Tina's throat. Her one thought was to crush the life out of her. Tina didn't resist, but Pally and Lucky were on Dalha's back and arms quickly, struggling to detach Dalha's strong grip from Tina's slender neck. Dalha fought to keep her grip with a single minded intensity. All she wanted to do was kill. To avenge Bobby. Then her own throat was constricted so she released her grip perforce. Her hands pulling ineffectually on the forearm tight around her neck. Pally had her in a choke hold that brought the helpless Dalha back to the floor.

"You probably didn't understand before since you are so upset," Pally said, "but I am a police officer. Now stand down. That's an order."

Dalha went limp gasping for air. Her rage gone as quickly as it had come. "Just kill me," she whispered to Pally.

"Just chill," Pally told her, letting Dalha loose from the throat crushing hold. "Tina, are you okay? Lucky?"

"I'm okay," Lucky said quickly.

"Looks like I'll live. Again," Tina gasped. "Rather than die again. Wow, Dalha. That was something. Just like old times. I remember an ugly cuss I called FistFace choking me like that. At least you're better looking than he was."

Pally pulled Dalha back to her feet and led her to the settee. "Here Dalha, sit next to Tina." Dalha felt Pally shove her into the small sofa next to the strange woman she had just tried to kill.

"Lucky, take your seat," Pally ordered, as the police officer remained standing.

"How's your hand feel?" Tina asked Dalha. "Not so good, right? Probably almost as bad as my cheek. You hurt me if it makes you feel any better, but I can teach you how to punch properly." Dalha could only stare at the strange woman.

"Okay, listen up," Pally said. "Chasing down this woman who killed Bobby is a police matter. Tina, you said it yourself that you're not chasing a story anymore. So like it or not, the job falls to me and the IS. Dalha and maybe Lucky, I want you both to make as long a list as you can of anyone you know involved in the Kashmir independence movement. Our mystery woman must be interacting with somebody."

"We don't like the authorities very much. For obvious reasons," Dalha said.

"You want to catch Bobby's killer or not?" Pally asked. "If so, you'll cooperate. Lucky get Dalha a pencil and paper."

"Two of my dads saw her," Dalha offered.

"Fine," said Pally. "Write down whatever you remember of their description of her."

"I'll still work with you, Pally. Like before," Tina said.

"No," Pally said. "I can't do my job well if I have to keep an eye on you so you don't kill the suspect before I can arrest her. Or even worse if you kill the wrong person."

"You don't seem to give me much credit," Tina said.

"Look," Pally said. "You three girls are hurting from Bobby's death. I get it. Though I only met him briefly and didn't get the chance to fall in love or lust with him, he seemed like a fine young man. So I will bring his killer to justice for you. Meanwhile you three stay out of it. Take time to mourn together. And ultimately heal together." Pally's cell beeped. "Okay, that's my ride. I've been ordered into HQ to report. So while I am gone, stay put. And work on your list of names and anything else you can think of. I or somebody else will be back soon enough for questioning."

As Pally reached the door, Tina said, "You're always at your cutest when in command. Can't wait to see you back in uniform. It shows off your ass."

Pally just rolled her eyes and left without another word.

After a moment Dalha turned to Tina, calmly this time, "So who the fuck are you?"

"And what the fuck are you?" said Lucky.

CHAPTER 16

DOROTHY

"Wait here, Airman," FBI Special Agent Miller told Air Force Airman Miller in the outer office, then went inside alone. She found IS Inspect Khera and Sub-inspector Agarwal already there. They both stopped talking as Miller entered.

"Welcome, Miller," Khera said, rising to greet her. "So what happened? We worked hard to get that tip for you and it seems you came up empty handed."

"Whether your tip was any good we'll never know," Miller said. "I was injured in the climb so we had to abort. Wasted trip. Maybe we can try again in a week or two when I am healed up."

"Who is that soldier you brought with you?" Pally said.

"Seconded to me from our embassy."

"What's he doing here?" asked Khera.

"If I go into high country again, I'll want him with me. He's good,"

"Not much need of that I should think," Khera said, "Still, if you wish to keep him as an Aide-de-camp you are welcome to do so."

Miller stifled a sarcastic response. It wasn't up to Khera and they both knew it. "So what do you have on your end?" Miller asked.

"We still have long distance surveillance on this rendezvous point they have been using. Someone came south two days ago. Maybe our mystery woman, maybe not," Khera said.

"Where is she now?"

"We lost her. She made a brief appearance at the clearing then disappeared back into the woods. Hasn't been seen since."

"Then she's still up there, either walked out or has some other means of travel," Miller said.

"She wasn't on the road I can tell you that," Khera said. Miller said nothing. "Look Miller," Khera continued, "if you hadn't botched your end we might be at the bottom of things by now. But Pakistan wouldn't let our people take that route through their country so you got the job. And you blew it."

"Fine," Miller said, rising. "I'm out. It's your security problem anyway, not mine."

Khera nodded to Pally. "Agent Miller," said Pally, "I learned today that Bobby Singh was murdered up north by our mystery woman so it very much is a USA problem, and yours." Miller kept standing, the urge to head back to the embassy and resign in rage was strong.

Khera said, "Sit down, Miller. Look we only had a general sense where they might be up there so even if you hadn't been injured you and your Airman would likely be still wandering about finding nothing. It was a long shot anyway." He took a deep breath. "India thanks you for the attempt. As I said, we couldn't try it ourselves. As far as we can tell it is impassable from our side."

"Only it isn't," Dorothy said.

"But even if we mounted an expedition, we couldn't do it in secret," Khera said, "The locals would see us coming. And probably the Chinese too. You were our only hope slipping in through the side door."

"We're glad you and your man made it back safely," Pally said. "Meanwhile, Bobby Singh's guide, and his lover, made it back and I think she is ready to spill. She is heartbroken."

"Then let's get her in here," Miller said.

"Agarwal is taking point on this," Khera said. "You and I stay back. I can give you some good news, Tina Marin is no longer a suspect. I don't know what she is, but she was definitely here when Singh was killed up north. Stay in town for Agarwal's report here tomorrow."

"Will do," said Miller, wanting nothing more at this point than to crawl into bed with Liam.

CHAPTER 17

SHE

She was staked out in Dalha's neighborhood in a position that would see her pass between that hole in the wall where Dalha's independence movement office stood and the tall girl's tiny flat. She had been waiting since before the start of the work day but no sign of Dalha so far. Dalha might be in great distress due to Bobby's death, so perhaps she was staying with other friends. This was patient work, but She was patient. It was a requirement of her profession.

As She waited, She reviewed her action north of the border. It had been a clean operation, only 24 hours within the valley itself. But it had been a grueling schedule through the mountains both ways without a rest and She was tired because of it. Not on the top of her game right now if there was action. Still, taking out Bobby Singh had been smooth. Leaving him alone had been a gift so She had taken it. If She had taken out Dahla too at the time it would have been far trickier and probably would have raised the roof in the entire valley. She might not have gotten out without a serious fight. But in retrospect, her final exit north after her mission was accomplished was now denied to her. Not that it really mattered since there were a variety of final exits from India. Undetected entry had been the challenge and that had worked.

Yet here She was with another hit to perform and She was already tired. It was in such a state that mistakes could be made. No, She needed to rest up, but She also couldn't leave Dalha floating around Srinagar with her story to tell. She had no doubt that IS was watching the independence movement closely. Not that Dalha was any friend to the police, but in her current emotional state She couldn't make that assumption. So the answer to all her problems would be easy and perhaps even pleasurable. She would renew her relationship with Dalha. Empathize with her loss, console her, seduce her, then when She was fully rested kill Dalha in such a way that nobody would be the wiser, just like with Bobby Singh.

It was early afternoon and the neighborhood was bustling. Plenty of traffic, foot, bike, moped, and car. She kept a sharp lookout for Dalha as She plotted next steps. Always have a full plan and always be ready with a variety of contingencies for the many variables that may arise. For example, right now She was in reactive mode rather than her preferred proactive approach. Waiting for Dalha did not bring her any closer to inciting a civil war. The more subtle approach had so far been ineffective. Like watching paint dry. And sooner or later IS would catch wind of her if they hadn't already. She needed to put them on their heels, get them in reactive mode again.

The bank heist had been a complete failure. Yesterday's news. Thanks to Tina Marin. Something about the American bothered She. No matter how well Marin may have been trained, her disguise couldn't be that good. She had been a part of the crowded onlookers who had tracked Tina Marin to the airport when Marin flew off to Greece. There was no evidence in her motions, her posture, her awareness that indicated a professional operative. Was Marin that good? And yet how Marin broke up her terrorist attack wasn't a fluke. That woman could handle herself. Whoever Marin was, She would find out after this mission was completed. She would have a chat with Tina Marin. And when She learned all that there was to be known, Tina Marin would disappear.

She saw Dalha round the corner in the direction to her flat. Moving slow. Not going to the office. Good, Dalha was in no condition to care about the cause right now. Still mourning for Bobby Singh no doubt. Missing his touch. Feeling lonely. She remembered the passionate few months they had shared three years ago. She moved into position to run into Dalha by accident.

***

So this is what death feels like, thought Dalha. This endless physically oppressive malaise, a weight on one's soul. It is your first awareness when you wake. It is with each step, everything you do, breaking you down until you collapse into sorrowful sleep. And the cycle repeats over and over again. Mum said it would end as suddenly as it had begun when they found Bobby frozen at the door of that abandoned hut. The horror was always there. Before her, within her. When would it end? It shouldn't. Bobby is her life partner and so the feeling should remain until she herself no longer is.

The climb back south from the home of her birth had been pointless. Dalha had wanted to die on that trek. Had begged her fathers to let her freeze in the waste as Bobby had done. But they had kept her warm. Had carried her through some of it, hauling her with ropes up and down the steep slopes like the sack of lifelessness that she was. Then Lucky and the other two women, the strange American and the cop, Pally, had taken her away. Just sitting there together in the car, in that barge, then Pally had asked her endless questions to add to her torment. Dalha hadn't resisted. She couldn't care enough to resist. Finally they had let her go so Dalha had wandered blindly through the city directionless until she found herself in her own neighborhood.

Dalha crossed the street to the other side of her office hoping nobody would see her. She didn't want to talk to anyone. Just get home to lie down and die, where nobody would stop her. One step after another. She tripped on the uneven pavement, instinctively regaining her balance, then somebody stepped into her knocking her down. Somebody else went down with her to the edge of the street in front of a shop entrance.

"Ouch!," a woman's voice said, "I should watch where I am going. Are you okay?" Dalha didn't respond to the woman sitting alongside her rubbing her elbow. "Here, let's get up off the street. Don't want to get trampled or hit by a bike." A firm hand was in Dalha's as she was hauled back to her feet. "That was my fault. You sure you are okay? Oh my god, Dalha? Is that you?"

Dalha looked down on the face before her. Mala! After all this time. Mala, to add to her misery. She stepped away, but Mala pulled her back by the arm in time to keep Dalha from stepping in front of a car.

"Careful, girl. Do you want to get yourself killed?"

"Yes. Leave me alone."

"Dalha, are you all right? I realize that you might not want to see me, but it was an accident. And I have been feeling so guilty about you. I used you badly and I am sorry. No, don't go. Now that we have found each other again like this, let me please tell you how profoundly sorry I am." Dalha just stood there dumb. "Girl, you do not look well. Here, let me help you home." Dalha let herself be led away.

***

From a discreet distance, Tina saw the woman bump into Dalha and lead her away hand in hand. The American had been following Dalha all morning to make sure she would be okay. In her state Dalha was in no condition to be on her own, but Pally had said they couldn't keep her at Lucky's against her will. So Tina had followed. Now Dalha had run into somebody who seemed to know her. The two women continued on together. Tina considered whether she should leave Dalha with this new companion, but the Spartan in her sniffed danger. So Tina followed.

CHAPTER 18

LUCKY AND PALLY

"So how are you doing, Lucky?" Pally asked after first Dalha then Tina had gone and it was just the two of them. "We've been focused so much on Dalha, but I know you must be hurting too."

"I'm just numb. That beautiful young man. My cousin. Gone. It was all such a game when we started; finding the bad guy, getting the scoop, then Bobby would become an acclaimed reporter."

"And for you, Lucky?"

"For me? I don't matter."

"Come on, Lucky. Spill. What did it mean to you, meeting your cousin Bobby and helping him with his investigation?"

"Helping him? Helping him? I got him killed! Don't you understand that?"

"Don't put too much on yourself."

"Don't you see? I told him about Dalha. He never would have met her without me. Then he wouldn't have gone north with her."

"It's not your fault, Lucky," Pally said. "We all have to take our chances in this world."

"I was bored, Pally. Bored. Then I heard from my mother that an American cousin was coming to town so I decided to intercept and seduce him. Because I was bored. And now he is dead."

"So who do you think did it?" Pally asked.

"I don't know. I've never heard of most of the names Dalha gave you and I can't think of anyone else that she didn't mention." Lucky sighed. "I was only on the periphery of the independence movement compared to Dalha."

"The resurrection of ancient Kashmir sounds surreal to me, Lucky,"

"Yeah well, you're not Kashmiri. Then there are splits in the movement. Dalha wants the ancient borders, but others want independence only within the borders of Indian controlled Kashmir politically, without starting a war with China and Pakistan."

"And where are you on that issue?"

"What does it matter now? Like Dalha, I find it hard to care anymore. Any other questions you want to ask me, Sub-inspector?" Lucky asked.

"Take it easy, Lucky. I care about you. Remember we were in bed together a couple of days ago. So I'll ask no more questions."

"You care about me? Really? Sex isn't love, Pally"

"I know. And love doesn't mean a relationship either, I learned that the hard way. But you fell in love with Bobby pretty quickly, didn't you?"

"Yes, because I opened my heart to him. One can fall in love, but one can also choose to love. I have that ability. But the sex we had with that crazy Tina didn't have anything to do with love."

"Look, that was a huge leap of faith for me too. With one word you can destroy my career. My life."

"I won't say anything. To do so would ruin my reputation too, you know. My family would disown me."

They sat in silence together, side by side on the settee. "As you know by now, I am a lesbian," Pally began, "You're only the second person that I have told. First Tina, and now you."

"Tina, what a piece of work. That is one fucked up individual."

"She's not an individual. That is why she has so many issues. I love her dearly and forever, but we have no future as a couple. Whatever her future holds, it isn't settling down with me. Here in India, America, or anywhere. I know that now."

"I think you are right to stay clear of her, but how does that make you feel?"

"Lonely. Desperately lonely. I'll be a cop in the closet for the rest of my life here in India."

"You like your work? It's important to you?"

"I love it. It's what I am meant to be, and I'm good at it."

"Good for you. You're one up on me. I have no such passion to carry me through my life in the closet."

"You're alone too?"

"There is another couple, to remain unnamed, that I love dearly and they love me. But I am definitely the third wheel."

"I envy you that, even in the closet. Since you can choose to love, do you think you could love me? And teach me how to do the same?"

Lucky took Pally's hand in hers. "Let's just hold hands for now. I am too deep in sorrow for anything else."

Just then, Pally's cell phone rang. It was Khera.

CHAPTER 19

LIAM

Liam snuggled into Dorothy's bosom, content after their lovemaking in Dorothy's hotel room, but dreading when she would send him away back to his own room before dawn when the hotel would start to awake. After their isolation on the adventure it had been difficult for him to maintain the facade of a professional relationship as her subordinate once they returned. Once back in India, Liam had returned to his unit in the embassy without any chance of interacting with Dorothy at all. He had been full of anxiety fearing he would never see her again. Then the next day, he was called to his captain's office and told he was temporarily detached to serve under FBI Special Agent Miller for an indefinite period of time.

"I don't envy you this assignment, Miller," his captain had told him. "That woman is a robot and a mean one at that. Still, you clearly did something to impress her. Stay on her good side. I wouldn't want that one as an enemy."

"Yes, sir."

Thrilled as he was to remain at Dorothy's side, it had been agony not to be able to touch her or even talk to her, except the bare minimum required by duty. Dorothy gave not even the slightest hint of affection for him the entire time and even though she had warned him in advance that it would be so, Liam had begun to doubt her love. He had relived all their loving and words of love in his head over and over wondering if he had misunderstood as he waited in lobbies and outer offices while Dorothy was closeted in meetings discussing unknown matters with officers and officials.

Then last night he had been sleepless in his hotel bed staring at the ceiling and seeing nothing when his phone rang. "Airman Miller, meet me outside my room, 420, in five minutes." Click, before he could say a word. then she had led him into her room and heaven had returned. Liam looked at his watch. They had another hour. He slid his hand down to her sex. Still moist. She put her hand over his. It was a stop.

"Liam, I have a confession to make. I want to have a baby. Your baby."

"Great. I love you, Dorothy. Let's get married," Liam said and locked his lips on her nipple.

"Hold it," Dorothy said. "We need to talk about this."

"Why? We love each other."

"That's the way your young heart and mind works and I love you for it, but things aren't that simple."

"I want to spend the rest of my life with you, Dorothy. It is that simple."

"Come on, Liam. I popped your cherry. Of course, that's how you feel. Now."

"You don't think I really love you?"

"Of course you do. I don't doubt your love for a second. And I am thrilled because I love you too. But let's be practical."

"Why? Why? Let's just go with the flow and see what happens. Right now. We don't have much time left." Liam began nibbling on her breast again. His erection was hard against her thigh.

"Okay, okay. Oh god. But then we talk," Liam felt her legs part.

***

Liam gave a final thrust deep into Dorothy and held it, feeling the surge within him and fighting to hold a moment longer. Finally, their eyes locked together, he shot into her with several eruptions, a grunt escaping his lips each time. Spent, he nuzzled into her neck still deep inside her. He felt her shudder as her muscles began to relax.

"Ready to talk now?" Dorothy whispered in his ear.

"If we must, but there isn't really much to talk about."

Dorothy rolled him off her. "No," he cried softly as he slipped out of her. She scutched herself into more of a sitting position lounging against the headboard. Liam followed suit. One look in her eyes and Liam knew she was all business again. He dropped his eyes to her magnificent breasts, waiting for it. Then he rested a hand on the thick black curls of her pubic mound, to keep connected.

"Okay, listen up young man," Dorothy said, but she allowed his hand to rest where it was. "We've had a lot of unprotected sex recently so I could already be pregnant. And say what you will, becoming a father at 21 is not in your best interests."

"Hey, my mom was only 21 when I was born and dad was only 23. It's the perfect age to become a dad as far as I am concerned."

"Great. Your mother is my age. That's like icing on the cake."

"Hey, my folks will love you, when they get to know you."

"And you're not worried about this first meeting?"

"Well, yeah of course I am but I would be nervous no matter what."

"You mean you'd be nervous even if you were bringing home a 21 year old white girl, right?"

"Okay, yes. But don't worry. My parents aren't racists, Dorothy. I think they'll be…"

"More shocked about my age? As well they should, Liam. I know I am. Do you have any idea how bad I am taking advantage of you?"

"That's ridiculous! I'm a grown man. And we fit together hand in glove. You know that."

"Yes, I do know that. And I admit the urge to continue taking advantage of you, marry you, and have your child, if we haven't already conceived, is almost overwhelming."

"Then listen to yourself. That is your heart talking. Where all your core wisdom comes from. Listen to your heart."

"When did you get so smart all of the sudden?"

"Not smart, Dorothy. Wise. Wisdom, it comes from the heart or from the soul rather. And my soul is telling me we should stick together and if we haven't made a baby already we should keep at it until we do." Liam couldn't repress a grin, "And then still keep at it, if you know what I mean."

Dorothy laughed, putting her head on his shoulder. "Oh Liam, what am I going to do with you?"

"Hold onto me. Never let me go. Fight for me against all comers. I'm worth keeping."

"I know you are, baby boy. I know," Dorothy said. They sat there silently together, leaning into each other as the precious moments slipped by.

"Let's come out in the open this morning, right now. And just make everyone deal with it," Liam said. "We can go to your next meeting hand in hand. As if it's the most natural thing in the world. Because it is."

"Wouldn't that be wild and crazy," Dorothy said. "But no, that's too crazy. We'd get into all kinds of trouble." Liam could see her mind working as she paused. "No, we will remain discreet, baby. We have to. We come out in the open now and we'll both get into all kinds of trouble that we really don't need. Okay, what I will do is contact HQ today and start the resignation process. I've got enough years in so that I don't need to have a reason, but I do need to finish this assignment as well as this specific mission I am working on."

"That we're working on."

"No it's just me now. Our suspect is back in India, probably in this very town. So no more mountain climbing. I have no reason to keep you with me. In fact, it's best I release you."

"Don't send me away, Dorothy. I could still be helpful somehow. And you don't have to send me back, do you?"

"No, I don't. I have discretion to retain you as long as I feel the need."

"And you don't feel the need?"

That made her laugh. "That's not the need the Air Attache envisioned, but alright. But we have to stay professional. Not even a hint."

"Oh god, that is such agony, Dorothy. You have such a poker face, I started to doubt. That I had imagined things."

Dorothy put her hands on his face and pulled him nose to nose. "Don't you ever have any doubts about my love for you. You have turned my world upside down. In a good way. A beautiful way. Because of you, it's like I am just starting to live for the first time."

"Then don't send me away. I can keep a poker face too. And as soon as this mission is over I will let the Air Force know that I am not going to reenlist."

"Okay then. Meet me in the lobby at 0800."

"Yes, ma'am."

Dorothy got out of bed, threw a bathrobe on while Liam quickly dressed. She stuck her head out the door. All clear. Liam gave her a quick kiss then slipped out into the hallway.

CHAPTER 20

SHE

"I don't know what's happened to you Dalha, but sleep is the best thing for you right now," She said. "You look exhausted." Taking Dalha's keys out of the tall girl's pocket, She unlocked the door to Dalha's flat while holding her around the waist with her other arm. The small sparse flat was just as She remembered it. Minimal furniture, but clean. The mattress on the floor, tucked along the wall behind the door, was neatly made. She led Dalha to the one chair in the room that went with a small desk and sat Dalha in it. On her knees before her, She gently took off Dalha's boots and socks, briefly massaging each foot. Then she helped Dalha out of her jacket and shirt so the girl was in her undershirt. She enjoyed the sight of the slight hint of nipples on the barest rounding of breasts. She knew the nipples below could protrude incredibly when aroused, a lovely mouthful. As She led Dalha to the mattress, She pulled the covering back and guided Dalha to lie down on her back.

"Just relax and go to sleep," She said softly. Dalha obeyed without comment or even recognition. "Let's get you more comfortable," She said, unbuttoning Dalha's pants and gently pulling both pants and panties down to Dalha's knees. "That's a girl," She whispered as She slipped the clothing off. The sight of Dalha's pubic mound almost caused a gasp to escape. Almost. But She was a professional. She then covered Dalha and tucked her in like a little girl. "Sleep, Dalha. I am here." She stood back up silently surveying the one room flat. the exterior door facing the back of the building, the one window overlooking the street from the second floor. the flimsy green drapes were pulled shut. The small bathroom to the side, the door slightly ajar. She sat down in the one chair, focusing on her breathing. Relaxing. Waiting. Eventually, Dalha fell into a deep slumber.

The American, Marin, couldn't know which flat was Dalha's. She had seen her tailing Dalha even before She had faked the chance meeting. That blonde head had stood out like a beacon. Another example of Marin's lack of expertise. Unless Marin wanted to be spotted. She thought that Marin was taking the facade of her cover too far, serving no purpose at this stage of the game. On the wall next to the bathroom door was a small range and a sink with a small cupboard over it. She found a small glass, then leaned it between the entrance door knob and door jamb. The slighted movement of the door would cause it to fall and shatter. She then slipped her silenced handgun from her jacket to rest it on the floor. She took one more look at the door and window, then making up her mind, She quickly undressed and slipped under the covers with Dalha. She touched Dalha gently, foot to foot. The girl stirred briefly then settled again with their feet still touching. She snuggled in a bit closer so their forearms touched lightly. Dalha did not withdraw. So lying on her back next to Dalha, with her outside hand resting on her sidearm, She fell asleep in bed with Dalha. She needed the rest almost as much as Dalha did.

***

Outside, Tina waited almost an hour for the strange woman to return back to the street from Dalha's flat. She was at a bus stop across the street and one building down. Close enough but not obvious. Maybe there was a rear exit to the building, most likely was but Tina couldn't check it out without leaving the entrance unguarded. Chances are the woman was still in there. What were they doing? It's not like Dalha would be in a conversational mood, but clearly the two knew each other. Who was she? Tina had just decided she would go in, find an occupied flat, and question the unlucky resident regarding Dalha's flat location. Afterall, Dalha had a singular look. Any resident would probably know her by sight and be able to ID which flat was hers. Just as she was about to cross the street, Tina saw Pally approach her with another man in tow. In plain clothes, like Pally, but undoubtedly a cop.

"Hi Tina," Pally said. "Dalha is home and she's got company."

"I was wondering when you would show up. Ready to go in?"

"No, we are holding off. Khera has agents placed in a block perimeter, the place is surrounded. It would be cleaner to take her when she comes out. After all, it might not be the person we are looking for."

"Too much of a coincidence to me."

"I agree and so does your buddy Khera, but if we go in blasting somebody is going to get hurt, including Dalha."

"Then I'll go in alone."

"No, you'll follow me around the corner to meet with Khera and Special Agent Miller from the FBI. Remember her?"

"I do. What do they want with me?"

"Right now they want to make sure you don't gum up the works. Come along, Tina," Pally said, then, "you stay here, Raj," to the other cop.

Pally led Tina a block away to an unmarked stepvan that served as a mobile command center. Tina saw Khera and Miller outside the stepvan as they approached. A tall redheaded kid loitered on the sidewalk at a discreet distance.

"FBI agents are getting younger," Tina said, "But very cute."

"He's not FBI really, but some Air Force kid that is serving as Miller's assistant. Although what he actually assists with I have no idea."

"I know what I would do with him if he was my assistant," Tina said.

"Hush up," Pally said as they came up to Khera and Miller. "Here she is, sir."

"So I see," Khera said. "Ms. Marin, what are you doing here in India? In Kashmir?"

"The same reason I came here in the first place. I am a reporter investigating possible Great Power interference in the Kashmir border problem."

"Then go do your job, You have no business here."

"I beg to differ. The source, or chief operative rather, of the disruptions could be just around the corner."

"Allow me to be blunt, Ms. Marin. This is a police matter. Stay out of the way."

***

She woke up with a start. Her hand immediately went to her weapon beside the bed but it wasn't there. She rolled off the mattress to the hard floor into a crouch position. Dalha was sitting criss-cross applesauce on the bed where She had put her to sleep. She's handgun was in Dalha's lap. She couldn't help but be riveted by the hint of curly black bush under the gun in Dalha's lap.

"You sleep deeply, Mala," Dalha said. "You must have been very tired."

She relaxed out of her crouch and returned to the bed sitting opposite Dalha in the same fashion. Dalha didn't hinder her.

"Be careful with that thing. It scares me," She said.

"It scares me too," said Dalha.

"I'm being watched, Dalha. And followed. By the police, but also by people I don't think are police."

"Why?"

"I don't know."

"Have you joined the militants?"

"No!"

"Then what's with the gun?"

"I was attacked about a month ago. By one of the people that follow me. I barely escaped."

"So if you are attacked again you will shoot someone with this?"

"Honestly, I am not sure that I can. But maybe I can scare them off."

"Where did you get it?"

"On the black market."

"With a silencer?"

"That's how it came," She said. "The man said that I could get away quietly if I… if I. I know it's crazy but I am afraid without it, and yet afraid with it too."

Dalha placed the gun carefully on the floor on her side of the mattress. "Strange that we just happened to meet."

"Yes, but I am ever so glad. I carry a world of guilt for how I treated you. I am so sorry. But what has happened to you? You are clearly in a bad way."

"I am, I won't deny it."

"Let me help," She said. She took Dalha's hands in her own. "Because believe it or not, I never stopped loving you." As She spoke, She surprisingly realized it was true.

Dalha's grief erupted in chest-heaving gasps, then the tears and sobs flowed. She leaned into Dalha, embracing the younger woman, crying with her. They fell over sideways back onto the bed crying and hugging together. Their tears mingled as She softly kissed Dalha's cheek and neck. Dalha pulled the older woman to her with a fierce tight clutching hug. She slipped a leg between Dalha's thighs throwing her other leg over the small of the girl's back.

"My girl. My poor girl. I am here and I will never leave you again."

She looked into Dalha's crying eyes then kissed her full on the lips. Dalha opened her mouth in response. She pressed her thigh into Dalha's crotch feeling hair on her skin as her tongue probed deeply in Dalha's mouth. Dalha responded in kind. Suddenly She rolled off Dalha and swept the gun into her hand coming to a standing position, She drew a bead on Dalha right between the eyes.

"I can't imagine you didn't figure it out," She said. Dalha just looked at her in bewildered shock. "Don't you see, Dalha? It was me. I am the one. I killed Bobby. And we're surrounded by police. It's over. I can't get away now. But no way can I let them take me alive." She paused, then continued more to herself than Dalha, "Even if I fight it out, they'll try to arrest me. And they might just pull it off. I can't let that happen. But what do I do about you? I can't kill you. I just can't." She twisted off the silencer. "You win, Dalha. Love wins. I love you." She thrust the gun into her own mouth.

"No!" Dalha roared.

She hesitated. Pulling the barrel out of her mouth, but not turning it away, letting the end of the barrel rest on her chin. Unconvinced. The anguish in Dalha's beautiful brown eyes seemed so real.

"I killed your Bobby," She said.

"And I hate you for it! Still, I love you. How can I not? So kill me first. I don't want to live."

She walked around to stand behind Dalha. Her weapon pointed to the ceiling, unsure.

"Do it, Mala," Dalha said. "Please."

"It will be quick and painless," She said. "I love you." She pointed the barrel at the back of Dalha's head, just a couple feet away. Still She hesitated.

"Do it, Mala. Please. If you love me, do it," Dalha said.

She stepped in and hit Dalha on the head with expert precision. Dalha collapsed on the mattress in a heap.

"No, my dear. I can not kill you," She said to the unconscious girl. "My mission is a failure and killing you won't change that. But maybe I can still escape."

She stripped her clothes off quickly, then rummaged through Dalha's sparse cleaning items under the sink. She soaped herself down, head to foot. With various cleaners, She mixed a small explosive, then opened some of her bullets to add gunpowder and tore some rag for a fuse. She put the makeshift bomb in the sink. She didn't want to risk Dalha, but needed a loud bang. A quick look into the hallway. All clear. She went back, lit the fuse, then raced out and down the hall to the garbage chute. She dropped her clothes down before her, then worked her way into the chute. It was a tight fit, then with her shoulders and head still in the hallway, her bomb went off. People would be pouring into the hallway in no time with the police from outside right behind. A burst of adrenaline helped her fight through the pain as She dislocated a shoulder to get fully in and the chute closed She into darkness. She heard shouts and doors slamming as She slowly worked her way into the vertical drop.

***

Pally was the first through the door to Dalha's flat with Khera guns drawn, both Millers, and Tina right behind. More police poured into the small room.

"All clear everyone!" Khera shouted. "Stand down!"

CHAPTER 21

DOROTHY

"Inspector Khera will see you now," the secretary told FBI Agent Dorothy Miller. With a glance of brief eye contact to Liam, Dorothy left him in the outer office. Khera and Pally were already there. Khera rose as Dorothy entered his office.

"Thank you for coming so promptly, Agent Miller," Khera said. "Please sit down. I won't keep you long." Dorothy sat without a word. Khera continued, "It's a bad business. One agent dead and the suspect escaped without a trace."

"And the gun that killed your man??" Dorothy asked. She saw Khera wince. "Sorry," she added.

"Nine millimeter. Silenced," Khera said, "We've got no ballistic match to the slug but have reached out to Interpol. I doubt they'll have anything either."

"A perfect shot between the eyes," Miller said, "She must have gotten close no matter how good a shot she might be."

"Agreed. But now we have a good artist sketch from the girl Dalha and a more accurate overall description than we had before secondhand from her fathers. And we know now that our suspect has been operating in India for at least three years," said Khera.

"I think you can assume that she masterminded that ridiculous bank heist that Tina Marin broke up," Miller said.

Khera said, "Not so ridiculous when you place it in context with other terrorist and criminal events that have occurred over the past three years. Maybe longer. We are reviewing past events looking for similarities and a pattern. Meanwhile the hunt is on. Either we'll catch her or chase her out of India, but we won't let her operate here like before."

Pally said, "We're even reaching out to the Kashmir independence community, sharing her description and warning them that she is armed, dangerous, and most importantly, not one of them."

"I doubt anyone will trust us enough to provide any intel but at least our suspect won't be able to hide among them as she did before," Khera said.

"I might have some luck, Inspector," Pally said.

"They know me and hate me," Khera said to Miller. "As you know, interpersonal skills are not my strength."

"Good move," Miller said, "You have a natural empathy, Agarwal."

"And we are going public through the papers and social media with the artist's sketch," Khera went on. "I want our suspect to know that everyone she shows her face to in India might recognize her and turn her in."

"That makes sense. It will keep her on the run. I can coordinate with our intelligence community. If you pass on your ballistic report, the sketch, and anything else you have or turn up I'll get right on it," Dorothy said.

"Thank you for your cooperation," Khera said.

"And what is our next step in the field?" asked Dorothy.

"For you, nothing," Khera said. "Since Mr. Singh was an American citizen, I will keep you informed as to our progress, but there is no field role for you."

"Very well," said Dorothy.

"And I was surprised that you and your airman followed us in, despite my instructions to the contrary. You were both unarmed and that boy isn't even a trained agent."

"He is young and athletic. He figures we are all too old and slow, which is true enough."

"You know better, Miller," Khera said.

"You're right, of course. I apologize."

"You're off the case, Miller. Both you and your airman. We won't have this discussion again," Khera said. Dorothy saw that he meant it, so nodded her agreement.

"Oh, there is one more thing you can do for me," Khera went on. "Please tell Tina Marin to stay out of it. If she disrupts our investigation, I will arrest her for obstruction of justice. And prosecute. I mean that."

"I'll let her know," Dorothy said as she rose to leave. "Good luck, Inspector. Good hunting." With a nod to Khera, Pally also rose and followed Dorothy out of the office.

"Agent Miller, may I have a private word?" Pally asked. Dorothy nodded her assent and let the policewoman lead her to Pally's small office. Once the door was closed, Pally spoke quietly. "You're not fooling anyone. You and your young airman. I know it's none of my business, but I just wanted to warn you."

Dorothy couldn't help but beam. "Thank you for that, but nobody will catch us in the open. And I have already started the resignation process from the FBI. I'm crazy I know, but," Dorothy said no more.

"Well, good luck," Pally said.

"You know, you and Ms. Marin aren't fooling anyone either."

"It's complicated, but I am safe enough with Khera. Believe it or not he's a closet liberal. Sort of. And Tina will be out of India soon enough."

"And then?" asked Dorothy.

"What can I say? Our love is eternal, but not our relationship." Pally stepped in for a hug and Dorothy embraced her fully. She felt the Indian woman's close embrace, chest to chest hip to hip. They held the hug.

"What's it like? With another woman, I mean?" Dorothy asked, whispering in Pally's ear.

"Indescribable. You should try it sometime."

"Maybe I will," reluctantly Dorothy loosened her embrace, but they didn't fully disconnect. Pally put a hand to Dorothy's cheek and gave her a soft kiss on the lips.

"I wish you joy, Agent Miller. Dorothy."

"You too, Sub-inspector Agarwal. Pally."

***

Liam was driving Dorothy through the streets of Srenagar. "Where to, Dorothy?" he asked.

"We're done here, Liam. I will be back to the States and out of the FBI as soon as I can. Then we can plan the rest of our lives. You'll need to go back to the embassy or wherever the Air Force sends you until your enlistment ends. Then we'll hook up and face the world together."

"But don't send me back to the embassy right now."

"Hell no. I am going to keep you on until somebody notices and tells me not to. Until right before I fly to the States. I want a baby more than ever. So as much sex as possible. Every chance we can."

"Then let's go back to the hotel now."

"In the middle of the day? Why not? There is no urgency in talking to Tina Marin, which is our last bit of business in Kashmir. Other than paperwork."

Dorothy saw the shiteating grin on Liam's face as he drove them though the streets to the hotel. His hand went to Dorothy's thigh and started probing. Dorothy spread her legs a bit, enjoying the petting, even if it was through her pants. "Stay focused on the road, young man. This backwards English style driving is tricky."

"Aw, it's easy enough. You just need to think everything opposite."

"Is there anything you can't do, I wonder?"

"Plenty, I am sure. And you'll have a lifetime to discover all my flaws and teach me better."

"Liam, there is one more thing I want to talk about."

"Don't bring up our age difference again because I am not listening."

"But it's real. We can't ignore it. Twenty years from now you'll be 40 and I'll be 63."

"So what, people can be fit and active at 63."

"So they can, but 40 years from now you'll be 60 and I'll be over 80. People aren't that active that old and you'll still be a very active 60. I will be a very old woman by anyone's, everyone's, standards."

"Why worry about 40 years from now? We have a lot of living and loving to do between now and then."

"And so we do, but it is something Pally just said to me."

"So what was that?"

"That love is eternal, but relationships are not."

"What does that mean?"

"It means that I want you to be open and ready for love with others," Dorothy said, "It doesn't mean I want you to dump me, it just means that I will be open to you accepting other partners in your life. I want you to have all the love that life can give you. I don't want to be selfish."

"You're going to be the mother of my child," Liam said, "I'm not going anywhere."

"First of all, we don't know that yet. We're going to try but we don't know anything. And second, I want you to experience love beyond me. Here I am 43 years old and you are just my second partner. I have wasted a lot of my love life."

"Are you saying all this because you want other partners?" Liam asked.

"No, of course not. I am thinking about you. Although I must admit I felt a little tingle when Pally hugged me goodbye. And she kissed me on the lips."

"So that's what you were doing in there. Should I be jealous?"

"No, and that's the point. You should never be jealous. And neither should I. Because our love is eternal. But I am beginning to think our capacities to love go beyond just one person."

"You got all that out of two minutes in Pally's office?" Liam asked.

"I did. I really did. It was a bit of an epiphany now that I think about it."

"Okay, as long as you're not breaking up with me because of your age obsession, I will do as you say."

"I will never break up with you for any reason. I just want you to live and love as many experiences as possible."

"Something tells me you're feeling a bit bisexual. Am I wrong?"

"First time I ever really thought about it, but you're not wrong."

"Boy, that Pally was busy." Liam started laughing and Dorothy joined in.

CHAPTER 22

SHE

From her hiding place on the roof of the house barge, She watched the black FBI agent approach the house barge with the young redheaded man in tow. He was dressed in the baby blue uniform of a USAF enlisted man. The woman's size and strength was obvious under her business suit. This was a complication that She could do without. The blonde American was already inside with the owner, the voluptuous woman who tried to disguise her beauty. The bedroom had a sunroof. After Marin had arrived, She'd had the pleasure of watching the Indian woman change out of her dowdy clothes into a fetching red sari. Seeing her naked as she changed in the bedroom had been an erotic pleasure. One of the most beautiful bodies She had ever seen. If all went well and She didn't have to kill her, She might enjoy the Indian beauty on her way out.

Tina Marin was her target, and with the element of surprise She was confident that a single silent shot would be easy enough. The other one wasn't a player. If she stayed out of it, She would let her live. The need for secrecy was gone. She just wanted to settle with Tina Marin then quit India for good. It was a matter of professional pride. But now there were three to contend with instead of one. Still, they were likely unarmed while She had her silenced nine millimeter plus her trusty knife.

She took her time to consider the situation. Her left shoulder was still sore and wouldn't be totally healed for a week or so at least. She had banged the dislocation back into place once She had gotten herself out of the dumpster that She had landed in from the garbage chute. Then after taking out the cop guarding the rear of Dalha's building, She had made her way to her nearest safe house to clean up, rearm and regroup. This job was a failure. Three years of work ending in failure. She wasn't going to get the final payment for her work and that was as it should be. She didn't like to fail and neither would her employers. They would come after her as a loose end to be cleaned up. So it was time to disappear. To retire. She could afford it.

She thought about the four people beneath her in the barge. She could look down into the bedroom and at this point it was empty. She had no idea about the layout of the living room or where each person was located. She had studied the videos of Tina Marin taking out those two fools from the bank heist. They were both easy marks, but it had been neatly done. Tina Marin was a woman to be reckoned with. That black woman was a professional warrior. She could just tell. And She would be giving up about 15 pounds to her. And some reach. When two evenly skilled fighters go toe to toe, size and weight matters. On the other hand, She was slightly bigger than Tina Marin. And about ten years younger. The young man moved like an athlete. He was the biggest, strongest, and fastest player in the game. Not certain what his skills were, She was confident that the redhead wasn't in the same league as the other two. With a surprise attack, he would hopefully take a precious moment to react. So the black woman first, then Marin, then the young man. And the Indian woman? If her location could be used to her advantage, She would take it. She leaned over to peak into the bedroom for one final look. All clear. Time to go in.

CHAPTER 23

ATTACK

"I don't care what Khera says. I will avenge Bobby's death. The world isn't big enough for that woman to hide," Tina said.

"I still don't get you, Marin," Dorothy said. "But be warned, your prey is a very dangerous person. A professional assassin. You hunt her and she might turn on you when you least expect it."

"Would anyone like tea?" Lucky asked.

"No thank you," Dorothy said. "I have done what I came for, to deliver Khera's message. You would do well, Marin, to find your quarry outside of India. You don't want to spend the rest of your life in an Indian prison. Inspector Khera wasn't kidding. He will lock you up and throw away the key."

"Why don't you stay for a bit?" Tina asked. "If I am to chase this woman around the world I would appreciate your advice."

"I don't know much, I am afraid," Dorothy said.

"You're a professional investigator while I am just a badass."

"Please everyone, sit at the table. I'll just be a minute. The tea is already brewing," Lucky said. "Young man, stop standing at attention or whatever it is you call it and sit down next to agent Miller."

"Call me Dorothy. It's okay Liam, sit here by me."

Tina sat across from Liam while Lucky bustled in her little kitchen with the tea. He was a good looking boy. Tina could see why the older woman kept him around. Tina also took another look at Dorothy. Much more relaxed than when they had met during the initial interrogations after the terrorist attack.

"So tell me about you two," Tina said to both of them. The boy blushed while Dorothy frowned at first then smiled.

"We're in love," Dorothy said. "It doesn't matter now. I am leaving the FBI and somehow this feels like a trust environment."

"Your instincts serve you well. This is very much a trust environment," Lucky said.

Tina heard the bedroom door open behind her. Liam lunged into a tackle of Dorothy, a soft whomp sounded past Tina's ear as crimson blossomed across the boy's back and Liam's weight took Dorothy out of her chair onto the floor with the boy on top of her. Tina whirled out of her own chair, grabbing and slinging the salt shaker back toward the bedroom. Another whomp as a bullet cut Tina's ear like a knife. Tina followed her salt shaker toss with a lunge grappling with the assassin before She could get another shot off. Lucky screamed, dropping the tea set to the floor with a crash. Tina had the gun hand with both of hers and head butted her enemy but the blow was softened as She took Tina's momentum to her advantage flipping Tina over her as they fell back into the bedroom. Tina kept a death grip with both hands on the gun hand as she flew over her assailant, twisting She's wrist. The gun broke free flying so Tina released her enemy's hand and curled into a roll back to her feet facing the fight. She was already up too with a knife drawn. Tina was just able to partially block the upward attack aimed for a death blow under her ribs. The blade cut lightly across Tina's ribcage, but using the momentum of the attack Tina turned She so that Tina could go for a choke hold with her left forearm. She pushed her weight back into Tina using her momentum as had Tina, throwing the both of them against the wall of the small room. Tina felt her wind knocked out of her from the impact with the wall. She smashed the back of her head into Tina's face as Tina tried to lock on her choke hold. Stunning Tina further, She was able to slip her head out of the hold and pivot for another slashing cut with her knife. Tina just barely blocked the blow, trying to get some maneuvering room off the wall, but another slash was already coming. Dorothy loomed up like a storm cloud behind their enemy. Then She was jerked off her feet like a ragdoll as Dorothy twisted her head with a two handed neck snap. Tina could tell by the sound of the blow that She was killed instantly. Dorothy dropped the lifeless body then turned running back into the other room.

"Liam!" Dorothy cried as she ran.

Tina fell to her hands and knees gasping for air, looking down into the lifeless eyes of her enemy. Checking her own body carefully, Tina discovered her cuts, bumps, and bruises and determined that none were life threatening. But the back of her head hurt something fierce. Relief rushed through her as fear subsided. Rubbing the growing lump on the back of her head, Tina looked down at the dead mystery woman then staggered to her feet, hearing sobbing from the other room. Her ear was throbbing and stinging too. Her hand came away from her head revealing blood on her forearm from her mangled earlobe. Oh yeah, she'd been shot. With a foot, Tina turned the dead woman's head so she could get a good look at it. Remembering that face. Definitely the woman she had seen with Dalha. The truth about She's mission and who hired her had died with her. Khera wouldn't like this outcome, Tina mused. Not that Khera nor geopolitics mattered to Tina anymore. Bobby was avenged, thanks to the big FBI agent.

CHAPTER 24

PALLY

Former police Sub-inspecter, now Intelligence Bureau Agent, Pallavi "Pally" Agarwal sat patiently in the cramped curtained ER cubicle. Next to her in a hospital bed, Tina snored softly, innocent as a cherub. Still adorable as ever.

Tina let out a soft groan as she started to wake.

"How are you feeling, girlfriend?" Pally asked.

Tina groaned again, not responding. Then she tried to move and suddenly realized she was strapped in restraints at her wrists and ankles.

"Hey, what gives? Not again!"

"Relax," Pally said.

"Pally," Tina said, coming into focus. "What happened?"

"Hi Tina, what do you remember?"

"Oh youngling, let's not go through that again. Just tell me. And please be a dear and scratch my left ear for me."

"No can do. Your ear has a big binding on it. Probably why it itches. But I hope this helps," Pally said, giving her a kiss as near to Tina's ear as the bandages allowed.

"So what happened, Pally? Why am I here, wherever here is?"

"To start with, you're in the hospital closest to Lucky's houseboat."

"Lucky! How is she? I remember she was a mess after the attack."

"So you remember that."

"Of course! Oh Pally, I was getting my ass kicked. I'd be dead now if it wasn't for Miller. But I don't seem to remember much after that."

"Well, you were still standing by the time we got there, but then you collapsed in my arms. You had a few knife cuts but your ear was bleeding a lot so we got an ambulance for you."

"And the redheaded boy? Miller's airman? He's dead, isn't he."

"I'm afraid so."

"So what's with the restraints? Talk about deja vu."

"You woke up in the ambulance on the way to hospital and started to tear up the place…"

"Oh no, I didn't hurt anyone, did I?"

"No thank god, they were ready for you and had a sedative shot into your ass before you could cause too much damage. And you were rather weak."

"Well thank god for small favors. So I am not under arrest, am I?"

"No, you're not but you need a psych eval before they can set you free. Into my informal custody."

"Thank you, youngling. What would I do without you?"

***

It was late in the evening before Tina was finally released from the ER. Pally drove Tina back to her hotel room.

"Welcome to my humble abode, Pally. Make yourself at home," Tina said as they entered her room. Pally plopped herself on the sofa. Tina joined her.

"I won't stay long. You need to get your rest," Pally said.

"Aw, I'm fine. Stay awhile, please."

"You've had another concussion, Tina, on top of all these cuts. You've lost some blood. The doctor said you should rest for a few days before you are fit to travel."

"That's fine since I'm not going anywhere anyway,." Tina said. Pally didn't reply, but Tina noticed that she appeared suddenly nervous. "What?" Tina said.

"I think it's time you head home, Tina. Once you've healed up, of course."

"Are you kidding? I still have a story to write. And even though our mystery woman is dead, I still have a lot of investigating to do. Who was she? And who was she working for?"

"Leave that to me. Khera has assigned me the job of figuring all that out, if it can be figured out."

"Great, then we're still working together."

"Go home and write your article there. You have plenty to write about already."

"Don't be silly. An investigative reporter needs to discover the answers. That's the job. For example, I'm sure you have ordered an autopsy. That might tell us tons."

"I have and I hope you're right. But this investigation is officially classified. I'm sorry but you have to stay out of it."

"And then there's her money trail to backtrack. That could lead us to who funded her," Tina went on.

"We already have a financial forensic team following up on that too."

"And there's all of the Kashmir activists she must have been interacting with. I mean, how did a nice kid like Rohit get mixed up with her? There's so much to explore."

"Tina, you're not listening!" Pally shouted. "Khera will revoke your press privileges if you push."

"My paper will create a diplomatic incident if he does," Tina shot back.

Pally jumped from the sofa, prowling around the room. Tina was on her feet too.

"What's the matter with you, Pally?" The younger woman's eyes were glittering wet. "Pally?"

"I can't do this, Tina. I just can't. Here I finally have a big case, a big promotion. You know how much my career means to me. And here you are ready to fuck it all up."

"Pally?"

"I can't do this! I love you. You understand? I love you. But you're a distraction. I can't have you here. Please, please, go back to America. Or Greece. Anywhere but here." She was openly crying now.

"Oh my poor girl." Tina enveloped Pally in a hug, tearing up herself as Pally blubbered in her arms, out of control. "That's it, let it all out," Tina whispered in her ear. Eventually Pally's sobbing subsided.

"On top of all that, Tina, I really look up to you. I can't be in charge with you around. I just can't." She took a deep breath. "And I need to be in charge!"

Tina stepped back but held Pally's hands in both of hers. They looked into each other's eyes in silence.

"You tell me you love me, Tina," Pally said thickly. "Prove it. Go home. Please."

Tina sighed. "Okay, I hear you, youngling. I'll go home. For a while. At least until you feel like you've established yourself. Meanwhile, you'll give me first dibs on any press releases, right?"

A laughing cry erupted from Pally in reply. "You got it," Pally managed to get out.

"Okay then that's settled. You know you owe me bigtime now, Pally."

"So what do you want?" Pally asked suspiciously.

"Take me to bed." They were in each other's arms instantly.

EPILOGUE

AT THE FOUNTAIN OF APHRODITE

Four Months Later

Tina swam over to sit on the smooth stone steps next to Thea, still shoulder high in the warm water.

"Thank you again, my Lady Amalthea, for welcoming my friends to the fountain," Tina said in ancient Greek.

Thea replied in the same language, "They all need the healing which, for each of them, is in consequence of the return of Agi to the here and now. I played a role in your return so of course they are welcome."

They watched the others still laughing and playing under the cascading fountain waters.

"It warms my heart to see smiles on the faces of Dalha and Dorothy," Tina said, "I was confident that Lucky would recover with Pally's support, but the other two, I was most concerned for them. Dalha particularly had a rough time on the trek with her fathers north to bring Bobby's body back to India for transport to America. That was a bitter parting for all of us when the plane left with Bobby's body aboard. But it is right that he was returned to his family back home."

"And Dorothy?" Thea asked.

"Her young man's body, Liam, too was sent home to his parents. The Air Force took care of that," Tina said, "but Dorothy is a warrior, as was her young man. It is no less painful for us, but we are more accepting of death. Death is the inevitable consequence of war."

"Because you know that truth, Agi," Thea said, "it is your mission, the mission of all warriors, to avoid war."

"I just go where my captains tell me to go, and kill whom my captains tell me to kill."

"No captain told you to fight for Helen. No captain told you to care for her and her sisters. You have a new captain now Tina of New York and Agi of Arcadia, and her name is Honor. As you go forth in this new world, always follow Honor. You lost her once, but you have found her again."

Tina's voice cracked through her tears. "Thank you, my lady."

After a moment, Ajita swam over and sat next to Tina. "I've been wanting to tell you, Tina, when we weren't in a crowd," Ajita said. She paused for dramatic effect, "I'm pregnant."

"That's wonderful! Stavros must be so proud," Tina said. They could see him not far away treading water, trying to flirt with Lucky.

"He is, although truth be told the baby may not be his," Ajita said with mischief in her eyes.

"So you have accepted the rituals of the fountain?" Tina asked.

"Like a fish to water," Thea interjected.

"It doesn't really matter," Ajita said. "Stavros will be the dad. We are going to be married and I will remain in Greece."

"And a child can never have too many loving uncles," Thea said.

"You should talk to Dalha about that," Tina said. "She has four fathers. And they all helped her through a very rough time."

"And what are Dalha's plans?" Thea asked Tina.

"Now that Pally has been transferred to Srinagar, it looks like Dalha will take a flat in the same building where Pally is setting up house. And Lucky will take a flat there as well. Although I am sure she will keep her houseboat too. I'm guessing that Lucky and Pally will need to help Dalha out financially. Because she too is going to be a mom."

Thea laughed, "And a child can never have too many loving aunties." Then, "It is time." Thea got out of the water and called everyone out to stand hand in hand in a circle on the grass around a small cluster of dripping red poppies. There was silence as Thea took the time to make eye contact with each individual: Stavros, Ajita, Pally, Lucky, Dalha, Dorothy, and Tina.

Then Thea spoke, "My friends, we have performed the rituals for those who have fallen, and for the healing thereafter. And we have cleansed our bodies and souls in the fountain of Aphrodite's love. So as with the cycle of life and death, comes life again. Hear all in this company that Ajita is with child and the child's name will be Rohit regardless of gender; Hear all in this company that Dalha is with child and the child's name will be Bobby regardless of gender; Hear all in this company that Dorothy is with child and the child's name will be Liam regardless of gender. And so will the fallen rise again."

"By your leave, my Lady Amalthea," Tina asked. Thea nodded her assent. "Rohit, Bobby, Liam: they'll be back," Tina told everyone, "Not only in their children but themselves as well. Look at me. Two thousand years later and here I am. Life never ends with death. They'll be back."

"Now everyone, back in the pool!" Thea shouted.

***

Thea watched Tina and the others frolic in the fountain from her place near the stone stairs. New additions to her flock. A calm contentment was upon her. She had retired from her law firm. Soon she would move from Athens and remain by the fountain for the rest of her days. And each day she would rise at dawn to perform the ancient rituals. For she was Lady Amalthea, priestess of the fountain of Aphrodite.

THE END

Other Books by D L Cooper

A Glimpse Through The Mist. Amazon.com, 2015

Converging Courses. Amazon.com, 2017

D L Cooper website https://dlcooperbooks.com/

Old Kashmir Borders

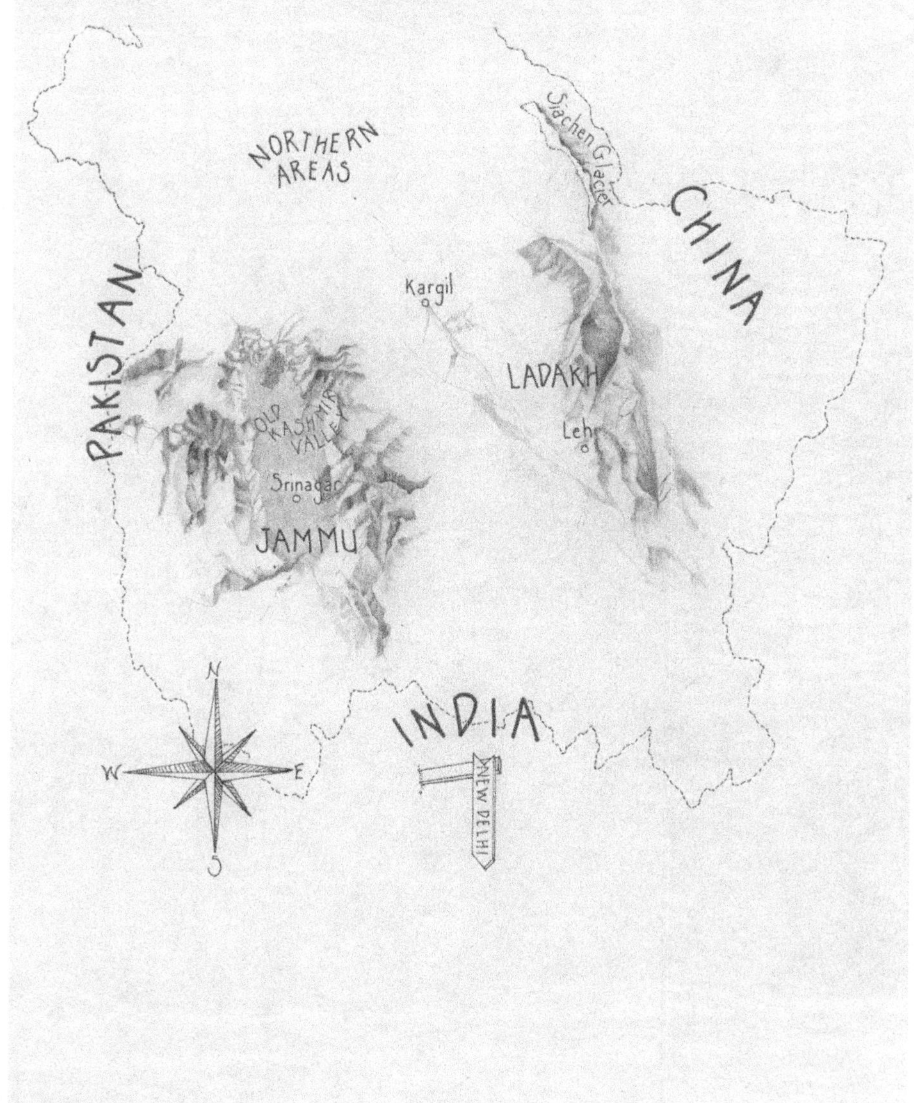

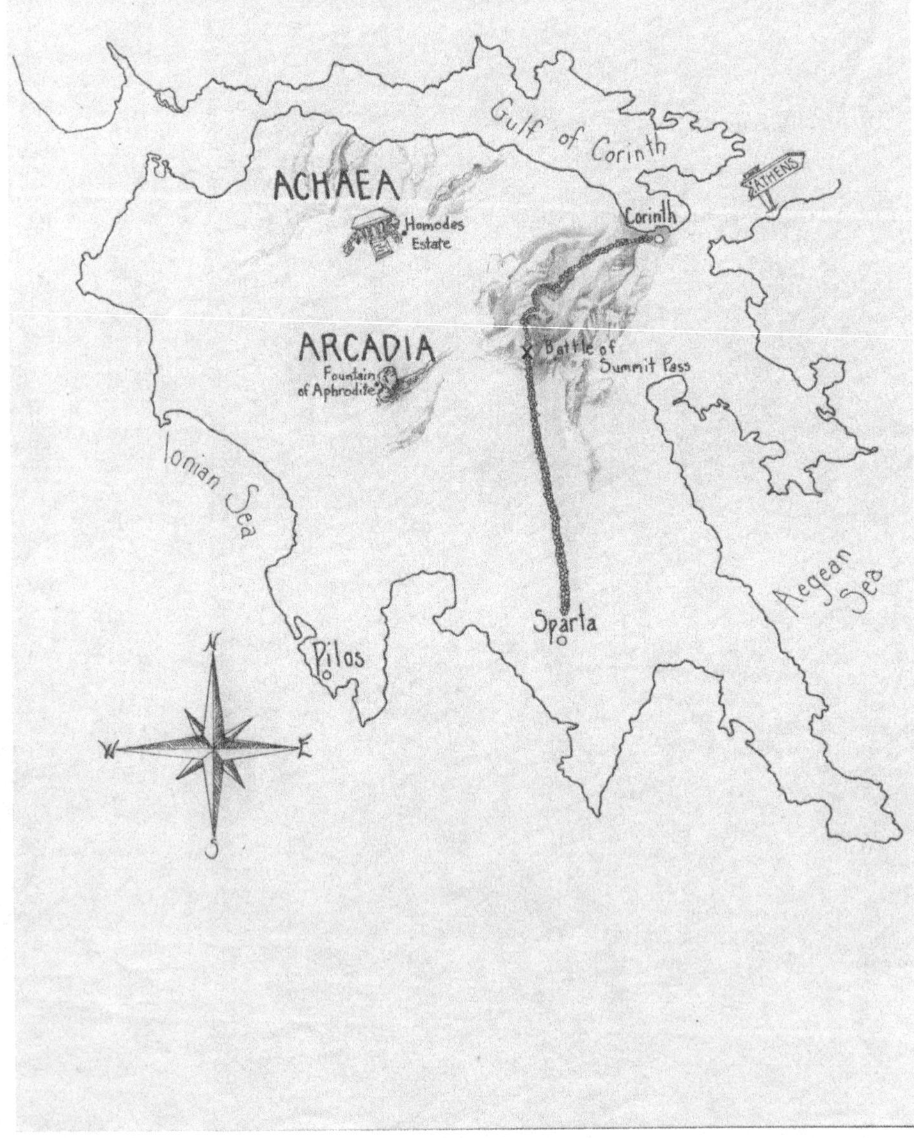
Part of Ancient Greece
Gulf of Corinth
ACHAEA
Homodes Estate
Corinth
ATHENS
ARCADIA
Fountain of Aphrodite
Battle of Summit Pass
Ionian Sea
Aegean Sea
Sparta
Pilos
N
W
E
S

ABOUT THE AUTHOR

Duality of Change / An Identity Odyssey is the third novel by D L Cooper following *A Glimpse Through The Mist* (2015) and *Converging Courses* (2017). Also a short story writer, you can find more about D L Cooper and his works at dlcooperbooks.com. Cooper earned a Bachelor of Arts degree in English Literature from the University of Maryland University College. He is also a lifelong sailor who, with Renée by his side, has sailed the Atlantic, the Mediterranean, and the Caribbean. Their home sailing base, along with their grown children, is the Chesapeake Bay.

ABOUT THE ILLUSTRATOR

A professional artist and illustrator of many years as well as former art teacher, Lucy Dirksen earned a Bachelor of Fine Arts degree in Illustration from Virginia Commonwealth University. She illustrated the cover art for D L Cooper's earlier novels, *A Glimpse Through The Mist* (2015) and *Converging Courses* (2017). Additionally, Dirksen is a jeweler and metalsmith. You can find out more about Lucy Dirksen, her art, illustration, and jewelry at lfdstudio.com. As an additional creative outlet and link to her indigenous roots, Dirksen is an avid hula dancer participating with her halau as both a performer and teacher.

Made in the USA
Monee, IL
03 November 2025